PRAISE FOR LISA TAWN BERGREN'S *THE CAPTAIN'S BRIDE* BOOK ONE IN THE NORTHERN LIGHTS SERIES

"I found myself immediately involved in the stories of Elsa and Peder, Kaatje and her wayward husband, Soren, Tora and her quest for wealth and power, and a host of other people who sailed with them to America to fulfill their dreams. Lisa Tawn Bergren has a straightforward, evocative style of writing that makes her characters breathe. They walk right across the page and straight into your heart."

—Francine Rivers, author

"Bergren at her very best! What an incredible tale of adventure, from Norway's sparkling fjords to the high seas of Cape Horn, to the rocky shores and plains of America in the 1880s. Even with such a panoramic backdrop, *The Captain's Bride* keeps its spyglass trained on the lives of people you'll care about deeply, from first page to last, as they wrestle with all the temptations of spirit and flesh we all know too well. Lisa Tawn Bergren's writing talents unfurl in this historical page-turner—I loved it!"

—Liz Curtis Higgs, author

"Pick of the month. 4½ stars! Lisa Tawn Bergren is a rare talent in historical fiction, writing with exquisite style as she immerses lucky readers in the powerful emotions of her full-bodied characters. Stay tuned for the next book to continue this exciting trilogy."

—*Romantic Times*

"Lisa Tawn Bergren has skillfully entwined the lives of the immigrants as they face opportunity and disaster in their adopted country. The characters capture the heart and parade through the imagination long after the book has been closed. *The Captain's Bride* rides the swells of history into the reader's imagination! Elsa is an independent-minded heroine worthy of imitation today. A triumphant saga!"

—*The Literary Times*

"*The Captain's Bride* is one of those rare pleasures…a terrific tale, told with extraordinary straightforwardness, honesty, and insight. In this, her first historical novel, Lisa Tawn Bergren, a remarkably gifted writer and student of human nature, has created a landscape filled with living, breathing characters. God's compassion and grace illuminate each page."

—Diane Noble, author

PRAISE FOR *DEEP HARBOR*
BOOK TWO IN THE NORTHERN LIGHTS SERIES

"The second historical romance in the Northern Lights trilogy should be at least as successful as its forerunner, *The Captain's Bride*. Bergren accomplishes this as she takes Norwegian emigrants to the Washington territory's Skagit Valley in the late 1880s. Bergren leaves readers eagerly awaiting the series' final installment, *Midnight Sun*, next spring."

—*Marketplace*

MIDNIGHT SUN

MIDNIGHT SUN

LISA TAWN BERGREN

WATERBROOK
PRESS

MIDNIGHT SUN
PUBLISHED BY WATERBROOK PRESS
5446 North Academy Boulevard, Suite 200
Colorado Springs, Colorado 80918
A division of Random House, Inc.

Scripture quotations are taken from the *King James Version* (KJV).

The characters and events in this book are fictional, and any resemblance to
actual persons or events is coincidental.

ISBN 1-57856-113-2

Copyright © 2000 by Lisa Tawn Bergren

Library of Congress Cataloging-in-Publication Data
Bergren, Lisa Tawn.
    Midnight sun / Lisa Tawn Bergren.—1st ed.
        p.   cm. — (The northern lights series ; bk. 3)
    ISBN 1-57856-113-2
        1. Missing persons—Alaska—Fiction.   2. Norwegian Americans—Fiction.
    3. Alaska—Fiction.   I. Title.

    PS3552.E71938 M54 2000
    813'.54—dc21
                                                                99-089444

Printed in the United States of America
2000—First Edition

10 9 8 7 6 5 4 3 2 1

To Andrea,
who inspired me with dreamy talk of one day seeing Alaska
and, since second grade, in many other ways as well.
With love.

Acknowledgments

It seems my books get more complicated with each one. A number of people helped me out with historical detail: the Alaska State Office of History and Archaeology; the Washington State Historical Society; and the medical part of my clan—Drs. Cecil and Nancy Leitch; Dr. Paul Amundson; and Ann Leitch (their personal medical librarian)—corrected me on wound description and helped me research treatment in 1888. Debi Wilson, a loving bookstore owner in Alaska, made sure this Rarely-Out-of-the-Lower-Forty-Eight-Author got things right in writing about the Land of the Midnight Sun and passed along the legend of Mount Susitna via Ann Dickson's *Sleeping Lady*. My husband, Tim, Tricia Goyer, Anjie Mote, and Liz Curtis Higgs read the whole raw manuscript and pointed out glaring errors. In addition, Sandra Byrd graciously allowed me to retell her story from her fabulous, moving, children's book *The White Pony* (you need a copy for every child you know). Last, but certainly not least, it must be stated that Traci DePree is my gifted editor and makes me look much better than I really am. To everyone I've named, or should have named, thanks.

contents

section one

The Eclipse

prologue

May 1888

*H*e had told her there was no singular Eskimo equivalent for the word "snow." There were words for "snow spread out," "old granulated snow," "snow like salt," "snow mixed with water," and multiple other variations, but nothing for what the Norsks simply called "snø." Kaatje glanced from the still-white banks of the Yukon River to her guide, James Walker, at the head of their riverboat, poling in tandem with his Indian friend, Kadachan, behind her. She shivered. She was glad that James knew this land like their native neighbors. It would be forever before Kaatje could get past the sheer, wild vastness of Alaska, let alone learn all the Eskimo derivations of "snow."

They had settled well in Juneau. Tora and Trent. Christina and Jessica. Kaatje. With the Storm Roadhouse open in the burgeoning city of Juneau near the end of the Inside Passage, and another about to open in Ketchikan to house and feed the growing number of tourists, she felt at home at last. She was financially secure, and after years of waiting and wondering, it was time to put her husband, Soren, out of her mind forever. To bury him in her heart.

If he was indeed dead.

James glanced back at her, and when she met his gaze, he quickly looked away, nodding toward a tree full of bald eagles. Kaatje sensed that she made James nervous. He didn't understand her or her mad quest to find the philandering husband who had abandoned her. Trent Storm did not understand either, but as a friend he had helped her convince an obstinate James into taking her. Her thoughts drifted back to that day in Juneau when Trent had brought James to the roadhouse.

"Let me get this straight," James had said, running an agitated hand through his golden brown hair. He reminded her some of Peder Ramstad. James paced back and forth, glancing from Trent to Kaatje. He directed his questions toward Trent. "You want me to take a...a woman into the Interior? Do you know what you ask of me? A third of the settlers there die within a year. A year. And you want me to take a *woman?*" He stared hard at Trent.

But James didn't leave; he seemed intrigued. What drove his interest? Kaatje wondered. The unique challenge or the generous financial offer to see her through?

"We know what we ask," Trent said, his face betraying his own doubts about what he asked. He had become an older brother figure to Kaatje, watching out for her and her girls as well as his fiancée, Tora. "Believe me, man, I know what we ask. I have gone through it all with Mrs. Janssen, time and again. She has to do this. For personal reasons."

James turned to Kaatje. Tora Anders, beside her, squeezed her hand in encouragement as they faced the rugged mountain man. "You'll have to tell me about those reasons," he said firmly, hands on his hips. "Before I put my life on the line—as well as yours and my Indian guide—you'll have to tell me."

She met his gaze, recognizing that their eyes were a similar shade of green. "They are personal."

"So is my life. Do you know that five miners were sent downriver last year, tied to a raft and their skin flayed open so the birds could peck at them all the way?"

"The miners must have done something to enrage the Indians. If it was the Indians. It is my understanding that most are friendly. We simply will pass through their land."

"Most are fairly cooperative. Tolerant. I wouldn't call them friendly. They only *put up* with our presence, for the most part. But sometimes they don't."

He was trying to scare her—she could tell. But hardly anything frightened her anymore. She had lived through too much to be afraid. It was as if this was her destiny: Finding Soren or his grave. It was her whole reason for bringing her daughters to Alaska.

"The Indians do not frighten you?"

"No."

Kaatje noticed how his chapped, red cheeks made his eyes seem brighter, as if sparking. His full lips curled in derision. He was so sure he could talk her out of this! "What about the bears?" he continued. "There are grizzlies so big that they could tear your pretty head off your shoulders with one swipe."

"Mr. Walker..." Trent warned, rising. Tora's hand squeezed Kaatje's again.

James held up a hand. "No. She needs to hear it. And she needs to be prepared for the dangers that wait for us—for her. This is no walk down the lane; this is survival. And if she isn't up to the task, she'll be putting all our lives at risk. If she intends to come along, she needs to know I won't coddle her." He leaned closer, daring Kaatje to look away. "If the bears don't get you, Mrs. Janssen, there are mosquitoes the size of hummingbirds that will eat at you all day and won't let you rest at night. To say nothing of the flies. And the gnats! They get so thick at times that you have no choice but to breathe in a whole mess of them! You'll sweat all day on the trail and shiver all night from the cold. We'll be walking for miles, each of us carrying a pack. That includes you. Kadachan and I can't manage *your* rations as well as ours." He looked her over from head to toe. "That's seventy-five pounds of pack, Mrs. Janssen."

"Mr. Walker!" Trent exclaimed, aghast at his lack of manners.

"No, Trent," she said clearly. "It is all right. Mr. Walker wants to know what he is taking on." She stood as tall as possible to reach every bit of her five feet six inches and stared at him, forcing James to take a step backward. "I understand the risks, Mr. Walker. I have lived here in Juneau for long enough to have heard every one of the horrible rumors about death and dismemberment that the miners spread. I understand that there are frightening things ahead of us, challenges we must face." She took a step closer. "But you need to understand this, Mr. Walker. You have never met a more determined woman than I. I have left my homeland in Norway to come to America. I bore a child on the plains of Dakota and traveled on to the Washington Territory after my husband abandoned me. I have broken virgin ground to plant crops and carried buckets of water to nourish them. With *these* hands," she said, raising them both to defy his incredulous look. "I have raised two children by myself, while finding a means to support us. I am not afraid of a hard task. Do you understand me?"

James looked unsettled at such revelations, as if he had assumed she was a society woman used to tea at four and a bed turned down by a maid at night. When Kaatje thought about it, though she still worked in running the roadhouse, she had become, in many ways, the woman he believed her to be. But down deep, she was still the same Kaatje who had shouldered too much pain to ever wither at the sight of danger or hard work again. She might not have been born strong, but life had made her fiercely resilient.

He crossed his arms and resumed his dubious expression. She had surprised him, but she had not yet won. "It will cost you a considerable amount. You are speaking of a journey of three…no, four months. We'll need provisions. And cash. Items to barter if we need assistance or goods from the natives."

"You will receive half before leaving," Trent interjected. "And half when you bring Mrs. Janssen safely home." He took a step forward, eye to eye with the guide. "And understand that if you fail to bring her home safely, you will pay for it."

"I don't take kindly to threats, Mr. Storm." James turned toward the door, clearly dismissing them and their insane proposition.

"No, wait!" Kaatje cried. She intercepted James and placed a hand on his forearm, thick and muscular beneath her fingertips. "Please. I must go. I must!" With her eyes she begged him to understand.

His eyes searched hers while he formulated his words. "Why? Why, woman, would you risk your life? Why would you leave your daughters to do this?" He dropped his tone. "Does the man owe you money? Why would you go to such great lengths to find a louse of a husband? Why not let him go? Divorce him. Heaven knows you have your reasons."

"Please," was all she said in response. "Please." He was the best guide available. It had to be James Walker. She felt it in her bones.

"Why don't you just send me and Kadachan? We'll give you a full report—"

"No. I must do this. I must be there when you find him...or his grave."

James looked over at Trent, desperation in his voice. "Tell her it's crazy. Tell her that women just don't enter the Interior unless they don't care if they'll come back."

"I have," Trent said, his voice resigned, miserable.

"Please," she whispered again, still staring at James.

He brushed her hand from his forearm, as if her touch had suddenly burned him. "Be ready in two days. The ice has broken. Kadachan and I'll go then."

She nodded, unable to say anything more as the tears choked her.

"I'll drop off a list of necessities by tomorrow." Then James said to Trent, "I need to know everything you know about this...man, if I'm to find him."

"We'll see that you do."

James paused as if wanting to say something more, then placed a well-worn, brown cowboy hat on his head, straightened the brim, and, after another long, searching look at Kaatje, left.

Trent stepped up behind her and put a supportive hand on her shoulder as she stared out the empty, open door of the roadhouse. "Are you sure, Kaatje? Are you sure this is what you must do?" Tora joined them and slipped her arm through Kaatje's.

"I have never been more sure of anything in my life." She did not look at her friends. "Trent, if I die, I'll need you and Tora to take care of my girls."

Trent paused. "Nothing's going to happen to you, Kaatje. But you know if something did, we would."

Tears again choked Kaatje. She ducked her head, whispering a "thank you" toward her friends and rushing up the stairs to her bedroom. She shut the door and dived onto her bed, giving in to the tears.

When they abated, she rolled on her back and wiped her face with a handkerchief. "Oh, Father in heaven," she whispered. "I have sworn to Mr. Walker that I fear nothing. For years you have been taking me to this place, to this day. But if I am so sure that this is the way I am to go, why am I suddenly so, so overwhelmed at the task before me?"

Nearly a month had passed since that conversation, and her life had changed drastically. Kaatje's attention jerked back to the present as a chunk of ice hit their riverboat broadside and pushed them. She bit her tongue, wanting to shout out, but the men had enough on their hands without screams from their troublesome cargo. The boat leaned left, threatening to capsize, and Kaatje instinctively leaned right with the men to counterbalance it. Their combined weight thrust them to the opposite side of the boat, tipping dangerously to the right. James let out a sound of intense exasperation. Kadachan remained silent. Miraculously the boat steadied, and with his pole Kadachan pushed the small iceberg away from the side, allowing them to resume their route upriver.

"I have told you," James said, after several long, tense moments, "to do only what I tell you. I did not tell you to lean right."

"I was only trying—"

"Only what I tell you." He never looked at her. In fact, Kaatje thought, in all the time they had been traveling, he looked at her only when absolutely necessary.

Kadachan said something softly in Tlingit to James, the sound low and guttural.

James looked about them and muttered something Kaatje couldn't make out. They were canvassing their surroundings, and James had obviously seen the soft bank up ahead, just past the hundred yards of limestone cliffs that climbed thirty feet above them. Were they going to land for midday dinner? Kaatje hoped so. Not that she would tell James. Not after that last little lecture he'd given. She didn't intend to ever speak to him again, after that rude display. Even if her stomach went on rumbling for hours.

Within ten minutes they reached the shore, the bow crunching against tiny rounded pebbles of whale gray and ivory white. James hopped out and hauled the boat more securely onto shore. There was a soft splash as Kadachan entered the water and helped him. As had become their habit, the men scouted up and down the riverbank while Kaatje untied the leather-wrapped provisions. She inwardly groaned at the thought of more jerky, dried fruit, and hardtack. What would it feel like to be eating hardtack after several months? Once in a while James took the time to fish with Kadachan, but that was rare. They were pushing hard, covering as many miles a day as they could. As it was, they would be hard-pressed to make it back to Juneau by autumn.

Setting the pack down at the tree line and pausing to stretch stiff muscles, she glanced at Kadachan, who met her eyes with a look of toleration and semifriendliness. The Tlingit Indian was nearly as tall as James, probably about five feet nine inches, rare for native men of the region. His skin was the color of the red chocolate cake the baker used to make in Bergen.

How faraway Bergen seemed to her now! Never in her life had she ever supposed she would be on a river in the Yukon, looking for Soren. Never had she imagined lugging seventy-five pounds of supplies—"a white man's burden," Kadachan called it, compared to the men's hundred-pound packs—over the White Pass. She thought back on it now with a smug smile. James had probably wagered that she would not make it to the pass. Midway, when she stumbled for the third time and took her boots off to rub sore toes, he had picked them up, broken the heels off, and handed them back to her. "That should help," he grunted, although for a moment Kaatje could sense a kindness in his look, as if he could see her vulnerability and wanted to protect her. But then the expression was gone, and he stood back with his hands on his hips, as if waiting for her to say, "You were right. Let's go back."

Well, she had shown him! She looked back toward Skagway. The mountainsides met in alternating fashion, like huge woven threads of the Master's creation. It amazed her she had made it up such a steep pass with a pack upon her back. She was proud of herself for making it so far, for proving James Walker wrong. She had reveled in her victory, all the way around the interconnecting lakes that led to Lake Bennett and, eventually, the river. But they were far from done, and the journey still ahead of them threatened to overwhelm her.

Kaatje looked over at James. "I am going…" She paused, still unused to discussing private needs with men. James nodded, looking out to the river. Unable to suppress a sigh, she turned and walked into the forest, searching for a suitable place to relieve herself. Afterward, she decided to give her legs a much-needed stretch. After a few minutes of ducking branches and squeezing between trees, she reached a meadow.

She welcomed the silence of her surroundings, the noisy rush of the river muffled by the span of trees. She stifled a feeling of guilt, remembering the many times Mr. Walker had told her to stay near them. It had been weeks, after all, since she had had any time to herself. Any woman would do the same.

She smiled as she stared over the lumpy tufts of grass, hot pink lapland rosebay flowering amidst it. Dark gray rocks, covered with light green lichens, stretched to the edges of the meadow. And Kaatje wondered if this place had once been a pond. She could almost see a bull moose, slowly raising his homely nose from the still waters, long strands of moss hanging from his mouth. To her right, the hillside climbed steeply. She knew the craggy peaks visible here and there from the river must be beyond them. How far of a hike could it be to that view? She never thought she would say it after the pass, but after two weeks in the boat, a climb uphill sounded heavenly.

Kaatje turned at once and began the ascent. If she hurried, she could get back to the river before the men missed her. Within minutes, she topped the first hill, and the sight made her catch her breath. There were indeed mountains above her, astounding, snow-covered peaks. Back home in Bergen, and even in the Washington Territory, most of the mountains had been climbed and named. But here in Alaska peak after peak had never been climbed and certainly never named. She grinned at the sight. She knew that if Soren had ever seen such mountains he would have smiled too. The wind rustled the dense bushes nearby, and for the first time Kaatje noticed that she was beneath a thicket of huckleberries. If only it were later in the year! The fat, sweet-tart fruit would be the perfect remedy to their boring fare. Oh, well. She turned around and could almost make out the bright silver river between the trees beneath her. It was the most satisfying sight she had—

"Go!" Kadachan whispered, suddenly at her side. She whirled in fright, wondering how her native guide had reached her so stealthily. *"Go!"* he repeated, still staring above her.

"What?" She looked over her shoulder. Beyond her was James, hunched over with his hat in his hands. He scowled over at them and signaled Kadachan to get her to the river. It was only then that Kaatje saw the bear.

A grizzly.

Her heart froze for a moment and then pounded in such a rush that she fought for breath.

Kadachan slipped his hand around hers, each finger testifying to his strength, and urged her to bend over, to look smaller. Kaatje's eyes went back to the bear above them and James ten yards away. The bear raised up on its hind legs, sniffing the air. A female. Worse, a tiny cub did the same beside her, mimicking her in a way that, in any other situation, Kaatje would have found charming.

No one had to tell her how bad it was to surprise a mother bear.

With agonizing slowness, they stepped backward, away from the bushes. No doubt, the bear was as frustrated as Kaatje that there were no berries to be had. *Leaving nothing to eat but us,* she thought desperately. *And James.* Her guide was clearly intent upon intercepting the bear, should she charge. *No! No, Father, please! It is my fault!* They were just beyond the bear's sight when Kaatje heard the crash of breaking bush limbs and the "hiyeeyee!" call of James.

"Kadachan!" she cried. But he was pulling her downhill, rushing her toward the trees as fast as he could take her. When it was clear she would reach the forest, and the gun in the boat if necessary, he turned and ran back up the long hill. It was then that she spotted the pointed lance now in his hand—the one he always carried with him in the boat. He held it and watched for James as he crested the hill, the bear almost upon him.

If Kaatje hadn't seen it, she would never have believed it. As if they had practiced it a hundred times, James wrenched himself into the air with a guttural cry, catapulting over Kadachan, who had crouched low over his lance. As soon as James had cleared, Kadachan raised his lance, the pointed end directed toward the rapidly descending bear, the butt of it pushed into the spongy soil.

The bear had no chance. With a roar she tackled the man at the same time that the lance impaled her. Over and over they rolled, bear over man, man over bear. By the time Kadachan and the thousand-pound bear came to rest at the bottom of the hill, the grizzly was dead, and, miraculously, Kadachan lived. Heart pounding, Kaatje looked up the hill, a line of bright-red blood marking their trail of descent. The tiny bear cub mewled at the top, making Kaatje want to cry.

James ran to Kadachan, pulling him from beneath the grizzly's haunches. Kadachan leaned his head back and laughed, displaying a terrific row of crooked teeth, and let out a victorious cry.

He had been attacked by a grizzly—should have been crushed by that grizzly—but lived through it. Somehow, Kaatje knew it wasn't the first time. James, as he looked over at her, did not seem nearly as celebratory. He marched toward her, a look of anger on his face.

Onward he came, never pausing, taking long, quick strides. His color was gray and his hands, as big as Kadachan's, were shaking and he raised one as if to clamp down on Kaatje. He was just about to find the words when she stopped him with two. "I'm sorry."

He paused and then paced before her, as if working to find a way to express his fury. Starting, and then stopping, over and over again. After several minutes, Kadachan approached them, watching. His expression was that of subdued amusement. James turned his back on her, a hand resting against the rough bark of a pine tree. With a shaking voice, he said lowly, "I intend to collect on my other half."

"Your...other half?" Kaatje was incredulous—all he apparently cared about was money! The mercenary! With a short laugh, she passed him on the way back to the boat. It was embarrassing, putting them all in mortal danger. She was ashamed of herself. But there was no way she would let James know that now. "You'll get your other half, Mr. Walker," she spit out. "You can count on it."

one

*J*ames knew she must be hungry. He stared at Kaatje across the firepit, the coals reflecting in her green, luminous eyes. He glanced back at the meat on the spit as fat dripped from it, then sizzled on the hot stones beneath. They had not spoken for hours, which was not uncommon. But this sort of tension was. He had regretted his comment about the money as soon as it left his lips, but it was the first thing that came to mind that expressed his anger at her thoughtless stroll into the woods, his fear that she could have been mauled, his confusion because he cared. It was stupid, what he'd said. But he could not find the courage to apologize. It was easier facing a mother bear in the heat of the moment than uttering soft words after hours of consideration. He stirred the coals and stubbornly avoided looking at her.

"You did not have to kill the cub," she said, the first to speak.

"We did. If we had not, she would have starved. Better to use the meat for good than to waste it."

"It was barbaric."

James snorted and poked at the meat. "This is barbaric country. What would have happened had that mother bear tackled you instead of Kadachan? What if he had not had his lance ready? Do you think she would have paused before eating us?"

Kaatje looked to the side, toward the forest. "It was my fault."

"Yes."

"You could try and make me feel better about it, you know."

"I know."

She rose and glared at him across the fire. Her hair was loose and flowing over one shoulder. It shone in the firelight, and James checked his emotions, forcing his eyes back to the roast.

"Mr. Walker, this can be an amiable trip, or it can be miserable. Do you not wish for us to get along?"

He went on poking his stick into the coals, watching as more bear fat fell to the pit. "We can get along, Mrs. Janssen. I have told you how that can happen."

Kaatje let out a sigh and paced before the fire. James dared to look at her, admiring the curves beneath shirt and split skirt. He had known it was a mistake to bring a woman. He knew it! Why hadn't he listened to his gut?

"You are downright rude, Mr. Walker," she began, looking as though she wanted to shake a finger at him. He stifled a smile. "You've been by yourself too long. You can't call Kadachan company either. He lives just like you. You cannot assume I think like you."

"Right," he returned. "I assume you think like a woman." He did not know why he liked to bait her. He just did. It amused him to see her rise to his challenges, just like—the thought brought him up short.

"What is that supposed to mean?"

"Not a thing, Mrs. Janssen."

"I doubt that. I suppose I deserve some reprimand for getting us into trouble with the bear today. I said I was sorry. But I do not intend to eat Kadachan's kill. Her cub was innocent! And he went out there and slaughtered her! How could you approve of such a thing?"

James sighed. "I keep telling you. You're speaking of that bear cub as if she had been a human child. To leave her be would've meant she would've just died a slow, miserable death. She would have starved. Did you want to see that?"

"She could have foraged for berries and roots! Eventually, she would have been big enough to hunt game on her own."

James rose and stared at the woman across the fire. Her expression wavered, as if she was unsure of herself under his gaze. "Mrs. Janssen. The cub was barely weaned. There are no berries yet, nor will there be for a couple of months. And without a mother to teach her, she would not have known how to hunt. I realize that you feel…guilty about all this. But honestly, we have to make the best of things. The bears' death will help us live. If we are to make it over this river, locate your husband, and make it back, you'll need to come to the same conclusion."

Kaatje glared at him, angry tears in her eyes. Tears. What was a man supposed to do with tears? But she knew he was right. He could see it in her face. Her lovely face.

Abruptly, he hunched down again, poking at the meat. *If I am to make it over this river, Lord,* he prayed silently, *I cannot look at this woman as…as a woman. Help me, Lord. Help me keep my mind on higher thoughts.*

She left the fire then, and for an instant James worried that she might run into the forest, foolishly throwing herself at the mercy of a cougar this time. But he had come to know Kaatje well enough that he realized that she would not do such a thing, not after a day like this one. He let her go, half relieved at her departure, half bereft. He needed to let her come to her own conclusions, in her own time.

The crunch of gravel behind him told him she was going to the river. He turned and watched her splash water on her face. Washing away tears that he caused, he wondered, grieved that he had caused her such pain. He did not intend to shame her more than necessary. But he did want her to do as he bid. Her life depended on it in country like this.

James threw salt over the roast and felt his belly rumble again. Fifty feet away, Kadachan stretched the mother bear's skin on a rack. They had decided to camp here for a time, allowing some of the butchered meat to begin curing into jerky and the hide to dry out a bit before again taking on the river. Kadachan would look for some edible roots to supplement their diet, and they all could rest.

Later that evening he sat back against his pack with a quiet groan. How long had it been since he had felt such stirrings in his heart over a woman? His belly full, his eyelids heavy with sleep, he still could not keep himself from staring at Kaatje Janssen. Laying his bedroll next to James, Kadachan nudged him, gesturing toward Kaatje, teasing him. James kicked gravel at his friend, but Kadachan's grin just grew larger.

James closed his eyes, as if falling asleep, but though he was weary, he could not resist looking again at his female traveling companion. He glanced first at Kadachan, his eyes now closed, and then back to Kaatje. Her hair fell over her face, creating shadows that danced over soft skin in tandem with the fire's waning flames. She was lovely. Not beautiful. But there was something about her quiet strength, in combination with her surprising softness, that made her lovely through and through.

He sighed and closed his eyes again. It had been years since he had been taken with a woman. Ever since…Rachel. His wife of seven years had died in a deadly fire while he had been away, filing a claim on the land they had made their own on the plains of Minnesota. And when he had returned, she was gone, his beautiful, vibrant wife. Everything was gone. It was only days later that James had hopped a train west and, eventually, made his way to the mountains of Alaska, away from anyone who could ever tear his heart in two again.

During the long winters, when the miners and trappers—Alaska "sourdoughs," as the pioneers were dubbed—flocked to dance halls and saloons, James was careful to steer clear of female companionship. Years in the frontier made a man desperate for a woman. The feel of a smaller hand in his, the tender touch of a woman called to him. But he had held firm, been strong. Until now, until Kaatje.

James grunted and rolled over. Last winter he had considered taking one of Kadachan's sisters as a wife. Indian wives were easy to keep in Alaska. They weren't demanding like their white counterparts. Their husbands often went to the wilderness or the mines to make their living. She could have stayed with her parents in the village, and since he regularly visited with Kadachan anyway, he could have had all the pleasures of home without any of the responsibilities. He had been drawn to the idea but, in the end, resisted it. Now looking at Kaatje—or rather, trying not to look at Kaatje—he realized he had declined the decision to marry the maiden because down deep, he wanted more. He wanted more of what he had had with Rachel, if he ever dared to have something like it again. He wanted love.

But Kaatje Janssen was taken. And being good at what he did, James would probably help her find the idiot who had left her. "Take away these feelings, Father," he beseeched his Lord in a barely audible whisper. "Take away my admiration for this woman who is depending upon me for all that's good and truthful and honest. Make me your vessel, Father."

He sighed again, heavily, and then threw off his wool blanket and rose. As Kaatje had done earlier, he went to the river and splashed his face with water that made his hands reflexively clench from the cold. After waiting for his Lord to speak to him, to give him some reassurance and renewed resolution, but hearing no word to his heart, he went back to camp and threw another log on the fire. Purposefully, he did not look again at the woman beyond it.

James picked up his stick and poked at the red-hot coals, glowing every time a wisp of wind stirred. He watched as sparks rose and floated into the sky until they disappeared, replaced by dancing stars that filled the velvet black carpet. "Lord, Lord," James whispered, looking up at the multitude of stars that his God had created and wondering how the Creator could consider James Walker and his concerns at all.

Tora stirred the coals in the potbellied stove, hoping to coax a little more heat out of it for the girls' room. Even in May, it was frigidly cold at night. Her thoughts went to Kaatje and how cold she must be out by the river in the middle of the wilderness. She shivered again at the thought of it.

"Will you brush my hair out, Auntie?" Christina asked. She was a lovely little girl of seven, already showing the promise of tomorrow's womanhood. Tora nodded and took the horsehair brush from the girl's hand, sitting down on the feather bed behind her. To her right, Christina's younger sister, Jessica, slipped into her nightshift and pulled her long brown hair from the neckline, then hopped onto the bed beside them.

Tora brushed out Christina's long, dark blond hair, admiring the golden waves, and then turned to do the same for Jessica. Jessica's was more unruly, holding a tight curl in its long, dark brown locks, the same color as Tora's. As was their routine, they each got a hundred strokes and a kiss on the cheek before Tora tucked them in to hear their prayers, just as Kaatje had done every night before her departure the month before.

"Do you think Mama is all right, Auntie?" Jess asked, her brow furrowed in concern. Sometimes it struck Tora odd that her own daughter called her "Auntie." Yet it was exactly as it should be. Kaatje was a wonderful mother to the girl. She never wanted to interfere with the bond Jessica and Kaatje shared; Tora was content to remain a beloved aunt. She had given up any right to be called the girl's mother when she left the babe at Kaatje's seven years prior.

"I think she is just fine, dear heart," she said, tenderly stroking Jessica's cheek. "She'll be back come autumn, just as she promised."

"In time to make sure we get our schoolwork done," Christina said with a giggle.

"That's right," Tora said, feeling the unnaturally bright smile on her own face. She had to give them hope, each night, every night, until Kaatje returned. Tora tried to picture Kaatje's homecoming. How good it would be to have her home again! But what if, by some miracle, she brought home Soren? What would it be like to see him again?

There they'd be: Soren's abandoned wife and children; his former lover; Trent Storm, her fiancé; and Soren—a man thought long dead. What confusion! The thought of it brought terror to her heart. It was not that she loved Soren; she had never loved him. Remembering the thoughtlessness of her act—her adultery—brought her sorrow. "As far as the east is from the west, so far hath he removed our transgressions from us," Kaatje always reminded her. *As far as the east is from the west,* Tora repeated silently.

"What if she finds Papa?" Jessica asked, voicing Tora's own fears. "I mean, what if he comes home to live with us? Wouldn't that be wonderful?" she asked wistfully. "I've always wanted a papa."

"I think Mama should just marry one of the men who's asked her," Christina said. "Frances Olman said her father said Mama's legally divorced anyway."

"Christina!"

"What? It's God's plain truth. No sense running away from it."

Tora stifled a smile at the girl's grown-up tone. "It might be the truth. But your mother lives by God's laws, not man's. She needs to know if your papa is alive or gone before she would consider marrying anyone else."

"If Papa loved her, why did he leave?" Jess asked.

"I do not know. Perhaps something beyond his control kept him from coming back to her—to all of you." *Like his own pride or his wayward desires,* she added silently. She pulled a nightcap onto each girl's head. "Now let's say our prayers."

Both girls obediently closed their eyes and folded their hands. "Thank you, Father, for thy holy grace and for putting us in this place," Christina led.

"And for thy holy Son, dearest Jesus," Jessica followed. It was the same prayer every night, just as Kaatje had taught them.

"Be with our mother, O God in heaven…"

"And with us until we are reunited on earth."

Tora added, "Keep Kaatje safe and warm. Protect her from the dangers she faces, and prepare her for what is to come. We trust you, Father, with our lives and hers. Amen."

"Amen."

"Amen."

Trent watched as Tora came down the stairs and into the sitting room, admiring the woman who would someday be his bride. He felt it was time to address the matter again—he was tired of waiting to make their love official. He glanced toward Charlie, a boy of twelve, whom Karl Martensen had taken in. After his last voyage, he'd left Charlie with them, asking them to "teach him to be a gentleman on shore." Trent had gladly accepted, happy to have yet another young person around. With three in the house now, the roadhouse teemed with life. His heart was full with all that God had given him; after all these years, he had some sense of a family, as ramshackle as it was. Kaatje's girls looked up to him as a beloved uncle, just as they looked upon Tora as a beloved aunt. And Charlie, or "Charles," as Trent had dubbed him, seemed content to stay with them for a while. Although he spoke often of returning to Karl and the sea.

The boy was asleep in a chair across the room, apparently able to sleep wherever he was placed. Trent's eyes went back to Tora as she sat down beside him on the sofa and slipped her hand into his. "I do not know what will become of all of us, Trent," she said in little more than a whisper, looking over at Charles.

"Pardon me?"

"If he does return, if Soren returns, what will become of all of us? Look at us! What a wild family we've become. Our ties are strong, but could we bear his entrance again? It would be so..."

"Complicated?"

As she weaved her fingers through his, her deep blue eyes went to his, as if grateful that he'd understood her so well. "I am sorry, love, that you might have to endure it. You've already endured so much."

"Tora," he said, pulling her next to him and placing his arm around her shoulders. "I love you and all you are now. What you once were doesn't matter to me at all. And everything I might have to 'endure' is nothing against the payment I get in being with you."

"If he comes back, I'm liable to kill him myself," Tora confessed. "Kaatje deserves so much more than him."

"I agree. But you never know how God can work in a man. Look what he brought us through. Look where we are, who we are. Could not even Soren be transformed?"

Her face belied her emotions—she clearly did not believe Soren Janssen would ever change. "I know I should not doubt my God, my Savior. Especially after all he has done with me. But I simply cannot believe…"

"It is not you who has to believe. It is Soren."

"True. And if he doesn't come back thoroughly changed, I'll wring his neck before I let him hurt Kaatje again."

Trent laughed. Tora's transformation had come full circle. She had completely given her heart to Christ, but being humbled by God did not mean she'd lost her spirited ways. She had regained some of her old temperament. He was happy to see it return, in tandem with her more mature faith. It made Tora all the better for him.

"Let us speak of happier things. Kaatje will soon know the truth about her wayward husband and once home will settle into life here in Juneau. My sense is that you feel you have fulfilled your duty to her. Am I right?"

"I still have the girls to look after."

"Of course. Until she returns. Then, finally then, is it our turn?" He looked at her earnestly, taking her hand in his. "I guess what I'm asking is this—Can we set a date for our wedding? When will you marry me, love?"

Tora smiled at him, glanced over at Charles's still-sleeping form, then gave him a soft, quiet kiss that promised much greater passion. "Can we set a date?" Trent whispered, inches from her face.

"We can," she whispered back. "It will take time to get the fabric that I want and have a dress made. I wish I had thought to ask Elsa to bring home a *bunad* from Norway!"

"A bunad?"

"A Norwegian wedding costume. There is one in our family home that three generations have worn. And I should have asked her to bring one for you, too! They have lovely white shirts and black vests and black knickers—"

"Ahh. I'm sure we'll find something else that will be suitable."

"Yes, I suppose so," she said with a sigh. "I have seen some wonderful patterns… Elsa should return by August. And hopefully Kaatje by September. Can we marry at the end of October?"

"That long?" Trent groaned. "Why not now? Surprise the whole lot of them when they return!"

Her eyes begged him to understand. "We have waited this long, beloved. Can we not wait another five months to have the wedding of our dreams? It just would not be the same without Kaatje and Elsa."

"Five months," he said, lowering his head to give her a mock stern look. "No more. I swear I will not wait longer than that, even for you. It's more than any man should be asked to bear."

She smiled benignly, and gave him another quick kiss. "I will give you this, Mr. Storm. Let's host a fine dinner party. Formally announce our engagement. It will distract the girls."

Trent returned her smile. "And give me a chance to test Charles on his manners."

Charlie stirred and grunted, opening his eyes. "I heard that."

"Charles!" Tora exclaimed. "How long have you been listening?"

"Long enough to hear you two lovebirds plan my public execution in a formal tie," he said, pantomiming a hanging.

Trent laughed. "I think, dear boy, that you'll somehow survive."

"I doubt that, sir," Charlie said very seriously, already drifting back to sleep. "I doubt that."

t w o

Bergen, 1888

Elsa reached across the sofa to still her mother's knitting. "Mother, will you not at least consider coming home with us?"

Gratia put down her needles, and the soft auburn yarn fell to her lap. Her eyes were kind and loving, the skin around them so weathered and sagging that it threatened to impede her sight. If only Amund Anders were still alive! Loving a man had kept Elsa's mother young. Elsa had seen the change in her. Gratia once took pride in her perfectly knitted sweaters; now she missed stitches, unraveling hours and hours of work after finally finding the mistake. There had been a slow unraveling of her health, too—it was painfully evident in the way she moved, so slowly, the way she would touch her chest and sigh when she thought no one was looking. How much longer would she live? Elsa longed to have her mother with her in her mother's final days.

"Come with me," Elsa begged, kneeling beside her diminutive mother. "Think of how surprised Tora would be to see you. I'm certain she and Trent will soon marry. Would you not like to be there?"

Gratia reached out to softly pinch Elsa's chin. "If I were a decade younger, I would go with you, dearest. I would pay a great deal to see my youngest daughter again."

"You needn't pay a thing! Come with us to America. To see our new home and your youngest child. I will bring you to Bergen myself when you wish to return."

Gratia focused on the mantel, but she wasn't seeing it. She was looking further, as if into the future. "No, Elsa. This is my home. This is where I was born and where I shall die."

"Die? Don't speak of such things! You have much for which to be thankful!"

"Ah, yes. I have much for which to be thankful. But I do not have many years left in me. Ach, look what good I am!" She pointed to yet another mistake in her knitting and began unraveling the yarn.

Pained, Elsa rose and left her mother, staring out at the fjord that met the mountains surrounding her birthplace. It had been harder than she expected to be home; memories of Peder, and the love forged there between them, assaulted her at every turn. Yet these months had also shown her that she was healing, getting beyond the constant pain. The memories made her more wistful than melancholy. *Almost two years, my love,* she said silently to the waters that had swallowed her husband on a stormy night at sea. *Oh, how much you've missed, and how I've missed you!*

"*Mormor*, I want some hot chocolate," Kristian said from the doorway.

Gratia smiled at her four-year-old grandson and then quickly at Elsa.

"Me, too!" Elsa's one-and-a-half-year-old daughter, Eve, pulled her bedraggled blanket behind her as she traced every move Kristian made. They were adorable, her children. It pained her to think that their *mormor* would not be there to see them grow up. It had taken eight years to get home. How long, if ever, would it be until she made the journey again?

She sighed and nodded her agreement. "One small mug of chocolate for you and then to bed! Tomorrow we sail for home, and I do not want droopy-doos for children."

"We won't be droopy-doos!" Kristian promised, racing to his grandmother and almost knocking her back to the sofa.

Elsa picked up Eve and looked over her shoulder at Gratia. "I need to spend a bit more time with the Ramstads before I turn in. You'll put the little ones to bed for me?"

"Of course."

"I want to go to Farmor Ramstad's!" Kristian shouted.

"No, no. It's late. A bit of chocolate and to bed with you." She handed Eve to her mother. "You'll say good-bye to your grandparents and cousins tomorrow at the docks. Good night, dear ones," she said, ignoring Kristian's petulant looks and kissing them each on the forehead. "See you in the morn."

"Bright and early!" Gratia added, herding them toward the kitchen. "Oh, it will be a sad day for me to say farewell to you Americans."

Elsa watched as they disappeared into the kitchen, Kristian happily chattering about America and Alaska. In many ways, it would be good to go home. But would she feel a true sense of home anywhere? She had houses in Camden, Maine, and Seattle. But would anywhere ever really feel like home? Her home was on the sea, just as much as in the homes she had occupied with Peder. It was at sea that she felt at peace.

She walked out into the brisk spring evening and glanced up at the stars that filled the sky above the fjord. How much life had changed in the eight years she'd been away. How much she herself had changed. Suddenly she felt older than her twenty-eight years. What would fill the next twenty-eight?

As she walked toward the barn, she remembered her wedding day to Peder. She remembered Karl, standing at Peder's side, and wondered at herself that she had been so naive to have mistaken his intense gaze as mere friendship. Now the two were friends again. But that friendship had been torn apart when Karl had kissed her and declared his true feelings. It had driven a wedge between Peder and Karl— friends that were more like brothers. After Peder's death, Karl came to her, begged her forgiveness. And she had given it willingly. But still he seemed distraught that he hadn't done the same with Peder before his death.

She looked out at Hardanger Fjord and wondered where Karl Martensen was. Memories of him now brought only warm feelings. He was as dear to her as he once was to Peder, and she missed him. Elsa made a mental note to look in on his family on the way to the docks in the morning. Knowing Karl, he'd want as much news of them as he could get. Last she'd heard he had planned to take a voyage around the Horn, taking raw materials east with him and new steamship materials back to Alaska. With any luck, they would meet again in Alaska come autumn. How grand it would be to see him! To talk and laugh and embrace—

Elsa stopped short, watching her breath fog into small clouds in front of her face. Embrace? She cast the idea of it away, immediately guilty at the thought. Since when did she dream about holding her friend? It was being home, she decided. Missing Peder and what they had had together made her lonely. Even to the point of romanticizing about a friend! She laughed aloud, disgusted with her wayward imagination, and turned her thoughts back to her in-laws.

She saddled a horse and made it to the Ramstads' home in ten minutes. After knocking, she waited and wondered about the girl who once expected Peder to answer it—the girl she had once been. Her thoughts went back to the last time she had come to this house, at twelve years of age, still able to knock on a boy's door without suspicion that she was anything other than the playmate down the road. At thirteen, she had been required to wait on the young men to call on her. But that year, she was young and free. She remembered Karl and Peder wrestling as they answered the door, both eager to see her, both shoving each other's face and arms away from the doorjamb. She had laughed then, and she giggled again at the memory as Helga Ramstad opened the door.

Karl had been as eager to greet her as Peder had been. But since their kiss, Karl had withdrawn from her, even more so since Peder's death.

Would he ever look at her with such eagerness again? She realized she wanted it now. After all these years. She wanted a man, a man like Karl, to open a door and see her and a smile to light up his face with joy.

"Elsa?" Helga said, and, by her expression, not for the first time.

"Oh! Forgive me!" Elsa said, embracing her mother-in-law. She wondered, as Helga led her to the formal parlor, if she needed to ask forgiveness for thinking of another man, a man who wasn't her husband. But strangely, she felt no need.

San Francisco
"Oh, Captain Martensen!" Mrs. Kenney called, turning from her group of fellow socialites. They were at the Society of Friends of the Less Fortunate Ball, a dance designed to bring in enough money to build a new house for the homeless and out-of-luck.

"Mother wants to introduce you to her new friends," Mara Kenney said, ducking her head toward him. His date for the evening was a beauty, and Karl was the envy of the dance. Why could he not feel more...pleased?

"Let us go and meet them then," he sighed, hating the displeasure in his voice. The Kenney family had treated him like a second son, and the senior Kenneys had welcomed his offer to escort Mara to the ball. They had been clear in their intentions to secure an honorable man's hand for their daughter. Somehow, Karl had always thought of himself as an older brother to their girls, not a potential suitor. Now in foolishly offering himself as an escort to the Kenneys' daughter—who had bemoaned that she would once again come in on the arm of her father instead of a beau—he had unwittingly opened them all up for pain. So what right did he have to feel used? It was his own fault for getting them all into this predicament. The longer he knew Mara, the more he hoped that stirrings of love for her would grow in his heart. Perhaps it was a fanciful young man's dream—to be in love with your intended.

Mara smiled at him, delight shining in her eyes. How could he squelch the young girl's pleasure? She was stunning; her dark hair was wound into a dramatic knot and pinned with a fanciful silk flower arrangement that matched another on the shoulder of her dress and still another where the bodice met her tiny waistline. And truth be told, it was gratifying for a man to be admired so.

Mara chatted on about how much "the girls" had mooned over her Nile green China crepe dress, made in the latest style to reach San Francisco society. Her arms were bare, and the low, square neckline had twin gauze strips that formed the shoulders of the dress and ran across her breasts to meet at her waist.

Karl's gaze moved toward her small hands in long suede gloves, holding an elegant fan. He wanted to dismiss her as being too much like his former fiancée, Alicia Hall. But deep down, he knew Mara to be nothing like the conniving, superficial, heartless woman to whom he had once found himself engaged.

"Captain Martensen," Mrs. Kenney began, "I would like to introduce you to some of our newest friends from the Society. You have been away much too long."

"For some of us more than others," winked a matron at Mara.

Karl glanced down at Mara. She was blushing prettily, the picture of propriety. "Well yes, I was in Alaska, and then back East," he said. "It is a pleasure to be here at last." He did not wish to embarrass Mara in the least. The Kenneys were, after all, dear friends.

Mrs. Kenney made the introductions, and Karl resisted the urge to shift uneasily.

Gerald Kenney joined the group and slapped Karl on the back. "It's good to have you home, son. It feels right, somehow, to have you here."

"Indeed," Mrs. Kenney said, smiling at Karl and then the group. She was like a proud hen showing off her chicks.

"Enough socializing with the women," Gerald said, puffing out his chest. "Let us gentlemen retire to another room for a bit of politics and cigars."

"By all means, take both to another room," Mrs. Kenney enjoined. She took Mara's arm, and the girl glanced at Karl a bit mournfully. *What have I done?* he berated himself when he saw her look. He turned away with Gerald, breathing deeply for the first time all night. Away from Mara's side, he at least would not dig his grave any deeper than it already was.

But his respite was brief.

"I would be in hot water with Mrs. Kenney if I did not ask your intentions for my daughter," Gerald said conspiratorially as they entered a huge parlor filled with the pungent aroma of cigar smoke and the lower, rumbling sounds of fervent male conversation.

"I am relieved to speak of it with you, Gerald," he said.

His friend turned and grabbed two crystal glasses from a passing waiter. Then he turned back to Karl and leaned closer to hear him amidst the din of laughter and dialogue. "Oh?" His merry look said that he had completely misunderstood Karl.

"Yes, I—"

"Kenney! Martensen!" Hayden Stover, an old captain of Karl's and colleague of Gerald's, joined them. "I hear you're just back from Alaska. Tell me, man, what is going on up there? I hear there's word of a man running some sightseeing trips along the Inside Passage and doing quite well for himself. What say you? Should we all become tour guides?"

Karl glanced at Gerald, but it was clear that his friend was as intrigued as Hayden Stover about the opportunities to their north and was no longer thinking about matrimonial prospects for his daughter. *Perhaps it is for the best.* Karl clearly needed time to think his way out of his predicament. He liked Mara but was in no way ready to declare his intentions to court her.

"A man named Smith is indeed doing a smashing business along the Inside Passage. I have colleagues that are in the midst of building an inn in Ketchikan, specifically to cater to those passengers. Have you been to Ketchikan? The totem poles there are remarkable."

"I bet it's Trent Storm who spotted a business opportunity like that so early in the game," Hayden surmised.

"Indeed, one and the same," Karl affirmed.

"Ha! I knew it. That man is always a mile ahead of anything I think of."

"Even so," Karl said, cocking a brow, "you manage to do quite well for yourself."

"Indeed," Gerald agreed. "Imagine how Storm is making out! I suppose you are investing in the inn."

"Sadly, no. Storm already allowed my friend Bradford Bresley as well as Kaatje Janssen to buy in. But I plan on giving Smith a run for his money. I'm picking up a new steamship in Panama next month that will top any other for luxury travel. It'll sail between Seattle, Portland, and Juneau, stopping at Ketchikan every two weeks."

"Now that's a dandy idea," Gerald said with admiration. "Won't Smith be steamed? Pardon the pun!" The men laughed along with him.

"I am certain there are many other opportunities of the like," Karl offered. "Along with the luxury steamer, I'm securing parts for several shallow draft steamers for the rivers. Alaska is untamed, remarkable territory, gentlemen, the best I've seen since coming to America. There are few riverboats, and more pioneers and miners by the day. Now is the time to act if you wish to capitalize on Alaska's riches."

"You're still in cahoots with Bresley?" Gerald asked.

"Yes, Bradford and I are doing a fair amount of business. Trent Storm has invested in a portion of the steamers I'll bring to Alaska via Panama."

"Humph," Gerald snorted. "Storm again. How come you didn't come to me, son, if you needed investors?"

Karl smiled and ducked his head. "I would have, sir, had I needed investors. Storm and Bresley and I have been partners in the steamship business since our days in the Washington Territory. Bradford has leaned more toward mining interests; I still have two sailers; and Storm, of course, has his roadhouses. These days, we combine efforts only when it comes to steam."

"You heading north soon?" Hayden asked. "I'd like to get the lay of the land, figure how I might take part of what is certain to come."

"Are you sure?" Gerald asked, looking about at the growing number of men around them. "Why, isn't that frozen monstrosity we purchased called 'Seward's Folly'? Some say that the man was a plumb fool for spending thousands of dollars on frozen tundra."

Karl watched the men react, amused at Gerald's incredulity. "I've heard tell of the same," he allowed. "But it's my opinion that the men who called Seward a fool are the fools themselves. Alaska is rich. Gold mines abound, and I'd wager it's only a matter of time until they have a rush that equals California's heyday. And if it isn't gold—there's a company doing a thriving business in sealskins. There are whales and salmon and other fish in the sea that would keep a hundred canneries in business…and the Interior." He paused and looked around him. "The Interior is so beautiful that it can bring a grown man to tears. Game abounds. Yes, it is harsh country, cold country, but I tell you, it's the future for the thinking businessman."

"Count me in on your next venture, Karl," Hayden said.

"Aye, me, too!" called another. It seemed all the men in the parlor, perhaps fifty or more, were listening now.

"And me!"

"Whoa, whoa. Slow down there, boys!" Karl said with a smile. "There's plenty for all of you, but I'm afraid you'll have to drum up your own business. I do not wish to share any more of my pie. If you like, I can point you in the right direction."

"Call him on it!" shouted a man from the back.

"Hear, hear!" called another, lifting a glass.

Laughing, Karl was jostled and pushed toward a map of Alaska. And as he began pointing toward the Inside Passage, pausing at certain breathtaking spots, his heart yearned to return.

Later that night Karl stepped out of the elegant George IV phaeton he had rented and reluctantly raised a hand to help Mara out. She rose from her seat in the carriage, and as she made her way down the two steps, she stumbled. Karl reached out to steady her, but she ended up in his arms. Helplessly, he looked toward the Kenneys' front door, but Gerald was busily hustling his wife inside.

He looked down at Mara, anxious to set her to rights and step away.

But she was looking straight up at him. Earnest, clear eyes staring at him with an unspoken desire flickering in their depths. How long had it been since a woman had looked at him that way? His body longed to kiss the girl, to envelop her in his arms. But his mind, his heart, warned that it would be a deadly mistake. He did not love Mara Kenney. And he never would.

Would he never love again?

At last, Mara laughed softly and looked away. "I'm sorry, Mr. Martensen. I am dreadfully clumsy."

"Not at all, Miss Kenney." He took her hand again and led her up the stone stairs to their front door, still open but unoccupied. "It was most likely my hand that left you unbalanced."

She paused before the doorway and turned to him, taking his other hand in hers. "Your touch, Mr. Martensen, I must confess, does leave me a bit...unbalanced."

Inwardly, he groaned. He had meant it to be a gallant statement, not a leading one. Once again, her chin tilted upward, her eyes pleading. She was lovely. Beautiful. And nothing like Alicia. Why could his heart not love her?

Karl dropped her hands, wanting to spare her any embarrassment, and gestured toward the door. "I had better get you inside, Miss Kenney, before you catch a cold."

Reluctantly, she turned and walked inside, her demeanor shouting out her disappointment. Karl bit his lip and followed her.

A month later, off the coast of Mexico, he still was berating himself for mishandling the incident. It was ten o'clock, the starboard watch was on, and Karl paced the decks, unable to sleep. There was

a brisk wind, uncommon at night, probably because a storm was passing to the south of them. The cold gusts off the water felt right to
Karl, as if they could slam some sense into him. He thought back to
that night in San Francisco for the hundredth time. He had decided
that he would have to address the issue with Mara in private. Surely,
if he told her there was no love in his heart, it would end her fasci-
nation with him. What girl would want a loveless marriage?

He had taken her for a stroll after supper. Looking over the San
Francisco harbor, he had turned to her and taken her hands.

"Mara, I must speak with you about a delicate subject," he began.

"Yes, Karl. Please, go on."

"I'm afraid that all I feel for you is kinship," he plunged in, not
trusting himself to wait any longer. "While I admire you in every way,
I do not have the feelings that I should have for a woman I intend to
court."

Mara's eyes filled with tears, but she did not look away. Instead,
she raised a small hand and stroked his cheek. He cursed himself for
the way she moved him physically. How he longed to duck his head
and kiss her pretty mouth! But it wasn't right, it wasn't true...

"Karl," she said, "I am willing to wait for you. You are a fine man,
and if, as you say, you admire everything about me, love can't be far
behind."

He took her hand from his face and moved farther away. "I am
more than ten years your senior."

"That matters little. Father is twelve years senior to Mother."

"I am often at sea."

"I understand. I would be willing to wait each time you leave my
side." She drew closer to him and took his arm, leaning her cheek
against his bicep. "Do not let this go yet, Karl. All I ask is for you to
give it some time. I understand you have some doubts—I understand.
Will you not even give me a chance?"

He had turned to her, determined to say no, to get out while he
still could. But one look at her luminous eyes, and he could not. Who

could say? Perhaps she was right. Maybe God would grant a love for her, in time. Would it not be wonderful to be a part of the Kenney family?

Karl groaned, remembering. He had failed once again, with people he truly cared about. As he had failed with his father. As he had failed with Elsa and Peder.

He gritted his teeth and made his way to the bow of the ship and braced himself against the railing, riding the oncoming swells like a bucking horse. Each slam and dip of the ship a flogging. He deserved all the punishment the sea cared to give him.

This is not the way. It was as clear as any audible voice.

Karl looked up, blinking against sudden raindrops. "Lord, Lord," he murmured. "I do not understand. Why do you allow me to hurt the people I love most?" His thoughts sped backward over the years to when he had kissed Elsa Ramstad and forever alienated his best friend, Peder. "Why do you not help me?"

This is not the way.

"What is not the way? Where I am going? How I mishandled the Kenneys?"

This is not the way.

Suddenly it struck Karl—it was not God's desire to watch Karl punish himself. It was dangerous, being out on the bow in the dark of night. How many times had he warned his crew not to do such a thing? If he wasn't careful, he would wind up overboard, just like Peder. Lost forever. A life taken by a cruel sea. That would not honor his Lord.

Carefully he made his way back to the bridge, pausing for a brief look at the binnacle, a chat with Lucas and the others on starboard watch, then retired to his cabin. He grabbed a linen beside his wash basin and dried his hair of the salt spray in the darkness, then struck a flint and lit his lantern. He sat down hard on his sea chest. "All right, Father," he said, resting his elbows on his knees and leaning forward, his hands on his face. "That was not the way," he prayed silently. "What is the way?"

You are on the right path.

"How? How can I be on the right path? With every step, I seem to hurt another."

Karl heard no response.

"Oh, I know. Perhaps it is not with every step. But must I hurt everyone I love?"

Again he heard no response.

Karl sighed and rocked in tandem with the ship for a while, relishing the great washing sounds of waves passing by and the creak of solid beams that groaned from the pressure but were certain to hold. He knew they would hold. This was a ship forged at Ramstad Yard, in Camden-by-the-Sea.

Camden. Was Elsa home yet from Bergen? He yearned to see her, talk with her, laugh with her. How long had it been since they had been together? Since Japan. Two years. How could two years have gone by? It seemed when he was back East, she was in Washington. When he was in the Far East, she was in Bergen. When she was in Camden, he was in San Francisco. *Are you keeping us apart on purpose, Lord? I can be trusted now.*

Or could he? Karl shook his head and stared at the lantern. Was the reason he could not fall in love with Mara Kenney because he still yearned for Elsa Ramstad? Impossible. Had he not proven his intention to do penance? To be only her friend? If Elsa was ever to be his, she would have to make the first move. She would have to walk up to him without faltering. Walk up to him without any hesitation in her step and *kiss him.* Yes, *she* would have to kiss *him.*

Karl flopped back on the bed and groaned again.

Because that was certainly never going to happen.

three

June 1888

The silence was getting to her. Kaatje had watched Kadachan pad off into the forest, presumably to see if he could find out any information from the tribe just upriver, while James went about laying a fire. They had traveled late into the evening, trying to cover more miles in order to reach the neighboring tribe and possible further information on Soren Janssen. Wearily, she pulled out the knapsack of jerky and hardtack, and then fetched a bucket of fresh water. The river was still icy cold, and even a quick dip made her wince.

When she returned, the fire was crackling, the warmth of it welcoming her back into the circle of silence. "Can we not speak?"

He looked up at her with a slight scowl. "Of what?"

"Of anything. The monotony of our travel is getting to me. Tell me of Alaska. Of the wildlife, your treks, your friends. Anything."

James grunted and stirred the fire. When he remained silent, Kaatje sighed and handed him a slice of jerky and another of hardtack, then sat down upon a wool blanket to eat her own boring fare. A half-hour later, feeling the cool June evening beginning to penetrate her clothes and chill her, she wondered if she should turn in. She had just picked up her blanket and wound it around her shoulders when James began speaking.

"Once, in ancient times in Alaska, there lived a tribe of giants along the Cook Inlet."

A story! James Walker was actually going to tell her a story! She sat down in stunned disbelief, a slight smile tugging at the corners of her mouth. He ignored her.

"The land was good and fruitful, and the gentle people wanted for nothing, content to live in peace with one another. In that day, there was a young couple named Nekatla and Susitna, and they were especially happy since they were engaged to be married." He kept his eyes on the fire, as if slightly embarrassed that he had begun the story at all. But as he went on, the words came more easily.

"The wedding day was nearing when bad news came to the tribe. A stranger came running into the village, crying, 'Run! Run! Warriors from the south are soon upon you! They are killing every person in their way, burning the villages! They have killed my family, my friends. I have nothing. Run, before you face the same!'

"All plans for Nekatla and Susitna's wedding were forgotten as the villagers gathered to discuss their strategy. Some thought they should stockpile weapons and prepare for battle; others wanted to hide in the forest until the invaders passed. Finally, Nekatla rose, waiting for his turn to speak. 'It has been our way for generations to avoid the ways of war. We are a people of peace. But to hide would be to allow the warriors to pass by, to go on to kill others in distant lands.'

"The elders conferred quietly among themselves and then turned back to him. 'Go on,' they said, 'we are listening.'

"'We must go south to meet this tribe of warriors,' Nekatla said, as tears of fear rolled down Susitna's face. 'We must carry gifts instead of weapons and show them that they have no reason to attack our village or our loved ones.' It was a bold plan, but the villagers saw the wisdom of it and quickly agreed. As the men gathered their provisions and the women the gifts, Nekatla and Susitna climbed to a nearby hilltop where they had spent many afternoons together. 'We will marry as soon as I return,' Nekatla promised her.

"'I will wait for you here,' she told him. 'I will not leave this spot.'

"Susitna watched as the men disappeared into the forest. She gathered her sewing needles, knife and baskets, nuts and berries. For days she camped on the spot where Nekatla had proposed, making baskets, sewing, and looking to the distant forest, hoping her beloved would soon return. When many days had passed, and Susitna grew weary, she said, 'I will lie down, just for a moment,' and quickly fell fast asleep.

"That night, word of a terrible battle reached the village. 'Nekatla was very brave,' reported the breathless runner who had escaped the fray. 'He led our men to meet the warriors, and when he went forward to speak, someone threw a spear and pierced his heart. At once, we were at war, fighting until all our men were dead or dying, along with many of theirs.' The women and children and old men wept as they found out that their loved ones were gone, never to return to them.

"A group of women climbed the hill to break the terrible news to Susitna, but when they found her asleep, they said, 'Let her rest. She'll have greater strength to bear this burden in the morning.' While she slept, they wove a blanket of soft grasses and wildflower blossoms, which they laid over her. 'May Susitna always dream of her love,' an old woman whispered. They left her then, returning to the village without joy or warmth. As the evening grew darker, and the air colder and colder, Susitna fell deeper and deeper into sleep. All around her, the fruit trees froze and died, like the men falling in battle. The villagers' tears became clouds in the chilly air, then returned as Alaska's first snowfall. Soon, all the land was blanketed in white, until Susitna and all her people were covered.

"Susitna still sleeps through the seasons, dreaming of Nekatla. If you come into the Cook Inlet in the winter, you can still see her beneath her white blanket. In the summer it is a green and flowered blanket."

James looked up at Kaatje then, his eyes curious. "It is said that when the people change their ways and peace rules the land, Nekatla will return. Then Susitna, the Sleeping Lady, will awake."

After a moment Kaatje said, "It is a sad story."

James nodded and glanced at the fire. "It is."

"Why did you share it with me?"

"You wanted to talk. About anything."

"That is not talk. It is storytelling."

"All right. Let's talk."

Kaatje sighed. *Why must it be so difficult with this man?* "Why did you share that story with me?" she repeated.

"The Sleeping Lady is a mountain south of us. Kadachan reminded me of it today."

"What made Kadachan think of it?"

"You remind him of her. You sleep, he said, until your husband returns."

"I am hardly asleep."

"Aren't you?"

Kaatje sat back, staring at him with a frown. Is that what he thought of her? "If I were like Susitna, wouldn't I still be on my Dakota farm waiting for my husband to return?"

"Perhaps," James said nonchalantly, stirring the fire with a stick. "There are many ways that people sleep through life."

"If I am sleeping, at least I'm trying to awaken! That is why I am here, out here. That is why you are here." Asleep indeed! This was undoubtedly the oddest conversation Kaatje had ever had!

James nodded once. His cool demeanor irked Kaatje. "What about you? What are you hiding from? A man doesn't come to this place," she gestured around her, "unless he's running from something."

He nodded again. "I suppose you are right."

"So?"

He considered her for a moment, his eyes sad. "I guess I was running from my own bad memories."

"Forgive me," she said, retreating a bit after seeing his expression.

"No, it's all right. You are not saying anything that I don't deserve. I had a wife once, Mrs. Janssen. A pretty girl named Rachel. We lived in Minnesota on a farm. We had just staked a new claim when she died in a fire."

"Oh, Mr. Walker. I am so sorry."

He shook his head. "It's been many years. I came to Alaska to sleep. Because I didn't ever want to risk waking to that pain again." He looked her steadily in the eye. "I didn't want any woman to ever come near me again."

She had felt that way when Soren first left, wanting to protect herself from the pain. She'd had no idea James had been there too— had known firsthand the cruelty of being the spouse alone, the one left behind. She looked over at him and smiled sadly. They'd been together all these weeks and she hadn't known.

"And then here you come, shaking me awake." His words interrupted her musings.

She looked up at him in confusion. Was he speaking of Kaatje as someone he wanted to be with? As a woman instead of an employer?

"Making me think about what I had once," he quickly amended. "What I would do if I were in your situation. I haven't thought this much in eight years, Mrs. Janssen, and I'm none too sure I like it."

Kaatje swallowed hard. "I think...I think God would rather have us be uncomfortable than asleep. I hope I'm not asleep, Mr. Walker. I hope that this whole journey is about waking from a long nightmare that began when my husband abandoned me. I want to put it behind me. To find out the truth and get on with living. I want to live each moment awake. Because as much as my life has been difficult, a lot of wonderful things have been given to me too. Do you understand that?"

"I do," he said with a nod, resuming his task of poking at the fire. "Yes, I think I do."

Kadachan still had not returned come morning, and after taking her daily river "bath," splashing her face and washing the rest of her body with a cloth as she hid behind a neighboring bush, she got dressed, packed her things, and sat down upon her sack back at camp.

"It could be a while," James said, looking over at her.

"I see."

"Might as well make the most of these few minutes." He went to the boat and pulled out two fishing rods. "You've been complaining about the jerky and hardtack. How about helping me scare up some fish? This part of the river is good for northern pike."

She raised an eyebrow in surprise. "Count me in. But I'll need a lesson. I haven't fished for years."

He gave her a small smile that warmed his eyes and revealed a dimple in his cheek. He pulled his head to the right. "Come. There's a nice fishing hole a few hundred feet upriver."

She followed behind him, matching his long strides with some effort as he jumped from one tree snag to another where the shoreline got mushy, then around an area of long reeds, sending tiny frogs leaping out of their way. James paused, bent down, and dug his hands into the muck, pulling long earthworms from their homes. Kaatje grimaced. She had forgotten about that aspect of fishing. James went on without speaking, and in moments they reached a group of towering pines, the river cutting under them, revealing their root systems. To one side, jutting out into the river, lay a large, sturdy logjam. The water grew deeply green and still in the small cove, and the spot in the shadows would be perfect for fishing.

"You know how to spot them," Kaatje said, making her way out on a silvered log.

"Careful."

"As always," she said. She sat down on the log, relishing the smell of the river, the cool breeze of morning off the water, the warmth of the log beneath her. It was idyllic and at last something to do besides sit in the boat. She looked up to watch James make his way out to her. "Do you think I could fish off the side of the boat?"

"It wouldn't be best. We're always moving around, getting set with our poles." He took her hook and jabbed a worm on the end, then let the string fly outward again, the worm jiggling.

"I could move around too."

"Let's just fish here, Mrs. Janssen, and I'll think on it." He baited his own hook and then found a spot he deemed likely to find fish.

"All right," she sighed.

"You're too far out," he said gently. "Pull your hook in toward the shadows of those logs. See? Did you see that one? They're down there, and hungry this time in the morn. Set your bait right, and we'll be eating fish for breakfast."

"I like that idea," Kaatje murmured, pulling it closer. It was a bit awkward, holding her pole out in order to get the string closer to the log pile. When a fish bit down on her hook right away, it surprised her, and Kaatje yelped.

"Got one?"

"I do! Oh!" The momentum of pulling up on the fish and trying to stand at the same time set her off balance, and she would have slipped into the water had James not grabbed her arm.

"Let go of the pole!" he said through gritted teeth, holding on to his own pole with one hand and to Kaatje with the other.

"No!" she said, laughing at her own stubbornness. "I have a fish!" She didn't know why she believed he could easily pull her upward with one arm; she just did.

He rolled his eyes and pulled her up to the log again, his face red from the effort. But Kaatje ignored him, quickly turning to the pole and the flapping Dolly Varden at the end. "Look at that!" she squealed. "She has to be eighteen inches!"

"Humph."

"Oh, don't be a grump, Mr. Walker," Kaatje said. "I caught a fish, and you caught me!" She grinned at him until he gave her a hint of a smile. She so liked how his rare smiles transformed his face. He really was quite handsome when he allowed himself to have a little fun. When his deep green eyes stayed focused on her a moment too long, she turned and bent, picking up the fish under its neck. "I'm off to fry my fish. Don't worry if you don't catch one of your own; I'll share mine with you. It's only fitting that I pay you for keeping me dry."

She started to edge around him, realizing too late that the log was barely wide enough for her to do so. She kept her eyes downward, suddenly uncomfortable, recognizing the strength in his wide chest, the clean, manly smell of him. He held on to her shoulder as she passed, still guarding her from a fall. She liked the protective nature of his gesture. She dared not look up at him, afraid of what she might see, or what she might not. Kaatje swallowed hard and made her way off the log, no longer smiling, never looking back.

When Kadachan came to camp that evening with word that a "curly-haired white man" had staked a claim a mile north, Kaatje felt as if an ox had sat upon her chest.

It had been years since she had even come close to getting word of Soren, let alone seeing him. What if he was on his claim, happily mining, believing his family safely tucked away on a distant Dakota farm? What if he was…there?

Her vision blurred, and she sat down hard upon a rock.

James leaned forward from the waist and gave her a searching look. "You all right, Mrs. Janssen?" He shifted uncomfortably and straightened. "You look peaked."

Kaatje's hand went to her chest. "I am fine." She took a deep breath. "Certainly there is more than one 'curly-haired white man' in the immediate area."

James's expression was not affirming.

The landscape swam before her eyes again. "It is not certain?"

James took off his hat and wiped his mouth with the back of his hand. He lowered his voice, as if being careful to break the news gently. "There are probably no more than ten white men within fifty square miles. And few men I've laid eyes on have curly hair."

Kaatje nodded, unable to speak.

"We can get to that claim tonight." He searched the sky. "This twilight will hold for another couple hours at least."

Kaatje looked away, thinking. "That is very thoughtful of you, Mr. Walker," she said, gazing at the river that might take her to her husband. "But we have had a very long day. I believe it would be best to wait until morning light."

James looked at her, apparently to see if she meant what she said, then shrugged and turned away. He spoke quietly to Kadachan in Tlingit, and they began finishing their chores for the evening.

Kaatje could not rouse herself to help. James seemed to understand, taking over her jobs of hauling buckets of water to the campfire, then gathering wood. All she could do was stare at the aquamarine river endlessly rushing against boulders in the center, striking them and cascading along the sides. How like the river was she? Endlessly pursuing Soren, striking up against insurmountable obstacles, then finding another way. Going on without him. Going on alone.

Well, she would go on alone if she had to. She had made it this far, hadn't she? She had God and friends and a solid means of support.

She didn't need Soren any longer.

Or did she?

They were on a Yukon River tributary, two hundred and forty miles downriver from the infamous Forty Mile—site of a huge gold strike two years earlier—when the trio came across the remains of an old cabin. It had once been perhaps ten feet wide by twelve feet long, but the roof had caved in. There was no sign of life around it; the woodpile was encrusted with lichens that spanned from log to log, and the forest floor showed no visible tracks. How long had he been gone from here? Kaatje wondered. If he had been there at all, she corrected herself.

Wordlessly James and Kadachan began stripping away the roofing material. The four side walls still stood, and now they could see that the roof had only partially collapsed. It struck Kaatje that Soren might have been inside when it fell. Would they find his corpse? His bones? The place had the air of death. Was it here that his life ended?

Within minutes the men had tossed the debris from the cabin. There was no body.

James picked off a cedar branch from the only table inside and looked back at her. "It probably was a heavy snow that did it last winter. Most cabins can't take more than a couple of winters. Come in, Mrs. Janssen. Have a look. There is nothing in here to hurt you."

Kaatje wasn't so sure. Hesitantly she stepped inside, looking from side to side as if she could feel Soren there. Was this place his? Had he truly been here?

Kadachan made a low guttural sound and picked up a picture. He blew off the dirt. Half of the daguerreotype was soiled beyond recognition, but there was enough.

Kaatje could see her own face, a portrait taken as a girl in Bergen just prior to marrying Soren. The only photo Soren ever had of her.

Her hand flew to her mouth, and she felt short of breath. It was Soren's cabin. He had been there, slept there. And he had kept her photo with him the whole time. Until he left, that is.

"Mrs. Janssen?" James asked, walking quickly toward her. He took her elbow. "Are you feeling faint? You look as if the wind has been knocked out of you. Here, sit down." He led her to the only bed, decomposing from the elements, and she gratefully sat down amongst the sticks and debris.

Soren had been there. There, right where she was.

A movement to her right caught her attention. Slowly, James lifted a worn buckskin dress from the other side of the bed. He glanced at her with sorrow in his eyes, and Kaatje knew at once what he thought. Soren had been there.

And so had an Indian woman.

She found her tongue. "Perhaps the woman lived here after Soren left." She rose and walked to the doorway. "Or perhaps he traded something so he could give that dress to me."

James nodded, but she could see he did not believe her words. She did not believe them herself. His look was kind and knowing, silently breaking the truth to her. He continued to poke around the cabin with Kadachan, but there were few other items left behind.

Soren had been with yet another woman. Kaatje raised her hand to her forehead, wondering if she was running a fever. She felt so woozy. Sick to her stomach. She rose and walked out into the woods, anxious for some privacy. There she was in the middle of the Yukon, looking for her philanderer of a husband. Defending him by making up excuses. James and Kadachan would think her such a fool!

Kaatje felt hysterical laughter build inside her. It really wasn't a surprise. The milking girl in Bergen, Tora, her French neighbor, how many had there been? *How many, Lord? And how long must I endure this humiliation?* Old pain was awakened, as if shaken from a long dormancy. *Why, Father? Why bring me so far to discover yet another dark sin of my husband's? What good does this do? What good?*

She began running, running as fast as she could through the woods. It was dark there by the cabin, since the trees were dense and the foliage formed a tight canopy hundreds of feet above. She wanted to get out of the darkness—it threatened to suffocate her.

Kaatje ran and ran, her skirts bunched in her hands, leaping over fallen logs, dodging low branches, until she could run no more.

Gasping for breath, her hands on her knees, she looked ahead. There was sunlight streaming through the trees there, and for the first time she felt as if she could breathe deeply. Kaatje wanted to cry but could find no tears within her. All she could feel was cold fury.

"Why?" she yelled at the sunlight as if at God himself. "Why?" she screamed again.

And at last the tears found her.

James motioned to Kadachan to silently back away. The woman had suffered yet another indignity; she deserved her privacy. With quiet hunter steps they left Kaatje, each taking a different flank hundreds of feet back. She could be alone, but she would be protected. When

she began her trek back to the river, they would beat her there, waiting as if they had been there all the time.

Her sobs tore at James's heart, and his breast filled with an anger
he had never known. How could Soren have done such a thing? Left
Kaatje and his girls and taken up with an Indian maid? Sure, he had
seen it a hundred times. Most of the mountain men and miners took
Indian brides, or at least tried to, whether or not they had a bride at
home in the States. But he had never seen the wives who had been
left. The women who had loved and lost their men. It gave the practice a whole new unsavory light. Before, it was none of his business.
Now, it was all his business.

James walked farther away, wanting to be far from Kaatje's gut-
wrenching cries. It made him want to punch something, and hard. He
clenched his fists and his teeth and bit back the cry of rage that built
inside his shaking body. How could Soren do such a thing? To Kaatje?

He paced back and forth, waiting for Kaatje's tears to abate.

He wanted to find Soren Janssen now.

He wanted to find him and give him a beating he would never
forget.

Kaatje headed back to the river an hour later. James and Kadachan
were by the boat as if they had never left. Kadachan whittled at a stick,
and James idly threw rocks into the river, at a loss for words.

"Did you find any letters?" she asked carefully, not looking at
either of them.

"No," James answered. What had she hoped Soren would have
received, there, in the middle of nowhere?

She did not explain.

James dug his heel into the rounded rocks of the small river's
beach, choosing his words carefully. "Would you like to go on? Or
head back to Juneau?"

"We go on, of course."

"Mrs. Janssen…"

She looked up at him then, her eyes bloodshot from crying, making the hazel green eerily vibrant. He glanced down and then over at Kadachan, silent. Quietly, James asked his friend in Tlingit to make further inquiries of the local tribe. Soren Janssen had been there at one point and time; perhaps they knew where he had gone.

Kadachan turned and ran off into the forest as if he knew this land like it was his own.

"Where is he going?"

"To ask the local tribe if they know anything more of your husband."

"You think me a fool."

"I do not understand your decision to go on."

"It is not your place to understand my decisions, just to abide by them," she ground out. "This is your job, Mr. Walker, and nothing more. You are being paid to lead me to my husband, dead or alive. What confuses you in this task? Why do you question me every mile?"

"I have not asked—"

"With your eyes. With your actions. You ask. Why not simply adhere to our terms and keep on moving?" She was shaking with anger.

"I do not understand a love that drives a woman to such lengths," he gently clarified.

She turned away and stared at the river for a long time. When she spoke, it was so softly that James could barely hear her over the water. "I wish him dead. Am I horrible?" Her eyes were intense, aching in their sorrow.

He considered his response. "No. I suppose I would feel the same if it were I. What if…what if we had found Mr. Janssen? Inside. Dead. What would you have felt then?"

"Released." She turned and faced him, her expression one of sheer exhaustion. "I would have felt released."

Kaatje watched James build a campfire. It was all she could do to sit upon a log and glance from the abandoned cabin to the fire to the river. James offered her food, and, as if in a dream, she dimly remembered declining it. Her stomach rumbled at the smell of sizzling trout, but she could not find it within herself to lift the food to her mouth.

Not wanting to speak anymore that night, she set out her bedroll and climbed under the wool blanket. James had spread fresh cedar boughs beneath her sleeping spot, and the sweet aroma filled her nostrils. He was sometimes difficult and surly about bringing her on the river, but he could also be thoughtful in small ways. Kaatje had to give him that. She closed her eyes and listened as Kadachan quietly arrived and spoke in low tones with James.

They talked back and forth for some time in Tlingit. At first Kaatje was irked that she was cut out of the conversation, but then she realized she was too exhausted to ask them to speak in English anyway. After all, Kadachan's English was rudimentary at best. He could understand them very well, but when it came to speaking, it was difficult to understand him. Through slitted eyes she watched Kadachan eat fried trout with his hands as he spoke, gesturing to the north over James's shoulder.

She raised up on one elbow to ask the one question to which she needed an answer before sleeping. "Is he alive?"

"We don't know," James said gently.

Kaatje nodded, discouraged, then seconds later fell fast asleep.

The next morning, before breaking camp, Kaatje explored the immediate vicinity. A hundred feet upriver, she discovered the traces. Soren had obviously labored here for many months, making his way into a cliff side after cutting through the rock on top. She heard James's whistle, his signal to rally, when a glint in the water caught her eye.

She leaned over and yet couldn't reach it, so she sat down to take off her boots and stockings. A minute later, she lifted her split skirt and waded a few feet into the frigid water, wincing as tender flesh met sharp rocks. Quickly, she dipped down and grabbed a golden rock that was as deep down as her shoulder. She rose and watched it as the water dripped away and the sun warmed it in her hand.

"It's probably fool's gold," came a voice behind her.

Startled, Kaatje whirled, stumbled, and almost fell, but James was already rushing in to help. She ended up against his chest, and she was surprised by the breadth of him, the hard muscles under her cheek. He held her as if she weighed nothing. "Are you all right?"

Quickly, she stepped away and up onto the rocky beach, then looked at the rock in her hand again, trying to push away the embarrassment of her stumble. "Yes," she said, feeling her cheeks burn. After the fishing-hole experience, James was liable to decide she couldn't stay on her own two feet. "Fool's gold, huh?"

James raised his eyebrows and nodded once. "Most likely. We can have it tested when we get back in town. If it's true gold, you'll have food on the table all winter."

"From just this?"

"Yes."

"But it's probably fool's gold."

"You never can tell. These mountains and streambeds are rich with gold waiting to be discovered. Your husband knew it. That's obviously why he was here."

"Do you think he found some gold? Maybe he found a solid streak and was taking a load to town. Perhaps he was intending to sell it and send for us. Do you think he might have been attacked, James?" Her heart leaped with sudden hope, a sudden prospect of a plausible and respectable answer to the whole sordid mess.

But his expression dashed it.

"What?"

"Kadachan and I explored his traces and the crevasse he was mining. There might have been gold once. But we didn't see any evidence of it."

"Could he not have mined it all out? I mean to say, it wouldn't be prudent to leave an open gold mine here alone, available for anyone to take, right?"

James pinched his lips together and looked to the river. "Mrs. Janssen, if I were a betting man, I would say he didn't find more than a nugget."

"Why?"

"Because everything I know about your husband tells me that he would have found some way to make it to town and brag about his success. Someone would have known about him. News like that spreads faster than wildfire. If he had been taken by Indians or claim-jumpers, he could have bought his way out of it, had he struck it rich. And once he bought his way out, he would have lived large, like he always wanted to, right? That kind of man is hard to miss."

Kaatje thought over his words for a moment. "Kadachan found out more about him, didn't he?"

He stared hard at her for a moment. "Yes. He took a local Indian maiden as his bride."

Kaatje swallowed hard. "And she is where?"

"We don't know. They both disappeared about two years back."

"Where?"

"The tribal chief said they were heading upriver. And they left just in time."

It was her turn to give him a sharp look. "Why?"

"Because the tribe was out to kill him."

"Pardon me?"

"Mrs. Janssen, they were coming to kill him because while he had been betrothed to the chief's daughter, he had also gotten her sister pregnant. It was the sister he took with him."

four

Christina and Jessica were already a big help in the roadhouse kitchen, Tora proudly appraised. They were both at the marble pastry counter, earnestly kneading bread, as Tora hurriedly dropped off dishes for Charlie to wash and took more steaming plates out to the restaurant. Ordinarily, she merely managed and greeted customers, but her three waitresses were so busy they could not keep up. Even Trent had pitched in and was helping the cook serve up hot pot roast, carrots, and mashed potatoes.

She grinned as she exited the swinging kitchen doors, taking good food to hungry men. Juneau was a hopping, rowdy place, and Tora loved it. She loved the frontier feel of the town, the awe-inspiring beauty of the mountains and fjords that reminded her of home. She cherished the chance to build a part of Trent's business alongside him again, and the sense of family that Kaatje, the girls, Charlie, and Trent gave her. This place, at last, was home.

The men flirted with her and left her generous tips, all of which went into a can that she saved for the children. She liked to spoil them with new clothes or treats. And although Charles was Trent's to care for, Tora wanted to mother him a bit too. She doubted he had ever spent much time with women, at least women of good morals.

And Tora Anders finally had her own good morals, she acknowledged to herself. Finding faith in God had radically changed the way she lived and saw others. It no longer mattered what others thought of her—at least, most of the time; she still had to work at it—but she knew God always found delight in her. It gave her a foundation of freedom and self-assurance that she had never known. Being Trent's bride-to-be was only icing on the cake. Her faith, her love with Trent, Kaatje, and the children had all added up to make her life just about perfect.

"May I have some more coffee, miss?" a heavily bearded man asked, holding up a white ceramic cup.

"Certainly."

"Got any more cobbler, Miss Anders?" another asked, obviously vying for her attention.

"I'll get that, Miss Anders," Bess, one of her waitresses, interrupted.

"Ah, Bess, I wanted Miss Anders to bring it by," the man grumbled good-naturedly.

"Yes, well, if you really want your cobbler, you'll just have to take it from me," the redhead sassed back. "Miss Anders is only helping us out since you boys all decided to take supper at the same time."

"We'll do anything to get your pretty manager out and among us!" shouted a young man from another table.

Trent came out wiping his hands on a dishcloth and perusing the room. The men grew quieter at the sight of him until one man yelled, "You're taking that lout as your husband? Look at me!" He stood, and the men laughed as he pretended to primp. "Don't you want a young man? Why, that old man probably won't be able to carry you over the threshold!"

Tora covered her smile while Trent glared at them all. "I'll show any man here that I'm twice the man he is! And I'm telling you, it will take twice the man to handle a bride like Miss Anders!"

The room erupted with laughter and shouts. Tora laughed with them.

"Who'll give me a decent run for my money?" Trent went on. He unbuttoned his fine shirt sleeves and rolled them up past his elbows. "There's a dollar here for any man who can beat me at arm wrestling!"

Several men rose immediately, eager to take the businessman's dollar with their miner's muscles. They jostled each other toward the table.

"Easy, boys, easy!" Trent called, Charlie suddenly at his side, eyes alight. "One at a time. I'll take as many of your dollars as I can. I'm working on that Ketchikan roadhouse now, you know! I can use the extra cash."

Tora had never seen such bravado in Trent, nor seen him so happy. But inwardly she groaned. Trent was tall and well built but lean, and he surely could never compete with the beefy muscles in the crowd. Still, she stood beside him, like a barmaid next to a seasoned card shark, watching what would transpire. Maybe it would be good for Trent to take a little beating on the arm-wrestling table. He was always so sure of himself…

Her mouth dropped open as Trent bent the first man's wrist and took his arm down to the table. Charlie hit the table, hooting out his approval and putting out his hand to take the loser's dollar. Abruptly Tora closed her mouth. It wasn't seemly to be surprised that one's intended could outmuscle another man, regardless of his enterprise. When he beat the following man, her surprise turned to pride, and she cast out her hands and raised her eyebrows in a silent, taunting dare to the remaining men in the crowd.

Trent beat three more men before the sixth man beat him. With that, he rose and smiled, waving to the customers. "That's it for me, gentlemen. I always quit when the tide begins to turn, and it appears that time has come." He rose, cheeks flushed and his hairline damp, making his dark hair, gray at the temples, curl a bit. Tora stared up at him in adoration, and before she knew what was happening, he dipped her for a low kiss.

She rose, gasping for breath and laughing in surprise. What had come over him? Trent was usually the picture of decorum! Today he was acting downright…unseemly.

"I take it back, Mr. Storm!" shouted a man in the back, the same who had challenged him earlier. "You're just the man for Miss Anders!"

"Hear, hear!"

"Hear, hear!" boomed the crowd.

Tora was still shaking her head and laughing about it two hours later. It was good to know that her love could still surprise her, she thought. It added some romance and suspense to their courtship. Intent on setting the kitchen to rights before turning in for the night, she gathered the canvas scrap bag and hauled it out to the back alley for the wandering dogs.

She tossed it from the back stoop and paused to search the night sky. The stars were brilliant, covering the black backdrop of infinite space with a powdered sugar sprinkling of glimmering orbs. Her breath fogged before her, and as she did each night with the girls, she prayed for Kaatje, that she was somewhere warm and safe. *Oh, come home soon, Kaatje.*

Tora missed her friend. She wondered about Elsa, too. Was she on her way from Bergen yet? Tora hoped so. She wanted both women with her when she said "I do." It just wouldn't be the same without them.

She smiled again and rubbed her upper arms, suddenly chilled through. She turned to go inside when a movement at the end of the alley caught her attention. It was pitch dark, but the lanterns outside the front of the roadhouse cast long shadows. A man stepped into the center of the alley, his back to the street, facing Tora. He stood stock-still, staring and staring.

By instinct, Tora threw back her shoulders and straightened. There was something eerily familiar about his stance and body. He was someone she knew... Who? Tora shivered again, this time not from the cold. Quickly she slammed the door shut and bolted it as if he were tearing at it from outside.

"Tora?"

She spun around, frightened out of her wits, and closed her eyes in relief when she saw Trent.

"Tora, what's wrong?" He rushed to her and took her in his arms.

"Nothing," she said, shaking her head. "I'm just being an idiot."

"What do you mean?"

"There was a man outside. He just stood there in the alley and stared at me." She felt increasingly foolish with each word out of her mouth.

"Did he come after you?" Trent asked, the muscles in his jawline tightening. "Did he threaten you?"

Tora sighed and took a step away from him. "No. It was nothing. I just thought…"

Going to the door and unlocking it, Trent pulled it open, then stood on the stoop outside like a marshal from the pages of a dime novel. He turned back to her. "He's gone, whoever it was." Then, after coming back inside, securing the door again, Trent placed one hand on her shoulder and the other under her chin. "You just thought what, Tora?"

Embarrassed, she shook off his tender touch. "Nothing. I was being foolish. Probably just tired. I'm going to go turn in now, Trent. I'll see you in the morning."

He watched her leave in silence; she could feel his gaze upon her back. Wearily she climbed the steps to the girls' room. She pulled their blankets up to their chins and kissed each on the forehead. Then she went to the window and looked out to the street. It was deserted.

I am being foolish.

She walked to her own room, pulled the pins from her long, dark hair, and brushed it out. Then she undressed and put on a loose cotton shift. Tora was about to climb under the covers when she decided to go to her own window and once more make sure the man was gone. She blew out her candle so there was no light to betray her presence, then slowly lifted the shade to one side.

The street was still empty.

I'm being childish. I just thought…

I just thought…

Finally, she admitted it to herself, voicing it for the first time in her head. *I just thought that he looked a lot like Decker.* The man who had kidnapped her in Washington Territory, raped her, and left her on a freight train bound for Seattle.

It looked an awful lot like Decker. She squeezed her eyes shut as if she could pinch away the memories and pulled the sheet and blanket over her head. He couldn't be here in Alaska.

He just couldn't.

Elsa Ramstad's newest steamship, the *Majestic*, had transported her passengers in record time to the Eastern seaboard of America. The steel-hulled ship was outfitted with three sailing masts, as well as a triple expansion engine. Elsa laughed to herself. She had spent too much time with Peder—he'd always been so adamant about the advantages of sails over steam, almost a purist about it. And now, she could not imagine a ship without sails. And they had proven useful. The sails helped dampen the Atlantic's tendency to roll a ship and, in tandem with the steam engine, had helped make their crossing a record in Ramstad shipping logs. A voyage that had once taken them six to eight weeks had been shortened to less than a month's time. Elsa noted the date in her logbook with some pride.

She relinquished the wheel to Eric Young when he came on duty and glanced upward at the yards of sail as she strolled the deck along with her eager passengers, waiting for their first look at America's shores.

"Kristian, come here!" she called, watching as her four-year-old climbed the rigging to one of the lower yards.

"Ah, he's a'right, Cap'n!" retorted a sailor. Elsa knew that she had gotten a reputation for being overprotective of her children, but then none of her sailors had lost a family member to the depths of the sea, had watched a spouse disappear forever among the roiling waves. "Kristian, come down at once!" she called.

"Ah, Mother," he complained. But he immediately complied.

When he reached the deck, Elsa breathed a sigh of relief and hurried him toward the main cabin. "Come, Kristian. Let us see what Cook has made us for our noon dinner."

"I hope it's brisket again!"

"Aye, that was a special treat last night, wasn't it?"

"Yes! And with carrots and potatoes and cabbage!"

Elsa laughed and placed a hand on his shoulder. "Nothing like a growing boy with an appetite. You've never seen food you didn't like."

They left the deck, and Elsa ducked her head to pass through the small cabin door. It was made of fine mahogany, like the interior, and she smiled as she gained sight of Eve and Riley, Elsa's loyal first mate, playing with a wooden train.

"Mama!" Eve cried, leaving the small table to toddle over to her mother.

The girl was in a pristine white dress. With her white-blond hair and big blue eyes, she looked like an angel. It was times like this that Elsa's heart ached for Peder, for a mate to share in the joys of parenting. How proud he would have been of his children! How he would have relished playing with them and seeing them grow. Blinking back sudden tears, Elsa pulled Eve close for a quick embrace.

"Go wash your hands, Kristian. It is soon time for supper." After bemoaning the task and getting a stern warning look from his mother, Kristian reluctantly did as she bid.

Riley studied her with a knowing look. "You still miss him, don't you?"

Elsa looked away, a bit embarrassed. Riley had become like an older brother or an uncle to her since Peder's death. "It's been almost two years, and it's much better. But it's times like this," she said, gesturing toward where Kristian had stood, "that I ache for him. He would've loved his children. And they would've loved him."

"Certainly." Riley rose and walked to the porthole, looking over the gray-blue waves of the Atlantic. "You said it's been almost two years, Elsa."

"Right..."

He turned and looked at her again. "Two years. Your grieving has been properly observed. Do you think...do you think that you can ever let a man into your life again?"

Elsa slowly shook her head. "Oh, I do not know. I don't know if I could ever take that risk again. The pain... Even the thought of losing another I love takes my breath away." She sat down. No one had asked her such a direct question before—the thought of finding someone she could love as fiercely as she'd loved Peder seemed impossible. Surely it would be selfish to think such a love could happen twice in one lifetime.

"Could you consider it for the children's sake?"

"For the children?"

"Yes. As you have said, they would love a father."

"It is not exactly like I have a hundred men at my door, Riley."

"It is not exactly like they can come knockin' when you're always at sea, Cap'n," he said, returning Elsa's sharp tone.

"The children have you."

"It is not the same and you know it. And it's not only for the children. You need a man by your side too. You're young and healthy. I know what you and Peder shared was somethin' special, but does that mean you will avoid love for the rest of your life?"

Elsa bit her lower lip. When he was so forthright, he was usually right, whether Elsa liked hearing it or not. The children came running back in then, eager for Elsa to inspect their hands. And Cook arrived with their meal, setting it upon the dining room table and leaving.

"Hurray!" Kristian cried. "It *is* brisket again! Can I have mine on a slice of bread?"

"Yes," Elsa said. "But you must first wait for us to say a blessing over the food." She turned to Riley and dropped her voice. "I will think about what you have said, Riley."

The man nodded once, obviously gratified.

A week later as they left Camden, Elsa worked on a painting of her mother, sister, and nephews outside her childhood home, with the harbor behind them. She had sketched out twelve prospective paintings while in Bergen, and wanted to get this one in color before it faded from her memory. As she worked, she thought of the portrait above the Ramstads' fireplace, the one of Peder and Kristian as a toddler in samurai costumes. That had been a glorious season, that year when they had first explored the Far East together. She smiled as she remembered going to the Saitos home in the mountains, an outdoor tub and a loving husband.

Elsa dipped her brush into the green-blue oil, then set it down. Her heart was no longer in the painting, and it never came out right if she could not concentrate.

That night in Japan, Peder had come to the steaming tub, picked up a bar of soap, and washed her hair, tenderly, thoroughly. She could still feel his strong fingers on her scalp, his lips softly touching her neck. It was one of the most intimate, treasured moments of their marriage. And even remembering it for a moment made her swallow hard in melancholy woe.

Could she ever let someone else in her heart like that again? When he had died, a part of her had died with him. They had been one. Not that they always were of one mind…but he had become her heart, and she his. Was there enough left within her to risk that loss again? *But look at what I've gained from the risk,* she thought, looking over at Kristian and Eve. They were playing skittles, a child's shipboard game involving a top and pins. As the top spun, Eve shrieked and Kristian giggled. The Swiss clock on the wall chimed seven times.

"Nooo," Kristian wailed, knowing what it meant.

"Yes, go get undressed. I'll be in shortly to tuck you in."

Cook ducked his head through the door and looked at her with an inquiring glance.

"Yes, I'd love tea, Cook," she said with a smile. It was their routine every night. She would go and tuck her children into bed—they had their own bedrooms and proper beds on the *Majestic*—tell them each a story, usually reading *The Adventures of Tom Sawyer* to Kristian and making one up for Eve, then she'd tuck them in and have tea in the parlor. Afterward, Elsa would stroll across the deck, talking to the crew, assigning tasks, checking Eric's charts. It was a good life. A fulfilling life. Did she really need a man to make it complete?

No.

But did she wish Peder were home with her again?

Yes.

One warm evening, Elsa sat down at her logbook table and moved aside a brass sextant—a gift from some anonymous friend—off the upper portion of an old, yellowed chart. The sextant was a fine instrument, the best she'd seen, and had been awaiting her in Camden a year prior, as other gifts had awaited her in Seattle and Bergen. Each time, when she inquired, no one knew their source. With the sextant, she had even gone to the maker in Boston—a temperamental craftsman named Gates—but he told her he had sold over a hundred of that make and hadn't kept records of who purchased them.

Elsa picked it up, feeling the heavy weight of the brass instrument in her hands. Whoever sent it knew her well, for she loved to take readings every night that there were stars visible, loved the methodical, dependable nature of the earth and sky and sea. Regardless of what happened in her world, those three elements remained constant. Like God in a way, she mused. The sea constantly showed her new faces, but deep down, it was always the same sea. An old friend, of sorts.

Hearing the bell clang for the fourth watch, Elsa rose, left her cabin, and walked the decks to the stern of the ship. She enjoyed observing the watch toss the foot-long Walker "Cherub" into the sea, allow it to drift beyond the *Majestic*'s wake, then haul it back in to measure their speed. The combination of rotating blades and recording dials indicated their progress with unfailing accuracy.

"How are we faring, Eric?" she asked as he raised a lantern to read their rate of speed.

"Very fine, Captain," he said with a smile. "She'll be one for the Ramstad record books, for sure."

"Good, good. Please report to me your findings before you turn in."

"Aye, aye."

She turned and closed her eyes as she walked back to her cabin, taking in deep breaths of the fresh salty air, loving the rock and roll of the sea beneath her feet. This was home to her, perfect in so many ways. She could almost sense Peder's arms around her, the warmth of his embrace. Almost. But he wasn't there. He would never be there again.

Perhaps it *was* time to be open to another. To look for the possibility that God would allow her to love again. "Perhaps," she whispered to herself, gazing at small swells across the water lit by a half-moon climbing the sky above. "Just perhaps."

five

After nearly two months on Soren's trail, Kaatje was so exhausted that she felt near to collapse. Life as a farmer had been taxing, but nothing like this day-to-day struggle to survive on the river and alongside it. They were moving fast and furious through the Interior of Alaska, stopping only to camp. They averaged fifteen miles a day, give or take a bit, and it was grueling. She had lost weight; her clothes hung on her lean frame. But there was no way Kaatje would ever let James Walker know she was struggling. While things had softened between them, there was still a discouraging air about him, as if he wanted to stay away from her but was stuck within close proximity of her, day in and day out.

They were trudging along an Indian path near the village of Tanana, portaging yet again where the river was impassable. The men carried the boat over their heads and small packs on their backs while Kaatje was left to manage the rest. The path wound around huge clumps of swamp grass and massive fields of flowers—wild iris and giant blue-bells, for the most part.

Kaatje wore a net under her hat, but still the huge black flies clung to it, hoping to find a hole and a way in. When they did, they bit, leaving red welts on her tender skin. Not so tender anymore. It was just as James had warned, but she refused to say anything, to complain. Where was the tenderness and consideration he had shown her now and then? He was a confusing and exasperating man. She stopped to shift her pack, lifting the straps that ate at her shoulders. The men trudged forward, never looking back. She felt irritable and abused, angry at her traveling companions—they called themselves guides!—and her absent husband. It was Soren's fault they were there; it was James's and Kadachan's fault they were on this path with these blasted woman-eating flies…

Memories of the mother grizzly plagued Kaatje, and she constantly looked about, sure they would soon happen upon another. They had seen several along the river, the bears fishing and dolefully watching the boat pass as if they knew the men had shotguns trained on their foreheads. Kaatje looked ahead. The men seemed to ignore her as they concentrated on their own load. As if they were the only ones carrying anything. *Why, a grizzly could come and haul me away right now, and the men probably wouldn't even notice,* she pouted, knowing she was pouting, unable to do anything else.

Kaatje rounded a boulder and immediately encountered a swarm of no-see-ums, tiny gnats that seemed to find their way under her net and leave bites that swelled to the size of chicken eggs as she slept. She could barely see the path before her, and swatted around her face blindly until they dissipated. James turned briefly, obviously noting her discontent, but then moved on.

What was she doing here, so far from her daughters, her home, her life? Why had God led her to this place to suffer so for a man who had mistreated her from the beginning? She grimaced and clenched her teeth, muttering a conversation between herself and her Lord. "He's dead. Here I am, in the middle of nowhere, on a path to nowhere. For what? For what? Yes, I needed to know about Soren. But couldn't there have been some other way? Couldn't I have sent James? Why bring me here?"

The old answer soon came to her. She needed to be there.

"Why? Why did I have to come? Wasn't it enough to come all the way to Alaska? Why did I have to do this? *With these?*" she growled, swatting away another wave of gnats.

Kadachan looked over his shoulder at her, apparently overhearing her muttering, and then whistled softly at James. Kaatje willed herself to be quiet. They rounded another bend in the path and the roar of a waterfall became audible. *Water.* The word alone gave her hope and courage. They neared the river again. How blessed water would be, driving away the sweat and heat and flies!

Fifty yards later, they came upon the edge of the river, and before them stretched a peaceful glacial pool with a fifty-foot-wide waterfall that cascaded down twelve feet, plunging bubbles to the bottom and then releasing them in an aquamarine cloud.

Oh, how she longed to dive in! To be free and clean! But she didn't suppose the men would consider it. No, they probably wanted to cover another ten miles before resting! They probably wanted her to take some more of their weight, or maybe carry the boat, too—

Kaatje felt her pack being lifted, and she looked over her shoulder to see James quietly easing it off. She felt ashamed of her childish whining, even if it had been to herself. Kadachan pulled off his calf-skin boots, and then his shirt. With a cry of glee, he did what she longed to do. He dived in.

He emerged twenty feet away, in the center of the pool, flicking his long, ebony hair in one glorious manly move. He pulled his head back once, inviting her in, as James dived in too. It took no urging. She bent, pulled off her mud-encrusted boots and stood, impatiently waiting for the men to turn. They did as she silently bid. Then, Kaatje unbuttoned her split skirt and dropped it to the ground, leaving her bloomers and shirt on. Last to go were the net and hat. She dived in then, loving every second in the bitingly cold, spine-tingling water as it covered her skin, easing away the irritating dust and flies and sweat and gnats, and eventually the frustration and aching muscles.

James swam over to her. He gestured with his head at Kadachan, who was now floating on his back. "He says you mutter and complain like the raven. The raven likes a cooling bath. And the water will wash away the smells that draw the flies in droves."

She splashed him in the face. "I suppose you do not smell and therefore do not draw flies?"

"They are not drawn to us because we spread bear fat over our chests this morning. As we suggested you do also, remember?"

Kaatje groaned. "Talk about smell! I'm amazed I could walk behind you two all day!"

This time, James was the one to splash her. He smiled, and Kaatje could not resist smiling back. It was one of the few times, in their two months together, that he had given her a full-fledged grin. His smile sent small laugh lines dancing at his eyes, and the dimple appeared again. His teeth were bright white against his tanned skin. She looked away, embarrassed to be wishing he would smile at her more often. It was such a pleasant sight, she told herself, such a relief in comparison...

"Come," he said, moving toward the waterfall. He swam over to it, and then looked back, waiting for her. Kaatje's heart sped up. What was that? she wondered. Did his look say what she thought it said? It was intimate, searching. He wasn't just looking her way. He was taking her in, drinking her in just the way he thirstily gulped in the glacial water. His glance was steady and meaningful. He was waiting.

Unsure of herself or him then, she moved to the falls, then followed James in a dive under the pelting cascade of water and beyond it to the other side.

When Kaatje emerged, she gasped at the beauty. The sunshine met water in a dancing, luminescent way that she had never seen before. James held on to a ledge before them, and she did the same.

"You are shivering," James said, still studying her.

"I am all right." She had to speak loudly to be heard over the waterfall, but the cavern gave each word a slight echo.

He gestured to the wall beyond the ledge, and for the first time Kaatje saw the petroglyphs. "What is it?" she asked.

"Kadachan showed me this place once. It's ancient. But the story still is passed along from generation to generation, among several of the tribes in Alaska."

She accepted his hand and smiled as he easily lifted her to the ledge. "Another story?"

"Yes," he said, staring at her. "A love story."

He didn't wait for her response. He simply turned and began narrating the story to her, pointing to each picture. "There was once an Indian brave who was destined to be chief. He didn't speak much, but everyone knew he had a big heart by the way he tended to his ponies. One day he decided it was time he should marry. There were several winsome maidens in the tribe—Gray Wolf's daughter, known to be the smartest; Sunlight, the most beautiful of them all; and Tiny Feathers, a girl who could find the best berries and roots. But it was Forget-Me-Not that caught his attention." James waved toward a rudimentary picture of several Indian maidens and then went on.

"He watched her closely. Although plain, it was she who touched him. She cooed to the babies and had a laugh that made him laugh too. It was she who was meant to be his bride. He knew it. So one afternoon, he approached her father, in the way of The People. He said, 'I would like to take your daughter as my wife. What will her bride-price be?'

"'This one is not beautiful or smart. I think one pony will be enough.'

"The brave and the father agreed, and the young man arranged to come back the next week to claim his bride." James pointed to a picture where two men clasped hands.

"That night, the other maidens talked of the day. 'One pony isn't much,' the beautiful one said. 'My father would ask for at least five. But, of course, Forget-Me-Not is not valuable as a bride.' 'It's true,' agreed Tiny Feathers. 'My love promised three horses for me!' Only one noticed Forget-Me-Not as she crept away from the edge of the fire, ashamed." James showed her an image of a great campfire, as well as the shadow of a woman.

He moved on to a group of men sitting in a circle. "The brave closed his door-flap to think and to sleep. The next morning he visited the old ones. 'What is the largest dowry a brave has ever paid for a bride?' The old ones talked and argued for a few minutes. Finally, one spoke out, 'It is said that twenty ponies were paid for Prairie Thorn.' The brave thanked them, then went to work. That week, he rounded up seventeen horses, all but his favorite. He walked through the village, trading for three more with all the possessions he had. Finally, he walked out to his horses, twenty in all. He stood and looked them over, great love filling his heart."

There were twenty-one ponies in a long, horizontal image across the wall. James pointed to the last, a white stallion. "The brave's favorite was a white horse he loved more than anything in the world. It was more valuable to him than all his things and other horses combined. After kissing the stallion's nose, he led him with the others to the tent of his new father-in-law.

"The entire village gathered around, wondering what occasion demanded such a spectacle. 'Here I am,' the brave announced, 'to bring my wife home.'

"Forget-Me-Not's father emerged at the tent's opening. 'What is this?' he cried. 'We agreed that one pony was enough.'

"'No,' said the brave, 'she is the bride beyond any price. She is my beloved.' He looked at her and smiled. And for the rest of her life Forget-Me-Not smiled, joyful because her husband prized her enough to give up all he had for her, not for what she had to offer, but because he loved her."

James looked at Kaatje meaningfully, and she sensed his care for her, his sudden intense feelings. It shocked her since there had never been anyone but Soren who had looked at her in such a fashion. "You deserve a love like that, Kaatje. You *have* a love like that."

He was professing love? To her? She did not miss the way he tenderly said her given name for the first time. It was like a song on his tongue.

"God loves you like that—you are the bride beyond price, Kaatje. He loves you with a sacrificial, no-disappointment-ahead kind of love. You know that, right?"

"Yes." So he wasn't talking about himself—he was talking of God! An arrow of sadness shot through her heart. And she realized that she wished it were James who loved her like that. What was wrong with her? She was a married woman; she shouldn't be thinking such thoughts! She was getting so cold her head was obviously growing numb.

His hand under her chin surprised her. She looked up at him with concern, but his face was calm. Her heart stopped for a moment. "You deserve a man to love you like that too, Kaatje. Soren has abused his rights as your husband. No one should ever treat a wife like that. One they call beloved."

Kaatje wrenched her chin away. She shook her head, wondering at the heat beneath her skin even as she shivered. "I am cold," she mumbled. "I had better get back to shore and get dressed." She dived under the icy waterfall without pausing and emerged on the other side. Kadachan gave her a knowing glance. She looked away from him, concentrating on getting to the bank and her pack and dry clothes.

As she changed into a clean pair of bloomers and a semiclean dress, grunting and wrenching cries from the pool made her anxiously peek out. They were wrestling. Kadachan ducked and sent James flying into the water again, the splash covering ten feet. James emerged, his muscles flexed in anticipation and dripping rivulets of water as he went after his friend again. Kadachan lost that time, and when James offered him a hand, Kadachan pulled him back in.

Kaatje bit back a laugh as James fell for the oldest trick in the book. It mattered not where men were. The world over, they were but small boys in men's bodies. What she had just seen she had witnessed a hundred times in Bergen, when Karl and Peder would do the same in a glacial pool where they all gathered as children. But the boys had been boys then.

James was all man. Kaatje ducked back behind the boulder and leaned against its rough surface. She drew a deep breath, thinking. He was kind and thoughtful. Kaatje sensed he had been watching out for her a hundred times in the last two months when she had not been watching out for herself. Even on the trail that afternoon, when she thought she was forgotten, James was pushing ahead, knowing this sacred, spectacular spot was within reach. Soren had never been so caring.

Soren also had never been paid to do so, she reminded herself. Why, Trent had practically threatened a public hanging if James did not deliver her home safely at summer's end! She had witnessed the deal herself. She made a low sound of disgust in her throat and shook her head.

James was her guide. Nothing more.

But why had his eyes told her differently in the waterfall cavern?

Days later, they arrived in Forty Mile but soon learned that the self-appointed sheriff Kaatje sought had been gone for two years and that no one had taken his place. At the trading post—little more than a log cabin of eighty square feet—the ancient, grizzled proprietor told her that "the miner's law rules in this country, and there ain't no need for a formal sheriff." Kaatje knew there was no legal jurisdiction for a "sheriff" in an ungoverned country anyway, so it didn't surprise her that "Sheriff" Jefferson Young had disappeared.

"We teach the injuns to keep to themselves," the old man told her while looking meaningfully at Kadachan. "Yes ma'am, when a miner gets out of line, we take care of our own. It ain't just redskins we hang from the trees," he said proudly, "We strung up Hard Luck Joe just last month for stealing Swift Water Bill's flour from his cabin. We can't be abidin' any stealing. Not when winters'll bring a man to eating bark rather than starving."

If she found Soren here, would he be as backward as this trader? He had been gone for seven years—perhaps she wouldn't even recognize him.

"Don't get many white women this way," the trader said with a smile that exposed several missing teeth and several more in the process of decomposing.

James took a protective step closer to her. His gesture sent a shiver up the side of her neck. "There is nobody else around that would know about miners in the area?"

"Nobody but me," the man said, hooking a thumb in each filthy suspender on his chest. "Know just about every man, least every white man, within a couple weeks' hike. They need me. I'm their flour and salt."

Kaatje nodded. "And you never met a man named Soren Janssen?"

"Now, I didn't say that, did I? We was talkin' about Sheriff Young and never got back to Soren Janssen."

"Get back to it," James said.

"Hmm. Now what was that we were gettin' back to?"

Kaatje sighed. "How much?"

"A dollar'd do it."

"A dollar!" James exploded. He leaned over the counter and took the man by the neck of his dirty undershirt. "Tell her what you know! For free! It's the decent thing, man!"

"All right, all right. Let go o' me!"

Reluctantly, James did so. The trader looked from him to Kaatje and back to James again. "Soren Janssen came this way 'bout two years back."

Kaatje sucked in her breath. "You saw him? He was here?"

"Yeah, with his squaw. They were headin' downriver toward Kokrine's."

Kaatje glanced at James. "I got a letter from the trader there. He said the last he had heard of Soren, he was heading this way about three years ago, to what I assume became his claim. He promised he'd write again if he saw Soren."

"Who was that? Malcolm Heffner?" the old trader gave her a

wheezy chuckle, as if privy to an inside joke. "Malcolm died of influenza three years back."

"So Soren could have passed through..." Kaatje began.

"Without anyone ever sending you word," James finished.

Tora Anders eventually decided that Decker, if it had been Decker, was probably just like almost every other man in Juneau, stopping in town only to stock up, rest, and find directions to Fortune's Smile. After several weeks of never seeing him again, she just knew he was gone for good. If it had been him at all.

"C'mon, Miss Anders," Charlie complained as she knotted a tie at his neck. They were in the general store across the street from the Storm Roadhouse. Tora was getting him new clothes suitable for church. Nearing thirteen, he was all long limbs and clumsy big feet, constantly outgrowing his clothes. Last week, he had started to get a few pimples. When she discovered the girls teasing him about it, Tora decided he needed some sprucing up. It would do his heart good.

"You stay still, Charles, while I get this right. Then I want you to look in the mirror and see the young man you're turning out to be."

"Young man?"

"Young man." She finished the tie and turned him by the shoulders to the full-length, oval mirror. He was already as tall as she. Tora guessed that he would eventually reach six feet, at the rate he was growing. "Look at you. Aren't you a treat? Pretty Cindy O'Malley will give you a second look this Sunday at church."

"You think?"

"I think," she said, peeking over his shoulder and flashing him a grin. "Now if we don't get back to the roadhouse and get ready for the supper crowd, we'll be behind all evening. I've picked out a new pair of Levi Strauss jeans for you and a couple of suitable shirts. That'll take care of you for work and school."

He turned to her with pure pleasure in his eyes. "Thank you, Miss Anders. For doing this for me."

"Well, you earn it, doing dishes and watching out for the girls and all. I know they can be pesky at times," she added in a whisper. "And I'm glad you've come to be with us for a while."

He nodded eagerly. "You think I'm learning enough that when Cap'n Martensen comes around again, he'll take me with him?"

Tora turned away and pretended to be interested in a cast-iron stove model, checking the price tag. Karl would take him to sea again someday, just not as soon as Charlie hoped. "I think Captain Martensen wants you to get a decent education as well as some manners. Didn't you two speak of graduation as the time you could sail with him again?"

Charlie groaned and picked at the end of a bolt of muslin. "Graduation? That's years away!"

Tora raised one eyebrow and looked him in the eye. "Could be four. Could be three. You're smart as a whip, Charlie. If you apply yourself to your studies, you could graduate at sixteen. Depends on what's important to you."

He met her gaze, understanding her challenge, and nodded once. "Three years I can take. Especially with Cindy O'Malley in town."

"Glad you can suffer us that long for a pretty girl," she said, chucking him under the chin. "You'll be a sailor yet!"

They bantered back and forth until they left the store, whereupon Charles offered her his elbow. Arm in arm they walked across the muddy thoroughfare, pausing to let two wagons and then several men on horses pass before them. Juneau became busier with each passing day, alive with the bustle and shouts of men on a mission of fortune. Tora had thought Montana was a land of opportunity; it was nothing compared to the raw wealth just beneath Alaska's surface. It surprised her when she thought about it. Once, she would've died for just such an opportunity. Now she was content to keep everything as it was—she wished she could freeze her life at this particular moment, like a photograph from one of the new Kodak snapshot cameras. It was perfect like this. Work was brisk and plentiful, and life with Trent, Kaatje, Charlie, and the girls had fulfilled her in a way she never thought possible.

It almost scared her, the thought of it all disappearing. *Lord, you've brought me this far. Don't forsake me now,* she prayed. What was this ominous feeling, this irrational fear that suddenly crossed her heart?

"Miss Anders? Are you all right?" Charlie asked, looking as if he was imitating Trent's expression of concern. They had crossed the street and now stood in front of the roadhouse.

"Oh yes, yes, Charles, I'm just fine. I have…a headache. Perhaps I'll rest a bit as you go and help the cook with preparations for dinner."

"Sure. Should I walk you upstairs?"

His chivalry touched her. "No. Thank you though. I'll be just fine. I'll see you at half past the hour." She left him at the main stairway, climbing to the private wing that housed her bedroom, Kaatje's, and the girls'. In the other wing were Trent's and Charles's rooms, plus the six remaining guest rooms. Jess and Christina were probably already in the kitchen, finishing their contribution for the evening: twenty batches of cornbread muffins. Yes, Tora could smell the roasted cornmeal already.

So she was alone and ready to figure out why she was feeling so strangely. *What is it, Lord?* she prayed silently. She dropped onto her four-poster bed, feeling the feather mattress gradually cease bouncing. *What is it? Am I to pray? For Kaatje? Is she in danger?* Was this the reason for her sudden unease? That God wanted her to ask for protection? It felt right, that danger was looming for someone close to her. Tora moved off the bed and to her knees.

"Father in heaven," she whispered fervently, her forehead against her knuckles, her eyes squeezed shut. "You have given me so much, and I am thankful. I praise your name that thou hast delivered me from my sins and made me free in thee. You have moved my heart today, and I do not know why. If Kaatje is in danger, please protect her. If you are trying to prepare me for something, open my heart. I am yours now, Lord. Thou hast made me thy servant. Show me the way. Show me thy way, Father. What you want of me. What you want me to do. Open my eyes. Amen."

Tora rose and wiped her eyes. It seemed she was given to tears of late, especially when something moved her as she had just been moved. She looked at her image in the mirror, shaking her head. "Enough. You cannot worry about it any longer, Tora Anders. Whatever is ahead of you is ahead! And you will get through it, good or bad, because God is with you." She unpinned the back of her hair, stroked it with a horse-hair brush five times, then wound it back into place and pinned it.

Downstairs, she entered the kitchen and soon found out that their hostess was ill and unable to come to work. "Never mind," she told Sara, a pretty Irish girl that Trent had hired. "I'll don an apron and lend a hand tonight."

Sara's eyes grew large in her gaunt face.

Tora laughed. "I was a waitress once too," she said. "Let's get the tables set and extra sets of utensils wrapped in napkins. Judging from last night's crowd, it's bound to be busy."

Tora was soon proven right. Shortly after the dining room's twenty tables were filled, a line began to form outside. Tora hoped the cook had made enough ham and vegetables, and that the cornbread muffins would last. It smelled heavenly, even outside, and it was bound to get ugly if the hungry men had to be turned away. Still, they managed well, serving a hundred in the first hour. She was perspiring, she was moving so fast, working to help Christina and Jess clear the tables as the waitresses served and collected payment for the meals. When the men had to stand in line outside for an hour, she poured each of them a complimentary glass of lemonade, thanking them for their patience. She knew a smile, a cool beverage, and a word of thanks went a long way toward maintaining a benevolent atmosphere. Many sat down in line, conversing with others, content to wait for the home-cooked meal.

She had just cut off the line at the end, refusing any more customers in fear they would run out of food, when her eyes were drawn to a rowdy table. The noisy bunch could be heard over the other seventy men in the room. It was typical, in a town as rough and tumble as Juneau, to draw the same caliber of men. But when she saw a large man grab Sara's apron strings and pull her backward to him, Tora became "as mad as a skinned rattlesnake," as Charles liked to say. How dare someone manhandle dear, sweet Sara!

Tora motioned to the boy clearing plates nearby. "Go get Trent and the cook," she said urgently, moving on without waiting for the others. She practically ran to the back table, where Sara was now struggling to get away from the man who held her, while his companions laughed.

"What is this?" she demanded, grabbing the man's long, thick fingers and trying to pry them off of Sara's waist. "What is this?" she demanded of the whole table. "You think this is a sideshow? Some house of ill repute? You may not treat our staff in this manner! Out! The whole lot of you! And never come back again!" She sensed Trent's presence behind her, and then the cook's. The men scooted their chairs out and rose reluctantly. She guessed that most were a decent sort, but they had crossed the line by allowing their comrade to behave in such a fashion.

Still, the man who held Sara resisted. Tora looked at him in outrage. "Did you not hear what—"

Horror swallowed her tongue. She shrank back against Trent, while Sara and her captor stared at her in surprise.

It was Decker. *Decker*. He was here, in Juneau. Right here! In front of her!

Didn't he recognize her? The woman he had kidnapped and raped? She was shaking her head, moving around Trent, stumbling backward, intent only upon escape. He looked confused by her sudden change

78

in demeanor. There was a flicker of recognition as Trent yelled, "You heard her, men. Out! All of you!" They were grumbling and moving toward the door as Tora disappeared into the kitchen.

Everything in her told her to run, run away, run fast from the worst nightmare of her life coming back to haunt her once more. The door swung shut behind her, but Tora kept backing up until she felt the rear door. Then she slid into a corner, under a counter full of dirty dishes. Dimly, she realized the children were staring at her, asking her something. But all she could do was shake her head. Shake her head and mumble, "It cannot be. It simply cannot be."

Suddenly Trent was in front of her. "Tora! Tora, sweetheart, what is wrong?" He shook her hands in frustration and gently slapped her cheeks. Tora pushed him away with dazed motions. "What is it, Tora? You're shaking! Are you ill? Tell me what is wrong!" Through the haze, Tora felt him wipe away the tears on her cheeks, his voice growing more frustrated. "What is it? Tell me!"

"She said she had a headache earlier," Charlie said.

"What's wrong with her, Trent?" Christina asked over his shoulder, looking as if she wanted to cry herself. Her expression made Tora want to pull herself together, to stand and be strong, but the wave of evil that had just reappeared in her life overwhelmed her. It was all she could do to keep it an arm's length away.

"I do not know," Trent said. He bent and pulled Tora up, lifting her and carrying her out of the kitchen and quickly up the stairs.

She looked wildly over his shoulder, mumbling, "Is he gone? Is he gone?"

"He's gone," he said reassuringly. They reached her room, and Trent gently laid her on her bed. He stroked her face and hair until she stopped crying. "Tell me," he said quietly. "Tell me, Tora."

But she could not. Despite all they had been through, all they had talked about, she could not bring herself to tell her fiancé that he had just met the man who had abused her and set her on a train like a common hobo.

Trent sat with her for an hour, and when she pretended to sleep, he sighed and finally left her side.

Tora felt ashamed all over again, reliving those days with Decker and his men. On Thanksgiving Day, they had kidnapped her from the teacher's cottage she lived in. After that, nothing had been the same with her again. Part of her rejoiced for the change it ultimately wrought in her, but not now. All she could think of now was what Decker had robbed her of: her sense of security and self-respect. The thought of ever seeing him again sent fear reverberating through her body, making her tremble once again.

She could hear the sounds of the restaurant shutting down, the staff leaving, the rattle of keys as the door was bolted. They had carried on, serving the men and cleaning up the kitchen, probably pretending that they were not thinking about Tora upstairs.

She rolled over on her back, staring at the high ceiling. As the night wore on, her trembling ceased and her head began to clear. She knew she had to get up and go tell Trent the truth—whom they had encountered. Otherwise, he was liable to find Decker to ask him himself. She shot out of bed at the thought of it, pausing briefly to regain her equilibrium. She heard the girls in their room, whispering. On the other side of the stairs, she could see Charles's light pooling under the door; he was probably reading. Trent's room was dark. As it was downstairs. Where was he? Her heart began pounding. Had she missed him? Had he gone somewhere?

"Trent?" she called softly, padding down the stairs. The restaurant and foyer were dark except for a lamp burning on the front desk, where Trent kept the books. It was the huge room's only light. She walked toward it, hungry for the safety it seemed to yield by simply burning.

Behind her, she heard the familiar sound of the kitchen door opening and then swinging shut. She whirled. "Trent?" she said, hearing her voice shake. She lifted the lantern above her head. The shadows were deep. Had someone ducked into the stairwell? "Charles?" she asked softly, her heart in her throat.

When there was no response, she backed toward the front door. She felt as if a vise were squeezing the breath from her lungs. The presence of evil was palpable. It was dark, foreboding, threatening to overtake her and make her disappear forever.

"The Lord is my shepherd," she whispered, in full panic now, still backing up, looking from one side of the room to the other. From what she could see, she was alone. But she didn't feel alone. "I will fear no evil." Behind her, she felt the knob of the front door and turned it. Locked!

"No, no," she whimpered, giving in to the terror surrounding her. She set the lamp down by her feet and slammed on the glass door with the palms of her hands. "No! No!" she screamed, certain she was being approached from behind. The street outside was empty. She madly tried the knob again, hoping against hope it would open.

But he was already there. Turning out the lamp. Rising to pull her toward him, covering her mouth before she could scream. Chuckling at her futile struggles, he simply waited for her to stop. Tears rolled down her cheeks, and she grew still, remembering how he always had liked it when she fought him. "Imagine my surprise," he whispered in her ear, his voice low, his breath warm. "Imagine! My sweet Spokane flower here in Alaska! I thought I sent you on a train to Seattle, and here you are. Or was it that you were missing me, sweetheart? Come looking for your man?" He pulled her away from the door, and all her hope receded with it. It was dark, so dark.

"Who's the man, beautiful? Word has it that it's Trent Storm. You weren't serious when you told me you were engaged to the famous Trent Storm, were you? Was that the man I saw today? Is he the man who's going to take you away from me?"

The click of a revolver being cocked froze them both.

"That was the man," Trent said.

Trent was here! Tora's pulse raced even faster. And he had a gun! He could save her! "Step away from Tora right now before I shoot straight through your stupid skull."

Decker moved as if he was going to comply, then whirled Tora between himself and Trent's revolver. He began pulling her away from Trent, toward the back. "Don't do it, Storm, or she'll be dead."

Sudden clarity overtook Tora. She knew she could not be alone with Decker ever again. She couldn't take it. She couldn't live though it again. "Trent, listen to me!" she cried. "Shoot him!" Trent walked after them, matching Decker step for step; she could make out his dim outline. "Don't let him take me, Trent. Don't let him. Shoot him!" She grabbed at chairs, at tables—anything to impede Decker's progress.

When they reached the kitchen doorway, the sudden light blinded her for a moment. She held on to the doorjamb, staring into Trent's eyes. His pistol was still aimed above her right temple. "Shoot him," she said, suddenly deadly calm. It was as if she were separated from her body, watching it from the outside.

He looked from Decker to her in that instant, and Tora knew she was lost. "I cannot," he said helplessly, and she knew it was fear for her safety, not a lack of courage, that kept him from it.

Decker laughed and pulled her through the doorway.

The swinging door was closing behind them, separating Tora from Trent for what seemed an eternity, when a shot exploded from Trent's pistol.

Decker convulsed and released her immediately, leaving her back strangely cold for an instant. As if in a dream, she wondered if she had been shot and felt her clothes for the telltale wet pool of blood. She turned and saw Decker on the ground, clutching his shoulder and writhing in pain.

He was swearing, screaming, but it sounded like a whisper to Tora. Then Trent was beside her, still pointing his revolver at Decker, while Tora turned away from her attacker and into his secure arms.

She felt Trent tense and noticed that Decker had quieted. Was he getting up? Coming after her again? She looked quickly. He was on his knees, seething with anger, his hand pushing against a gaping wound in his shoulder. But Trent stopped him with the pistol, mere inches from his face.

"Move again and you'll be dead, man," Trent warned, his voice even. "It's only because I'm a man of God that you're not dead already. But I am still only a man. You have two choices. Die now. Or go to jail and await your sentencing. One way or another, you will pay for the crimes you have committed."

He stepped in front of Tora and bent lower, taking the man by the collar. "I will see to it myself," he vowed. "Do you hear me?" His voice rose to a scream. "I will see to it myself!"

seven

July 1888

Elsa paced as Riley brought the *Majestic* into the Panamanian harbor of Cristobal. She was anxious to get ashore, to bathe and have her feet on solid ground. For as much as the sea had stolen her heart, coming into port never failed to excite her. Or her children. They bounced up and down around her, pointing out different things on the verdant, tropical shore and yelling in their excitement.

The sailors at the capstan released the heavy chain, and the anchor left the ship with a tremendous splash, followed by the clunking *whir* as it descended to the harbor floor. Riley reversed the ship's engines, bringing the giant steamship to a halt.

"Come, Mother," Kristian begged, pulling at her hand. "Let us be on the first launch ashore!"

"All right, all right," she said, laughing. She self-consciously smoothed her tailored walking dress of brown plaid and then nodded again at her children. "What do you want to do first?"

"I want to go to the Taylors' to fish, and I want ice cream at Señor Manuel's!" Kristian said.

"We will go for ice cream after our noon meal," she returned. "And I will send a note to Mrs. Taylor asking if we may call upon them." Adrian Taylor was the American consul general to Panama.

Elsa and Peder had been introduced to Adrian and Isabella a number of years prior, and Elsa and Isabella had become fast friends. The Taylors' son, Michael, had a birthday within days of Kristian's, and the boys got along splendidly. Elsa knew that as soon as the Taylors heard she was in port, they would invite the Ramstads to stay. She looked forward to their visit with pleasure.

"Cap'n?" Eric Young, her second mate, called. "You and the young'uns want to be first ashore?" Eric had joined her and Riley on her first voyage out of Seattle after Peder's death. At first, Elsa had wondered if he would challenge the authority of a female captain. But the glint in his eye proved only to be a mark of good humor and quick wit, rather than defiance.

"Aye, Eric. If I do not, I fear a mutiny among our smallest mates."

Eric laughed and then grabbed Kristian, hanging him upside down. The boy screeched in delight.

"Not before I throw this pirate over the side!"

"Let go o' me, you filthy bilge rat!" Kristian yelled.

"Kristian Ramstad!" Elsa reprimanded. "You know better to say that, even in jest."

"Ah, now, Cap'n," Eric said, coming to Kristian's defense. "That isn't the worst the boy hears."

"Please, do not remind me. In any case, he is a Ramstad, and my son. I expect him to speak in higher regard to the second mate of this ship, or to any elder, for that matter."

"Captain—" Eric stopped as he met her determined glance, then he set Kristian to rights. "Better mind your step, Kristian," he said, ruffling his sandy hair, "or the cap'n will tar and feather you." He bent down and whispered something in the boy's ear, and Kristian laughed.

"I will choose to ignore that," Elsa said. She was sure the comment was at her expense, but she valued the rapport Kristian had with the crew even if it meant a little chafing on her behalf. They were his father figures, after all, the men he would eventually emulate. And Eric and Riley and Cook were all admirable men. She accepted Eric's proffered hand and climbed aboard a small boat that was tied at the side of the ship, then reached for her children.

When Riley and several select sailors were aboard with them, those still aboard began the process of slowly lowering them to the turquoise sea. There were small waves today as the wind was up, and they lapped against the side of the boat once it rested.

"Heave ashore, men," Riley directed.

Four men, each at a long oar, did as he directed, singing a sailing song that kept time for their rowing. Elsa smiled at the sound of the men's voices blending in a nice harmony. It warmed her heart like the sun on her broad-brimmed hat, these men and their solidarity. They were sound company, but still it would be good to be with another woman. Her smile broadened as she thought of Isabella Taylor. In some ways, the woman reminded her of Kaatje, with her fierce loyalty and steady composure. In others, she reminded her of Tora, with the proud way she held her shoulders back and her chin high.

Perhaps they needn't wait through the formalities of an announcement of their arrival and an invitation. No, she would simply surprise her friend. After taking their noon meal at a restaurant, of course. She wouldn't want to impose. But remembering Isabella's warm smile, Elsa doubted it would ever be an imposition. They had met at Lady Bancock's ball in Honolulu, then later in Japan, and still later in Maine. Isabella's husband, a Mainer, had been a sea captain like Peder before turning to politics. After a brief term as a United States senator, Adrian Taylor had accepted the post as consul general in Panama.

Elsa knew that a large part of his job was to oversee the overland trade that Americans were doing in Panama. There was talk of a canal someday, but for now a huge amount of cargo was carted across the isthmus via railroad, saving shipping companies weeks in transit time. Adrian worked constantly at bettering the labor force, the equipment, the track, and the relations with Panamanians.

Within minutes they were at the local docks. Riley helped Elsa, and then the children, to the rough, salt-eroded planks.

"Lewis and Smyth," he said to two of the more burly sailors, "I want you to accompany the captain and her children about town and north to Aspinwah. You can have extra shore leave in exchange for your time now."

"Riley, I don't really think that is necessary," Elsa protested under her breath. She was as tall as her wiry first mate, and she looked him in the eye.

"Cap'n, we've been through this."

"But, Riley, I know this town. I know the people."

"You knew Yokohama too." He referred to that day in Japan when Mason Dutton had kidnapped her right outside the trade building in which Riley had been doing business. The memory still obviously agitated her friend. But after almost two years, his overprotective nature was getting a bit tiresome.

"Will you ever forget that day?" She knew she could insist they go on alone. She was, after all, still captain. And yet as much as she hated it, it was probably wise to have an escort with her.

"No, Cap'n. And I don' think you should e'er do so either."

"Very well, Riley. We will return at, say, four o'clock? To get back to the ship."

"Aye, aye, Cap'n." He nodded once, acknowledging her command, but Elsa could see the glimmer of pleasure at her acquiescence in his eyes. As much as it irritated her, it was why she insisted he be her first mate; Riley always looked out for her and her children.

"Come along, boys," she said to the two bodyguards. "I'll buy you a meal in town." They followed behind, and Elsa balanced Eve on her hip as she took Kristian by the hand. On the boardwalk that led to Cristobal's main thoroughfare, the ground felt leaden and foreign after weeks aboard the *Majestic*. But oh, how happy she was for the new sights and smells! She found herself staring into shop windows with the same eagerness as her children. Quickly they made their way to the restaurant they had not eaten in for over a year.

After lunch, Elsa asked Paul Smyth to hire a coach for them for the day. "An open one," she added. "I do not care to be inside on a day such as this." The afternoon's heat combined with the tropical humidity made Elsa's dress chafe at the collar. She was unaccustomed to fussy clothes such as these; aboard ship, she wore simple cotton dresses with split skirts. Still, she was determined to greet Isabella in proper attire.

Smyth soon pulled up outside the restaurant, and David Lewis helped her and the children into the carriage. She settled upon the leather-covered bench, melting under the hot sun's torturous glare, and David then climbed on the back. Smyth flicked the reins over a mismatched pair of horses, and they were off. A mile north of town, past fields of sugar cane, at the top of a long, grassy hill that overlooked the Caribbean Sea, stood the Taylors' understated, elegant home built in the Spanish colonial style. Even the sight of its soothing adobe made Elsa feel a bit cooler. Outside, under a canopy of thick vines and beside a small table, sat Isabella, Adrian, and a man who looked vaguely familiar.

Her driver pulled the horses to a stop at the end of the lane beside the house, and the trio at the table rose.

"Elsa!" Isabella called in delight. "Elsa Ramstad!" She hurried over to the wagon and pulled Elsa into her embrace as soon as she descended. "And this cannot be Kristian and Eve!"

"It is!" Kristian said earnestly, as if the woman were truly confused. "Is Michael at home?"

Isabella laughed, the light sound of it bringing another smile to Elsa's lips. "He is down at the beach, Kristian. He hooked up a rope to a tree down there and sails high over the water, then drops in. If your mother approves, you may join him."

"May I? May I?" he asked, his eyebrows high. Something in his expression reminded her of Peder, and a pang of melancholy shot through her heart.

"Is it safe?" she asked Isabella.

"Quite. No more than a few feet deep. Michael will show him."

"Oh, please, Mama," Kristian begged.

Kristian was an incredible swimmer for his age, and Elsa assumed Michael must be too. If Isabella trusted her son… "All right," she gave in. "Be sure to take off your finery before swimming!" she called after his slim form that was racing away from her as fast as he could go.

"Go, go!" Eve begged, reaching after her brother.

"Oh, sorry, darling. You're not old enough to go without me."

"Never mind swimming," Isabella jumped in. "Come up to the house, Eve. I have a wonderful assortment of dolls and a tea set just your size." Isabella and Adrian's tiny daughter had died of consumption, Elsa remembered. She wondered at the pain of losing a child, surely an even greater pain than losing a spouse, putting a tiny body in a grave. No doubt, Elsa would have clung to Eve's toys and clothes too had a similar tragedy befallen her.

Isabella raised a hand. A maid appeared from the shadows and after a brief word took Eve up to the house, presumably to play with toys. "Elsa, Elsa," Adrian said, interrupting her thoughts as he drew near and took her hand with both of his. "It is a delight to see you."

"And you, Adrian," she returned.

He gestured toward his companion. "I believe you know Lucas Laning."

She looked to Luke in surprise. "Mr. Laning! It's been years." She found herself looking over his shoulder for his captain, Karl Martensen, and, knowing it was rude, forced her gaze back to him as he took her hand and kissed it.

He looked back up at her with a smile in his eyes. "He is not here."

Elsa pretended confusion. "Pardon me?"

"Your friend, my captain. Karl Martensen."

"Oh yes, of course." She battled to keep the sorrow at such news from her voice. It had been so long since they had seen each other. What a delight it would have been to chance upon him here! "He is off to some other waters, I take it?"

"He took a steamboat around the Horn and is on his way to San Francisco. I am overseeing the shipment of parts for two shallow draft ships across the isthmus and tomorrow will accompany them to Alaska. Karl is using the giant steamboat for those travelling to Alaska on holiday, and the two smaller boats for business along the river ways."

"A wise plan."

"Indeed," Isabella said. "Come. You must be desperate to escape the sun. I am! Let us go back to the table and drink our tea."

"That sounds divine," Elsa returned.

Isabella linked her arm through Elsa's. "Tell me. Tell me where you have been, where you are going."

"Well, I just returned from Bergen."

"To see your mother?"

"Yes. I tried my best to convince her to come home with me, but she wasn't willing."

Isabella nodded in an understanding way. "I miss my own dear mother. It is terrible to be so far away from loved ones."

"But I am so thankful to have been able to see them. To introduce my children to their grandparents—we saw Peder's parents, too— and aunts and uncles and cousins. Many never have such a chance after leaving their home country."

"That's one of the good things about shipping," Adrian interjected as they sat down at the table. "Since coming here, we have seen none of our family."

"But friends from far and wide come through here," Luke said. "It is a good place for that."

Elsa studied Karl's first mate. He was handsome, with dark, almost black hair, and eyes to match. *He and Karl would be a striking duo,* she thought, *just as Peder and Karl once were.* He returned her look with interest, and Elsa quickly drew her attention to Isabella.

"Does it feel like home yet?"

"It does," Isabella said. "We really could not be happier."

Adrian sat back and raised his glass of iced tea toward Elsa. "If you people with Alaska connections could get us more ice, it would be perfect."

"I had heard there is a company doing just that. The Greater Alaska Ice Company, I think."

"And expanding a ship a month," Lucas added.

"It's not fast enough," Adrian said. "There are many in these parts who would pay a good bit for regular ice shipments. We were fortunate to get a new block last week."

They chatted on for the next hour, about shipping news, the weather, politics, until Isabella suggested they go and check on the boys. Elsa agreed. As they entered the house together, Elsa asked, "Wouldn't a dip be fun? Why don't we join the boys? I know that Eve would love it."

"Oh, let's do. The cove is very private, and I have a bathing dress you could borrow."

Elsa laughed. "I would never fit into your tiny clothes." Isabella was petite whereas Elsa was quite tall. "If it's private, I'm sure I'll be fine in my bloomers, if Adrian has a shirt I could borrow."

"Very well." They turned into a tiny playroom filled with fine miniature toys. Eve sat at a small table, serving tea to a stuffed bear.

"Want to go with us, Evie?" Elsa asked.

She practically fell over her chair in hurrying over to her mother. And Elsa picked her up with a smile. They followed Isabella out a side door to a long, covered, tiled patio. They stopped at a bathing house to change clothes, then went on down the hill.

Following a winding path, they walked down the hill to a small, secluded cove. Elsa sighed. It was idyllic, surrounded by a dense tropical forest. Palm branches waved along a white sand beach that formed the tiny harbor. The women could hear the boys before they could see them.

When Elsa caught sight of Kristian, her heart stopped. He seemed to hang in midair for seconds as the momentum of the rope counteracted gravity. Then he fell with a "whoop" to the water five feet below. Still on the path above the boys, they could see down to the sandy bottom of the cove; there appeared to be no reef, just endless sand. In the deep shadows of the afternoon, it was cool, but once they were out on the point where the boys played, the warm sun caught them again.

"Want to go out on the rope?" Isabella dared.

"But it's not deep enough."

"Not where the boys let go. You have to ride it to the end. Then it's six, seven feet."

"If you will first," Elsa returned.

"Come on, Mama!" Kristian called. "It's fun!"

Elsa disrobed as Isabella marched up to the rope. She grabbed hold and swung outward without a second glance. Elsa's breath caught as she let go, and Isabella fell to the water in a slim line, holding her nose. She came to the surface at once, her long, auburn hair floating about her in waves.

"Come, Elsa! It's your turn!" She swam over to the bank and reached for Eve.

Elsa walked over to the rope still swinging toward the bank and grabbed hold. "Watch your mama!" she cried, picking up her feet and swinging outward. "Hoo-hoo!" she yelled, falling to the warm tropical waters. She stayed under for a moment, relishing the feeling of total immersion. When she came to the surface, the boys, Isabella, and Eve were all clapping. Kristian and Michael raced toward the bank to be next.

Eve cried, reaching for her.

"All right, Eve. I'm coming." Elsa swam over to the bank. Directly underneath, the water was only a few feet deep. Elsa took her from Isabella and swung her around, getting her more and more wet as they circled. Eve giggled so much that Elsa giggled with her. Then Elsa waded out to Isabella, who floated on her back.

"Doesn't it feel divine?" Isabella asked.

"Divine," Elsa agreed.

Isabella turned her head to the other end of the cove. "Did you see the men followed suit?"

For the first time, Elsa noticed the two small figures at the other end of the intimate cove, swimming as if in a race. "Guess it sounded good to them, too."

"Adrian takes a swim every day." Isabella threw her a teasing glance. "Too bad that handsome Lucas Laning is so far away. You could get a better look at him."

Elsa crossed her eyes at Isabella.

"Why would you want a better look at Mr. Laning?" Kristian asked, suddenly beside them and dog-paddling.

"Maybe Mrs. Taylor doesn't think he's a good swimmer," Elsa evaded.

Isabella choked on a laugh and then dived underwater.

"Do you want to go back to shore?" Elsa asked her children.

"Yes, please. I would like to collect sand dollars and seashells!"

Elsa laughed. "Where will you put them? The *Majestic* is about to sink under the weight of your collection."

"Mama, you're silly."

Elsa accompanied him to the shallows and watched until the boy walked out of the water. Michael immediately joined him in the hunt. Then she returned to Isabella, who was floating in the water. "What was that all about?"

"Nothing," Isabella said, raising an eyebrow. "I merely thought you might be ready to enjoy some male companionship again."

Her frankness made Elsa blush. "That's nonsense. I am surrounded by men every day."

"Men you command. When was the last time you were around a man who simply commanded your attention? A man as handsome as Lucas Laning," she added in a whisper.

Elsa snorted in disgust. "I am around men I do not command all the time."

"When? Where?" Isabella's entire countenance was one of complete assurance. "Men with whom you do business? When was the last time you went on a stroll with a man who was your equal? When was the last time you went to a ball?"

"I have been to many society dinners in the last couple of years," Elsa protested. It was as if Riley and Isabella were conspiring against her.

"But when was the last time you were with a man alone?"

"It isn't proper to be alone with a man."

"Oh, come now. You're a grown woman. A widow." Her tone softened. "Is your sorrow not…easing after all this time?"

Elsa searched the tropical shoreline and then the fluffy clouds that passed above them, thinking. "Not enough to consider anyone else. Sometimes I wonder if I shall ever be over Peder."

"It's been two years?"

"Yes. I've counted every day. In here"—she gestured toward her head—"I think I should be past it, over losing him. But in here," she said, bringing her hand to her heart, "I cannot imagine letting go of the loss. It's almost as if that's the only thing I have left of him."

Isabella sighed along with her, and they silently turned toward shore, pausing when it was waist deep. Elsa crinkled her toes, burying them in the fine granules.

Isabella studied her, obviously weighing her words. "Sometimes, my dear friend, the only way out of sorrow is to plunge into happiness. Peder would want you to be happy, not holding on to his memory like a shield."

"I am happy. I have my ship, my children. It is a good life." She pulled Eve closer.

"But not a full life. I know your heart. And it is big enough to love still another."

Elsa swallowed. "It might be big enough. But I don't know if I could withstand the pain of losing another love."

Isabella nodded. "When we lost our baby daughter, I thought I would never recover. But I know now that if I was blessed enough to carry another, I'd embrace that new love. Despite the chance that she, too, might die."

Elsa gave her a sorrowful smile and looked down toward where the men walked along the beach. "But Lucas Laning. I don't feel the stirrings in my heart for him that I believe you should feel for a man."

"Then he is not the right one." Isabella took her hand and Elsa met her glance. "But, Elsa, darling, when you feel those stirrings again, promise me."

"Promise you what?"

"Promise me that you will not ignore them. Consider them God's thumbprint, a gentle push."

Elsa's heart raced at the thought. Could she dive into a relationship again? Could she risk losing another piece of her heart? For the first time, she thought about the pleasure of a man's touch, the warmth of an intimate conversation between a couple bound by marriage. She yearned for that kind of love again. She missed it.

"Promise me," Isabella repeated.

"I promise."

Karl felt badly about not contacting the Kenneys when he reached San Francisco. *But I'd feel worse if I got in any deeper.* He still had not thought of a way to dissuade Mara from her apparent feelings for him or how to speak to Gerald. Every time he tried, Gerald misconstrued his meaning, reading into Karl's comments that he was indeed pursuing his daughter, and acted very pleased at the thought. Karl felt flattered that the Kenneys apparently wanted him as a son-in-law, but that was the last thing Karl wanted. He decided it was better to stay away until he thought his way out of this mess.

He walked into the carpenter's shop, his mind on Mara, but his task the steamship. The carpenters and woodcarvers in San Francisco were some of the finest in the world, and he was there to have his new ship outfitted in grand fashion. Especially the small ballroom—Karl wanted carved panels on the walls. He knew the Italian carver, Antonio Marzilli, would be perfect for the task.

Antonio greeted him warmly, and looked over the blueprinted plans.

After a quick assessment, he said, "It will take two months."

"Two months? I cannot wait here that long!"

Antonio threw him a puzzled glance. "Why not? You have friends here, no? It is a fine city in which to wait."

Karl sighed. There was no possible way for him to avoid the Kenneys for two months. Word would reach them that he was in the city, and they would be terribly hurt.

"Do your best, Antonio, to get it done sooner. I'll pay more for the rush. I'll plan on the glassmaker coming to install the chandelier next month, as well as the hallway and cabin lamps." The steamship was wired for electricity, one of the first to be outfitted in America. All they were missing was the glassware and bulbs.

"Very good, very good," Antonio said in his heavily accented English. "I will send word to you when it is ready. You will be at the Saint Ignatius Hotel?"

"Yes. But I will come and check on your progress every week."

"Very good, Captain Martensen. I will set five men at work on it by next week when we finish our current project. And I will have a design drawing and cost estimate to you by Thursday."

"Good," Karl said, shaking the man's hand. He walked out of the shop and resignedly hailed a cab to see the Kenneys. There was no sense putting off the inevitable, and he couldn't bear the thought of offending them.

It took thirty minutes for the stout horses to climb the steep hills from the wharf to the Kenneys' home. As they approached, Karl saw Mara strolling down the street with a gentleman in a top hat. His heart leaped with surprised pleasure. Could it be that she fancied another? He took care not to make unnecessary noise as he paid the cabby and climbed the stairs, still looking after the couple who grew smaller and smaller as they strolled down the street.

He knocked and Nina answered the door, covering her mouth in guilty surprise at the sight of him. "Captain Martensen! What are you—Mara's not here!" she confessed in a hurry.

He smiled gently. "That's fine, Nina. Are your parents at home?"

"Yes, yes." She opened the door to let him in and showed him to the parlor. It seemed she could not escape fast enough. In short order, Gerald arrived, welcoming him with a friendly embrace.

"Karl, Karl. I thought you were not due home for another few months."

"I decided to have my new ship outfitted here in San Francisco. She's getting a ballroom complete with paneled walls, parquet floors, and a chandelier. And she has electricity."

"Electricity!"

"Yes. I didn't dare put in the glassware until she was 'round the Horn."

Gerald laughed. "No, you wouldn't want to pay for that twice."

Karl laughed too and shook his head. "Not that it matters much after paying for the *ship*."

Gerald's laughter grew louder. "No, no, sir. She's a beauty?"

"Pretty enough," he said modestly. "Nothing compares to the sailers, I'm afraid."

"Give the shipbuilders time, man. The steamships will rival the sailers someday." He gestured toward two chairs. "I'm glad you came by, Karl. I wanted to talk with you, man to man."

"Yes," Karl led. Finally they would get things out in the open.

"Please, as my friend…as someone who could be more to our family. I'd like to know about your intentions for my daughter."

Karl leaned from the edge of his chair, resting his forearms on his legs and twisting his hat in his hands. "I'm so glad you asked, Gerald. I've been meaning to—"

"Why, Karl Martensen!" Mrs. Kenney cried from the parlor doorway. She rushed in to embrace him. "Nina told me you were here, and I couldn't believe it. I know Mara wasn't expecting you back for some time." She shifted, as if a bit uncomfortable at the mere mention of Mara's name.

"I saw her out for a stroll," Karl said. "I take it she's seeing someone?"

"Oh, no one like you," Mrs. Kenney said, taking his arm. "He's harmless. Don't you worry."

Karl coughed to cover his unease. Just then, the front door opened and Mara came in, pretty as a schooner on a brisk spring day. He smiled softly as she rushed to him and took his hands, chattering immediately. Behind her, a young man took off his hat and looked Karl over from head to toe. *He's thinking I'm the competition,* Karl assessed. *If he only knew...*

"Why did you not send word, Karl? I would've been home had I known you were coming to call."

The man behind her took a step forward. He obviously wasn't one to turn tail. A good thing in a man, Karl thought. The rival cleared his throat.

"Oh, forgive me," Gerald said. "Karl Martensen, please meet our dear friend Arthur Hairston. He's just in from Boston. Going to settle here. His family and ours go way back."

"Mr. Hairston," Karl said, shaking his hand firmly.

"Captain Martensen," he returned, matching Karl's searching gaze.

His use of the title told Karl that Arthur knew more about him than he knew about Arthur. "How long have you been in town, Mr. Hairston?" The man was of average looks. Brown hair, brown eyes. But Karl liked the sparkle; he was clearly a man who enjoyed life.

"For about a month. Long enough to take an interest in Miss Kenney, here." *And a man who likes a challenge,* Karl added to his mental checklist.

Mara laughed prettily, coyly taking a step between the two men. "Now, gentlemen, I am sure we will have plenty of time to all become friends. There is no need to draw a line in the sand."

"I agree," Karl said, looking at Arthur meaningfully. "There truly is no need."

"Very well," Arthur said amiably. "Shall we take a ride? It's a beautiful day for a carriage ride down by the water."

"That sounds delightful," Mrs. Kenney said.

"I am afraid you all will have to go on without me," Karl said. "I have some business down at the waterfront. Need to see to the parquet floors for my ballroom." He ignored Mara's sorrowful expression and gave up on finding a moment to speak with Gerald alone. Again. Perhaps he wouldn't need to anyway. If Arthur Hairston swept Mara off her feet, maybe no one would need to be "let down easily."

"That is unfortunate," Arthur said, his tone denoting no sorrow. "May we drop you somewhere?"

"That would be most kind."

"Good enough," Gerald said. "Will you return to join us for supper, Karl?"

"Yes, do," Mrs. Kenney said.

"I'm afraid not. Perhaps later in the week?"

"Name the date, son."

"Very well."

"Oh, and, Karl," Mara said. "There's a ball in three weeks. You must come."

Karl smiled down at his hat. "I shall have to see. It really will depend upon progress on the ship. Besides, I'm sure Mr. Hairston has dibs on your hand for the evening." He bit his tongue. Why did he have to play it this way? It would be so much better just to be honest! To have it all in the open! But every time he tried it came out all wrong. And he never wanted to hurt Mara...

Arthur tucked Mara's hand into the crook of his elbow. "I truly would be honored if you would accompany me to the ball."

She glanced away and answered in a monotone. "You do me an honor, Mr. Hairston. But Captain Martensen promised me months ago he would escort me."

Arthur nodded once toward Karl, as if in silent acquiescence. "Indeed, I see you plan ahead, Captain Martensen. Shall we?"

"Sometimes," Karl said, walking alongside the young man, "I find I still don't plan well enough."

eight

August 1888

*K*aatje had become used to their pace, the endless paddling or poling or walking. She had become used to the heat of the day and the chill of the night. She had become used to James and Kadachan. Her life in Juneau, her girls, seemed far, far away. All she seemed to be able to focus on was the search for Soren. The endless path.

They had traveled over most of the Yukon River and several of its tributaries, backtracking from Kokrine's Trading Post, all the way to Fort Yukon, looking for Soren. Someone in Kokrine's had said they thought Soren and the squaw had gone to the fort years before. Thought they had seen them there. Twenty miles from the fort, they met a trapper who spoke of a blond man who had operated the trading post there.

"Blond, curly hair?" Kaatje asked. "About this tall?" She raised her hand above her head.

"Yes, yes," the old trapper said. "Go to the fort. See for yourself."

James quietly thanked the man, and they were off. Perhaps to find Soren at last. With each step they took toward the fort, Kaatje's mind grew thicker with wild thoughts. What would she say to him? What would he say? And would the Indian woman be with him? As his *wife?*

Two days later, they stood outside the fort, and Kaatje could not seem to walk any farther. She stood as if planted in the ground as firmly as the fir trees that surrounded her.

"Kaatje?" James asked. "Kaatje?" he repeated softly, bending to look her in the eye. To Kaatje he looked as though he were underwater, his face swimming before her. "Are you all right? Do you want Kadachan and me to go in and see if he's there?"

"No," she said, finding her voice. "I must do it myself."

"Are you sure?"

"I am."

Tentatively, he offered his hand, and she took it.

His hand on hers comforted, gave a strength she wouldn't have had on her own. They made their way past several vendors inside the courtyard of the fort, selling tools and jerky and other items. But she never looked away from the trading post. In seconds, they stood inside the darkened doorway, waiting for their eyes to adjust.

Kaatje swallowed hard. Directly in front of her, a man stood with his back to them. Dimly, she felt James's hand on her shoulder. But her concentration was on the trader—about Soren's height, with hair almost the color of his too. Could it have darkened in the years apart?

"Sor-Soren?" It came out in almost a whisper. "Soren?" she then said too loudly.

The man turned in surprise.

Even with a beard, he was obviously not her husband.

"I'm sorry." She turned and fled the building. The tears found her as soon as she was outside.

James did not hesitate. He followed her and pulled Kaatje around the corner of the trading post, away from the curious stares of onlookers. Then he pulled her into his arms and let her cry. How long he had wanted to do just that! She came willingly, her tears dampening the front of his shirt. On and on she sobbed, as James stroked her long, shiny hair and kissed her crown. "Shh," he whispered. He desperately wanted to stop her crying, to ease her pain. He didn't know how he should feel.

After several minutes, Kaatje looked up at him, and the sorrow in her eyes made him want to cry too. "He's gone, James. And I'm done."

"You're done?"

"Yes. I want to go home. I want to bury Soren and get on with my life."

"But you said you wanted to find either him or his grave. Can you be sure—"

"I'm as sure as I need to be. He's dead. Or so far gone that we'll never be reunited. The judge will come to Juneau next fall, and I'll ask him to make a formal declaration."

James pulled her into his arms again, unable to speak.

"Take me home. Will you take me home?" She looked back up at him, and James fought off the overwhelming desire to kiss her right there and then. Her hazel eyes were beautiful, innocent. It was then he knew that he was in love with Kaatje Janssen. That his heart was in her hands, whether she knew it or not.

"Yes, Kaatje. I will take you home. To your daughters, your home. Your new life."

They began walking when James pulled her to a stop, holding her small hand in his. "But, Kaatje, are you sure? You've come this far…"

"I'm sure, James. He's dead. Or dead to me anyway. It's over."

James nodded and then took her back to where Kadachan stood over their supplies. "I think we'll camp here for the night. We can get rooms and baths and then resupply." He looked over at Kadachan. "We're going home. To Juneau."

Kadachan's eyes reflected no surprise. "Through Saint Michael?"

"Yes. We'll catch a steamer there to Juneau. It'll be faster than overland."

Kadachan switched to Tlingit. "I will ask about the river between here and Saint Michael—how she's running. Where we can expect to portage."

"Good. And I will secure us two rooms for tonight."

He turned toward Kaatje, who stood, looking out the fort doors as if looking at a different world. Her stance, her expression, was that of a woman once imprisoned who had been released. He put a hand on her shoulder again, but she did not look at him. "I will get you home, Kaatje. Just as soon as I can."

"Thank you, James. It will be good to be home. Oh, it will be so good to be home."

Kaatje was not a single woman yet and wouldn't be until the judge made his declaration—that Soren was dead. James wanted to stare and stare at the beauty in her, her eyes looking about as if seeing her world for the first time. But his soul told him to turn away and keep his distance. He had to. Or he might take her in his arms and never let her go. James forced himself to turn away and inquire after rooms for the night.

Tora paced back and forth in her room. For a month Decker had been in Juneau's small prison down the street. In the fall the judge would come and decide his fate. For now, he sat inside, probably pacing the small cage, thinking about how to get even with Tora and Trent. The thought sent a shiver down her back. She punched her fist into her other hand. Why, why could she not rid herself of him? Why could she not forget he was in Juneau and get on with her life?

But an irrational fear had set in. She hadn't slept more than three hours for the last few nights, certain that every sound was Decker coming to get her.

Fear is not of God, she told herself. *Fear is of the devil. I will fear no evil. I will fear no evil. I will fear no evil.*

But she was deathly afraid.

She fell to her knees every night, praying that God would lift the oppression from her shoulders. She wanted to be free, to feel confident again. But still, she found no peace.

On the fourth night, she again climbed out of bed and went to her knees. "Oh, please, Lord. Please. I need to sleep, to feel your peace. I need to feel...quiet. My heart seems to be wrenched in two when I should at last feel whole. He is in prison, and I am safe. Why does fear surround me?"

Go to him, child. Go to him.

Tora stood stock-still.

No, no, no. She must have misunderstood. She had to have misunderstood. Her God, her Savior, could not ask her to go toward the mouth of the devil.

Go to him.

"For what?" she whispered, tears streaming down her face. "For what?" she cried, looking up at the ceiling of her room. "Please, Father. Don't ask it of me."

Go.

Tora shook her head and rose, walked to her window, and stared at the street. She no longer wanted to hear from her Lord. He hadn't given the answer she sought. Or was she losing her mind? What good could possibly come from seeing Decker?

Trent did not understand her. "You want to go see *him?*" he thundered, furious at the thought. "Why?"

"I do not know," she said miserably. She looked up at him, her luminous blue eyes staring into his. "All I can tell you is that God has asked me to do so. I haven't slept in days—"

"Exactly," he interrupted. "It's your exhaustion that has led you to this. A rational woman would not want to see her *rapist.*"

The word seemed to cut Tora, and Trent immediately regretted using it. But he could not help himself. The thought of her within Decker's presence made him crazy.

She closed her eyes, as if trying to summon some strength inside her. He knew Tora Anders well enough to know that when she had made a decision, he had no choice but to move out of the way. But how could he now? When she wanted to be near the man who had threatened her life? Taken her body? He clenched his hands at the thought. If only he had shot Decker in the heart that night. If only he had not feared for Tora's life.

He paced away, pulling at his hair. What was he thinking? He wanted to have the blood of a man on his hands? Even one as evil as Decker? He stopped at the window and stared out. "I realize I cannot stop you from going, Tora. But you will not go alone."

Trent could hear her rise behind him. "You will go with me?" He knew she held her breath in hope.

"I cannot. Do not ask that of me. But I will send two men." Her pause told him his answer hurt her. "You will have to... You will have to give me time to come to terms with this, Tora."

"I have not yet come to terms with it myself," she said, suddenly near him. She took his hand and rested her head on his arm. "I do not want to go. But I know I must. It is just as it was with Kaatje. Everything in my head told me to go off with you, to marry you. But everything in my heart told me to go to her, to make restitution. It is the same with Decker."

"Decker is hardly like Kaatje."

"And yet God's pull is the same."

Trent nodded slightly. Her words, though they pained him, were heard. "I cannot bear it if he abuses you, even verbally."

"I do not think God asks that of me. Let me go. With your men. And see what it is that God has set before me." She put a small hand on his chin and turned his face toward her. "I know enough of our Lord to know that he doesn't set needless tasks before us. Good will come of this. Somehow."

Trent nodded again, but could not summon the strength that Tora had found. "I wish Kaatje were here," he said. Kaatje Janssen would have a word of wisdom for them, an understanding touch for each.

"I know. Me, too," Tora said.

"When will you go?"

"I don't know. Not yet. I can't yet. But I am sending a man to deliver a Bible to him today."

"There's probably not a man in Juneau who needs it more."

Three days later Tora found the strength to go. When she stopped at Trent's office on the way, her hands were already shaking. "I need to go."

Trent's face grew white, and he rose. "I will call my men. They are not to leave your side. Under no circumstances. Right?"

"Right."

"And if he becomes abusive, I want you to come straight out of there."

"Right. Oh, Trent, can you not come with me?"

"I can't, Tora. The sight of him makes me crazy. I have my own peace to make with him and God, and it won't happen today. If you're to go to him today, I cannot go with you."

Tora pulled a handkerchief from her waist pocket and crumpled it in her sweaty hands. "Call your men then. I must go right away, or I won't be able to go at all."

Trent's eyes told her he understood. "I will go with you to the jailhouse. And I will wait for you right outside. But I cannot go in."

Tora agreed. He took her hand, and they walked toward the jailhouse, stopping only at the railroad station where two burly men who worked loading cargo agreed to come with them. They asked no questions, and Tora looked away as Trent paid them each a dollar. "You will see that Miss Anders is escorted out if the prisoner becomes unpleasant? Your presence should persuade him to be decent."

Their glance at each other told Tora that they thought it an odd mission. But mission was what it was. There was no way she could get around it.

The men followed behind them, not speaking, and they walked into the jailhouse. A deputy sat outside, in a chair by the door, dozing. Trent cleared his throat, and he stirred. "Mr. Storm. Good to see you, Mr. Storm."

"A pleasure, deputy. My fiancée would like a word with her attacker. I would appreciate it if you would escort her and her bodyguards inside."

"Sure, Mr. Storm. Want to give him a piece of your mind, lady?"

"Something like that," she murmured as she walked through the open door.

Decker was sitting on his dirty cot, staring at her through the bars as if he'd expected her to come calling. He rose and nonchalantly walked toward the only thing that separated them, wrapping a bar in one of his huge hands, the other still encased in a white sling to keep his shoulder still. "Well, hello."

He leered at her, and the men behind her stepped to her side.

"'Fraid to be alone with me anymore, eh?"

"Miss Anders," said one of the men, "shall we leave?"

"No," she said, clearing her throat when the word came out too quietly. "Give me a moment."

"You will address Miss Anders with respect," her second bodyguard demanded.

"Got your package," Decker said, ignoring him, his eyes only on Tora. "A Bible. Never had a Bible before." With that statement she could see a crack in his harsh facade. It dawned on her that he was a person, just like her. Suddenly her fear of this evil man receded a bit—he wasn't someone to be dreaded; he was someone to pity.

"I hadn't carried a Bible before I got to Seattle either," she said in reply.

His eyes searched hers, and she stalwartly refused to look away. He did first.

"Don't know what you want with me. I'm as good as hung. With the pretty fiancée of Mr. Trent Storm pointing her finger at me anyway."

Tora swallowed hard. "That may well be. But perhaps that's the best reason to open that Bible."

Decker laughed. "For what? To find out God wants me hung and gone as much as you?"

Tora shook her head. Suddenly she knew why she was there. Why she had to be there.

"No, Decker. For mercy. For mercy on your soul."

"Ah, Tora." He clutched his breast melodramatically. "Your thoughtfulness touches me. But I don't need mercy. There's no mercy for men like me. I'm on a train straight to hell, and I'm gonna ride it in, hootin' and hollerin'."

"You cannot mean that. No one wants to be eternally damned."

He gave her a condescending look. "I'm at ease with it." His eyes searched hers, and Tora could take no more. She turned to go, then paused, her bodyguards by her side.

"Start with John, Decker. If you open that Bible, start with the book of John."

"I'm not makin' any promises."

She left without another word.

Trent was waiting outside. "Are you all right?"

Tora nodded, but reached a shaking hand out to him. She felt, rather than saw, him dismiss the men.

"I'm glad. Let's get you home. It's over."

Tora had not the heart to tell him he was wrong.

It had just begun.

❧

September 1888

They were off the western coast of South America, having
sailed successfully around the Horn, and the September noon
skies held as much heat and moisture as they did in July in Camden.
The *Majestic*, however, sailed through the calms of Capricorn on steam
power, ignoring the still waters as if the winds were pushing them at
eighteen knots. At this rate, they would reach San Francisco by month's
end, another Ramstad shipping record.

Elsa pulled an embroidered handkerchief from her waistband and
wiped her brow. Perspiration trickled between her shoulder blades
under her dress, sending a shiver down her spine. As had become their
custom these last few days, she walked with her children to the bow
to take in whatever breeze they could. Thank goodness they wouldn't
have to sit in these waters for days on end again as they had when
solely under sail power.

It was then that they heard the thundering explosion below, the
impact of the sound taking Elsa's breath away. The ship shuddered
as if grounded, and, pulling Kristian close, Elsa instinctively ducked
and covered Eve with her body. Splintering wood shot past them and
into the water. She grunted as another chunk hit her squarely on the
back.

"All hands! *All hands!*" Riley screamed, blowing three short blasts on his whistle.

"All hands on deck!" Eric echoed.

Men swarmed everywhere, and though Elsa wanted to help, she also wanted to keep her children clear of the possible fire. She knew boiler explosions could be deadly, taking a whole ship and her crew down in minutes.

Preparing for the worst, she set her children against the foremast and sternly told them to stay there. Then she ran back toward the boiler room, squinting her eyes against the smoke to ascertain just how bad it was. The boiler room and deck had a massive hole in it. Fire shot upward, and a chain of sailors had made a bucket brigade. Others battled the tongues of flames with wet blankets.

They were in a race. A race for their lives.

Since she could not leave her children unattended for long, and the men were doing all they could to put out the fire, Elsa set about preparing the lifeboats in case they had to abandon ship. She went from one to the other, working on all ten boats' ropes to make sure they could easily slide down to the cooling Pacific waters below. She scanned the coast five miles east. Judging from her maps, there wasn't a town within thirty miles.

She continued to glance back at the foremast, making sure the children were staying put. They did, eyes wide.

"Cap'n," Riley said, suddenly at her side. "It's bad, but we have a chance. I think we can get it under control."

"Good. Hold on to her if we can. Lifeboats are ready."

"Very well."

"How many dead, Riley?"

"We had two men down in the boiler room. If they're alive, they're prayin' they'll soon die."

Elsa swallowed hard and nodded once. "Any injuries?"

"Two others."

"Bring them aft, and I'll tend to them."

"Aye." He ran away to do as she bid.

Elsa moved back to her children. "Kristian, I need you to do me a favor. Riley is bringing back some injured sailors. They'll be in a lot of pain. Can you keep your sister busy? Teach her some knots?"

Kristian nodded obediently, lips clamped in a worried expression.

She reached out to squeeze his shoulder. "I want you to stay near and try to keep Eve from seeing the sailors. But I want you nearby, in case we have to get into the lifeboats, as we practiced."

He nodded again.

The men came then, one sailor screaming in agony, the other moaning. Eve covered her ears in fright, and Kristian hurried her to the front of the ship. Elsa, feeling torn, turned to the sailors and examined their wounds. "Get their clothes off of them. They might still be smoldering!"

The sailors immediately set to their task.

"I need my bag from the cabin. Can you get to it safely?" She looked up at Samuel, a broad-shouldered man who had been with them for a year.

"Aye, Cap'n. Think I can."

"Good. Go."

She turned to another. "We'll need some fresh water and clean sheets. Fast." He left without further command. "You two, stay here and try to hold these men down. They're hurting themselves with their writhing." The others did as she bid, and Elsa carefully examined the wounds on the man who screamed in agony. She grimaced. There were serious burns across his face and chest. The other one, the one semiconscious, had similar burns across his back.

"These two were outside," explained a sailor. "This one turned in time, but was knocked into a mast by the explosion. He might not be right in the head."

Elsa nodded. She wiped the sweat from her brow and dimly noticed her perspiration dripping down on the man's wounds. Samuel returned with her huge bag, and she quickly opened the black leather case. In one corner was a wooden box that Elsa carefully lifted out. She flipped it open. Inside were many glass bottles, and she desperately searched for laudanum to sedate the still-screaming man. His cries were getting to her, threatening to break her like nothing before. Her hand shook as it passed each one. *There.*

She poured some onto her handkerchief and quickly held it over the man's nose and mouth, holding her breath as he gasped, practically pulling the thin cloth into his mouth, exhaled, and then breathed in again, immediately calming. In moments, he dozed. "Is he still breathing?" she asked, moving down to his chest.

Samuel bent at the sailor's mouth and listened. "Barely."

"Good. Do the same for the other man." She examined the man's chest, grimacing as white and black skin peeled away like burned roast. The smell of roasted flesh threatened to make her gag. "Where is Cook?" Cook often tended to the ill on her ship; he would know what to do.

"He's on the bucket brigade. Said he'd come if you wanted."

She shook her head. "I think we're all right. There isn't a whole lot we can do for these men but calm them and clean their wounds. Then we'll wrap them."

"Mama?" came a timid voice behind one of the men around her.

"Kristian, it's all right. We'll be all right. Now go back to your sister." She didn't look up while she spoke, intent upon cleaning the wounds and getting the men bandaged before they awakened again.

"But, Mama, Eve has to use the toilet."

"Kristian!" she said, losing patience. She looked up—smoke swirled around her child. "I cannot help her right now. Tell her she'll have to wait."

The sailor's skin pulled away as she touched it with a cloth and water. Elsa shuttered, suddenly unsure. Was it better to leave it, or get rid of it? It seemed logical that it would be best to strip the blackened skin away, leaving the wound clean and ready for healing. Old, rotting skin would only complicate matters, right? "I need Cook after all," she said to Samuel. "I'm afraid I'm making a poor decision."

"Right." He was off.

As he left, Elsa glanced toward her children. They were not there. "Kristian?" she cried, rising. She couldn't help the panic in her heart. Last time she had looked away from her family during a crisis aboard ship, she had lost Peder. Forever. *"Kristian? Did anyone see the children? Kristian! Eve!"* She looked wildly about.

"Ma'am," said a sailor. "He was talkin' about his sister and the necessary…"

"Oh no. No! They've gone to my cabin. Stay with these men and wait on Cook!" She ran toward her cabin. The fire was nearing the door, the heat so fierce it was difficult to push past it. Could they have gone in there? Or were they turned back by the fire? She didn't want to go in and get trapped herself if they weren't there. *"Kristian! Eve!"*

She glanced at the fire brigade and wondered if it was her imagination or if they were actually making progress. It was then that she heard a muffled "Mama!" and a child crying. She ran to the tiny cabin window, but the velvet curtains were pulled shut. "Kristian! Call if you're in there!" If only she could see inside!

"Mama!" It was louder this time and coming from…behind her. She whirled in relief, running to the lifeboat at the side of the ship. She whipped back the tarp and gasped at the sight of her children huddled at the bottom.

Kristian looked up at her in misery. "She couldn't hold it, Mama. She's all wet."

"That's all right, darling," she said, holding out her arms. "Come. It's not time to abandon ship yet."

"Is the *Majestic* sinking?" he asked in wonder as he jumped to the deck. "We came back to the cabin to go to the water closet and saw the fire."

She reached out her arms again for her little girl. Her dress was wet at the bottom, but Elsa didn't care. She was there! Alive! "Children, I must go help those sick sailors. Come with me. They're not screaming anymore."

They hurried forward again, and Elsa glanced over her shoulder and suddenly stopped. "It's out! The fire's out! They've done it!" She let out a cheer, lifting up her arm as she did so. The sailors who heard her cheered too. After seeing Cook tending to the men at the bow, she ran to the middle of the ship again, her children firmly in tow.

Her smile quickly faded. It made her heart sink. There was a terrific hole in the center, out of which a huge column of smoke arose. With a crew of twenty-five, Elsa could barely believe that they had only lost two, with two more injured. Here and there, she spotted a crew member with a bleeding brow or forearm, but nothing serious.

Riley came up to Elsa. "Fire's out, Cap'n. For good. We saved her." His white eyes and teeth beamed at her out of a blackened face of soot.

"Very well, Mate," she said, clapping him on the shoulder. "A fine job, Riley," she said, more softly. "Who'd we lose?"

"Ian Dougherty and Elmer Simms. Fine men."

"Aye. Let's retrieve the bodies and prepare them for a funeral on the morrow."

"I'll see to it, ma'am."

Elsa watched briefly as he walked away. What would she have done without Riley? Or Cook? She had given Mrs. Hodge shore leave for the voyage to Norway, and they were soon to pick her up in Washington. This proved that Elsa needed another woman about to help mind the children. *Oh, Peder. I wish I had you around.*

She shook her head. There was no use pining for a dead husband. He was gone. And Elsa was left to make the best of things, on ship, on shore. She stood there, watching the men continue to douse the smoldering fire, the carpenter surveying the damage, Riley shouting orders. And she was suddenly bereft. Lonely. Alone. She longed for a man at her side, the steadying heartbeat against her own in an embrace. She wanted to be held as her children clamored for her to hold them now. To be loved. To be comforted. To be known.

Karl awakened in a cold sweat, searching his cabin walls in a frantic effort to ascertain that all was well. He was sure he had heard a boiler explosion. He went to his cabin window and threw open the sash, letting in San Francisco's early morning light. Below, he already could hear the men working on the ballroom.

He didn't know why he had felt the need to leave the hotel in the city last week. But he could not help himself. Between his days spent avoiding the Kenneys, and his nights of anxious dreams, he felt like a listing ship. Between wind and water. Exposed. Off kilter. Maybe it was the deep desire to be at sea again, on his way to Alaska. Instead, he was stuck here—here in a place where Mara hovered near and he seemed to get more and more stuck in the mire of his own making. Perhaps if he stayed on his ship, he reasoned, it would encourage Antonio's men to work all the harder. Karl had sidestepped Mara's invitation to the ball, saying he thought he would be putting out to sea by then, but with each passing day, he knew that he would not get out of California in time. He went to the private bathroom that featured a copper washtub and a matching wash basin, splashed his face, and washed his hair. He took a cloth, soaped it, and washed his body. Being clean made him feel ready to take on the day.

Donning a smart suit of trousers and a jacket, and pulling on a bowler hat, he glanced in the mirror and guffawed. With his hair reaching his shoulders in gentle waves and an earring in one ear, he looked like a pirate dressing up as a gentleman. Karl picked up a leather strap and quickly pulled his hair into a neat ponytail, tucking the ends under his jacket collar. Then he pulled the wide gold loop out of his earlobe and left the cabin, heading directly to the ballroom.

"You wantin' breakfast?" called his cook from the galley as he passed.

"Not today, Cook!" he returned. Today he was going to get his ship in order. In order so that he could leave the bay within the month.

Before the Harvest Ball. His city clothes felt restraining, and once again he longed for the freedom of the sea. For shirts open at the collar, for hair free to wave in the wind. He sped down the circular wrought-iron stairs, the shortcut to the ballroom, and opened the huge mahogany doors, both at once.

The workmen paused to look back at their employer, then went back to work. There was progress, yes, but not as much as he had hoped.

Antonio hurried over to him. "Captain Martensen, have you—?"

"I thought you would be three-quarters of the way done by now," he said, exasperation just under the surface in his voice. He could see that his pacing only made the workmen nervous. But they should have been so much further along!

"Yes, but—"

"We are scheduled to be out of here by month's end. Will you be on schedule?"

"We are doing our best. We ran into—"

"I'm not sure of that, Antonio. You and I made a deal. You saw the plans. You know what I expected. Are you now telling me that I cannot leave because you cannot fulfill your part of the bargain?"

"No, I am not saying—"

"Are you telling me that I will have to remain here, possibly missing my first scheduled trip out of Seattle, because your carvers can't put in a little extra time?"

"They are already working—"

"Enough!" Karl said, putting up one hand. "See to it that they pick up the pace!"

Antonio's face grew red with embarrassment. "Yes, Captain Martensen."

Karl turned on his heel and left.

Later, walking along the waterfront, he felt ill over his actions. Antonio and his men were clearly doing their best. He had misplaced his anger. His anger was at himself, for his own inaction when it came to Mara. He stopped at a store window and stared at himself in the mirrorlike glass, not seeing the goods beyond it. He only saw a man of thirty-two, with ash-blond hair and large gray eyes that looked empty.

Karl sighed and leaned his forehead against the glass. "I've done it again, Lord," he confessed in a whisper. "I've left without you and gotten into a mess. Help me, Father. Help me see my way out of it. Amen. Amen and amen."

It was then that he saw it. His eyes focused beyond the glass, to the jewelry on the black velvet behind it. A necklace in a huge teardrop form, a sapphire. A sapphire exactly the color of Elsa Ramstad's eyes, the color of an island cove's water at dusk. He had to have it. For her.

Immediately he entered and purchased the necklace, unflinching at the price and tucking the velvet case into his breast pocket. He never stopped to think about why he purchased gifts for his old friend; he just knew there were things he came across occasionally that were meant for no other. He didn't remember when he started buying them—he supposed it started with the Italian Galli glass "fish pot" painted with water lilies that brought back memories of Elsa in the Far East. And then there had been the Japanese cloisonné palace vase painted with a dragon and phoenix images, reminding him of how far she had come and grown since losing Peder; the Scottish agate bracelet with immense colored stones set in gold and silver, that reminded him at once of her strength and her beauty.

And now the huge teardrop sapphire on a slender silver chain. How it would bring out her eyes! He knew not where or when or how or why he would give his old friend this gift. He only knew it was meant for her. Just as the others had been.

t e n

September 1888

ora convinced herself she should go to Decker again. Ever since she had seen him in the prison the previous month, she had begun to realize how lost he was. At first she had fought it, grumbling against God for his urgings. Surely he would allow her to hate this man who had torn her life, her security, into pieces. And yet God nudged, reminding her of his infinite mercy, his forgiveness toward her when she had been so unlovable. And even though Decker deserved whatever punishment the judge rendered, God offered his Son for everyone. Even Decker. She felt pulled in half. Her heart was relieved at the thought of seeing Decker sent away to pay for what he had done to her, yet the image of him hanging because of her pointing finger left her…unsettled. It was the unsettled half of her heart that made her determined to go to the jailhouse.

She decided she would not tell Trent—the whole thing would just upset him. Besides, there would be a deputy inside the jailhouse. And she did not care who overheard their conversation because she was going solely to share the gospel. Or was it more? The notion nagged at her. Did she need to do this to conquer some inner fear? The fear that awakened her at night in a sweat? Perhaps she had two reasons to go. In any case she was going.

Tora rose from bed and considered her dresses in the armoire. She pulled her most subdued dress from its hangar, a yellow-brown plaid work dress she had worn the last time she went to see Decker. Once she had her drawers and corset on the best she could by herself, she pulled the dress over her head and then brushed out her long, dark hair.

Staring at her image in the small oval mirror on the wall, she decided to pull it back in a severe bun, hoping to make herself as unappealing as possible. She decided not to use any color on her cheeks or the lip balm. *No use dangling a carrot before the horse.* She winced at her own internal analogy. But that was what she was to Decker, at least at one time. A carrot, something he wanted to get with a singular purpose…

She swallowed past the lump in her throat, squeezing her eyes shut and willing the memories of those awful days away. But it was no use. They came in a bombardment as thick as her sisters' old snowballs on a clear winter day in Bergen, pelting her without mercy.

Tora felt ill and out of breath. She sat down on the edge of her bed, then sank to the floor, gasping for air as the memories came on… He was on her, tearing at her clothes, whispering lewd things in her ear. He laughed when she cried, told her no one could hear her when she screamed. She struggled, but he was so strong…

She cried for an hour or more, unable to stem the tears. "How could he?" she whispered, wiping her face. "How could he?" She looked up. "How could you let him?"

No voice welcomed her. No mellow tone from within told her the answer.

"I know he is lost. I know I was too. But how can I give a man who did such hateful things to me a second chance?"

I am the God of second chances.

Tora sucked in her breath. "But can you not get to him some other way?"

This is for you, as much as for him.

"Please, Father. I have done my penance, have I not? I went to Kaatje. I asked forgiveness and she granted it. Must this be too?"

It must be you.

Tora did not want to pray anymore.

God only gave answers she did not want to hear.

And he led her to a path that terrorized her.

"Auntie Tora, where are you going?" Christina called from the kitchen. Judging from the flour on her apron, she and her sister were working on their bread.

"Just out for a minute. I will be home within the half-hour. Bye," she called, before they could ask her anything else. She shut the glass door behind her and prayed for strength. *I'll just pretend. I've pretended to be more than I am before. Now I'll just pretend I'm brave and fearless.*

She strode across the street, shoulders back, head held high. She concentrated on her breathing, trying to calm the trembling in her hands. But when she reached for the jailhouse doorknob, she saw that her hands still shook. Biting her lower lip, she opened the door.

"Deputy," she said to the man rising behind his desk. "I would like to have a word with your prisoner named Decker."

"Certainly, ma'am." He turned to lead her down the short hallway to the three cells. "I'll have to stay with you since you don't have no menfolk with you this time."

"I would be most appreciative."

A long whistle greeted her. "You can try and make yourself look unappealing, Miss Tora, but it ain't no use. You're a siren in any dress. No matter what you do with your hair."

Tora resisted the urge to turn tail right there and run. "I would like a word with you, Mr. Decker."

"Seems like you just had seven or eight."

"Don't be smartin' off to the lady," the deputy warned. He turned to Tora. "You sure you want to talk with this no-account?"

"Yes. May I have a chair?"

"Be right back, ma'am." He left right away.

"See?" Decker said, still lying back on his cot. "Even the deputy has an eye for—"

"Decker," she said sharply, cutting him off. "I have come for one reason. Have you opened that Bible I sent to you? To the book of John?"

"You sure didn't seem like a churchgoer when I met ya. Sure you were a schoolmarm and—"

"*Decker*. Have you read that Bible?"

He looked at her strangely. "I don't believe I have."

"You ought to," she said. "There is an incredible message in there. Someone…cares about you."

He rose and walked quickly toward the bars, leering at her. "That you who cares about me, Miss Tora?"

The deputy came then with the chair and rapped him on the knuckles where they lay exposed on the bars. Decker backed off, rubbing his hands with the look of a wounded tiger.

But Tora stepped closer to him, infuriated. "Certainly *not*. Sadly, I cannot muster one *ounce* of care for you, Mr. Decker. Everything in me *hates* you. Hates what you did to me. I *want* to see you hang! I want to cheer when they string you up!" She turned, letting out a sound of pure frustration. Then she turned back to him. "But my God, our Lord, won't *let* me hate you in peace. He won't let me forget that you abducted me, used me, until I do this. He wants me to *forgive* you, which, I confess, seems a long way away from me right now, but he wants you back in the fold. Isn't that just *dandy*? Here I am, a woman who has every right to revel in her hatred of you, especially now, now that you're *caught*. And I'm supposed to lead you home."

Her hands splayed as she let out another sound of frustration. She shook her head. She'd said what she'd come to say—whether or not he took it was up to him. She rose and left, knowing that the deputy and prisoner watched her go.

Tora was halfway across the street, so deep was her consternation, before she noticed the trio in front of the roadhouse. It was a moment longer before she noticed who it was.

"Kaatje!" she cried, running the rest of the way. She embraced the woman, ignoring the grime and weariness that shrouded her pretty face. "Oh, Kaatje, Kaatje!"

"Tora!" she returned, squeezing her tightly. "It is so good to see you! How are my girls?"

"Just fine, just fine. You won't believe how they've changed in the four and a half months you've been gone."

"Don't remind me," she said sadly, wrinkling up her brow. "I am glad I went, but I will always be sorry I missed these days with you and the rest of my family."

"I'm so glad you're home!" She burst into tears, the strain of everything proving too much.

"Tora, are you all right?" Kaatje pushed her slightly away, wondering at her expression.

"Yes, yes. I'm sorry. I'm just so, so glad you're home!" She gave Kaatje another hug. "Quick, let's surprise the girls around back. You wait there, and I'll send them out to feed the poor and homeless!"

James and Kadachan laughed, and Tora focused on them for the first time. "You all look like you've been traveling a long while. Please, we'll get you a good meal, a bath, and a bed within the hour. But give me the pleasure of surprising the girls!"

They agreed, but reluctantly. Tora could feel their incredible weariness. They had covered untold miles and who knew what they had discovered. She resisted the urge to ask as they turned to walk around back; she would find out when Kaatje was ready to tell them all.

She smiled, feeling weary herself from the drastic change in emotions, and her neck tingled with excitement at the approaching reunion. She could hear the girls in the kitchen as she entered the restaurant. Trent sat at a corner table, reviewing papers and accounts. When Trent looked up, she motioned him to follow.

"Girls," she said, as she entered the tiny kitchen, "there are people in back asking for a bite to eat."

"Must we feed everyone who comes around?" Christina groused. Tora guessed she was hot and tired.

"I think you'll be glad you did."

"Yes, Auntie Tora," Christina said obediently. "I know. I always am." She gathered up a hot loaf of bread while Jessie brought a chunk of cheese from the larder. Together they went outside and a moment later shrieked in joy.

Tora grinned at Trent's curious expression and led him outside. Kaatje was embracing one girl and then the other. Then both at the same time.

It was then that Tora looked at the men beside Kaatje and saw something unmistakable. James Walker and Kadachan looked on with care in their eyes. But something in James's expression was different— it held an intensity, the way his eyes trained on Kaatje, followed her every movement. It was as if he couldn't take his eyes off her.

Clearly James was in love with Kaatje.

While they ate and ate and ate that late afternoon, Trent suggested a town dance, held in honor of Kaatje's safe return.

"Killing the fatted calf, are you?" she quipped, as if the prodigal had at last returned. "At least wait until Saturday. I need to sleep for days. And soak in a tub for about as long."

"Saturday it is," Trent agreed. "We'll put on a party that will only be outdone by our wedding reception."

"It is coming soon enough," Tora evaded, coyly smiling back at him.

"It is? When?"

"You silly, we decided on October thirtieth, remember? If my sister isn't home by then, she'll just be missing Juneau's biggest celebration."

Trent laughed, his scalp tingling in exhilaration. "October thirtieth it is! She's kept me out to pasture so long, I can't even remember the date!" He unbuttoned his sleeves and rolled them up. "I guess we ought to get busy. Two parties to manage within six weeks…"

Kaatje rose. "Forgive me, but you will have to plan this first one without me. If I don't get to bed right now after a quick bath, I will fall asleep here, and the supper crowd will just have to step over me!"

James laughed, but Trent wondered if he looked a little sorry at the idea of saying good-bye to her. There sure was a difference in the way the man looked at Kaatje from when they first met. He had been surly and irritated with her obstinateness before, but now he looked…smitten. But, he reminded himself, it was like that with Kaatje. Anyone who got to know her had to love her. He swiftly glanced back to the man. Love her? Was James Walker in love with Kaatje?

She had not mentioned whether or not they had found sign or sight of Soren. Instead the hour had been spent eating huge quantities of food while the girls chattered on about what had kept them busy these last months.

Christina stopped talking as her mother rose, and when there was a pause, she asked, "But, Mama. What about you? We want to hear all about your journey! And about—"

"And you shall," Kaatje said, bending over to pinch her chin, "very soon. But for now, I must go and bathe and get to bed. I'm very serious—if I do not, I feel as if I could sleep right here."

"Your bath is ready, Mrs. Janssen," Charlie said from the stairwell. "I took up eight buckets, so it'll be nice and deep!"

"Thank you, dear," she said, passing him by. She paused on the stairs, suddenly remembering James and Kadachan. "Oh, forgive me." Her hand went to her mouth, apparently moved at the thought of her friends' departure. "We've been together so long, I can't seem to remember how to say good-bye."

"No need, Kaatje," James said tenderly, twisting his hat in his hands. "We'll be about for some time. At least for the weekend's party."

"Would you like to stay here?" Tora volunteered. "I told you we'd give you a room, bath, and a bed."

"No need, Miss Anders. We always stay down the street. We don't want to impose—"

"Never you mind about that," she interrupted. "Charles, please see to warming more water. The gentlemen will be staying in the third and fourth guest rooms upstairs." Charlie groaned, but she ignored him. Trent hid his smile and looked back at Kaatje.

The news that they planned to stay seemed to ease the wrinkles from her brow. She gave them all a small smile and said, "It is so good to be home. Good night, dear ones."

They said good night as one, but Trent stared at James instead of Kaatje.

There was no doubt about it; the man was in deep.

Kaatje did not rise for forty-eight hours. The girls went by her room every hour, it seemed to Tora, worrying that something was wrong.

"Why doesn't she get up?" Jessie asked. "She's slept for days."

"She's practically snoring, her mouth's so dry. Don't you think we ought to awaken her again and give her some more water?" Christina added.

"She's so awfully tired," Tora answered. "She needs to let her body rest and recuperate. She's been on a very rough trail for months. No doubt she has many adventures to tell us about. And all that can make a person terribly weary." She remembered her days on the streets of Seattle, when she had been without a home or a bed, always on the move, and how weary she had become. She supposed Kaatje felt just that way. "Now off to the study with you. I'm sure you both have some homework, right?"

"Right. But, Auntie," Jessie said. "What about Father? Do you think she found him?"

Tora looked to the floor, then back at the girls. "I'm afraid that her return without Soren, or any word of him, must mean she did not. I'm so sorry, girls. I know you wanted to meet your father."

The two looked at each other and then back at Tora. "Can we go and ask her?"

"She'll tell us in her own time. Now off with you. Go get your studying done."

"Yes, but what if Mama needs—"

"She's fine. Really. She didn't get all the way home to die on our doorstep. You'll see—"

"That's right," Kaatje said from the stairwell. Tora smiled at her. "I intend to stay with you all for a very long time. I've been in the wilderness, but I'm home now. I'm home!"

The girls rushed up the stairs and hugged her close.

"Now you won't believe this after seeing me eat last night, but I'm hungry again!"

"There's a reason for that," Tora answered, sitting on a stair beneath the trio. "That was two nights ago."

"Two nights! I've slept for two days?"

"Yes ma'am. And I would wager that as soon as we feed you again, you'll be off to bed once more. By tomorrow, you'll be feeling like your old self again."

"Or somewhere near."

"Would you like some ham and potatoes?"

"That would be wonderful, Tora."

"Let me get it ready while you girls catch up with your mother."

"Oh, Tora," she called. "What day is it?"

"Friday."

"And did Trent say there's a party tomorrow, or did I dream that?"

"There's a party tomorrow. In your honor."

"And...and James? Will he be invited?"

Tora's smile grew broader. She *knew* it—Kaatje had feelings for the man. "Of course. He's already asked to be your escort."

The next night Tora came to her room to help Kaatje prepare for the dance. She wound Kaatje's hair into an elaborate knot, using her own pearl-and-ivory combs to hold the style in place. Then she pulled a dress from behind the door as Kaatje watched in the mirror.

Kaatje gasped and turned to look. She had planned to wear her old wine-colored dress, but this dress was amazing! And Tora seemed to be offering it to her. "Is it yours? When did you get it?"

"No, it's yours," she said. "I ordered it for you when you left, knowing there would be many causes for celebration when you returned."

Kaatje rose, her hand at her throat. Never had she owned anything so elegant, so luxurious. "Is it proper? I mean, for a town dance? This is something that you or Elsa would wear to a ball."

"Certainly. You're the guest of honor, after all. No one should outshine you tonight."

Tora sat down on the edge of Kaatje's bed and looked her in the eye. "Kaatje, you haven't said. And the girls have been dying to ask…"

Kaatje turned away from Tora and looked at her image in the mirror. "I did not find him. I found his cabin, his claim, places he'd been. But not him. He had taken an Indian wife, and then apparently disappeared. He's dead. Or gone. Dead to me anyway. I intend to have him declared as such when the circuit judge comes to town."

Tora rose behind her and came near. She rested her hands on Kaatje's shoulders. "I am sorry, my friend, but glad you've made a decision to move on. The circuit judge will be here next week."

"Next week?"

"Next week. There's something I need to tell you. We have a prisoner in our jailhouse."

"Oh? Another miner stealing flour upriver? An Indian falsely accused?"

"No." Tora's tone made Kaatje turn to stare at her. "Decker. The man who abducted me outside of Spokane."

"What?" Kaatje's heart raced at the thought of it. "He's *here?* However…? Whatever…?"

"His travels apparently brought him here, and I ran into him. Then he came after me—can you believe it? And Trent shot him and—"

"*What?*"

"Yes, he came after me again. He came right in here and threatened to take me away. Tried to take me away until Trent shot him."

Her story chilled Kaatje to the bone. "Oh, my goodness. I cannot believe… Are you all right? Did he hurt you?"

"Yes, yes. I am fine. And his trial is next week. I'll tell you the rest of it tomorrow. We have to get you ready for the party now. James will certainly be early. I believe he fancies you."

"Tora Anders! First you talk of your kidnapper in such an offhanded way, and then you move on to James. Are you trying to make me scattered?"

"Not at all. I simply think you should be prepared for love to finally find you again."

Kaatje held her breath as she stared at Tora. "Love?"

"Love."

James looked away and glanced back to the stairway to make sure his eyes did not deceive him. Kaatje descended in an elegant silk ball gown that plunged at the neckline. It was the exact color of her eyes—a delicate green. Over her shoulders was a small Spanish jacket of black velvet that matched the long gloves over her arms. In her hair, a dramatic style atop her head, she wore two bands of pearl and ivory, reminding James of pictures he had once seen of a Greek goddess.

She approached him with a smile that tore at his heart. Perhaps tonight was the night to declare his love. If she was ready. If she gave him any hint.

"Hello, James," she said softly. "I've missed you."

"You look amazing," he returned. "And there's no way you could have missed me more than I missed you. I've become…used to you, Kaatje." He hoped the way he said the words told her that he felt much more than that. It just had been so long since he had had to find a way to talk to a woman, especially a woman who had become closer than any other to him. It was different here, in town, so much more formal than he had felt with her on the river.

She smiled sweetly and glanced away, taking his arm as she did so. Did he note a trace of shyness? Perhaps it was being in all that feminine finery after months of Levi Strauss jeans and split skirts. She probably felt like a doll, all dressed up like that. She looked like a doll. Perfect, just perfect. He could not help himself; he kept staring at her and then making himself look away.

He stared at her all through dinner, an elaborate affair with every imaginable kind of food. It seemed the whole town had turned out; there was even a platform set up in the middle of the street for a dance. The band—an odd assortment of fiddles, a cello, a bass, and banjos—was already playing. Anyone who could play was up there. Several boys, led by the one Tora called Charlie, lit the torches set about the platform at around ten o'clock. James's stomach did a little flip at the thought of stepping on Kaatje's toes through a waltz, but he was ready to risk it to hold her in his arms. He'd been aching to touch her again ever since he had held her in Fort Yukon, in the Interior, when she had given up on her no-account husband at last.

The band stopped as Trent climbed the platform to make an announcement.

"Ladies and gentlemen," he called. "We are here to celebrate the safe return of Kaatje Janssen and the heroic measures James Walker and his companion, Kadachan, took to get her here. They have made a grand journey and have stories to tell, from bear attacks to long days on the river. Let's applaud them all for their courage and gumption."

The crowd erupted in applause, obviously impressed by such exploits. James wondered if any of them knew or cared why Kaatje had taken such a journey. Or if they did, they cheered her loyalty and fierce resolve. James knew he did anyway. He looked over the crowd and found Kadachan enjoying a plate full of food as he spoke to several Inuit women dressed in Western style.

"And now," Trent called, "I'd like to invite Mr. Walker to escort Mrs. Janssen in the first dance to start us off for the night."

"Gladly!" he called, feeling eager.

Several onlookers hooted and hollered. "I'm next!" called one. "Then me!" yelled another.

"Everyone wants a chance at the lovely Mrs. Janssen," James said lowly. He had stopped himself from calling her the Widow Janssen, as he had heard others refer to her. He did not think Kaatje would be ready for that for some time, regardless of what she had decided.

The band found the key for "Clementine," and to his surprise James soon found his step, remembering lessons from long ago. "Mother would be so pleased."

"So pleased?" Kaatje asked, looking up at him with interest.

"Yes. That I remember my dance lessons."

"You're a fine dancer, James."

"And you're a fine woman, Kaatje." They turned and swayed with the music, and it felt to James that they were the only couple on earth. "I want to tell you something, Kaatje."

The look of love in her eyes encouraged him. Maybe, just maybe, she felt the same way.

"I've wanted to tell you something myself, James, for some time—"

"Excuse me," thundered a man as he jumped up onto the platform. The boards bounced beneath him. The band ceased playing. Kaatje and James turned toward the intruder. "But I believe that's my wife you're dancing with."

Kaatje raised her hand to her mouth.

"Soren?" she whispered.

James thought he must have misheard her. But then she said it again.

"*Soren?*"

It was then that James knew all was lost.

section two

Solar Flare

eleven

September 1888

"We need to find a harbor in which to moor," Elsa said to Riley, the night after the explosion. "Someplace to rest, find fresh water, while the carpenter ascertains what needs to be done."

"I agree, Cap'n," Riley said. They pored over the charts together in her cabin. Elsa could still smell the smoke that had permeated every cushion and curtain in the room.

"It looks as if we can get through the reef here," Riley said, pointing to a shallow harbor. "It would gain us some protection from the trade winds as we go about our repairs. Might even be a stream of fresh water."

Elsa perused the map. There were no markings within a hundred miles showing fresh water or any semblance of a town. They were on their own. She sighed. "I guess it's as good as any. There doesn't appear to be any perfect place along this stretch of coast. And that one mast could use a replacement. The fire burned it half away. I wouldn't trust it in a storm."

"Aye," Riley agreed. "Though I doubt there's any suitable timber along the coast."

"We may well have to wait until we can get to Ramstad Lumberyard to replace her. Can you get us through that reef, Mate? It looks tricky."

"Sure enough," he said with no qualm in his voice.

"Then go about it."

"We'll be there in time for you to take the children for a swim." He winked at her and left her cabin.

But as quickly as the thought of a swim gladdened her heart, the thought of the delay saddened her. By the time they repaired the deck and mast, it would put them a week behind, to say nothing of sailing with no auxiliary power. Stopping in San Francisco for a new boiler and Washington for the mast would put them further behind. Tora would most certainly give up on Elsa ever coming home, and Elsa would miss her sister's wedding. Surely Trent had talked her into moving forward by now.

Elsa sighed heavily again, suddenly homesick for family and friends in North America, until her children came to retrieve her for a game of hide-and-seek.

Karl smiled as he walked along the ballroom walls. Ornate carvings of scrolls and grape leaves made the room truly elegant.

"We shall complete the carving within two weeks," Antonio said, walking alongside him, "Then take them back down to sand and finish them."

"Very good, Antonio," Karl said. He had given up on the chance to escape San Francisco before the ball and determined to have a heartfelt talk with Mara and Gerald. It was well past the time he needed to be forthright, and it was cowardly of him to be thinking of escape instead of honesty. God had made him see it at last. Taking it head-on bolstered his confidence. "I will plan on leaving the first of October. Let me know if anything changes with your plans or progress."

"Very good, Captain Martensen." The older man turned to leave.

"And, Antonio?"

"Yes?"

"Please accept my apologies for yelling at you yesterday. My anger was misdirected, and I'm afraid I was unjust."

"Apology accepted, Captain." The man's eyes crinkled at the corners as he smiled. He put a hand on Karl's shoulder. "If I'm not mistaken, I'd guess you have woman troubles."

Karl smiled ruefully and shook his head. "Sadly, you're on the mark, my friend."

He left directly after the noon meal for the Kenneys', hiring a cab at the wharf. He leaned his head back against the black leather, feeling the gentle heat of it through his hair while the breeze cooled his face. It was a beautiful autumn day. The young trees planted along the boulevard were turning color, and his mind raced back to a fall day in Camden-by-the-Sea. That day he had come across Elsa, high above the Maine coast, sitting atop a granite boulder. She had been in tears, angered that Peder did not see things as she did.

His mind shifted to Mara and the task at hand. Would he make Mara cry today? Would he make her as angry as Peder had made Elsa? He hoped not. If he did, he prayed that her sorrow and fury would soon be assuaged. Perhaps Mr. Hairston would soon turn her heart toward him. Karl had purposefully dressed formally today, knowing that Mara was attracted as much by his rough seafaring image as by the man inside. He had left the earring behind and pulled his hair into a neat ponytail.

All too soon, he was there. "Please Father," he prayed silently. "Help me to find the words, the right expression, the demeanor that reaches Mara and Gerald in a way that honors you." The cabby turned around when Karl didn't exit, a silent question on his face. "I am going," Karl said with a brief smile. He pulled a coin from his jacket pocket and flipped it at the young driver. "Good day. Give your horse a carrot on me."

"You ha' a good one too, sir," the young man said, his face brightening.

So simple, Karl thought, *to make someone's day. Now I go in to ruin another's.* He climbed up the steps, forcing himself to go quickly, as if he looked forward to the encounter ahead rather than dreaded it.

All too soon the maid opened the door and showed him to the parlor.

"You wish to see Miss Mara?" she asked.

"No. Please. First I would like to call upon Mr. Kenney."

"Certainly," she said, with a brief bob of a curtsey. She left the room.

Shortly thereafter, Gerald entered the parlor. "I didn't remember that you were calling today, Karl."

Karl shook his head. "I had not warned you, I'm afraid. Just decided this morning that I must come and speak with you and Mara without further delay."

Gerald sat down in the chair across from Karl, a knowing smile on his face.

Oh no.

"I knew this day was coming. Let me tell you, son, I could not be more pleased—"

"No. No, Gerald. I am afraid this news will not please you."

The older man's face fell. He shifted in his seat, and there was an uncomfortable pause. "Well, man. Out with it. There have never been secrets between us."

Karl tried to swallow but found his mouth dry. He twisted his hat in his hands. "Gerald, please first accept my apologies. I never meant to hurt you or your daughter."

Gerald's face clouded in consternation.

"Somehow, I fear I have misled Mara. And each time I tried to tell you about my true feelings, we were interrupted. But that is no excuse. I should have found some way, someplace to tell you, man to man. And then to tell Mara the truth."

"You do not have feelings for her." Gerald's tone was flat.

"I do not," Karl said, looking him dead in the eye. "I love her as a sister, and believe me, I would have loved nothing more than to be a part of your family. You all mean much to me. But try as I might, the feeling that I think I ought to have for her, the spark I think she deserves, just isn't there."

Gerald sighed as heavily as Karl had found himself doing of late. His hand went to his mouth, his elbow on the armrest, as he stared out the window beside them. Then he looked back to Karl. "I cannot tell you I am not disappointed, Karl. I really hoped you were here to ask for her hand. But I agree with you—a marriage needs more than a brotherly love to get it going, keep it going. Friendship is the best basis, but if that spark of romance hasn't lit by now, it isn't likely that it will."

Karl breathed a sigh of relief, the burden lifted, at least partially. "Thank you for understanding, Gerald. And please forgive me for not getting the truth out on the table sooner. My intention was never to mislead. I simply got in deeper and deeper."

"Understood, man. We Kenneys didn't help matters either. Encouraged you both."

"Thank you. Now if you think it best…I'd like to tell Mara myself."

Gerald considered his request and then gave his ascent. "I will go and fetch her. May I prepare her with a few words?"

"Whatever you think is best."

"Very good." Gerald rose and straightened his vest while he stared at the door, as if already choosing his words. Then he paused beside Karl and put a hand on his shoulder. "Let her down easy, son."

"As easily as I can. Remember, Gerald, I truly do care about her."

Gerald nodded and left the room.

Shortly after, Mara came into the room in a lovely rush of lavender silk and crinoline, silently taking both of Karl's hands in hers and lifting her cheek for a kiss. Her brows were furrowed in consternation. "Karl, my father has said some disturbing things to me."

"Yes," he said. He gestured toward the settee, and they sat down together. "Mara, I fear I have misled you."

"Oh?"

"Yes. I should've told you how I truly feel a year ago. I tried but…" He stopped himself, unwilling to make any excuses. He sat up straighter. "I care for you, Mara. Deeply. But I'm sorry to say that the love I feel for you is more of a brother than a suitor."

Mara pulled her hands from his and looked away. A moment later she turned back to him, her eyes damp and wide. She was so lovely! Why couldn't he love her?

"Your words wound me, Karl."

"I know. I never intended to hurt you, dear one."

"Perhaps…if we only give it a little more time. You told me you would give it, give *us* time."

"No, Mara. I *have* given it time. I would love nothing more than to find myself…with deep feelings for you, to be a part of your wonderful family. But I do not. And the time has come to be honest. So that you can look for another." He knew that both of them immediately thought of Arthur Hairston.

"But I have told all my friends that you will be escorting me to the Harvest Ball."

"Cannot Mr. Hairston escort you?"

"No! I mean, he is a dear friend, but it is you I want at my side at that ball. All my friends—"

"But, Mara," he interrupted. "I had wanted this to be a clean break. For us to move forward in honesty."

"Please, Karl," she said, taking his hands in hers again. She pulled them to her cheek, and he felt her tears. "Please. It will be such a disgrace for me to show up with anyone else but you." She stared into his eyes. "As my friend. As a departing gift. I know that there will be nothing beyond that dance. But please, for me, won't you escort me?"

His heart screamed to him to say no, to walk away, finish it. But her eyes tore him in half. "You understand that it will be our last social appearance together? That we will be there only as friends?"

"Yes, yes," she assured him. "Only as friends."

What harm could it do? Taking her to a silly ball? This was merely his last act of kindness, soothing the break. Then he would be free. Or would he?

The cove reminded Elsa of so many others she had visited in her years upon the sea. Riley had fashioned a looking glass of sorts, in the middle of a floating wood frame. The glass cleared the water surface of ripples and let Kristian explore the sandy bottom as if there were no water at all. They had spent hours huddled over it in less than a foot of water, both staring down at fish every color of the rainbow, a sudden scuttling crab, perfect shells. It made the entire sea bottom a treasure trove.

Elsa sat in the shade beneath the waving branches of a palm, taking a well-deserved hiatus from the *Majestic* along with half the crew. As Riley had predicted, they discovered a small stream that let them refill their casks with sweet, clear water while men trekked up the small mountain in search of a tree that would yield a decent mast until they reached Ramstad Lumberyard off the coast of Washington.

Elsa didn't have high hopes for a good match. Here, in this part of Chile, the trees were short and scrubby. They would most likely have to pray for amazing winds to power them northward on the sails of the two remaining masts, fore and aft. She dug her toes into the dark sand, thinking of many other sailing expeditions. "We have done it before; we'll do it again," she murmured to herself. Eve sat beside her, studiously pouring sand from a tin cup to a tin plate, then poking sticks and shells into the new pile.

"Mama! A sand dollar!" Kristian shouted, holding the treasure up from a dripping hand.

"Wonderful!" she called, thinking of the hundreds of others aboard ship. Every once in a while, she convinced her son to pitch his sea-birthed treasures over the side, relinquishing them to the sea bottom once more, oftentimes oceans from their origin. She liked to think of them making it to shore, puzzling the beachcombers there with the discovery of a shell they had never seen before. Peder's old trunk was already full of them again.

"You had better come out of the sun!" she called. Even with his bathing costume that covered him from neck to knee, she knew that his fair skin was susceptible to burning at the forearm and calf, not to mention his head and face. Kristian obediently turned and walked through the shallows toward her. His hair had been bleached from the sun, and he had huge freckles across his nose. Elsa knew that her mother would groan, especially if she saw Eve with her own brown skin and spotted face. But to Elsa they looked healthy and vibrant. Oh, how she loved them!

Kristian drew near, his damp, small feet covered with a layer of sand. She greeted him with a towel she had purchased in Egypt, made of their finest cotton. The children sat on either side of her.

"This is a great place, Mama," Kristian said. "I'm almost glad the ship had to be repaired."

"Kristian," she chastised. "Two men died in that blast."

He lowered his head in shame.

"I am sorry," Elsa said. "I know you were only talking about how good it was to swim and have fun again. But we must remember to honor those sailors' lives."

"Yes, Mama. Mama," Kristian asked, "are we going to sail all autumn?"

"No. I am hoping we'll reach San Francisco for a new boiler within a few weeks, then stop at Ramstad Lumberyard for a new mast."

"Can we go to the house in Seattle?" he asked hopefully.

"We'll stop there for a night or two and pick up Mrs. Hodge. Then we're off to Alaska, hopefully in time for Auntie Tora's wedding!"

"Can I be ring bearer?" Kristian asked.

"I know Auntie Tora would like nothing better."

"But first we pick up a new boiler in San Francisco," he said.

"Yes. First things first."

The *Majestic*'s carpenter had organized the sailors into two teams working 'round the clock, and within days the deck was sufficiently repaired to ward off any storm that might wash over it en route to San Francisco. The wind, as if divinely orchestrated, had picked up, and Elsa ordered all sails set.

"All sails set!" Riley echoed.

"All sails set!" returned the men, climbing masts and ropes to do as Elsa bid. Within the hour, they were underway. The ripple and *whoosh* of the sails as they filled soothed Elsa, and she found herself almost happy that the boiler was not churning out smoke and noise. She walked alone to the bow of the ship, welcoming the breeze upon her face as she retied the floppy, wide-brimmed Mexican sun hat to her head, and tightened a sloppily belayed line. She looked up again at the great sails that powered the *Majestic* toward home. It was glorious, being under tarp alone again, the only sounds being those of the crisp, taut sails filling with wind and the ocean beneath their keel.

"Yes, Peder," she said under her breath, "I know. I know why you always loved sailing over steam. It is so peaceful, serene. We're going home to Washington, darling. Then I'm taking your children to a place you always wanted to see, but never did. Alaska."

She walked over to the other rail. "You see? We're doing just fine. All three of us. You needn't have worried about us being at sea with you. We're just fine."

She lifted her face to the breeze, trying to remember Peder's touch as he caressed her skin. But the memory was fading. She frowned and looked down at the blue-black water. The realization that she couldn't remember what it felt like to be touched by her husband made her melancholy. Bereft all over again.

"Forgive me," she whispered, suddenly feeling disloyal for forgetting. "Forgive me, Peder. I want to remember. I want to hold you close."

A Chilean seagull swooped low, barely five feet away from her, then over the waves of the sea. The bird looked free and light, undisturbed by the *Majestic*'s presence, or anything else for that matter. Elsa found herself yearning for the bird's freedom, the ability to fly. Without the burden of sadness or guilt. Truly free.

What happened next surprised her, took her breath away. Because suddenly, as she watched the bird, she became certain Peder would not be angry if he knew. He had loved her—he would want her to fly, to soar unchained to the sadness of the past.

It was as if it was all right with him that his memory was fading. But not forgotten. Never forgotten.

t w e l v e

September 1888

*S*oren gathered Kaatje up into his arms and swung her around in a circle. "Kaatje, Kaatje, darling. It is you! It is!"

"*Soren?* Soren! Please! Please put me down!"

He did as she bid, and Kaatje backed away, kept backing away, until she bumped up against James. She could feel his warm, reassuring hands as they rested on her shoulders. But she could look nowhere but toward the man who claimed he was her husband.

Who looked like her husband. Who was her husband.

"Kaatje. I know this is a shock, but do you not know me?"

Kaatje, as if in a dream, looked away from him, not willing to answer his plea. She looked at Juneau's townspeople, some women covering their mouths in wonder at the drama before them, some men looking angry, ready to pounce. Then she looked back to him. To...her husband.

Even with a closely trimmed beard, she would have known him anywhere. The curly blond hair, the mischievous eyes. He had aged in the years they had been apart, but, if anything, he had only grown more handsome.

"Kaatje?" He took a step closer, and Kaatje leaned against James as if retreating. "Please, *elskling*." When he lapsed into their native

Norwegian, it robbed Kaatje of her last reserves. She started crying, so broken, so overcome, she feared she would never again be able to stop.

That was when James intervened. He moved in front of her, between them, and held a hand out toward Soren. "Wait just a minute."

Soren ignored him, staring at Kaatje with pleading eyes. "My *dyr* one. Kitten. You know me, right? Right?" He tried to push past James, but James held Soren back.

"Kaatje?" James asked over his shoulder. James shoved Soren away. Soren took several steps backward until he regained his balance. They were about the same height, Kaatje judged, with a similar build. Funny how one woman could fall for two men so similar in stance, yet so different in countenance. She drew strength from James, his concern for her evident in his eyes. He stood there, her protector, ready to pounce if she so much as gave the signal.

"Kaatje?" James repeated. He ran a hand through his hair, and for a moment Kaatje felt like her heart would break. He glanced down as if he knew. Something in her eyes must have told him, told him that this would be good-bye, that their love would never have a chance to bloom. "It's him, isn't it, Kaatje?"

She didn't remember nodding, but she must have, since James closed his eyes as if pained and then turned toward Soren. He leaned to him and said something no one else could hear. Then he raised his hands to the crowd and said, "Kaatje Janssen, after searching the length of the Yukon for him, has just been reunited with her husband. I think we should all head for home and give them some time alone."

Soren heard what James had said, the word of warning and love and frustration in his tone, and he knew. The man was in love with his wife. Too bad that he had showed up in the nick of time, Soren gloated. He would be one to watch. No doubt Mr. Walker would be looking for any shred of evidence that Soren was less than he appeared.

Now that they were alone, Soren stared at his wife. She had grown lovelier in the years they'd been apart, and a familiar desire stirred within him. He had been a fool to leave her. When he found out that she was seeking him in Fort Yukon, he had followed the trio, watching them from afar. It did not take long for him to discover how she had the means to hire Walker and his sidekick as well as offer a reward for information on his whereabouts. Days later, he learned that she had a serious investment in the Storm Roadhouse in Juneau, as well as in Ketchikan. It was that, coupled with the jealousy of seeing her with another man, that made him follow them along the river and to Juneau.

"Kaatje? After all this time, can you not even embrace your husband?"

She turned away, and he stared at her profile, that perfect nose, those wide eyes with long lashes. Only her slight lack of chin kept her from being beautiful. And he could see from the dress she was wearing that childbirth had spread her hips but left her waist trim, making her even more enticing. "No, Soren, I cannot. I must know why you've...reappeared. After all this time."

"I heard you were looking for me and came right away." That much was true. "I didn't even know you were in Alaska until someone told me you had been in Fort Yukon."

She whirled toward him. "I have been gone for months. I left our girls to find you. Just when exactly did you intend to come find *me*?" He hadn't missed the fact that she had said "girls." But her anger had to be dealt with first.

"I kept thinking that I'd find my fortune and bring you up. I knew you were safe—"

"No, Soren. I was not safe. Your family was not well. Did you even know that we left Dakota for Washington Territory four years ago? Did you know I had to scavenge for buffalo bones to sell for fuel in order to afford the train fare? Did you know I tilled twenty acres of soil in Washington by myself?" With each question she drew nearer to him, until she was jabbing a finger in his chest.

She was petite, yet strong, and Soren fought the urge to gather her into his arms, to kiss away her questions. He was about to do so when she asked, "Did you know that Tora brought me a child that you fathered on the ship of our crossing? Left her for me to raise?"

The others he was prepared for. This took his breath away. "She did what? She brought who?"

"Your lover's child," Kaatje spit out. She took several steps away from him on the platform, and it struck Soren that they were performing a delicate dance. If he was not very careful, one of them would fall. "It is by God's grace," she said over her shoulder, her tone notably softer, "that I fell in love with the girl as if she were my own."

Soren carefully crossed the span between them and, with a shaking hand, touched her shoulder. When she did not flinch or move away, he placed his other hand on her other shoulder. Still she did not move. Then he wrapped her in his arms, feeling the warmth of her small, curvaceous body against his. Why was he such a fool? Why had he left this strong, courageous woman?

"I thought you were dead," she said in a monotone. "I was going to have you declared dead next week when the circuit judge came to town."

He leaned his cheek gently against her head, smelling the clean scent of her hair, the lavender perfume on her neck. "Sounds like I arrived just in time," he quipped.

She moved away then and whirled. Again Soren was reminded of a dance as her skirt flared and then fell. "This is no laughing matter, Soren."

"I know. I *know*."

"I do not think you do know. Abandoning the girls and me on the Dakota farm was one thing. Staying away all these years is another. You have created a crevasse I don't believe can ever be crossed, Soren."

"Do you believe in love?" he asked softly.

"What?"

He took a step closer to her again and gently caressed her cheeks. "Do you still believe in love, Kaatje?"

"I…I do not know if I believe in it anymore."

"I do. Kaatje. Kaatje, Kaatje." He pulled her chin back toward him and waited for her eyes to meet his. "I do, *elskling*. You and I were born for each other. You cannot deny it. Behind the hurt and sorrow in your eyes, I still see the love." He was lying now, desperately fishing for what he hoped was there.

She looked away, obviously unconvinced. He needed something...more. It came to him in an instant.

"I have come to know a greater love than ours, *dyr* one."

Her hazel eyes immediately met his.

"Yes, Kaatje. It is as you prayed. God found me, and I welcomed him at last."

His heart sped up when he noted a flicker of light in her eyes. A warmth spread through his chest as he sensed her defenses faltering. "Is it not how you prayed?"

"Soren. Oh, Soren, of course I prayed for you. That you would find the One who could bring you peace. But I never thought... I always wondered..."

"If it were truly possible?"

"Yes." She gave him a searching look.

"It's possible." When she said no more, he asked, "Where are my girls? May I see them?"

"No," she shook her head immediately. "No, it would not be good. I'm sure Tora took them home."

"Why? Why can I not see them?" He worked to squelch the flare of anger in his chest. He hadn't seen Christina in six years and had never met—he didn't even know his other daughter's name.

"Why?" she asked, her face portraying her exasperation. "You ask me why?" Her own anger grew. "You might think you can reemerge now, Soren, and resume our life together, but it is not that easy. I was ready to declare you dead. Now here you are standing before me, acting as if you have every right to see our daughters. You abandoned them. You abandoned us, Soren. No, you may not see my girls. Never. Not until I am convinced that you are home to stay. That you are home to stay with *me*. I won't put them through what I have been put through with you. I will not risk their hearts."

"Kaatje, I am changed."

"Time will tell."

"Yes, it will. I am changed, Kaatje." He reached out and stroked her shoulders. She was all lean muscle and bone beneath her gown. He hadn't known she was such a woman before, a woman of strength and character. Her strength drew him. Challenged him.

She shook her head and then her arms, turning away from him. "It is too much. I need to go away from you, to think."

"I understand. May I see you tomorrow?" She was scurrying down the stairs as if he was pursuing her. He was, in a way.

"I do not know," she said over her shoulder, dismissing him.

It was odd that she didn't welcome him back right away, he thought. After searching the entire Yukon for him. Soren had thought it would be much easier. That there would be some groveling, sure, but not this rebuff. Why, she had left him out there in the streets! Without a room! The least she could've done was offer him a room at her roadhouse! He kicked the stage in frustration and paced, thinking. What would it take to win Kaatje back? To get his old Kaatje back?

He turned and walked down the stage stairs, looking each way for the nearest hotel other than the Storm Roadhouse. Spotting it, he took his time in getting there, laying his plans to make Kaatje his own once more. He was at the hotel's frosted glass door before the idea first struck him. Was Kaatje in love with James as he obviously was with her? Soren repeatedly slapped one fist into the palm of his other hand, turning away from the door as he thought about it. Never. Kaatje would never have given her heart away to another before she knew for certain that he was dead. Not his Kaatje. She was loyal to the end. He had come back just in the nick of time.

"Kaatje." Her name emerged hoarse from his throat. He had run after her, racing to intercept her before she went inside the roadhouse. She turned halfway, not daring to look at him, and the beauty of her pro-file made him close his eyes in anguish. "Kaatje, I must speak with you."

"James, we cannot. It is too much. I already have so much to think upon."

He sighed. "Yes. I know. I hate it that I am here, but I cannot help myself. I was about to tell you on that dance floor… I only wanted you to know…" He turned away, biting back his words. He could not tell her he loved her now. It wouldn't be fair. She had to make her decisions about Soren first.

When he turned back to her he discovered her on the stair, hold-ing on to the rail as if she would faint at any moment. The sight of her made him want to weep.

"I know what you were about to tell me, James."

"You do?"

"Yes."

"How?"

"Because I feel the same." There was no joy in her words, as there should have been. Only regret and sorrow. Only good-bye.

He gasped for breath, feeling as if he were being held underwater. Once more he had found love. And once more, he was left alone.

She stared at him, her eyes shimmering with tears, then turned and walked to the door, crying already.

Kaatje was gone. Soren had stolen her away.

"You had better heed my warning, Soren Janssen," he whispered angrily through his tears as he left Kaatje's home. "You hurt her this time, you'll be accountable to *me*."

t h i r t e e n

Late September 1888

By some miracle, the *Majestic* made incredible time to San Francisco, even with the loss of one mast. The ship's carpenter had brought the broken white pine log down, cutting the base in a way that a new mast could be easily grafted on once they reached Ramstad Lumberyard. The prices in San Francisco for a sizable mast would be exorbitant, and Elsa refused to purchase one there when, after a week's further sail, they could pick one up for no cost at all. No, in San Francisco, they would simply replace the boiler and get back to sea. Elsa twisted her hands as the ship was brought into the wharf by a small steamer tug. They might still make Tora's wedding if all went well.

She accompanied the children into town, agreeing to explore Chinatown with them. Eric came too, ostensibly to sightsee, but more likely acting as a self-appointed bodyguard. Or responding to Riley's direct orders, she mused. Riley stayed back to oversee the purchase of a new boiler and, hopefully, negotiate an immediate installation. Oh, how she hoped that he would receive good news and that they could soon be underway!

The children requested dim sum—a light meal of finger foods—for their noon dinner, and Elsa agreed with an easy smile. Being in the hills of San Francisco with the smell of hot oil in the sea breeze and the bustling of people in traditional costume made her remember pleasant times in the Far East. It was interesting to her that her first thought was not of Mason Dutton and his attack upon her, but of fragrant lotus blossoms and friendly people. Of rickshaws and heavily wooded mountains...

"Captain?" Eric was asking, looking at her with a slight frown.

"Oh, forgive me. I was in another world. What is it?"

"Is this restaurant suitable for the children and you?"

"Yes, yes. And please, won't you join us?"

"I will be fine, ma'am. I'll just stand outside the door while you eat."

"Nonsense! You're eating with us. Captain's orders!" She smiled as she said it, then took his arm as he opened the door for the children.

He grinned back at her. The sun had spread freckles across his fair skin, making his teeth all the whiter. Distantly she considered Eric as a potential suitor. Just two inches taller than she, he was bright and quick on his feet, as fast with a joke and a tender word as he was in directing the men as second mate. No, it would never work, she decided, chastising herself for her fanciful imaginings. Even if he was interested in her, she did not feel that certain tug in her heart that she should feel toward someone she could grow to love. And any man would have a difficult time seeing his superior, his captain, as a...woman.

As Eric pulled out her chair and the waiter passed them menus, Elsa wondered just who would ever pursue her. She was fairly well-to-do now, with holdings in Camden and Washington, not to mention the twenty Ramstad ships that floated the high seas, two having been sunk during severe storms. She spent the majority of her time on the seas herself, taking her away from any potential suitors ashore. Just who would ever match her?

"Are you having dim sum too?" Eric was asking her, looking over the menu.

"I think not," she answered. "Orange peel beef sounds good to me. And what do you think, children? Shall we have rice, snow peas, and mushrooms, then caramelized apples for dessert?"

"Yes, yes," they said, bobbing their heads.

She turned to the waiter and pointed to what they wanted, using scattered Chinese when she could.

When the waiter looked confused, Eric stepped in, speaking in fluent Mandarin.

"Eric!" Elsa said. "I never knew you spoke Chinese!"

"I lived in Beijing as a child."

"Beijing! Whatever took you there?"

"My parents were Christian missionaries."

"Goodness. Americans, I take it."

"Yes."

"How long were you there?"

"I was in a missionary school until I was seven. My parents were killed by an influenza epidemic in '65. America was at war then, so I couldn't go to my grandparents' in Virginia. Instead, an uncle, a captain of an old brigantine, took me in, showed me the lay of the sea."

Elsa's hand went to her chest. "I had no idea, Eric. I feel so sorry for the child that was you."

Eric nodded and placed his elbows on the table. "They were trying times. But I didn't really know my parents. They had left me at the school when I was three, along with an older brother."

"And your brother? Where is he?"

"He turns a coin as a lawyer in Boston. I see him from time to time. He has a family of eight."

"Eight!" Kristian exclaimed. "I wish I had that many brothers and sisters."

The four of them said grace, and then the children picked up the flat, angular spoons and began eating.

"I bet they love to see you, hear your stories of the sea and distant lands."

"The children do. Not so, my brother. I think he had his fill of distant lands in those years at the school. He still blames God for taking our parents."

"And you?" Elsa asked carefully.

"I think we live in a fallen world. Disease is a part of it. And disease was what took my parents, not our Lord."

Elsa enjoyed the rest of their meal, their conversation, and their walk back to the cable cars. When she pushed herself, she had to admit she liked the more intimate male companionship. She was constantly surrounded by men aboard ship, but they were under her command. Eric, too, was under her command, but that day in Chinatown, she felt they were on equal terms, at least for a few hours, and Elsa liked it.

San Francisco was truly a wonderful city, Elsa mused. Part of her wished she could stay longer, call upon old friends who now resided there. But she was anxious to get going northward.

And yet it was not to be. Riley had succeeded in obtaining a new boiler but could not secure delivery for three days.

"You tried paying them a rush charge?"

"They said they'd take the money, but couldn't guarantee any sooner." His Cockney accent grew thick with his frustration. "There was no budging 'em, Cap'n. The boilers are in much demand, and there just aren't enough to go around. I was fortunate to be able to get one at all."

"At what price?" she asked, trying not to cringe as she awaited an answer.

"Double what your boys in Camden paid, I'm sure."

When she groaned, he said, "I ha' something that will lift your spirits."

"What?" she said miserably. Suddenly she was weary, anxious to get home, to land for the winter. To be with her friends and family in Juneau.

"This was waiting for you at the harbor master's office." He pointed to a wooden crate she hadn't seen until now. "Did I miss your birthday?"

"No," she said in puzzlement. There was no return address, just a typed label with "Captain Elsa Ramstad" and the harbor's address on it.

"Harbor master said it's been here several months. They were taking bets, wondering what one sent the Heroine of the Horn."

Elsa gave him a look reminding him she did not care for her old moniker. She'd given up her column a year prior, feeling as if her time for writing was simply over. She concentrated on her paintings instead, developing a new style that was more representational than her old realistic depictions. It entertained her. But now her thoughts were only on the crate.

She grabbed an iron bar as Kristian entered the cabin. Spotting her with the box, he ran over and jumped up and down. "What is it, Mama? What is it?"

"I do not know," she said, clenching her lips together as she pushed on the reluctant lid.

"Want some help, Cap'n?"

"No, Riley, thank you very much. I think I can handle…this."

The top gave way, the nails squeaking in protest. Elsa lifted the lid and set it aside, careful to point the exposed penny nails downward so Eve wouldn't crawl over them. The boy was already digging through the straw. "There's a box, Mama! A box!"

"Well, lift it out." She was as excited as her son but tried to hide it.

The elegant box had a Parisian label on it. Riley lifted one brow.

Elsa opened it and unfolded the tissue inside. Underneath was the most exquisite silk ball gown she had ever seen. It was the color of ivory, with the hint of gold spun into the fabric. The low-cut bodice was heavily decorated with pearls and lace.

"Is it a wedding gown?" Kristian asked.

"No, darling. It's a ball gown." She lifted it out and spread it before her as she looked in the full-length mirror. "The most beautiful ball gown I have ever seen." And as she stared at her reflection, a lump formed in her throat.

"What is it, Cap'n? Tell me."

Eve came to her and patted her knee.

"It's...it's nothing." She shook her head, tears welling in her eyes. "Well, almost nothing. It's just that no one has bought me a gown since...since Peder."

Riley awkwardly came near and patted her on the shoulder.

"There's no note? No card?" Elsa asked.

"No. I have to say, ma'am, that I think all these gifts you've received are troublin'. You don't know who sent them or why. Any friend of yours would be certain to at least tell you that it was from them."

"Oh, Riley, you're so suspicious. Mason Dutton is dead. I have no other enemies. Sometimes cards get lost. Or harbor masters lose them. These gifts are fine, from fine friends."

"And expensive."

"Yes. Please...let me enjoy it. Don't ruin it!"

"All right, all right. I just don't like it. Something's not right. This makes, what? Five gifts with no notes?"

"Seven, counting the Stetson hat from Denver and the Persian rug."

"Seven."

"All right, Riley, I understand you. We'll figure out who sends me these things. It must be Tora. She's an imp when it comes to surprises. And she has the means now, with the new roadhouses and all."

"It doesn't make sense," Riley said, shaking his head. "It's been going on since before they reached Alaska. Miss Tora had no means before then."

"Nonsense! Trent has been pursuing her for years. Please," she said, turning toward him. "Let it go. We'll figure it out."

"You bet we will. I have something else for you," he said, changing subjects.

"What?"

"It's an invitation to the Harvest Ball from Mrs. Jones. She must have found out you were in town. So now you have a place to wear that pretty dress."

"Oh, I couldn't."

"Yes, you could."

"But I have no escort."

"I'm sure any one of the men, including me, would be happy to escort you. You might have to buy them new duds, but they're all itching to get into town, even if it's to some highfalutin society ball."

Elsa laughed and stood again to look at her reflection in the mirror. "I do not know if I even remember how to dance," she said.

"Can I practice with you?" Kristian said helpfully.

Elsa laughed again, then turned to Riley. "Do you think Eric would accompany me? Is it too much to ask?"

"No, woman," he said tenderly. "I'm sure he'd love the chance to dance with the beautiful Captain Ramstad." He stepped closer to her. "And I'm sure your beloved Peder, God rest his soul, will dance up in heaven at the sight of you in that dress, having fun again."

"Do you think so?" she whispered.

"I know so."

She was out for a walk the next afternoon with the children, when she spotted the elegant steamer in port. She stopped a man who had just exited the gangplank.

"Excuse me, sailor, but from where does the *Fair Alaska* hail?"

"She's a Ramstad Yard ship out of Camden," he said, looking her up and down.

Elsa ignored his brazen stare. "I knew it! I knew she must be a Ramstad! And her captain?"

"Why, that'd be Captain Martensen."

Karl! "Captain Karl Martensen?"

"Yes'm." The man straightened up when he realized she knew Karl by name.

"Is he aboard?"

"No ma'am. He left this morning and hasn't been back since."

"Any idea when he will return?"

"No. I'm not a part of his crew, just doing some woodwork installation in the ballroom."

"The ballroom?"

"Yes ma'am. This steamer is going to be the prettiest on the Pacific. Word has it that Cap'n Martensen aims to please the high-society crowd anxious to see the glaciers up in Alaska."

"Ah, yes. That is a good plan. He'll have little competition."

"Say, you look familiar. You're not... No, it couldn't be. You don't happen to be—?"

"No, I'm sure I am not," she quickly interrupted. "Come, children." They walked away, down along the piers that made up San Francisco's wharf. The air was filled with the scent of fish, creosote, rotting wood, and ocean air.

"Whose ship was that, Mama?" Kristian asked.

"Why, that's Uncle Karl's."

"Uncle Karl's?"

"Yes. He's been designing his own ships these last three years, and that must be his latest."

"She's very nice. I like the lines of her bow."

Elsa paused, amazed at the adult tone of his statement. "You've been paying attention to lines, have you?"

"Yes. I like them. Will we see Uncle Karl?"

"I hope so. It's been too many years since we had the chance. But it sounds like we'll have many this winter. Uncle Karl appears to be setting his sights on taking tourists along the Inside Passage. Surely he'll be stopping in Juneau and Ketchikan where Auntie Tora and Kaatje have inns. We'll cross paths all the time!" She felt herself grinning and wondered at herself when she couldn't seem to stop smiling.

She hailed a cab when they reached the harbor master's office, intent upon finding suitable slippers to wear with her new gown to the ball.

Karl went to the window of the harbor master's office, sure he had just seen Elsa Ramstad. But she was in a cab and off down the block before he could make his way to the door and outside. He grimaced and shook his head. He must have been mistaken. But he couldn't quite shake the sense that he had really seen her. He strode back up to the harbor master's desk and inquired, "Pardon me, but can you tell me if a Captain Ramstad has entered port?"

"Don't even have to look at the books on that one," the young man drawled. "The Heroine of the Horn arrived yesterday and is set to leave in a few more. You know her?"

"I do," Karl said, stunned. "Tell me, did she retrieve a package here?"

"Her mate did. First day in."

Karl smiled. She had received the gown. Would she be at the ball? Would she wear it? He hoped so.

At the cobbler, Elsa had been intercepted by Mrs. Smith, a prominent San Franciscan and an old acquaintance, and had accepted her kind invitation for supper. She sent a cab with a note for Riley, informing him of where she and the children were, knowing he would fret if she didn't return on time. She had such a good time with the Smiths, she didn't leave until ten o'clock that evening, sent home in the Smiths' own coach. It was too late to call upon Karl then, she realized, disappointed. It would just have to wait until the next day. Eric appeared at her side on the wharf and helped her with the slumbering children, wrapped in wool shipping blankets.

She awakened the next day to a clear autumn morning. The breeze off the water was brisk, and she dressed the children in their warmest traveling costumes. No doubt she would be too cold in her gown that evening, and her dress coat was so out-of-date. Once more she hailed a cab and headed to town, this time without the children, intent upon finding the perfect shawl. It had been years since she cared about what she wore, and now she found herself acting like a silly girl in dressing up for the ball.

But if Karl was there, she wanted it to be…she wanted it to be…perfect. The idea that her reunion with Karl excited her beyond the normal bounds of friendship finally pierced her heart.

What was this? Some sudden interest in an old friend? Or was it merely the hope of meeting a man who was truly on her level, a man she could admire?

Karl agreed to dance with Mara once again, wearily aware that she played a game with her friends, putting on a face of love with him even though he knew her to be deeply angry with him. It came out in small asides and demands that made the evening long—just an hour into it.

Elsa still had not arrived.

He escorted Mara out onto the dance floor for another turn, then politely asked if he could get her a glass of punch.

Petulantly she agreed, taking his arm and pulling him close as if they were inseparable. It was her youth, he supposed, that pushed her to pretend so. Grateful to her for taking his rejection with a fair level of maturity, he played along. They chatted with friends of the Kenneys, who chided him in roundabout fashion for not making a proposal to Mara at an event like the ball, where they could all enjoy it.

Suddenly Karl was anxious to get out on the dance floor again away from the speculation.

Elsa gasped when she saw him. Eric looked every bit the gentleman as he took off his top hat and bowed deeply to her. The men were grouped around him, eager to see their captain in her lovely new dress. When she appeared at the door, they cheered.

"Ne'er had a cap'n that was a looker, too!" one called.

"If Eric fails ya, come back for me!" shouted another.

They all laughed together.

"Oh, Mama!" Kristian cried. "You look like a princess!"

"Aye, ya do," Riley said, drawing near. He took her hand and kissed it. "Won't get too close. Don't wanta dirty your dress. But you're a sight, Cap'n. A sight."

Elsa smiled, a bit embarrassed at the attention. It was like having forty older brothers seeing her off to the dance. No doubt dear Eric had taken his share of ribbing.

"You'll get the children right to bed?"

"Soon as you're off the gangplank, Cap'n. Go have fun."

"Three cheers for the prettiest cap'n on the Pacific!" shouted one of her men.

"On all the seas!" corrected another.

"Hear, hear! Hear, hear! Hear, hear!" They rumbled as one.

Elsa was sure she blushed the color of Riley's red handkerchief around his neck. "All right, boys. You've earned some shore leave for that send-off. Riley, assign ten men to stay on watch until ten o'clock. Those men that have to stay on get the whole day ashore tomorrow. Then I want the lot of you aboard tomorrow night by ten, because the next morning we sail." She felt a bit foolish taking command in her finery, but she could not help it.

"Bye-bye, Cap'n!" called a sailor in a high-pitched voice above her. Elsa looked up and saw about ten men on the lanyard. She laughed. They were all dressed as voluptuous women, wharf girls with dark, red painted lips, in blankets that simulated tawdry dresses. They delicately waved white silk handkerchiefs at her in an obvious imitation of society women. "Think they'd welcome us at the ball, Captain?" one asked in his falsetto.

"I think not."

"Hmm," sniffed another. "Just because a girl ain't got the right dress, is that it?"

By now some of the men below were rolling on the decks they were laughing so hard. Riley wiped away tears from his eyes while Elsa grinned.

"Not all of us get dresses delivered from mysterious admirers," sniffed still another man.

"Apparently all of you are not as deserving as I," she tossed back.

The men laughed. Elsa laughed with them. They were boys in men's clothing. And "women's."

"Ta ta!" called one, waving his handkerchief. "Ta ta!" echoed the rest on the lanyard.

Elsa laughed even harder, waved back, and then shook her head. From the side of the ship, they hooted and hollered as she took Eric's arm, and then again when she grasped his hand to climb into the phaeton cab. Eric laughed. "You can put the boys in different clothes, but they're boys no matter what," he said.

Elsa looked at him strangely. Hadn't she just thought something similar herself minutes ago? Maybe they had more in common than she knew.

They arrived after a ten-minute ride to the Saint Ignatius Hotel. The hotel boasted of its new electrical capabilities, and Elsa gaped at the huge crystal chandelier above them in the foyer, warmly lit by hundreds of tiny flickering bulbs. "Just think, Eric," she said, leaning closer to him. "In a few years, we'll see many like that. Can you imagine? A whole city lit up like midday!"

"It will be remarkable. Shall I check your coat?"

"Certainly," she said, admiring his formal language. She remembered that underneath that sailor's exterior he had been raised to be a gentleman.

They walked down a long hallway, following the noise of music and revelers, and, after turning again, spotted men and women in elegant dress entering and exiting the grand ballroom.

Elsa smiled in appreciation as she entered. There were hundreds of people present, dancing underneath the tiny white lights and streamers of fall-colored leaves. The light cast a warm glow over everything. Elsa found herself immediately scanning the crowd for him. For Karl Martensen. But there were so many people that Elsa despaired of ever finding him.

She had been dancing with Eric for over an hour before the master of ceremonies called for a cotillion dance, in which everyone would take part. "I don't know if I know this one," she whispered to Eric.

"I do. Follow me!"

Elsa wondered again at her second mate. Just where did he learn the cotillion? He laughed at her confused expression. "My uncle was a sea captain, but a gentleman through and through. He had me take dance lessons every year. Now follow me."

He took her hands in his big, rough ones. His touch was gentle but sure. It felt good to be touched again, even by a friend. Few touched her other than her children. And nobody with the assurance of a man leading a woman on the dance floor. "Now lift your hands," he said, gently lifting them upward and over her head. "Turn halfway," he said in time with the music. "And again. Now around me." When she came back around he held her at the waist and pulled her closer. "Thank the Spaniards for their influence," he said, smiling into her eyes. Then he turned her around for two quick twirls. "Now, my dear captain, you are on your own."

"What?" she gasped as he left her, and suddenly she was in front of another. A bit late, she lifted her arms, then caught up on the half turn.

"Are you Elsa Ramstad?" the man asked.

"I am," she said as he twirled her around.

"It's a pleasure. Alfred Cummings," he introduced himself.

"Mr. Cummings." She nodded once, as she met up with her next partner.

Three partners later, she lifted her arms, getting into the cadence of the dance, enjoying herself, when she stopped, letting her arms slowly drift to her sides as she stared. "Karl," she breathed.

"Elsa," he greeted her, slightly shaking his head and smiling. "Elsa Ramstad. You're as lovely as ever."

She was lovely. The loveliest woman at the ball in that dress of ivory and spun gold. Just as he knew she would be when he'd seen the gown at the shop in Paris. It was meant for her. Her hair, the color of a harvest moon's reflection in a glass of champagne, was the exact same hue, and it made her blue eyes seem bigger somehow. "It's been too long, my friend."

"Too long indeed. Come, let us get out of the way of the dancers."

"Oh yes!" he said, suddenly aware of others in the room. For a moment, it was only he and Elsa. He took her hand, slender and yet strong in his own, and led her off the floor. They each retrieved a glass of punch and walked to a small archway off the dance floor.

She stood away from him as if suddenly shy.

"Elsa Ramstad, you're the most beautiful woman in this room." He couldn't help himself. She was.

"Surely not."

"Disagree if you must, but it's the truth. Who escorted you?" he asked, scanning the room.

"My second mate, Eric Young."

"A good man, I hear."

She lifted a brow but let his comment go. He'd have to be more careful; she'd find out how much he kept track of her and her crew.

"And a surprising one. I keep finding a new reason to like him more."

Karl faltered at her candor. Was there something between them? Did he have any right to the sudden jealousy in his heart? He supposed no one would ever be right for Elsa, in his eyes, other than Peder. Or himself. And there was no chance of that ever happening!

"And you?" she asked.

"I escorted Mara Kenney." He held his tongue, suddenly anxious to explain the true nature of their relationship. But she had not asked, and to volunteer such intimacies would seem ungentlemanly.

"A fine family. I met the elder Kenneys at another ball, years ago. The girls were just..." She broke off, apparently embarrassed.

"It is all right, say it. They're still girls."

"That's true. Why, she must be half your age!"

"A bit scandalous, no?" He was teasing her, wondering what her reaction would be. He couldn't help himself. "Plenty of men take brides much younger than themselves." It was out before he could stop himself. He wanted to know how she would take it, if she cared at all. If she would be jealous, as he had been at the mention of Eric Young.

"I suppose they do," she said, turning slightly away.

"Elsa, I—"

"Karl Martensen!" cried Mara, suddenly at his side. "I look away for one moment, and suddenly you're talking to another woman!"

He bit back a sharp retort, wanting to send her back to her mother where she belonged. "Mara," he said instead, "I would like to introduce an old friend. Captain Elsa Ramstad, meet Miss Mara Kenney."

"Elsa Ramstad!" Mara gasped. "Karl, I had no idea you knew the Heroine of the Horn! Wait until I introduce you to my friends, Captain Ramstad! Oh, it will be just wonderful!"

"I am sure," Elsa said vaguely. She shot him a look that said "This *is your love interest?*"

He smiled in frustration. There he was, wanting nothing more than to stare at Elsa in that dress, to catch up on old times, and instead he had immediately gotten off on the wrong foot. Before he would allow Mara to drag Elsa off to meet her friends, he said, "Mara, would you excuse us for one moment? As you know, I had Ramstad Yard build my steamer, and I need to speak with Captain Ramstad about it."

"Oh, Karl. This is hardly the place for business."

He flashed her a smile. "I know. Forgive me. Give me just one minute, and the captain and I will join you and your friends."

Mara reviewed her choices. "Very well. *One* minute," she stated.

He turned away from her with a sigh and back to Elsa. She awaited him with a knowing smile. "Got yourself in deep again, didn't you, Karl?"

"Yes. I have a bad habit of that."

"You wanted to talk business?"

"No! No," he said, taking her hands in his. "I simply wanted one more minute with a dear friend I haven't seen in years. It is so good to see you, Elsa. Truly. Are you here long? I saw your ship yesterday and inquired after you, but you were in town."

"As I inquired after you," she said, pulling her hands from his to take two crystal cups from a passing waiter's tray. She gave one to Karl. "That's quite a beauty our yard turned out for you. And I hear she has a ballroom."

"Indeed. Perhaps you'll come and join me for a dance sometime."

"You're going to Alaska?"

"I am. As fast as I can."

"Then we'll be in a race. From Washington to Juneau, as soon as we replace our mast."

"What? Truly? You're going to Juneau too?"

"Trent and Tora are soon to get married, if they're not already. I want to be there. As soon as we stop off for a new mast at Ramstad Lumberyard and for Mrs. Hodge in Seattle, we're heading north." She brought her crystal cup to her lips. Karl loved her lips. Even settled, they looked as if they had a slight smile to them. He reminded himself not to stare. Besides, she was a friend, and a friend only. If ever they were to be more, it would be up to her. Never again, as God was his witness, would he make an unwelcome advance upon her. The last time he tried, it had torn them apart and killed his friendship with Peder.

"Oh," he sighed, "Mara is waving at me. We had better go. So it sounds as if we can meet up in Seattle? Go from there to Juneau together?" He took her hands again. "Think of it, Elsa. We can get to know each other again, rekindle our friendship. I would love to know your children."

She smiled then. "I'd like that too. So next week in Washington?"

"Next week in Washington," he whispered, suddenly able to lead her to others when he knew he would soon have her all to himself.

Elsa danced the rest of the evening with Eric, with Alfred Cummings, with any man who asked. But never with Karl. Why did he not come to her, invite her onto the floor? Gradually her gay mood faded as she brooded over the fact that he never asked, but instead twirled the lovely, but so young, Mara Kenney about the floor. She saw them laughing together, whispering another time. And still later, she watched as Karl bent and kissed her cheek. They were a striking couple, she had to admit, but something just didn't settle right.

On the way home in the cab, Eric turned to her. "Are you all right?"

"Oh yes. Why?"

"You've become more and more quiet as the evening went on. In fact, I would say it all started when you ran into Captain Martensen. Yes, that's when I noticed the change."

"You noticed no such thing," she directed, suddenly the captain again. "I am fine. Nothing changed." She was irritated at his perception, for being put on the spot. Consciously, she gentled her tone, knowing he thought he had hit the nail on the head. "It was a lovely evening, Eric. Thank you for agreeing to escort me."

He turned to her and grinned. "It was my pleasure. Do you know how much I'll get out of this? The boys will be begging me for stories all the way to Juneau."

"You're a good man, Eric."

"And you're a fine woman, Cap'n. The prettiest at the ball. I was a proud man tonight."

She looked down at her lap then, to the beaded purse. His words echoed in her head, bringing back memories of Karl saying he, too, thought her pretty. It made her sick to her stomach. Why was that? Did she not want her old friend admiring her, giving him a chance to "rekindle," as he said, something more than friendship? No, that wasn't it. He was handsome and smart and obviously well established, by the look of his new ship. What was niggling at her?

Elsa thought back to watching Karl and Mara, unable to enjoy her own whirl across the dance floor as she did so. Why was she not happy for them, a couple who were so beautiful together?

Then the thought struck her dumb.

She was jealous.

Jealous of Mara Kenney.

"You're a sorrowful mess, Elsa Ramstad," she whispered.

"What?" Eric asked.

"Oh, forgive me. I'm just talking to myself."

"An odd habit," he said, giving her a wink.

"An odd habit, indeed." But she wasn't thinking of odd habits. She was thinking of Karl Martensen, with his ponytail undone, his hair waving in the wind. She was thinking of a gold loop through the hole in his ear and his collar open a few buttons.

Elsa was thinking of what a fine man he was and how she wished it had been she, instead of Mara Kenney, that he had whirled across the dance floor all night.

f o u r t e e n

2 October 1888

*P*lease, Tora. Won't she see me?" he asked, once again at the door of the Storm Roadhouse. Tora was as eye-catching as she had been on the *Herald* eight years earlier, but Soren was determined never to let her know he thought as much.

"No. And I hope she never will."

"It has been days."

"It'll take years for her to get over what you did to her."

"I did not hurt her on purpose."

"Oh no?" she scoffed. "You thought that leaving her alone on a Dakota farm with a baby was helpful?"

"I sent her money."

"Once." Tora was like a bur under a horse's saddle.

"Strange."

"What?" she asked, suddenly wary at his tone.

"That a former mistress of mine would deposit a child on my wife's doorstep and then years later act as a soldier at her gate. Seems to me that you've done your share of hurting my wife."

"It's true," she said, her face falling. "I hurt her badly. But we've built our bridges—"

"As I want to do," he interrupted. "Is that fair? For you to be allowed to ask forgiveness and heal that rift, but not allow me to do so?"

She said nothing.

"I'm a changed man, Tora."

She laughed then in derision. "I doubt it."

"And you, Tora? How have you changed? I didn't force you to my bed."

Tora shook her head slightly and then glanced over her shoulder. "You do not fight fair."

He raised his hands in surrender. "I do not want to fight. Truly. I'm a changed man. I just want to see my wife. If she'll see me."

Tora looked him in the eye for a long moment, apparently contemplating his words, and Soren refused to look away. Without a word, she went into another room, but she left the door ajar. He assumed it meant that she was going to ask Kaatje if she wanted to see him. He suddenly wished he was a praying man, because it seemed an opportune moment for a talk with the heavenlies to get Kaatje to at least speak to him. *A little "inside" help,* he thought wryly.

When she returned to the doorstep, she gave him a look that reminded him of James Walker's word of warning. *Don't hurt her,* he'd said, *or you'll have me to deal with.* How could little Kaatje have won such fiercely protective friends? There was much he had to learn about his wife.

And suddenly she was there, a sliver of light illuminating her hazel eyes.

"Please. Please, Kaatje. Won't you come and sit with me? Here on the porch?"

Kaatje still felt as if it were a dream. Or a nightmare. She couldn't decide. Just when she had given up on her husband, here he was, asking her to come and sit with him on the porch. But all the love she thought she had for him was absent in her heart, surprising her. She couldn't get over the fact that she felt nothing toward him except indifference…emptiness.

Mutely she followed him out to the front porch where Tora had placed two sets of rocking chairs. The other set was empty.

He gestured toward the near one for her, then quickly sat down on the other, twisting his hat in his hands. "What can I say to you to convince you to give me a chance?"

She shrugged. What could he say? She didn't want to hear his excuses. His lies. And yet there she sat, riveted. Just like old times. She disgusted herself.

"What if...what if we start over?"

"Start over?" Kaatje found her voice, each word becoming stronger. "How could we possibly start over?"

Soren cleared his throat. "Perhaps we have to go back a bit. Let me explain—"

"No. I don't want to hear your explanations. There is no excuse for leaving your family for years without a word. Without a word!" Her anger surprised her. Maybe there was more in her heart than she thought.

"I staked a claim, Kaatje," he said, going to his knees before her, seemingly uncaring of who saw them. "I thought it would be our future. Instead it was just another dead end." He looked saddened, beaten. "I wanted you with me. Every month, every year. I was determined to make something of myself, so I could return to you and make you proud."

"I was proud once, Soren. Those first months on our Dakota farm...that's what I wanted from you. But it wasn't enough. It was never enough."

"I know. I know, *elskling*. Every month it became harder to write to you, harder to let you know where I was, what I was doing. I was wasting my life; I didn't want to waste yours."

"What did you think I was doing? How did you think I would survive? Alone? With our child? Your children?"

He shook his head in misery. "I know. I know!" He licked his lips. "I thought the Bergensers would look after you."

She sighed and pursed her lips in disgust. "Get up. Get up, Soren, and sit. People are watching."

He glanced toward the street and then did as she bid. She knew he saw her comment as giving him an opening, a chance.

"I know it's been so hard on you, kitten. If I'd known..."

"If you'd *known?* How could you have possibly assumed we would be all right?"

"I was a fool."

"You were," she agreed.

He paused, then forged onward. "With each passing month, my future looked more grim. How could I have brought you to that? Somehow I became convinced that you would have divorced me, married another."

"How could you think that? I have never believed in divorce."

"You had a good reason. I had abandoned you. You thought I was dead."

She was silent. Had she not been ready to do just that? "Why not just return home? To see?"

"With my tail tucked between my legs?"

"Yes. Exactly. You were too proud, as usual, to come back. Weren't you? Or was it your Indian lover that held you back?"

His eyes flew upward to meet hers. "How do you know about the woman?"

She shook her head. Nothing changed. Nothing ever changed with Soren. He would confess because he was caught, not because he wanted to change. She rose. "I'm going in now."

He stopped her with a hand to her arm. "Wait."

"No." She shook it off, suddenly remembering being a newly married girl in Bergen, catching him with a milkmaid. *Why, Lord? Why? Why put me through this misery?*

"I've changed, Kaatje. The girl, the Indian girl—she was being hurt by her people. Abused."

"Abused? That is not their way. Why would she have been abused?"

"She was beautiful and betrothed to one man. Another caught her eye. When she refused the man she was betrothed to, he claimed she went to him one night to seduce him. She was an outcast."

Kaatje laughed, a mirthless sound. "And she came straight to you."

"No. It wasn't like that."

"It wasn't? No, it wasn't. I know more, Soren. You not only were with one Indian girl, you were with two."

"No! That is not true! Who told you that?" Her look must have told him. "Him? Walker? Why, the man's in love with you! He'd say anything to win you from me. Please. *Please.* Kaatje, we have more than ourselves to consider."

"What?"

"Our children. For the girls. Will you not at least give me a chance?"

His words sliced her. Only the girls could make her feel vulnerable again. "Where is the woman?" she asked through clenched teeth, not looking back at him.

"Away. At Saint Michael. There's a Catholic priest there. Russian Orthodox. He finds such women work, shelter, food. He'll take care of her." He moved back in front of Kaatje. "There is nothing between her and me. Nothing. Please. Please, Kaatje. Give me a chance."

James followed Soren every day, watched through bleary eyes at night to make sure he wasn't sneaking out. As far as he could tell, Soren was living the life of an upstanding man. He rose at seven, ordered a bath from the hotel manager—at least Kaatje had not let him stay at the roadhouse—and then took his breakfast at a restaurant down the street. He had taken a job at the mercantile the day before, loading supplies into wagons at the back, and bringing new shipments in. It appeared that he meant to support himself and was prepared to wait however long it took for Kaatje to welcome him back.

But was that all it was? Appearances?

James's gut told him it was so.

It wasn't a coincidence that Soren Janssen showed up in town the week before Kaatje was to declare him dead. He was up to something. Down and dead on his luck, James assumed, no doubt Soren had heard of the woman who looked for him on the river and had learned of her means in Juneau. Kaatje had made something of herself in the new territory, was suddenly the wife Soren had wanted all along. Maybe he had finally given up on finding the mother lode himself and had decided to ride on his wife's coattails.

If only he would go to the saloon! Pick up a woman! Buy a pint of brandy! That would prove to everyone what James could feel in his bones about the man. Instead, this morning Soren had even gone to church, quietly sitting five pews behind Kaatje and Tora and Trent, never attempting to talk to her. But James was sure that he had made a point of pausing outside, making his presence known. Was it all an act? Or had the louse actually changed?

James groaned and slid to the ground outside the hotel's wall. What was he doing? If Kaatje was going to give him a chance, it was up to her. He rubbed his face, suddenly conscious of how wearing the last days had been. As he sat there, he noticed a bulge in his coat pocket. He reached inside and grasped the bundle and pulled it out. There, inside a handkerchief, was the gold nugget that Kaatje had found outside Soren's abandoned claim.

He smiled a little bit, examining the glint of it in the dim, overcast light. It didn't look like fool's gold today. Maybe he should have it examined. He smiled. Pleased to have a new mission, he set out for the alchemist's shop. In minutes he would know. And if it was truly gold, he planned to have the last laugh on Soren Janssen.

He rose and hurried down the street. Inside a small man sat hunched over his work with his back to James. The shop was dark, with only one kerosene lamp lit over the books the alchemist kept. "May I help you?" he asked over his shoulder, not looking back.

"I'd like you to inspect this nugget. Tell me if it's real or fool's."

The man turned around, and James saw that he was in his latter sixties, with silver hair that covered his face as well as emerged from his nostrils and ears. He wore half-glasses low on his nose and clothes that were old but clean. He reached out for the nugget, his face expressionless. In Alaska, he probably had ten men a day asking the same thing of him.

But he paused as he looked over the nugget, about the same size as the tip of his index finger. He pursed his lips in concentration and reached for a bottle of liquid behind him. Then he pulled a leather glove on his hand and put the nugget into a glass dish. He allowed some of the liquid to fall to the surface. It spattered and sizzled but made no dent.

The man looked over his half-glasses at James.

"That, my man, is pure gold."

James laughed. Couldn't stop himself from laughing. Could it be? Could Soren have stumbled upon a claim that was worth something and abandoned it before it was fully explored? He had heard stories of miners working for years on mines, mere inches from a gold streak as big as a man's thigh.

The alchemist was staring at him. "That'll be two bits for my trouble."

"Sure. Sure!" James pulled out a coin and slapped it on the wooden counter.

"Want to sell that gold?"

"Not yet."

"That claim registered?"

"You bet," James said. It would be. By day's end. And if Soren was as foolish about letting the claim go as he was about his wife, he would lose two treasures by his own stupidity.

James was whistling as he left the land office, shaking his head at Soren's ineptitude. He had let his claim lapse, and James had signed Kaatje's name to the deed. If he was right, and there was more gold on that claim, Soren's wife would be richer than Soren ever dreamed.

But before he found out, James had to ascertain what Soren had up his sleeve. James wouldn't let him use Kaatje as he had in the past, only to be discarded again. He was as crafty as a traveling gambler; James was sure of it.

He was returning to his hotel, bent on the idea of a bath and a big meal, when he caught sight of Soren, crossing the street to the restaurant, presumably for supper. He looked James's way as he crossed the muddy avenue and paused to wait for him. James bristled. Why would Soren wait for him? What would he have to say?

As James drew near, Soren said, "Saw Kaatje today."

"Oh?" he returned, feigning indifference.

"Yes." He leaned closer. "That thought must eat you alive."

James seethed inside, squelching the desire to shove Soren to the ground, smash his face in the mud. But he was careful to keep his expression composed. "I don't know what you're talking about, Janssen."

"I know it's hard to give up a woman like Kaatje, Walker. But face it. She's mine. Or she will be mine again shortly. It's already begun."

James stared him in the eye until Soren walked away, whistling.

What was he after? It had to be more than Kaatje. She had never been enough to keep him home before. Just what was Soren Janssen after?

fifteen

The sudden rapping at Elsa's cabin door startled her. The steady beat of Washington's rain, her children's rhythmic nap breathing, and the dim, warm light of her cabin had lulled her as she painted a new canvas with muted colors to match the day's mood. She quickly stood, almost upsetting her chair, and went to the door. Odd, the knock. Her men always knocked twice, then announced who awaited her.

She twisted the brass knob and pulled the swollen door from its jamb.

"Karl!"

"Oh, hello," he said, stifling a smile. "I'm here to call upon Master Kristian and Miss Eve. Are they at home?"

She smiled and gestured inward, closing the door behind Karl and shutting out the curious looks of her crew. "I will go and awaken them. They're just in the next room."

"They're asleep? I'm sorry. I can come back later—"

"Nonsense. They've slept for two hours or more. If I don't awaken them now, they'll complain later that they missed Uncle Karl and will never go to sleep again!"

"Does Kristian even remember his uncle?" he whispered.

Elsa stifled a shiver as his warm breath tickled her neck. She

176

stepped away. "Very little, I'm afraid. It's been so long, Karl." She hoped her eyes told him that she had missed him as much as her son had. Suddenly embarrassed at being so forthright, she turned. "Have a seat. I'll just be a minute."

Elsa hurried from the room, wondering if Karl was watching her walk away. She sighed, wishing she had worn her gold waistcoat, rather than the drab day dress. She walked to Kristian's narrow bunk bed. Eve slept beneath him. "Kristian, wake up. I have a surprise for you."

"A surprise?" he asked, sounding so clear she decided he must have been well ready to awaken.

"Yes. Let us wake Eve, and then I'll show you.

"Eve," she said lowly, squatting to look at the tiny girl on the lower bunk. Her daughter wasn't as ready as her son to rise. "Eve, sweetheart. I have a surprise for you. It's time to get up. You can go to bed early tonight if you wish." When the girl didn't move, Elsa suppressed her irritation. She was so eager to get back to Karl! To see him again, talk to him again!

"Come on, darling." Kristian hopped noisily to the plank flooring beside Elsa. "Kristian, I've told you a thousand times to climb down the ladder, not jump. You'll go right through to the crew's quarters next time." Was that a muffled laugh she heard from the next room? Quickly Karl coughed to cover it up. Elsa smiled. She probably reminded him of his own mother's reprimands years ago. Karl and Peder had been wild—active and playful. Much like Kristian.

She helped Kristian get his arm through one hole of his shirt and then pulled Eve's lilac day dress over her slip. Then she combed both heads of hair.

"Now, Mama? Now?" Kristian begged, hopping up and down.

"Now," she said with a grin. His enthusiasm was contagious. Not that she needed any assistance in that matter. "Look who's here to see you!"

They both crowded around her to see Karl, and then Eve went back behind her legs when she discovered she did not know her visitor.

"Hello," Karl said, his cello voice at once soothing and welcoming.

"Hello, sir. I'm Kristian Ramstad," her son said formally, sticking out his small hand.

Karl rose, bowed, and shook his hand. "It's a pleasure, Kristian. I'm Karl Martensen."

"*Uncle* Karl?" Kristian asked in surprise.

"Why, yes," Karl chuckled. "You can call me that."

"Uncle Karl!" he said in glee, encircling his waist with an exuberant hug.

Karl laughed, but his eyes were on Eve, peeking out from behind Elsa's skirts. "And you must be Eve," he said.

Eve smiled shyly.

He pulled out a wooden box and forlornly stared at its inlaid lid.

"What is it? What is it?" Kristian cried, his shyness suddenly forgotten.

"Why, I don't quite remember. Why don't you open it, Eve?" He gestured toward the box, and Eve slowly opened it. Music immediately began playing, and her tiny face lit up. She shrieked with joy when she saw the ballerina, dancing atop the highest platform—made of a child's block with the letter *D,* presumably for *dancer*—a monkey scratching his head on a lower one with the letter *M,* and a man riding a bicycle on the other one painted with a *B.* She laughed with delight.

"What'd you get for me?" Kristian asked.

"Kristian!"

"That's all right, Elsa. Now let me see… Did I bring something for Kristian?" he asked rhetorically, looking puzzled. He absently patted all his pockets and looked around the room as if he had lost it, then found another box at his feet. It was larger than Eve's. Kristian greedily took it from him. Elsa smiled her apologies, but Karl seemed unperturbed.

Kristian ripped the brown paper from the surface and whooped his pleasure at the sight of his favorite Oriental game. "A mah-jongg! He got me a mah-jongg! Thank you, Uncle Karl!"

"You're welcome, Kristian. Do you know how to play?"

"I do! Jeremy Bergerson taught me when his dad's ship was moored in the same harbor as ours."

"Ahh. Which harbor was that?"

"Renoit Bay."

"Very good. Well perhaps you can get it set up while I take your mother for a stroll around the deck. It sounds as if the rain has stopped."

"Better yet," Elsa said, thinking of all the curious stares they would get from her crew, "why don't you show me your ship? I've been anxious to see it."

"Certainly. But I was hoping you would come aboard for supper. And the children, too, of course."

"That sounds lovely. Where are you moored?"

"Just three piers north." They were in Seattle's busy harbor, about ready to set sail again. The central mast had been repaired at the lumberyard; the new boiler worked perfectly.

"When do you plan to leave for Alaska?"

Her question seemed to surprise him. "Why, just as soon as you do."

"Oh yes." He was there just to see them! Even though she knew they had planned to meet in Washington, the idea of it all thrilled her. For once, business was not pulling them apart to separate seas, but rather bringing them together. And they could remain together for a while!

"You had mentioned a race to Juneau..." he led.

"I was only joking—"

"No, I like it. What if we do this," he said, rising. "Tonight we dine on my ship. When we leave, we will race northward for the day. Whoever is in the lead at five o'clock will reef their sails and await the loser; then the loser shall feed the winner's entire crew."

"Their entire crew!"

"Their entire crew."

Kristian clapped in excitement. "Oh yes, Mama! A race! Every day! We'll be at Auntie Tora's in no time at all!"

Elsa laughed and shook her head. "That'll be a lot of food you'll have to shell out for my crew, Karl," she warned playfully. "But you'll only use two of your boilers, not all three, to make it a fair race."

"Three?" He raised his eyebrows and then lowered them in mock confusion. "Whoever told you I had three?"

Elsa smugly crossed her arms. "I am yet the owner of Ramstad Yard. Kristoffer informed me of his task as builder of Karl Martensen's latest design, as he has on every ship that comes out of Camden-by-the-Sea."

Karl grinned and stared into her eyes. "Two boilers. But all masts."

"Fair enough. Your ship is heavier and will lag behind our *Majestic*."

"So you think. I take it we have a wager?"

"A wager indeed."

Elsa fussed with her hair and combs for a long while before supper, wanting to get the gentle wave just right. When it fell yet again, she groaned and stared at herself in the mirror. "What are you doing, Elsa Ramstad?" The thought of leaving the *Majestic* for Karl's *Fair Alaska* made her hands perspire and her mouth dry.

She had to admit that her reaction to Karl was more than that of a dear friend. He was the equal she was beginning to wonder if she would ever find, a potential suitor that, as a friend, could be a perfect match. But could they ever get past their troubled history? To Elsa, it seemed like a dim memory now, but it was still present. Not because it bothered her any longer; he had long since proven himself to her as a good friend above all else. He had always been a gentleman, his resolve to never hurt her again showing in his every action. But it also seemed a barrier of sorts that kept him from her. Would his intentions to remain pure keep them apart forever? What if…what if Karl was the one she was meant to love?

"All buttoned up?" Mrs. Hodge asked, ducking her head into Elsa's room. Elsa was glad to have her back aboard the *Majestic* to care for the children. "My, don't you look lovely!" She came all the way in, followed by Kristian and Eve.

"Can't we go with you tonight, Mama?" Kristian asked with a begging tone. "I heard Uncle Karl invite us, too. *Please*."

"Now, now," Mrs. Hodge said. "We've been all through this. Your mother has obviously let you stay up until all hours, and it's time to get back into a suitable routine. To bed by eight, up at sunrise. If you're living aboard ship, you ought to live as the sailors do. Besides, I've gone and made my finest pumpkin pie. If you're good, I'll even whip some cream."

"Winning them over with food again, Mrs. Hodge?" Elsa teased.

"Whatever wins them, I say. It's good to be back with you, Elsa. I've enjoyed my time at the house, but I was surprised when I found that I not only missed you Ramstads, but also the sea."

"It grows on you," Elsa said.

"You children go and wash your hands before supper," Mrs. Hodge said. After they scampered off, she turned to Elsa, taking the ivory comb from her hand. In seconds she had the stubborn segment of hair perfectly in place, firmly secured with the comb. "Peder gave that comb to you, didn't he?"

"He did," Elsa said, feeling guilty all of a sudden for her excitement over supper with Karl.

"He'd be glad you're wearing it tonight. Moreover, he'd be happy you're having dinner with Karl."

Her reassurance eased Elsa's heart. But one thing held her back. "Mrs. Hodge... Tell me. What if it was more than just supper with an old friend? What if I found myself with...feelings for Captain Martensen?" She held her breath, afraid of Mrs. Hodge's answer.

"I'd say it was high time." Mrs. Hodge stared into her eyes via the mirror. She put a hand on either shoulder. "You've honored his memory, Elsa. You'll continue to honor his memory. Why, you and the children just visited his grave. One can't ask for more than that. Peder would not have asked for more."

Elsa nodded once.

"You see? Peder Ramstad will always hold a special place in your heart. Always. He will always be your first love, your husband, the father of your children. But that doesn't mean there isn't room for another."

Eric insisted on rowing her over to *Fair Alaska*, apparently chagrined at the thought of escorting his beautiful captain past the rough-and-tumble crowd that frequented the wharf. "Besides," he said, "it'll give me time with a crew besides these louts," nodding at those on deck.

"It is most kind of you, Eric."

"Shall we?"

"Let me kiss the children good night."

"Right away. I'll get the skiff ready."

After bidding her children a good night, she accepted Riley's hand and climbed into the boat before it was lowered to the surface. At the bottom of the net, another sailor waited for them, and then stepped aboard. Elsa looked upward. "Two men? Isn't that overdoing it a bit, Riley?"

He grinned down at her. "Nothing's overdoing it when I'm sending my fair captain to another ship dressed as if she were attending a society luncheon."

She shook her head, embarrassed to be caught, and then nodded her assent to Eric to carry her onward and away from the laughter of her men aboard ship. Eric sat at one long oar and sang a low sailor's tune to help the other sailor keep time with him at his own oar. They said nothing, and Elsa felt a bit uneasy in front of the other sailor. Especially with her mind on Karl Martensen.

He was waiting at the rail when she arrived, as somehow she knew he would be. They tied up beside the massive *Fair Alaska,* and Karl carried a ladder down to the pier for her, then lowered it to the skiff. She carefully climbed up, wanting to curse her bulky crinoline for making her feel clumsy, and accepted his hand. He bent low to kiss her fingers, then turned to shake Eric's hand.

"Weren't you the one who escorted Captain Ramstad to the ball?"

"Indeed," Eric said, measuring Karl with his eyes. "Eric Young, Captain Ramstad's second mate."

"Yes, I was sorry not to have made your acquaintance the night of the ball. I know of you, Mr. Young. You have a good reputation. If you ever tire of working for Captain Ramstad, look me up."

Elsa looked from one man to the other. They seemed to admire each other, but there was a smell of competition in the air.

"If you don't mind, I'll accompany my captain to your ship and stand outside the door should she need anything."

"That's hardly necessary. I have plenty of crew members to see to her every need."

Eric stood firm, unrelenting, staring only at Karl, never at Elsa.

"You might as well agree, Karl," she said, taking his arm and breaking the awkward moment. "I have assembled the most wonderful, loyal crew on the seven seas."

"Apparently," he said, tucking her hand more securely on his strong forearm. "And the other man?"

"He'll stay with the skiff," Eric answered from behind them.

"I'll send some supper down!" Karl called back.

"Much obliged, Cap'n Martensen!" the man called back.

Once aboard the *Fair Alaska*, Elsa dropped her hand from Karl's arm and brought it to her mouth in astonishment. "Why…Karl, she's *beautiful*."

"You haven't seen the half of her." He stared down at her, and Elsa sensed that he wasn't only admiring his ship. "Come, this way. I'll give you a tour of the main deck and then we'll end up at the dining hall. You, too, Mr. Young."

They began at the impressive bridge, twice as large as Elsa's on the *Majestic*, then proceeded to the boiler room. Karl's arm waved in the air as he explained the inner workings of the ship.

"They're half again as large as ours," Eric murmured in her ear when Karl's back was turned. "She has to be twenty tons." Elsa's crew had heard of her wager with Karl and was eager for their journey north, and their race, to begin.

"Twenty-two," she whispered back, remembering Kristoffer's report from the Ramstad Shipyard in Camden.

She waited until Karl was finished and then, ignoring what he had just said, stared into his eyes. "You think you have us already, don't you? Simply because your boilers are such monstrosities? You probably had a good laugh when I demanded you only use two."

Karl's eyes sparkled in merriment. "A wager's a wager."

"Indeed," she said, turning to lead them out of the noisy compartment where one of the gigantic steam engines slowly chugged, even though the ship was idle. She supposed it was to generate the electricity that lit the entire ship. That electricity would eat up a lot of Karl's precious steam, she thought with a smirk. And the sheer bulk of *Fair Alaska* would take a lot of power to push it northward. He hadn't won yet.

They went down a great, curving staircase to the guest's quarters, forty rooms that bragged of elegance by their ornate furnishings. There was even a tiny water closet and shower attached to each room, and electric lamps in each of the bedrooms. "My, Karl, she's lovely. You really think you can attract enough paying customers to make it profitable?"

"I'm sure of it. John Muir has written countless articles on Glacier Bay, piquing society's interest. Word has it he's even contemplating a book, he's so wild about the terrain. Trent Storm is already organizing rail trips from the Midwest and East to Seattle, where I'll pick up the passengers and escort them to his roadhouses in Ketchikan and Juneau. You wait and see. It'll be the rage."

"You're most likely right," she answered, a bit miffed she hadn't thought of the plan herself. It was perfect. A gem of an idea.

He took them back to the main deck's receiving area, an enormous parlor meant for his guests' recreation with huge portholes that boasted of terrific views, even in foul weather. Then they walked along a narrow covered walkway that arced over the deck like a small bridge, presumably to allow crew members easy access while protecting his high-paying passengers from the elements in their formal dress. On the other side was a massive dining room; Elsa imagined the tables set with white tablecloths and silver. Crystal and china were neatly displayed in cabinets at the end of each long row of tables.

"You really think this will work?" she wondered aloud. "You're obviously going to have to charge these people exorbitant prices to treat them this well. You'll dine on what? Pheasant and duck? Pour the finest wines? Really, don't you think it's a bit ostentatious?"

"Not at all," he said. "I think it's the next wave of sailing. People will get up out of their armchairs and see the world, not just read about it. And if we can give them all the comforts of home, they'll be all the more pleased to tell their friends that they must go too."

"I hope so," she said with a laugh. "Because if they don't, you won't be able to pay your Ramstad Shipyard bill."

"Not at all."

She looked at him quickly, confused.

"I paid cash for *Fair Alaska*. She's mine, free and clear."

Words could not express how glad Karl was to have Elsa aboard *Fair Alaska*. And he was even more glad when he smugly gestured toward the table outside the ballroom and could finally shut the door on the watchful Eric. It was more than loyalty that made that man such a watchdog for Elsa, Karl was sure of it. But tonight, tonight Karl would see if there was even a chance for him.

She paused when she tore her admiring gaze from the ballroom panels and saw the beautiful table. It was set with the finest sterling and china and crystal that Karl had, with a crystal candelabra already alight. She laughed in amazement and turned to him in surprise. "I had better leave."

"Leave?"

"Yes. You must be expecting the governor."

"Better," he said, taking her hand. "An old friend that I've missed for far too long."

She glanced away, her cheeks reddening with his praise, looking toward the gilt-edged mirrors on the walls and Antonio's incredible carvings. "Where did you have these done?" she asked. "Last I knew, Ramstad Yard wasn't doing such work."

"San Francisco."

"Ahh," she said knowingly. "Convenient."

"Convenient?"

"Yes," she said, still running her hands over the carvings, avoiding his gaze. "All that work had to be done, right there near young Miss Kenney."

Was that a hint of jealousy in her voice? Was she fishing for information? Surely not. "Yes, it was good to be near all the Kenneys. They're fine friends." He never wanted to say anything disrespectful about his friends, regardless of what he wanted Elsa to understand, that there could never be anything between him and Mara. He hoped Elsa read between the lines.

"And what would young Miss Kenney think of this?" she said, waving toward the table for two. She sounded a bit indignant. And for the first time Karl wondered if he had gone too far, too fast.

"I would tell her the truth," he said. "I'd tell her that we are old friends who had dinner for the first time in two years and that I used every resource on the *Fair Alaska* to make it a memorable reunion."

Her expression eased a bit, and she almost looked a little sorry at his explanation. Women! Who could figure what they wanted? Unable to think of what else he should do, he went to the phonograph, wound it up, and set the needle upon the metal disk. Music wafted into the air, and Elsa's expression softened. "Do you have a phonograph?" he asked.

"Hardly. This is the first one I've seen."

"You'll want one after you hear a few disks."

"I want one now! And the children would love it."

"Take mine back with you."

"I couldn't."

"Yes, I insist. Borrow it until we reach Juneau."

"You're sure?"

"Absolutely."

They paused, both watching the revolving machine and listening to the notes leaving the fluted horn that broadcast them. "Would you care to dance?" he asked, instantly chastising himself for his forwardness. Of course she didn't. She was there for dinner, not romance!

"Certainly," she said.

A second later, he faced her and offered his hand and arm. Slowly she walked toward him and took his hand in hers, placing her other hand on his shoulder. He whisked her across the ballroom floor, smiling. This was what he had longed to do as soon as he saw the completed ballroom. To take a woman into his arms, a woman who fit him as Elsa did, and float across the entire length. He caught glimpses of them in the mirrors, the hollow between her shoulder blades, his own intent face, her glistening hair. She was so beautiful. He wanted this moment to last forever, but all too soon, the music stopped.

She looked disappointed too, if he wasn't mistaken. "Thank you, Karl. I was sorry we didn't have another chance to dance at the Harvest Ball."

"I, too. Come, let us sit. The food should arrive any minute." He escorted her to the table and pulled out her chair. Then he sat on the other side and raised his crystal goblet. "I'd like to make a toast."

"With an empty glass? Is that like an empty promise?"

"Not at all." She raised her own crystal flute and waited. "I'd like to make a toast to friendship." Her smile faltered a little, even as they touched the glasses together for a bell-like *ding*, and it was only then that Karl thought of the application to Mara Kenney as well as to Elsa. He was about to say something else, to amend it, when she spoke.

"And I'd like to make a toast as well."

"Of course."

"To dining like this every night of our journey to Alaska. The crew will love it."

Karl raised his eyebrows. "You really think you can beat my ship, eh?"

"Every night. She's the prettiest ship I've ever seen, but she'll also be slower than molasses. She's too heavy."

"We shall see. To the *potential* of dining on the *Fair Alaska*."

"To dining on the *Fair Alaska*."

Their glasses met again.

s i x t e e n

‸

ora Anders was hot. *Stifled* was a better word for it. She felt ill at ease, agitated, and could not seem to sit still through her attacker's long-overdue trial. She fought the urge to pull at her high-necked collar, trying in vain to keep her hands in her lap. The small schoolhouse was packed with every townsperson who couldn't wait to hear what the respected Mrs. Storm-to-be had to say against her assailant. Tora could hear the gossip already.

It was all his fault.

That she was here.

That she and Trent and her friends had to bear this.

Decker.

Dirty, despicable…she cast about for the last descriptive word that would define her assailant. *Lost.* Lost? The word stunned her. It had a quality of empathy that she did not care for. Lost? Yes, lost to this world. Lost to her. She should be happy. After today, Decker would be out of her life forever. What judge would dare to question Trent Storm? Once he took the stand, it was all over, regardless of what Tora's past had been. He was Trent Storm, after all. And it was his testimony that would send the man to the gallows. Tora was certain of it.

Decker looked at her, and Tora immediately looked away, but not before she identified the look in his eyes. Gloating? It was he who would have to face the gallows. Not her. So why would he gloat? The man didn't even have an attorney. There were few solicitors in Alaska. It was up to the judge to exact justice. And Tora aimed to turn the judge in her favor. If she dropped her eyes here, teared up there, he'd play right into her hands.

You are thinking of your old ways, came the Voice.

Tora swallowed hard. *But this is justice, Father. He tried to take me again! And his intentions were not holy!* Tears came to her eyes. It wasn't fair. She was created with certain physical attributes, attributes that may have contributed to his abuse of her. So shouldn't she be able to use her looks in her favor to exact justice? To help justice prevail? The tears fell to her cheeks.

Trent looked at her. "Are you all right?" he whispered, his eyes filled with concern.

She nodded, trying to sort out what she was feeling. *I need to concentrate on the facts,* she thought. *Decker is just playing me. Using me emotionally as he once used me physically. I will not play into his hands again! I will not! This time, he pays.* "He pays," she whispered, summoning every ounce of hate she had ever felt for Decker.

Her attention went to Sara, the waifish waitress Decker had assaulted at the roadhouse. Seeing her on the stand, shaking as she took the oath, one small hand on a black Bible—seeing her tremble as she reached for a tepid glass of water, hearing her voice crack as she fought to speak up as the judge asked her to do—made Tora furious all over again.

And then when dear Trent took the stand, spoke of that horrendous evening when Decker tried to abduct her again… Seeing his ashen face and clenched lips made her even angrier that Decker had hurt not only her, but the man she loved.

Even Christina and Jess had lost sleep for a week, afraid that he might get out of jail. He was a monster, and there was no way to reach him. And yet, hadn't she tried to reach Decker? Hadn't she gone above and beyond the call of duty? It was up to him now; she'd done all God had asked of her. Even though her heart had resisted. His eyes told her he was lost. Well, for good reason. He *was* lost. And none of it was her fault. None of it.

Decker's afternoon-long trial ended with Tora's testimony. The judge gently asked her to point toward the man who had kidnapped her, "manhandled" her, and then set her off on a train to Seattle with no money or food or water.

"There," she said, pointing toward Decker. It surprised her that her finger did not shake. She rose, suddenly uncontrollably furious. "That is the man!" she spat out. "He told me not to look out of that...*cattle car* or he would blow my 'pretty little head off.' What choice did I have? He's an animal, Your Honor."

The court erupted with the loud murmurs of the onlookers. The judge rapped his gavel on the desk and yelled, "Order, order! Get control or I'll throw the lot of you out the door!"

It immediately quieted, and Tora took her seat. "He deserves any punishment you give him, Your Honor," she said, turning back toward the judge and clutching her handkerchief. She wanted Decker to hang, to be out of her life forever.

"When exactly were you abducted, Miss Anders?" asked the kindly judge.

"Thanksgiving 1884."

"Nice day you chose, Mr. Decker," the judge said.

Tora dared to look at him. The prisoner did not deny his deeds. He just smiled.

"And there is no doubt in your mind that this is the man?"

"No doubt," she answered clearly. But inside, her heart began to dread what was happening. But why? Wasn't this going exactly as she wanted? Wasn't justice about to be served?

The judge turned toward Decker when he took the stand. "Mr. Decker, what defense have you?"

Decker smirked and leered at Tora, then said smugly, "I ain't never seen this woman before, or her fancy boyfriend until he shot me down when she and I were having ourselves a conversation, gettin' to know each other one evening at the restaurant."

Tora gasped at his blatant lie. Decker's eyes turned to her with a leer. Her gasp had given him a sense of control, and Tora dropped her eyes, refusing to give him the power.

The judge went on questioning him. "How do you account for your bullet wounds?"

"Her boyfriend was just jealous when he found her making eyes at me."

The judge sighed heavily, as if tired of his obvious lies. "Do you have anything else to add, Mr. Decker?" the judge prodded.

Decker looked up as if in a stupor and said, "What more is there to say, Your Honor? If I ain't done it, I ain't done it."

"Well, by Miss Anders's testimony and Mr. Storm's testimony of Mr. Decker's second attempt at kidnapping and aggravated assault, I have come to a decision."

Tora's mouth was dry.

"Frank Decker," he said, staring at the prisoner. "You have erred for the last time. You will be hanged in the public square at noon tomorrow." He pounded his gavel on the desk.

But all Tora could think about was Decker's name.

Frank. It was such a plain, honest name.

His mother had looked down at him as a child and caressed his cheek and called him Frank.

The next day, Frank Decker was led to the gallows hastily constructed on the same platform that had been used for Kaatje's celebration four days prior.

Trent stood at Tora's side, with an arm protectively around her. Kaatje was there too, the girls firmly told to stay at home with Charlie.

The deputy and two volunteers led Decker up the stairs to the platform. A pastor in a clerical collar read some Scripture verses, and then the deputy asked Decker if he had any last words.

He laughed under his breath and shook his head. For the first time, there was some hint of hesitation on his part, as if he dreaded what was to come.

Tora held her breath as two men turned him toward the noose. One slipped it over his head while the other tied his hands behind his back. Someone offered him a hood, but he shook his head, his lips clenched together.

Now is the time. Forgive him. For you as much as for him. He is paying the price, God spoke to Tora's heart.

Tora tried to say something, but quickly clamped her lips shut. *He wronged me,* she silently screamed. *He hurt me!*

Now is the time.

But he wronged me, Lord. He killed a part of me. He robbed me of…me.

He killed the part that held you from me. Now is the time.

But stubbornly she kept her lips clamped shut. She would not forgive him. She would not!

Frank Decker searched the crowd, found her, and winked. He winked, of all things! Trent's hand tightened on her shoulder, and she could feel him tense.

Tora turned toward Trent then, burying her face in his chest, wanting to run away from the scene before her. She kept listening though, unable to turn and watch the platform floor open beneath Frank Decker, his body descending, the crowd ogling, the rope growing taut, or his neck breaking. But she heard it. Everyone heard it.

Tora sat on the porch, rocking fast, refusing to speak to Trent, to anyone. Kaatje let her sit awhile alone, until the sun set and her breath fogged into small clouds in front of her face. Tora had to be cold, chilled to the bone by now. Quickly Kaatje poured two cups of tea and headed out. The restaurant had been closed for the day, the proprietors more interested in the day's events than commerce.

She thought it incongruent, somehow, that the sun could give such a brilliant display as it left the horizon. This day, of all days. It would have suited better to be socked in with clouds, the sun leaving their part of the world with a muted, understated good-bye.

Kaatje sat down in the rocker opposite Tora and stretched out her arm with the other mug of tea. "Here," she demanded, "take it."

She waited for a few seconds before Tora seemed to come out of her stupor and reached bluish fingers toward the mug. "Do you not think it's time to come in, Tora?"

"In a bit," she mumbled.

Kaatje took a sip of her own tea, wrapped her shawl more snugly around her shoulders, and then sat back to rock. After a moment she spoke, carefully choosing her words. "I expect that what happened today is very difficult for you."

"You know nothing of what I'm feeling," Tora shot back, then said, "I'm sorry."

Kaatje let her words sit for a moment, continuing to rock. "Do you think you reached him at all? Do you think he might have believed?"

Tora said nothing, staring through the dancing tendrils of steam that rose from the tea, toward the farrier's place across the street or beyond. "I don't know. I doubt it. He never gave me any indication that he had."

Kaatje rocked with her in companionable silence. "It's a question that's plagued me of late. I can't decide if Soren has honestly changed and if I should give him a chance, or if I should send him packing."

"At least you still have the chance."

Kaatje looked down at her tea. So that was it—Tora was feeling guilty. "He committed crimes against you. He deserved his fate."

"And I wanted him dead," she whispered, so low that Kaatje almost missed it as a team of horses pulling a wagon drove by.

"Sometimes hate is hard to overcome. Why don't you give yourself some time? He did some hateful things to you. You're feeling the first vestiges of forgiveness—that's hard stuff after hating someone for so long."

"Like Soren?"

"Like Soren."

"Like you hated me?"

Kaatje paused for a moment. "Yes, like you once."

"Kaatje," Tora asked, looking her in the eye for the first time. "What would you do in my position? If God had called you to speak to him, to reach out to him, would you have done so?"

"I expect so. But it would've been one of the hardest tasks I ever faced. Tora, there was no hope for Frank Decker to clear his name. He was to be hanged, regardless of what you said." She reached out and grasped her hand.

Tora nodded, but there were no tears. "It's not that I thought I could stop the hanging. I only wonder now if I should've forgiven him before he…died. Maybe if I had found the courage to say it, say it out loud, he might have seen God for the first time."

"That would have been a tall order."

"It was. And I failed him. I failed God." She sat silent, morose for a while before she said, "I think I'll go in. Suddenly I'm very, very tired."

"All right. Tora?"

"Yes?"

"It won't be the first time you've failed God. But we live with a God of grace. He'll give you another chance."

She paused, not turning back, but she had obviously heard her. "See you in the morning, Kaatje."

"Tora, there's one more thing."

"Yes?" she asked quietly. This time she looked at Kaatje.

"I want you to think about something. Think about that day you came to my farm. Think about what it would've been like had I not offered you a chance at redemption, even if you had never come to me. At some point, it would have kept *me* from moving on. And then give yourself some time to do the same for Frank Decker. It's too late for him. But not for you."

Tora stood for a moment, then left the porch without another word.

Soren watched as Tora walked inside. He stepped forward and then back, unable to decide if it was a wise time to approach Kaatje. But her expression and stance seemed mellow, open somehow. He had been practicing his words all evening, ever since Frank Decker's neck broke at the end of the rope.

Decided now, he waited for a horseman to pass, then two girls, then he crossed the street. Kaatje still had not seen him, apparently lost in reverie. He stepped up on the deck. "Penny for your thoughts."

She looked at him in surprise, then away. "My thoughts cannot be purchased."

"Fair enough," he said, taking off his hat. "May I sit?"

"Go ahead," she said dully.

"Kaatje, I've been thinking. I was there today at the hanging." She didn't answer. "I saw that man up by those gallows, and I couldn't help but see him as me, that rope as the death of our marriage."

Soren swallowed hard and knelt before her. He took her hands before she could pull them into a ball in her lap. "When he was hanged, the life gone from his body, all his opportunities were gone. That was the end of it. In the same way, I can't get past the idea that if you don't give me one more chance, our marriage will die too."

She looked up at him then, her hazel eyes staring into his soul. He fought to keep his eyes on hers, afraid that she might see the truth there, the truth that he didn't deserve Kaatje Janssen as his wife. But his future depended upon them being together. Their future. "Kaatje, give me one more chance. Please. I know it's the last time. I know it. One more try."

Kaatje stared into his eyes and then looked across the street. Suddenly she pulled her hands from his, and Soren fought the urge to swear. He could feel it; he was losing her. His eyes followed her gaze across the street.

To James Walker.

That was it. Soren had had enough. James was in his way. And he had to be removed.

It was his only chance to get to Kaatje.

That night he waited for James to follow him from the roadhouse back to his hotel. He was aware that James or his Indian sidekick followed every move he made. But tonight Soren had a surprise for him. He walked straight down the street, then disappeared through the swinging doors of the Hanging Moon Saloon. He waited for a minute, ignoring the bartender's request for a drink order, then headed back out the doors.

Just as he suspected, James was walking toward the saloon, as if checking on him.

Soren headed straight for him, never wavering. "You want a fight? Let's fight! You can watch me all you want, Walker. Watch me take back my wife and leave you in the dust." With his last word, he shoved James away from him. "It's eating you alive, isn't it, Walker? Watching me with her, touching her."

Dimly, he was aware of passersby stopping to gawk.

"Back off, Soren," James warned, rubbing his mouth with the back of his hand. "I don't want to fight you."

"Don't you? Don't you? Everything in me says different. No, you don't want to fight me, Walker. You want to remove me. But that's not going to happen."

"I only care about Kaatje. You, I could never care about." James watched Soren from the corners of his eyes.

Soren could tell James wanted to hit him. What would it take to get him there?

197

"No? What if I told you that Kaatje would be mine again soon? She's my wife. Mine. I'm going to lose patience soon and just kiss her, take what's mine. It's my right. And I'm going to tell her I saw you out with a whore last night. That'll end any feelings she has for you. What would you say to that?"

Soren didn't even see the punches coming. One went to his stomach, driving the breath from his gut, a second to his face, splitting his upper lip.

If he hadn't been fighting for breath, he would've laughed.

Everything was working out perfectly.

Just as he planned.

James was confused. Soren looked as if he were laughing at him, even though he fought for breath. Oh, how good those punches had felt! He had longed to drive the breath from Soren's greedy gut, do some damage to that perfect face. And now he had. What was that sudden, stabbing feeling of remorse? James couldn't get past the idea that he had taken a drastically bad step, regardless of the primal, physical pleasure it brought him.

"What? What?" he screamed, kicking dust at Soren's shoulder. "What are you smiling about? What? I'll wipe that smile from your face—" Suddenly Kadachan was there, pulling him away from Soren, telling him to calm down. He couldn't make out the words; he understood his intent from his friend's tone. Kadachan took him to the nearest porch, where he sat James down and retrieved his hat.

He brought it back, brushing off the brim as he purposefully blocked James's view of Soren. Last thing James saw, someone was helping the slime off the street. Next time Soren came into view, he was heading down toward Kaatje's, throwing that same sinister grin back toward James.

James groaned and leaned back on the porch, covering his face with his hands.

"What is it?" Kadachan asked. "Are you hurt?"

James was silent for a moment. Then, "Nothing I didn't do to myself. That man has been begging me to slug him ever since he showed up."

"And?"

"And so tonight I did. And I knew right away in my gut that something was amiss."

"What?"

"Look where he's going," James said, unable to watch with his friend.

"To Kaatje."

"Exactly. She's been barely warding him off. The wounds I've inflicted tonight will drive her straight into his arms. There's one thing she can't resist, and that's the bruised and broken. He's got the broken act down, and now I've added the bruises."

seventeen

Mid-October 1888

The crew was wild in their excitement; for eight days running, the *Majestic* had beaten the huge *Fair Alaska,* and the crew had dined in her fine quarters every evening. Elsa strode across the deck, hands at her lower back, children following close behind. Today Karl was giving them a run for their money.

"Think he's been letting us have the lead this past week?" Riley asked.

"I doubt it. It's cost him a fortune in food, to say nothing of the damage to his male pride."

"They're setting all sails!" cried the sailor in the crow's nest, who had been watching the competition more than anything else.

"Set all sails?" Eric asked, his eyes alight.

Elsa frowned. The wind was stiff. Setting all sails was a dangerous proposition, but one that might well put them more firmly in the lead; if they did not match sail, it was certain that they would be serving the crew of the *Fair Alaska* this night. She glanced at Riley, and he gave her a small frown, a subtle shake of the head.

"Set all sails," she said firmly, keeping her eyes from Riley.

"Set all sails!" Eric yelled. The crew scrambled across lanyards high above them, anxious to give their boilers a boost and win the day again.

Elsa looked above at the streamer that showed the wind's direction. "She's coming from the southwest, Riley. In another fifty miles
or so, she'll switch to a northwester. It almost always proves true. If I
were a gambling woman, I'd guess that there's a fair chance Karl doesn't
know of the change. He hasn't traveled much in these waters."

"And you distracted him from his charts last night," Riley said,
giving her a knowing look. "So we'll let them pull ahead a bit near
the changeover and prepare the *Majestic* for the drift."

"Yes. And we'll catch the wind and swoop by them just in time
for supper," she said, clapping her hands together in excitement.

"I still don't think it's wise, ma'am," Riley said discreetly. "The
wind's stiff. We're putting the ship and her crew in danger."

"We have the best, Riley," she said. "If it gets rough, we'll reef the
royals and gallants."

He still looked unsure. The ship noticeably leaned with the wind
just as the highest sails came down from their lanyards and into
place.

She rested one hand on his shoulder. "Be at peace, Riley. If need
be, let the *Fair Alaska* win this night in order to keep us safe. But give
them a run!"

His smile returned. "Aye, aye."

She leaned closer and whispered, "I'll tell Cook to prepare for the
worst, and if it doesn't happen, we'll have his fine meal for noon dinner tomorrow."

He nodded and looked upward, ordering a crew member here
and there while letting Kristian take a turn at the wheel.

"Eve!" Elsa called. "You come with me. You need to stay by my
side in these seas, or in the cabin. I'll not have you falling overboard.
Come, come inside. We'll get Mouser out."

That sent her running. Her pet cat was allowed out once in the
morning to play with Eve and then stayed mostly belowdecks all afternoon to hunt for rats. Surprisingly, considering the sizable rats Mouser
killed, he was very loving with Eve. Elsa, he could take or leave. And

he openly despised Kristian; Elsa suspected her son had pulled his tail once too many times as a kitten.

Since he was given to shredding her linens, Mouser lived in a fairly large crate, which Eve carefully lined with an old baby blanket. He gave them a *meow* combined with a yawn as they entered, and pounced on the ball of yarn that Eve wiggled in front of his now-open door.

Elsa sat down to draw the child and pet. They both were in such high spirits that Elsa could do nothing else. She wanted to capture this moment forever. Someday she wanted to get one of those new Kodak Snapshots for moments such as these. Imagine! Having the chance to take a picture rather than to draw it!

She opened her box of coal pencils and put a large canvas on her easel. Then, before the moment was over, she sketched the main por-tions of body stance and several details of expression. As had become her habit, she would create the rest from memory as cat and girl moved on to hunt for dust balls underneath her four-poster bed. Some details she would make up from sheer familiarity.

By noon dinner, the *Fair Alaska* was leading by half a league or more. The crew, dog-tired already from their busy morning of reefing and unfurling sails, dragged into the dining hall and wolfed down all the food Cook and his three assistants put before them.

"Look at 'em, Cap'n," Riley said to her in an aside. "We'll never get ahead of Cap'n Martensen now."

"Sure we will. Inform the crew of our plans. A little food in their bellies and being in on the idea will rejuvenate them."

"Aye, Cap'n," he said with a wink.

Elsa left him to oversee the portion of the crew who had already eaten. "All right, listen ho!" she called. "We need all men pulling extra sails out of the poop deck storage room."

"But Cap'n," one dared, after eyeing his silent but uneasy mates. "The *Majestic* canno' handle any more sail! Why not say we're done beat for today and just ready supper for the other crew?"

"Agreed on one count, sailor. But we're going to beat the *Fair Alaska* this eve, if we're crafty enough. We need the extra sails to throw them off. We'll hang them as decoys on one side of the ship, so they cannot see us tacking. They're so bent on beating us, that the mate and I are wagering that they're not consulting their charts, nor anticipating the change twenty miles distant now. By the time the sailor in the crow's nest scouts the wind on the sea, and the crew gets the ship turned, we'll be past 'em!" she said with glee, slapping one hand past the other.

"Three cheers for the cap'n!" one called.

"Hey-oh! Hey-oh! *Hey-oh!*" they called as one. Then they immediately set upon their task. They might question her a bit more than a male captain, Elsa mused, but when she explained herself, they went along with her decision. And in a crisis, they never faltered when she ordered them about. All in all, all was well aboard her ship.

"What *are* they *doing?*" Karl muttered, still staring through the telescope back at the *Majestic*. For two hours now, their sails had been fluttering in the wind as if not tied down. Were they not even making use of the sail that was unfurled? And even at this distance, it seemed to him that they were tacking already, but in doing so, already falling behind. It made no sense. It was as if they were preparing...

"Luke, did you look at the wind charts last night?"

His first mate shifted uneasily. "I'm sorry... I merely took down notes of speed and distance covered. I was going for the charts when the crew of the *Majestic* arrived and you called me out." He swallowed audibly. "I'm sorry, Cap'n. I confess I didn't get back to them."

"Come with me," Karl said urgently. Elsa had something up her sleeve; he was almost sure of it. And didn't the wind change direction at about this latitude?

A sailor's call from the crow's nest cut their walk short. "Cap'n!" he shouted. "Wind change ahead! Wind change ahead!"

Karl took off his hat and threw it to the ground. On the very day he was going to beat the *Majestic*! Luke gave him a knowing look. He knew it would end the race. He ran back toward the bridge. "All hands! *All hands!* Tacking for a northwester! Prepare to come about! *Prepare to come about!*"

But Karl was already looking through his telescope as the wind waned and his sails flapped like dying fish. As they wafted back and forth above him, and the crew began untying ropes and hauling them around capstans, only the boilers kept them from being left dead in the water. He grimaced. The desire to win and lack of preparation had been their downfall. How often had that duo hurt him in the past?

As he watched, sails on the *Majestic* were dropped to the ground, undisguised now as her remaining sails caught the new wind, and the *Majestic* jolted forward, running dangerously between wind and water, yet holding her course. Within minutes, they were alongside the *Fair Alaska*, and after half an hour more, well ahead of them as their own sails were finally in place.

Karl groaned and then shook his head ruefully.

There was no doubt in his mind how bad the evening would be; Elsa's crew would crow like roosters and make them *eat* crow all night.

"Good evening, Captain," Elsa said sweetly, as she took his hand and climbed aboard ship.

"Uncle Karl! Uncle Karl!" the kids cried as they climbed in beside her. "Wasn't that great?" Kristian cried. "You thought you had us beat when *whoosh*, we passed you!"

"*Great* wasn't the first word that came to my mind," Karl said, ruffling his hair.

Elsa couldn't help but grin. "You thought you had us in the bag. Proves that all is not always as it seems."

"Yes, but have you seen our open spit? I doubt you can afford the deck space for such extravagance."

Elsa raised her eyebrows and took his proffered arm. "No, I cannot. But I can smell something divine. Did your cook put it on about three?" she asked, referring to when they passed the *Majestic*.

Karl looked rueful. "I'm afraid so. We'll have to wait on supper for a few hours yet. Until then, the men want to do some singing on deck. While we wait for the singing and dancing, how about accompanying me to the game room?" Karl invited. The children readily agreed. Under a portion of covered deck, there were several shuffleboards, as well as checkers and backgammon. As the children took up their mallets and began playing, Karl helped Elsa to a deck chair.

"Well, our ship is not all this, but I'd say she's faster," Elsa taunted her friend. He was handsome tonight; he remained in what she assumed were his day clothes, with a soft white cotton shirt open at the neck, allowing soft tufts of chest hair to peek out. His shoulder-length, sandy hair was coming loose from the ponytail, and again she could imagine what it would look like down, softly waving. And he wore a gold earring through one lobe, something she had seen only once or twice before.

He caught her staring, and she quickly looked toward the children, feeling the heat climb up her neck. "Going a bit more casual this evening?" she said, unable to come up with something better to fill the silence.

"I thought it best for a pig roast."

"You do not fear a fire with an open pit aboard ship?"

"No. Kristoffer had it lined with iron and suspended. There's nothing to burn."

They sat in companionable silence for a while, watching Eve and Kristian, laughing with them.

"You're proud of yourself today, aren't you?" he asked.

"And you're ashamed. I can feel it."

"Foolish of me, not checking the wind charts myself. I even knew they were coming. I was just so taken with actually winning the day that I didn't research the best tactic of all." He waited until she looked at him. She could feel the heat of his stare. "You're a fine captain, Elsa."

"As are you, Karl."

"Thank you. My wounded pride will accept any frivolous compliment you care to toss my way."

"No, truly. You made a mistake today, as we all do from time to time. But your crew obviously loves you, respects you."

"Not as much as yours."

She accepted his words in silence. "They are remarkable, my men. God has blessed me to find them all. As a female, my life could be very difficult as a captain. Instead it is a dream with the men I've chosen."

He paused, as if wanting to comment, and Elsa thought back on her words. Was he thinking about the men she'd chosen? About choosing one man? She let it go, uncomfortable at the thought of trying to get him to express what he was thinking. There was an electricity between them, something beyond anything she had ever experienced before. The side of her arm that was nearest to him felt warm, and she longed for the brush of his skin against hers.

"What about Mara Kenney?" she blurted out, instantly regretting her words.

He looked confused. "What brought her to mind?"

"Nothing. I was just thinking. What does she think of you shipping off for distant lands? Are you considering marriage? Will she move to Alaska?"

Karl laughed under his breath at her barrage of questions and cocked his head. "Why so curious?"

"Oh, no reason. But as your oldest friend near you, I felt as if someone should ask."

"Someone. Hmm."

"You know, in looking out for you."

"For me."

"Stop repeating what I'm saying, Karl Martensen! You're twisting my words!"

"Am I?"

She stared at him and blinked rapidly. Oh, he was infuriating! Did he love Mara or not? She couldn't seem to get it out of him. One minute he was saying they were just friends, the next he was commenting on how dear his friendship was. And what better foundation for a marriage than friendship was there?

The thought stopped her, and she stared dead ahead. Not only was Karl her equal, someone she could easily respect, he was also one of her oldest and dearest friends.

Lucas interrupted her thoughts. "Captain, we're ready to start. Care to join us?" His question was for all of them, but his eyes were on Elsa. He was handsome, she thought again, as she had in Panama, but then she looked at her old friend as he helped her to her feet.

Luke was no Karl.

Karl held her hand, held *her* close for a moment longer than necessary. Elsa quickly stepped away. The children bounded away with Luke, racing ahead of him, already knowing the ship as well as their own. The door swung shut behind them, and for a second Elsa and he were alone. He pulled her to a stop and turned her back toward him.

She looked up at him in confusion, her blue eyes huge in that perfect, sculpted face.

"Venus," he whispered, caressing her cheek.

"What?" she asked, her eyebrows furrowing.

"Elsa, I've tried to tell you so many times. And so I'll just do it now. Mara and I are only friends. Only friends. Her family is dear to me, but when I was in San Francisco last, I told her that there wasn't anything in my heart more than friendship." He forced his hands to his sides, not wanting to touch her if she did not want to be touched. Never again would he force himself on her as he had that night he kissed her.

"You're not...to be engaged?"

"No."

"There is someone else?"

"There is."

She studied him intently. "Me?" she whispered, her eyebrows rising. He could barely nod, feeling as if his feet were frozen to the spot.

She let out a sudden breath of air, like a laugh of relief? But he had no time to further consider it as she ran her hands up his arms and cupped his cheeks as if she were cherishing the moment. Was he dreaming? Was this real? She reached up behind him, her body coming closer as she reached for his ponytail strap and released the leather.

Her body was so warm, and fit so well against him! He fought the urge to put his arms around her until invited.

As if reading his thoughts, she whispered lowly, "Hold me, Karl." He could feel his hair fall to his ears as he looked down at her, slowly, reverently pulling her close.

"I don't want to push you," he said through gritted teeth, closing his eyes, fighting for control. "I never want to push you again. You mean too much to me, Elsa. As my friend."

"You're not," she said, running her small hands around him, pulling him even closer. She raised her chin and stared at him with lowered lids. "Kiss me. Kiss me, please."

He needed no further invitation. He kissed her with all the passion of love lost, and love found again. And he pulled her to him with all the desire he had found rekindled since seeing her again in San Francisco in the ball gown he had purchased for her a continent away.

Finally, their lips parted, and Elsa gazed up at him in wonder. "I thought I would never find love again, Karl. I thought I would never again know passion. I'd forgotten. I'd forgotten what this feels like."

"I won't let you forget it again," he promised, caressing her brow and hair, wishing they were married, wishing he could hold her into the night and forever. "Never again, Elsa."

And it was she who kissed him then.

The sound of singing brought them up for air, and they took a step away from each other. "We have much to discuss," Karl said.

"Yes," she agreed, smoothing her hair. "Let's take some time, and we'll have dinner tomorrow night."

"And the next."

"And the next," she said with a smile. She took his hands in hers and grinned up at him. "This makes me so happy, Karl. Truly."

"And me, Elsa. More than I can say. You must know that I never planned to pursue you unless you came to me first."

"Because of…what happened."

"Yes."

"I understand that. I understand your heart," she said, placing a hand on his chest. "I was married to your best friend. Is it so odd that we would find love too? After all, there is much you and Peder had in common."

Her words concerned him. "I am not Peder."

"I know that," she said with a small laugh. "I do not expect you to be Peder, except for the ways that you are. You're loyal and smart and dear, just as he was." She laughed again. "But hopefully not as pigheaded."

"Not nearly as pigheaded," he said with a firm nod and smile.

She shook her head with a slight smile. "Oh, Karl. Oh, Karl!"

"Come, love," he said, taking her hand. "We've tarried long enough to get both crews talking. No doubt they're having a laugh on us."

She leaned her head on his shoulder as they walked. "Let them laugh. I feel like laughing and never stopping myself."

eighteen

"Anyone home? Hello!"

Tora frowned. It was early yet for any customers, just three, she saw, glancing at the kitchen clock. And that voice sounded familiar... No, it was too much to hope for. But it sure sounded like Elsa. Tora was just wiping her hands on her apron, telling Kaatje and the girls that she would see to the woman, when Elsa burst through the kitchen door.

"Surprise!" she shouted, opening her arms wide. Her face was pink with merriment, and she was as beautiful as ever, Tora mused, rushing toward her for a hug.

"Elsa! Oh, I'm so glad you're here!" she exclaimed.

"As am I!" She turned toward Kaatje and then the girls, giving them each a hug as well.

"When did you arrive?" Tora asked, weaving her arm through her sister's.

"Never mind that!" Elsa said. "Have I missed it?"

"Missed what?"

"The wedding!"

"No, it isn't for two weeks yet."

Elsa sighed and smiled. "I'm so relieved. I was afraid you'd given up on my return and gone ahead with it."

210

"Much to Trent's chagrin; he wanted to elope long ago. But Tora was bound and determined to have her sister here," Kaatje said, placing her hands on Elsa's and Tora's shoulders. "Trent would not have put up with yet another postponement. You came just in time." She paused for a second. "And we've had other things going on around here."

"Oh?"

"We'll talk about all that later. Where are your children?" Tora asked, evading the issue.

"Out in the restaurant. We ran into Trent, and they're with him and Karl."

"Karl? Karl Martensen?" Kaatje asked as she winked at Tora.

"Yes," Elsa said.

"You're falling in love," Tora said, crossing her arms and circling Elsa in examination.

"What?"

"Why yes, that's it," Kaatje added, looking at her from the other side. "That high color, her demeanor…"

"I don't know of what you speak," Elsa said, lifting her chin, even as she smiled.

"Oh yes, you do," Kaatje returned.

"You and Karl finally put two and two together," Tora said. "It took you long enough."

"Tora, we just were reunited," Elsa said as if cross. "And I've been in mourning."

"Yes, but you would never have given him a chance before."

Elsa looked down at Jessica and Christina, who were glued to the women's conversation. "Shouldn't you two go and see my children? They've been asking after you for weeks!"

The girls left the kitchen, giggling and exchanging knowing looks.

Elsa took a step away, wiping her finger through the flour on the baking table absent-mindedly. "It's true. It's only recently that I felt…ready. I'm still not sure of what I'm doing. I am still not sure it's love," Elsa confessed.

"Of course you're not sure of yourself; you are in love," Kaatje said. Was that a wistful expression on her face? Tora examined her friend for a moment. Kaatje deserved to find that kind of love, the kind she and Trent had, the kind she could see blossoming in Elsa's eyes. But was she thinking of her lout of a husband or of James Walker? Soren had certainly been persistent in pursuing her in the weeks he'd been back—but there was still something wrong, something underhanded about the man that she couldn't quite pin down. On the other hand, Tora could sense a tension between Kaatje and James whenever they were together, as if something had happened between them those months on the trail. Poor Kaatje! Tora didn't envy her position.

Tired suddenly, Tora pulled Kaatje in and hugged both Elsa and her friend at the same time. "Now I am ready to get married," she said. "You are both here!"

"I am glad," Elsa responded. "Because Mother sent a special present home with me."

"Not a wedding costume," Tora blurted out. Oh, how she had wished for one!

"Yes. The one that Grandmother, Mother, Carina, and I all wore. There is a lot of love represented in that costume. It will be perfect for you and Trent."

"If only Trent would wear a bunad too!" Tora said, chuckling.

"Oh, he will. You marry a Norsk, you become a Norsk by marriage. It is only fitting that he wear a costume to match yours."

Tora shook her head. "No. There is no way. Even you cannot convince my future husband to wear a bunad."

"Tora Anders!" Elsa exclaimed, her slim eyebrows lowering in consternation. "We have been apart far too long! Have you forgotten? I am a captain on the high seas! I brought one home, just for him. Just give me some time—"

Kaatje laughed and nodded. "Yes, she's used to ordering men around!"

A knock at the back door brought them all to silence. Kaatje walked toward it, her step light. Elsa's arrival had lightened her burdens; Tora could see it in her face. But when she opened the door, her shoulders slumped. It was Soren.

If only they had had a chance to warn Elsa! She shot her sister a look, hoping to convey a bit of information in silence, but Soren was already coming through the door. Tora couldn't bear to look at him, so great was her disdain. Instead she focused on Elsa and saw in her sister all that she felt.

"Why, if it isn't the great Heroine of the Horn," Soren said, opening his arms as if to embrace her.

"Soren," she greeted him flatly, a bit breathless in her surprise. She made no move toward him.

He dropped his arms. "When did you get in to Juneau?"

"Just today." She quickly found her lung capacity again. "The better question is, when did you? Or did your wife have to cover the entire Yukon before you came out of some cave?"

"Elsa!" Kaatje exclaimed. "Please..."

"Please what?" Elsa asked her, her face a mask of confusion—combining all the fury and fear that Tora had experienced these last weeks. "Please welcome the man who abandoned you? Oh, Kaatje! I knew you were looking for him, but frankly, I hoped you would find...forgive me." She turned toward the kitchen door as if to flee. "I cannot be trusted not to say too much." And with that, she left.

"Excuse me," Tora said, wanting out as much as her sister. But Soren stopped her with a gentle hand.

"Are you never going to give me a chance either?" Soren asked.

"Let go of me, Soren."

He dropped his hand obediently and raised it as if to show he had meant no harm.

Tora sighed. "I cannot speak for the future, Soren. I can only speak for today." She shot a look at Kaatje, begging her forgiveness for what she had to say. "And today, I cannot give you another chance. I fear that you are not as changed as you claim, and I fear for Kaatje." Then she passed through the doors and walked across the restaurant floor to Trent and the others, forcing a smile.

As if sensing her mood, Trent raised one arm beckoning her, and she gratefully sank against his side. His touch felt warm and protective. And after Karl and Tora briefly greeted each other, he went on chatting with Karl about the trip.

"You look wonderful," Karl said gently to Tora. "It must be your upcoming nuptials."

"Thank you, Karl. And you look wonderful too. Could it be that there's love in your life as well?" Trent nudged her, and Elsa narrowed a look in her direction.

"It could be," Karl said, slanting a glance at Elsa.

Elsa smiled uneasily, clearly uncomfortable, and then leaned toward Tora. "Come. I must know about Soren. Excuse us," she said to the men. The children had evidently gone off to play outside on the swing and seesaw Trent had constructed for them last month.

"Tell me," Elsa said, sitting down at a table for two by the window.

"He showed up last month," Tora said. "And I've been wrestling with it the whole time. Kaatje is too. Think of it! She journeyed the whole trip along that river—was gone for four and a half months! And no sight of him. She came home ready to have the circuit judge declare him dead."

"Truthfully?" Elsa asked in wonder, obviously not doubting Tora's word, simply trying to digest all of it.

"Truthfully. Worse, she was falling in love with her guide, James Walker."

"What?" Elsa gasped, her eyes widening. Her hand went to her mouth, and then she looked as if she were ready to cry. "Oh, how can it be? Finally Kaatje finds someone worthy of her...and then he decides to show up!"

Tora nodded.

"Where is the other man? James..."

"Walker. James Walker. Oh, Elsa, he's wonderful. Everything Kaatje deserves. And so wounded. He walks about town looking like a beaten dog."

"And unable to do anything because Kaatje's husband is here."

"And Soren's been trying to win her back."

"Why? Why now? There has to be a reason. After all this time."

"I think Kaatje wonders too. Trent and I do. In fact, Trent has hired his private investigator, Joseph Campbell, to come out and check on Soren's story. We want Kaatje to know everything she can before she makes the decision to reunite with him. I hope we get word from Joseph soon. Kaatje is warming up to Soren. I can see it."

"What was his excuse for being gone so long without a word?"

"He says he thought she would have had him proclaimed dead a long time ago. That she would've moved on. When she came along the river leaving word everywhere about the man she sought, he claims he came right away."

Kaatje came through the door alone. Elsa chanced one more question. "How did he split his lip?"

"James helped him with that one," Tora whispered.

"Are you two talking wedding plans without me?" Kaatje asked, a thin smile upon her lips.

"No. But we should be," Elsa said. "Come on, you two. The dress is in the coach. Let's go and fetch it!"

Two weeks later Elsa helped Tora into that same dress. Her younger sister was so nervous she was shaking. Elsa laughed. "I do not think I've ever seen you tremble, Tora Anders!"

"If there's any day that's appropriate, it would be a girl's wedding day," Kaatje said in defense, pushing Tora down into a chair and stroking her long, dark hair that reached her tiny waist. It was the color of the sea at night, Elsa mused. So striking, around her dark blue eyes. That blue was the only thing she and her sister shared, or at least that's what she used to believe. Now she knew that Tora was as fiercely loyal and devoted to her Lord as she, and it gave them a bond they'd never had before.

Elsa turned toward the bed and gestured toward the box. Jessie turned, retrieved it, and passed it along to her, a question in her eyes. Elsa pulled her head back, inviting them to watch.

"Tora, Mother sent something else for you for this day."

Tora looked up at her, and Elsa was surprised by the tears in her sister's eyes. How much she had changed! She had been utterly transformed! Elsa thought back to her own wedding in Bergen when she had worn the same dress. There were signs of generosity and true spirit in her sister then—she had hiked high into the hills around Bergen to find Elsa's favorite flowers for the church—but she had been largely self-indulgent and spoiled. Greedy. But there was none of that in her eyes now. It made Elsa choke up.

She knelt by Tora and watched as her sister opened the box. Inside, under the tissue, was a headdress made by hand, with elaborate needle-work over the crown. "She made it just for you, Tora. There was the family headdress, but she wanted to send something that would convey to you all the love she has in her heart. She worked for months on this."

Tora's eyes overflowed, and she quickly wiped the tears from her cheeks, apparently afraid that they would fall upon the incredible headdress.

"I told her, Tora," Elsa said, taking her sister's hand. "I told her that you were more than beautiful now, that you were...*skjønn*. That you were lovely from the inside out and that the Spirit of our Lord shines through you."

"Not always," Tora said, looking away.

"That's the thing," Kaatje said. "We don't always acknowledge him, but he's always there, shining whether we realize it or not."

"You seem shiny today, Auntie Tora," Jessica said, taking her hand. "Why are you sad?"

Tora laughed under her breath and wiped her eyes once more. "I am not sad, Jess. This day is the happiest in my life. I have all of you around me, and today, finally, Trent will make me his bride."

"You're the prettiest bride I've ever seen," Christina said.

"Just wait," Elsa said, rising. Kaatje finished Tora's hair, brought up in thick coils to a high crown, on top of which Elsa pinned the headdress. The threads from the fine needlework glinted in the lamplight. The girls said "ooh" together, and Kaatje sighed in appreciation as Tora stood. She turned toward the mirror. "Oh, Mama," she whispered. And then she turned to embrace Elsa.

"Come, it is time," Elsa said, taking her hand.

"Wait!" Tora turned to dab some color on her lips and pinch her cheeks. The girls giggled together as the music downstairs began to play. As Americans, and marrying an American, Tora had taken some of the new traditions. White fabric had been draped down the center of the nearly one hundred chairs, creating a luminous path side lit by dozens of candles. Tora would come forward to the minister, and Trent would be standing at the front of the restaurant before a cascade of fall flower arrangements in hues of yellow, orange, and red.

"Ready?" Elsa asked her, feeling a true bond with her sister, and a twinge of envy. "You look perfect."

"Thank you." She took Elsa's arm, her head only reaching her older sister's shoulder.

"I am sorry Father couldn't be here to do this American escort thing."

"Never mind. I'm glad it's you anyway. I couldn't tell Father that my stomach is threatening to leave without me. He would've never understood."

"Father was tough, but more loving than you ever gave him credit for being."

"We never…understood each other."

"It was a pity." They walked to the top of the stairs, and they could hear the crowd's whispering and the music jumping into sharp clarity. Jessie and Christina, at Elsa's cue, began their walk down the stairs, distributing flower petals as they went.

"He always favored you," Tora whispered, a tender note of jealousy in her voice.

"But it was you he always wanted close to him."

"No." They took the first steps behind the girls.

"Yes. That is why he didn't want you to come to America with us."

"No. It was because he was afraid I'd be a burden. Which I was—"

"No, Tora. He didn't want you to go because you were his baby. And he hadn't had the time to show you how much he loved you. How much you two had in common."

"Really?" Tora asked at the bottom of the stairs.

"Really." She smiled back at her sister and squeezed her hand. At least, that's what she hoped Amund Anders had felt. Amund had never been one to talk of anything personal unless pushed, and yet he had been the one to tell her of the northern lights and how they danced as David had danced in the streets of Jerusalem. How they whispered that God was near. Her father would've liked Alaska and her frequent view of the aurora borealis.

"I do not believe it," Tora whispered, as a new song entered the air around them, signaling Tora's turn to walk the aisle. She let out a delighted laugh.

"What?"

"You found a way to get Trent into a bunad."

Karl observed Tora across the other attendants, even held his breath for a second at the sight of her as she walked up the aisle, but found himself slightly irritated that she partially blocked his view of Elsa. Only the sight of the traditional Norwegian wedding dress brought him up short. The last time he remembered seeing the costume was on Elsa, the day she married Peder. The thought sobered him.

He concentrated on Bradford Bresley's shoulder instead of Tora's bridesmaid. As Americans, they had each asked two people to stand beside them this day; Tora had Kaatje and Elsa beside her, and Trent had Bradford and Karl. Bradford, Virginia, his wife, and their toddler had sailed up the Inside Passage the day before from the Storm Roadhouse in Ketchikan in order to take part in the festivities. Karl was almost as eager to catch up with them as he was to dance with Elsa that evening. Duties aboard the *Majestic* had kept them from each other the evening prior, and already he was missing her company.

The ceremony was soon over, and the hundred guests cheered as Trent finally got to kiss his bride. In his delight at the moment, Trent tenderly picked Tora up in his arms and swung her around, kissed her again as the people applauded, and then gently set her down. He gestured for silence. "A lot of you know that I've waited years to marry this woman, and today I have finally done it. In honor of the happiness I have in my heart, we've arranged a celebration that shows just how happy I am. Please join us in the tent behind the restaurant for a feast and dance before I steal my bride away for the night."

Karl smiled more broadly as Trent's neck colored a bit. Rarely had he seen the man blush. Happily, Karl waited to escort Elsa back down the aisle, following the bridal couple and Kaatje and Bradford. Perhaps one day he would be able to take Elsa down the aisle himself... He shook his head. He was getting way ahead of himself. Only the sight of Soren, sitting in the crowd, put a damper on his mood.

He hadn't had a chance to speak to the man alone yet. But he was dying to do so. His hands opened and clenched at the thought of it. How could the man have abandoned Kaatje, then shown up after all these years? If he was going to pretend he was dead, he should have had the decency to stay dead! Elsa pulled him forward as he paused and stared for a tiny moment, wanting to call Soren out. She seemed to sense what he was feeling and whispered in his ear, "This is Trent and Tora's day. Let us not do anything that might ruin it."

He nodded once. "I will be able to concentrate on them and their pleasure if you stay by my side."

She smiled and looked at the floor. "All right," she agreed quietly.

He escorted her around the roadhouse, gazing up at dark storm clouds that threatened the day with a fall shower. "It could even hail."

"Shush. Don't let it hear you. This tent can tolerate some rain, but not much else."

He tucked her hand more firmly in the crook of his arm as he caught sight of Soren ahead, at the opening of the tent. Somehow he had beaten them. The man actually had the audacity to reach out a hand as if to shake his, and Karl looked at him in disbelief. He pulled Elsa to a stop and shook his finger at Soren. "Watch yourself, man. Watch yourself very closely. Kaatje has many friends now. Many friends who do not appreciate the fact that you abandoned your wife."

Soren picked up his chin, and his smile disappeared. "Whatever the case may be, she is still my wife."

"Lus," Karl growled under his breath, as Elsa urged him forward. "We'll speak again. In private." How he longed to punch the louse in the mouth! He was no better than the bedbugs that plagued sailors on ships.

"I shall look forward to it!" Soren called, lifting a hand and smiling as if Karl had just invited him to his ship for supper. Just then, Kaatje reached him and accepted his hand. The sight of it grated on Karl's nerves.

"It is her business, Karl," Elsa said firmly. "Her business. Whatever she decides, we need to support her."

"Maybe several of us men should help make her decision easier. Make him disappear again. Forever."

"Karl Martensen!"

"I am only joking. That man gets under my skin like no other."

"He's a tick all right," she said. "Come." She walked backward, leading him forward with both hands. "Isn't it wonderful?" She gestured all about them, and Karl finally looked around, casting out Soren's image.

"It is," he said, shaking his head. Trent had spared no expense. The entire tent was made up of intimate, round tables set for four, with thousands of candles and greenery with small white flowers that proved to be jasmine. No doubt Trent had ordered it carefully packed and shipped to Alaska directly from Hawaii. Their fragrance filled the air, even if they were a bit wilted. In all four corners, wood stoves were blazing and pumping heat into the outdoor ballroom. A small orchestra was playing on one side, mostly soft chamber music as the guests milled about finding their seats.

The china was Limoges, the crystal Baccarat. There were sterling silver place settings at each of the hundred seats. "Trent's wedding gift to Tora," Elsa whispered, waving over it all. Karl whistled lowly. "Just one of them. He is taking her to Hawaii and then Japan for an extended honeymoon."

"After all these years, they deserve it."

"Amen," Elsa said.

Where would he take Elsa on a honeymoon? Karl thought. She had seen much of the world as a captain, but he didn't think she had been to Egypt. Perhaps Cairo, and then a cruise down the Nile. There were archaeologists there, rumored to have found a valley full of ancient cities and artifacts. Luxor on the Nile, they were calling it. Yes, it would take something like that to be worthy of her... *Quit, Karl,* he told himself. *Quit it. Your relationship has yet to begin, and you are already planning a honeymoon?* He laughed aloud.

"What?" Elsa asked, her lips spreading over perfect, white teeth.

"Nothing," he evaded.

"Tell me," she demanded lowly, leaning closer to him.

Bradford saved him. Almost. He interrupted them by saying, "You had better not let Mara Kenney see you two like that."

Elsa looked at Bradford in surprise and then at Karl in confusion.

"I've ended things with Miss Kenney, Bradford."

"I see," Bradford said, smiling at Elsa.

Tora came then and whispered in her ear. Elsa immediately rose to go. "I had better see to the bride. See you soon," she said softly to Karl.

Bradford and Virginia nodded, looking at Karl meaningfully as Elsa walked away.

Karl sighed. "I suppose you two want to know what has transpired between me and Elsa."

Karl did not catch up with her until much later that evening. Kristian had taken her seat, apparently at her behest. Elsa lingered at her dinner table, talking intently with her companions, and then was passed from one dance partner to another before he could make his way across the crowded room to her. Their eyes met occasionally, and she looked as if she were missing him too. His frustration just made his anger toward Soren all the more intense, and he purposefully avoided the man all night.

Finally Elsa paused at the opening of the tent, watching as the last of the rainstorm ended. He neared her. "At last a moment alone," he whispered in her ear.

"It's been torturous, don't you agree?" Another man came to offer his arm for a dance, but she graciously declined.

Karl looked about them, noted they were being observed, and urged her out into the waning rain. "Come before ten others try and steal you away from me!" She shrieked as they splashed through mud puddles and her gown got soiled. But he didn't care. Fortunately, she was laughing by the time they got to the house.

"What are you doing?" she cried, still smiling as he pulled her into his arms. Rain washed down her face, leaving huge droplets on her eyelashes.

"I want this straight, Elsa Ramstad, right now," he demanded, blinking water from his own lids. "I am only interested in you. In you. There are no other women. Are you still interested in me?"

"I…I am."

"Only me?"

She smiled. "Yes. Only you. It was foolish of me in there… I guess I am simply afraid. Afraid that this isn't real and will disappear. That you'll disappear. Afraid that what we're…*discovering* won't hold true."

He kissed her then, drawing her to him. He could feel her shivering, and he wanted to warm her with the heat that seared through his body. When he released her, he gazed into her eyes. "Elsa, what we're discovering *is* true, and I aim to prove it to you every day for a long time to come. Now quit dancing with anyone but me, all right?"

"All right, Karl. All right."

n i n e t e e n

November 1888

After Trent and Tora made their tearful good-byes and headed south the day after their nuptials to catch a luxury ship to Hawaii, everyone else settled into some semblance of a routine. Kaatje continued to see Soren, despite numerous silent protests from Elsa and Karl. She could read their disapproval in their faces, the way their eyes met when Soren was at the door. *His true colors will come through eventually,* Kaatje decided, *if he has not changed.* And if he had, perhaps there was a chance for them. In any case, she was in no rush to decide.

She walked over to the mercantile the day before Thanksgiving, needing a freshly slaughtered bird, some yams, and cinnamon. The hills surrounding Juneau were mostly green now, the deciduous trees having dropped the last of their autumn leaves the week before. The smell of snow lingered in the air.

Her heart skipped a beat at seeing Soren today, just as it always had at his handsome face. He had been promoted from loading supplies to assisting customers at the front, and Kaatje could see why. As she entered, he was climbing down the fifteen-foot ladder, a can of beans in hand. "Here you go, Mrs. Laninger." He flashed her a grin that Kaatje was sure would sell fifteen more cans, if he asked her if they were needed. "Anything else, ma'am?"

"No, no thank you, Mr. Janssen."

"Have a pleasant day and a wonderful Thanksgiving. I'll just put those beans on your account."

Blushing a deep red and with a silly grin upon her face, Mrs. Laninger turned toward Kaatje and passed, not even noticing her.

Kaatje shook her head. "We should have known long ago that you would be perfect for retail."

He flashed her a broader grin than he had given Mrs. Laninger. "Ah, my love, I hoped I would get to see you today. And yes, this is a good job for me. I like it, and the customers seem to like me. At least, most of them."

Kaatje knew that Elsa and the others came in from time to time and largely ignored Soren. "They have little reason to give you another chance. They all care for me and want to protect me from being hurt again. Now could I trouble you for a box of cinnamon?"

"Certainly." He turned and moved the ladder on rollers to another spot in the shelves, and took one step up to grab the metal box that had a picture of a cherubic Indian girl on the front. He jumped down and placed it on the counter. "Anything else?"

"I do not suppose you have any fresh turkeys that are plucked."

"We do. They're hanging in the meat locker. Shall I fetch you one?"

"Please. I'm looking for one of about fifteen pounds."

He raised his eyebrows briefly. "Sounds like you're feeding a crowd."

Kaatje swallowed hard and studied the grain of the counter's wood. She wanted him to come. She had wanted to invite him for a long time. But James and Kadachan, Elsa, and Karl would not be pleased at the additional guest. "Do you have plans, Soren?"

"*Nei*," he mumbled in Norwegian.

"Well then, I'd love to invite you, but you see, it's…"

"Awkward?"

"*Ja*." How easy it was to lapse back into their native tongue. It felt comforting, comfortable. She longed to have an entire conversation in Norwegian, sharing the intimacy with Soren again. He left her to fetch the turkey and returned to wrap it in brown paper.

"I needed something else," she said, racking her brain. Seeing Soren had apparently knocked it out of her head forever. His bright blue eyes sparkled and studied her in glimpses as he wrapped the turkey and tied it with string.

"Here, I've made you a handle for it."

"Wonderful. Now what was that last item?"

"Why, Mrs. Janssen. Are you simply pretending to forget in order to spend time with your husband? There is no need, Kitten," he said more lowly and reached across the counter to stroke her cheek. "You only need ask."

"Soren," she said in exasperation. "I really have forgotten." Her cheek felt warm where he had touched her, and her heart had tripled its beat.

"Okay then. Let's see. You're making what for supper?"

"Turkey, potatoes, bread, beans—I already have mine—yams, yams! That's it!"

"Fresh or canned?"

"Oh, fresh, if you have them. About twelve."

He left the storefront and disappeared into the back room. She wandered nervously about, eyeing fabric that she really wasn't seeing. She was only seeing the snappy blue of his eyes in a calico, the wind-chapped red of his face in a muslin. Suddenly he was at her shoulder.

"I was thinking this would look wonderful on you," he said, picking up a rich bluish green velvet. "For a Christmas dress."

Her hand went to the soft pile, and a shiver went down her spine as Soren placed a hand on her left hip. They had not touched since the day he arrived in Juneau. She pretended not to notice. "Oh, I couldn't. Maybe for the girls."

"No, for you. You deserve a new dress as much as the children."

"But, I really shouldn't. It's…how much?"

He looked at the end of the bolt and told her.

"Oh no, I could never spend that much."

"How many yards would you need for a gown?"

Her eyes scanned the ceiling as she visualized a wonderful dress and tiny coat that she had admired in *Godey's Ladies Book*. "For the dress I'd like to make, I'd need eight or nine yards. You see? It would be much too much to spend. An extravagance."

Soren didn't push her any further. "Is there anything else, Kaatje?"

"No. You'll put these groceries on my monthly bill?"

"Of course." He went and retrieved her things. "Would you like me to carry them across for you?"

"That's not necessary. You're alone here. I can manage."

"Very well. Have a nice night and a happy Thanksgiving if I do not see you."

There was a touch of sorrow in his voice that cut Kaatje to the core. "Listen, why don't you join us tomorrow night? We can all be civil and make it a decent evening."

"Now, Kaatje, you said yourself you didn't think it was wise. And James Walker and I—well, you saw what happened last time we were too near."

She felt her forehead furrow in consternation. That was true. Last time they met, James had struck him down in a rage. That kind of behavior would not do on a day of thanks. Especially with young, impressionable children about. She quickly decided on her course of action. "I will simply tell James that I have decided to invite you, the girls' father, to join us for Thanksgiving. If he cannot abide by my decision, then he will have to find other plans."

"Oh, Kaatje, I don't think—"

"No, Soren. I have decided. We'll see you tomorrow night at seven. The restaurant is open for a buffet supper from five to seven, then it'll be just us."

James took the news that Kaatje had invited Soren with a face that he hoped remained stoic. It had only been a matter of time before Soren got to her. It was his whole mission for residing in Juneau: to woo Kaatje back. And it looked as if she was moving in that direction.

When the hotel manager had come to tell him there was a lady awaiting him in the lobby, his heart had thundered in his chest. Knowing few women but Kaatje and her family, he wondered what she wanted or needed. He had smoothed his hair down and straightened his tie, pulled on a vest and then his jacket before hurrying down the stairs.

She was waiting in the parlor, pacing, clearly uneasy about something. "James, I uh… You see, I've made a decision…" His heart paused as he worried that she had made a decision to reunite with Soren, so he actually breathed a sigh of relief when she told him it was just for Thanksgiving. And it gave him the courage to bow out. She didn't need him lingering around if she wanted Soren there, and besides, it would simply be too painful for James—to see the woman he loved sucked back in by the scoundrel.

"I've been thinking that I ought to see some friends who also invited me," he lied, trying to spare her the pain of this moment. "I've been so busy with my business," *watching Soren,* he thought silently, "that I haven't even had a chance to call upon them and share a meal. Since you've decided to have Soren over, I'll just go do that." He forced a smile. "You know how well your husband and I get along."

She gave him a troubled, but slightly relieved, look. "Well, if you're sure. It probably would be best to keep you two separated. How about the day after tomorrow?" The thought brightened her expression. "Care to join us then for supper?"

"Sure, sure, Kaatje," James said, awkwardly reaching out to pat her on the shoulder. "That would be great." He pulled his hand back, not trusting that it wouldn't pull Kaatje to him as he had longed to do for months. She was someone else's wife; her husband was alive and well and bent on winning her back. James's ethics, his morals told him not to interfere, whatever his heart might say. "You have a happy Thanksgiving," he went on when she still hesitated. *Go, go on now!*

his heart screamed. *I can't stand it any longer! Go before I kiss you and never let you go again!*

"You have a blessed Thanksgiving as well, James." He watched as she turned and walked out the door without looking back, and then he gripped the staircase rail, feeling ill.

"Are you all right, Walker?" the hotel clerk called, pausing over his paperwork to study his frequent guest over his half-glasses.

"Fine, fine," James mumbled with a weak wave, turning and wearily walking back up to his room.

When they sat down at last for supper, they were all thankful that they could have the excuse of full mouths, if nothing else, to cover up their lack of conversation. Never had a table been more silent in the Juneau Storm Roadhouse, Soren surmised, than theirs that evening. And yet it mattered little to him, so victorious was his heart that Kaatje had dared to invite him, as well as uninvite James Walker. She was close to giving him another chance. Close to welcoming him home, to her fine rooms upstairs. To her bed. He could feel it.

He made up for the lack of conversation between the adults by talking animatedly with the children. He soon found out that Eve had a kitty and that Jessica was gifted with animals. Much as his own mother had been, he mused. He learned that Christina liked to bake bread, and the boys liked to eat it with a thick layer of sweet cream and butter. He carefully made note of their Christmas wish lists: Eve wanted a doll; Kristian, a wooden train set—complete with rails and a bridge; Christina, a silver brush and mirror set she had seen in the mercantile; and Jessica, a wagon. Even Charlie would get a gift from him—a model ship.

He would gladly play Saint Nicholas this year, buying his way into their young hearts to win them over. He truly liked the children and was drawn to his girls. But he knew they sensed the adults' reticence about him, and he needed a way to counteract it. The gifts would be just right. Kaatje had carefully kept the children away from him while she weighed her decision, but the girls had sneaked over to the mercantile one day, just to tell him that they always wanted a father and were glad he was near. He knew that the children would likely be his greatest ally, his most opportune avenue to winning Kaatje back. Because she wanted a family most of all.

As always, there was a part of him that wanted it too. A house of their own, a roaring fire, a chance to tell the girls Norwegian folk tales his mother had told him as a child. Beyond the wealth that Kaatje was accumulating, he liked the prospect of having a hearth and home. And perhaps he could choose a new business, spend a little of Kaatje's cash on it, something that would entail travel, so he would not tire again of that hearth and home. A little excursion now and then would be just the thing, giving him the best of both worlds.

If she would just let go of her fears and give him one more chance. He was so close. At least Tora and Trent were gone, he mused, stuffing a moist piece of turkey into his mouth. They were difficult, those two. It increased his odds, having them depart on an extended honeymoon. With any luck, he'd have Kaatje and his ducks in a row by the time they returned, when it would be too late for them to protest. He knew Kaatje and her loyal heart; once she decided on him, it was done. He wiped his bread in the last remnants of gravy, then sat back in sated pleasure. "That was wonderful, Kaatje, Elsa, girls," he said, nodding at each of them. "A fine, fine meal."

"Yes," Karl echoed. "One of the best in a long while."

"As it should be," Kaatje said, rising. "I will go and get the cream whipped for the pumpkin pie."

"Pie!" Kristian squealed, pinching his younger sister in his excitement.

"Mama!" she complained.

"You two—in fact, all of you children—help us clear the table. You, too, Charles. You can bring back dessert plates and forks." They obediently rose as a group and followed the women out to the kitchen.

When the door swung shut behind them, leaving Karl and Soren alone for a moment, Karl stared over at him.

"You have something to say, Karl?" Soren asked, pleased by his own bored tone.

"At least one thing. Watch your step."

"I've heard that before."

"I bet you have. It's because everyone but you knows that Kaatje is a treasure. As I see it, you're little better than a pirate."

"Did you work all day to come up with that?" Soren asked in disdain. "Surely you can do better."

The children came back through the doors, armed with small plates and forks, as well as coffee cups and saucers. Soren chanced one more comment. "You think you know me. You have no idea who I am."

"That's what I fear," Karl returned, never looking away.

James watched them through the restaurant windows, even as the snow fell. He couldn't shake the feeling that Kaatje was in greater danger than ever now that she was closer to giving in to Soren. And all he could do was stand guard and watch. He was like a soldier with no weapon, even kept from using his fists. All he could hope for was that his spirit, head, and heart would win someday over Soren. But how? And was it terrible for him to wish for such a thing?

He was a man of God, a man who prided himself on his ethics. And here he was, pursuing a married woman. Not actively, of course, but with the diligence of a first love. Kaatje seemed that way to him; he had been married before, and to a special woman, but this time it was fresh, new again in a way he would've considered impossible. "I'm like a new-broke horse," he muttered to himself. "Learning the ways of love all over again, after years away from it."

James wished he had never ventured giving his heart away again. It was much safer, and much less painful, to stay by himself or in the company of Kadachan. On the river, in the mountains, he had never felt this kind of fear, something that threatened to break him in two.

Not the mother grizzly, nor a terrible lightning storm. Not the ice floes that nearly toppled their boat, nor the rapids that pulled men under and held them there until they had no more breath to hold. This, this thing he felt for Kaatje had been like climbing a mountain peak and gazing over a verdant, unexplored valley…a summer sun's warmth on his chest. But now he was falling from that peak, the sun searing his skin.

Shamed by the tears on his cheeks, he ducked around a corner and gazed up at the gray sky releasing fat snowflakes that hit his face and melted. "Lord, Lord," he cried, "help me. Help me to make wise choices here. I fell in love with Kaatje, but is it better for me simply to leave? Am I getting in the way of a marriage you once blessed?"

There was no answer to his heart, just the muffled silence of a late fall snowstorm.

He turned and held his body away from the building with his forehead, the slight pain from the pressure expressing a tiny bit of what he felt inside. It was ripping him apart, this thing between him and Kaatje, or rather the thing that had only had the slightest first breath before a windstorm stole it away. It was like a faint memory, a hope against the odds. And now it was over.

"It's over, James," he told himself. "It's over. Get on with your life. You saw him there tonight. He's made it. He's made it in. The rest will be easy."

But as he turned to walk away with one last glance toward the Storm Roadhouse, the children laughing, the women serving pie, he could not leave.

What was wrong here? Why could he not make a decision and stick with it? Everything in his upbringing, his morals, told him to remove himself, that a woman belonged with her husband, and that was that. But Soren Janssen had broken all the rules, leaving her for years with children—on a farm, of all places—to fend for themselves. He took up with another woman. And he showed up only when Kaatje had come through town, boasting of a reward and, therefore, showing she was a woman of some means. No, James just couldn't leave it alone. He knew something was wrong, something more than just unrequited love.

He continued to pace back and forth for hours, watching when Soren went home, and later Karl, until the front lights were turned down and the front door was locked up for the night. Still energized from the tips of his toes to the ends of his fingertips, he decided he had to find an outlet or he would never sleep. Next door, a man left his snug little house, letting the door slam shut behind him, and walked to the side where he chopped a log into kindling. After a few minutes, he returned inside without ever spying his silent watchman. Chopping wood. Suddenly, it sounded like the antidote this dying man needed.

James strode across the street and around the Storm Roadhouse. He knew that Kaatje and the girls resided on the far side of the hotel; he hoped his chopping would not awaken them. He envisioned Kaatje arising to find a cord of freshly cut wood in the back, and it gave him even more energy.

He was halfway through his fourth log, however, when the back door swung open, bathing him in warm light. He panted in his exertion, small clouds of steam arising before his face. Without speaking, he turned back to the log and with a loud *thwack* split it in two.

"Easing your stomach of a heavy Thanksgiving dinner?" Kaatje asked gently.

"Of sorts," James evaded, sending the half-log into a neat quarter.

"Are you going to chop wood all night?"

"I hope not."

"You didn't eat much dinner, did you, James?"

He rammed the axe down into the stump and rested his hands on the handle. "Not much."

"Come in, James. Quit before you wake the neighbors."

Obediently he followed her indoors. Truth be told, he wanted to be nowhere else.

"Sit," she said, waving toward a chair. She was in a breakfast coat, from which descended a smooth nightdress of deep red. He averted his eyes, staring at the table while she put a plate before him and on it stacked sliced turkey, dressing, yams, a slice of bread, and then corn. She sat down across from him as he ate. "You don't have friends who invited you over, do you, James?"

"No."

"Why did you lie to me?" Her tone told him she knew the answer.

He shrugged a little and chewed his food as he studied her. "You had made your decision. I wanted to make it easier for you."

"Where do we go from here, James?"

He thought her question over, looking around the table. His eyes rested on a gift box, in which a generous length of blue-green velvet lay. "From him?" he asked, trying to keep the note of accusation from his tone.

Her eyes told him yes.

"I would say that it is not up to me to decide where we go from here, Kaatje." He set down his fork, no longer hungry. His stomach was in knots. "I do not trust the man, Kaatje. I want to go away, leave you two to your business, but there's something amiss..." He leaned back in his chair and blew air out of an *o* through his lips while he ran a hand through his hair. "Maybe it comes from looking out for you for months on the river, but I can't stand to leave you alone with him. I'd as soon walk away from you now as when that mother bear came tearing toward you."

Kaatje looked away, biting a fingernail. When she looked back at him, her eyes were sad. "You can't protect me from every bear out there, James."

"I can sure as well try. If you'll let me."

"I think you had better go, James. If I come to some conclusion, I'll let you know. For now, know that I'm as confused as you."

He agreed in silence, heading back toward his hotel without looking back. One more glance at Kaatje and he was liable to break down in front of her like a newborn baby. What was wrong with him? Clenching his lips in consternation, he decided that the following morning he would find six men to go and work Kaatje's mine on the Yukon. And if God was with them, they would strike gold. News of a gold strike from a mine that was once his was bound to flush Soren Janssen out, much like smoke in a fox's hole. Yes, like smoke in a fox's hole.

James smiled for the first time in weeks.

Kaatje sat on the edge of her bed, staring out the window. Her tears matched the softly falling flakes outside, slowly, gently descending. Her throat closed around a soft sob, and she threw herself into the down pillow, not wanting anyone to hear her cry.

How confused was her heart! One moment she had almost decided to give Soren a chance, a real chance, the next it skittered back to James. How she longed to enter James's arms to claim him as her own! To send Soren, and the accompanying confusion, away. To know James's steady ways, his slow smile, his tender look, again on a daily basis. Oh, how she missed him!

And yet she couldn't. Soren was her first love, her husband, and he was trying. With each day, her trust grew, little by little.

Still, it did not ease her pain at watching James leave her side, step by step. When would he simply give up and go away? And what right did she have to hold him?

section three

Daybreak

twenty

᪥

Elsa did not know when they had started to assume that Karl would dine with her every night. It had all started on board their ships, in the race to Juneau, and had simply never stopped. It was comforting, much like the snow that began on Thanksgiving Day and continued on, getting deeper and deeper, just as their love deepened. The drifts had grown to five feet high beside the restaurant by December.

Every morning she awakened to the sound of Soren shoveling the front porch and walk. It was thoughtful of him; she had to give him that. As she languished in bed, her thoughts went from Karl the night before, laughing at something Kristian said, and then whipped back to Soren. With each skid and slide of the shovel, Elsa winced. It was as if he was shoveling his way back into Kaatje's heart. Yesterday she had come downstairs to see Kaatje give her husband a steaming cup of coffee before he left for the mercantile. She even allowed him to kiss her on the cheek. Since when was Kaatje allowing him to kiss her? It sent a shiver down Elsa's back.

Never mind that she had let Karl kiss her on the lips as often as he asked. Karl had never betrayed her. She was thinking of *Soren.* Soren, who had disappeared for years, who had cheated on a wonderful wife, had a child with a lover.

She sighed. It was not her place to judge. And she could see that Kaatje was taking it slow. She just hoped that Trent's detective would get proof once and for all that Soren was either the snake in the grass she feared or a changed man. "Help me to keep an open mind, Lord," she whispered as she scooted out of bed and her warm toes met frigid wood floor. She quickly pulled on her housedress and breakfast coat, trembling as she did.

It was cold, bone-chilling cold, in Alaska. Suddenly she longed to be aboard the *Majestic*, sailing to Hawaii like Trent and Tora. Warm sands, warm waters, green tropical forests… She clamped her lips shut. All in all, it was better to be here. She knew the children needed some time off the ship, though their life in a snowbound home was much like life on a ship. It gave Kristian a chance to attend school, the teaching task something Elsa dreaded. It would be fun to watch her child learn his letters and numbers, but she doubted she would enjoy enforcing study habits. And Eve loved being with Kaatje's girls. Christina was like a mother hen, watching out for the child, telling on her when she wasn't behaving, teaching her the art of doll care, taking tea, and other ladylike pursuits.

Many in her crew had elected to stay in Alaska and try their hand at mining. Rumors of gold had long since caught their fancy. By spring they would be good and ready for the sea again, Elsa expected. Riley had shipped out with the remaining crew and other new members, picked from miners who already had gold fever beaten out of them. He would return in April for her, providing Elsa was ready to leave.

Elsa walked to the window and pulled aside the curtains. She liked Juneau, its vibrant pace and growth in the midst of winter. It was a healthy city, destined for great things. Elsa could sense it. Gold strikes all around continued to feed the growth, though few of them were long-lived. Everyone was seeking the next California of 1849. There were also thriving timber and sealing industries, as well as the commerce that followed them.

It was a cold place to winter, but a good place. The thought of Karl Martensen warmed her. The windowpane fogged up as she leaned her forehead against the glass. The street below blurred as she thought of him, dressed in his favorite Irish blue wool sweater and gray-gold pants. He was a striking man, and her attraction to him so overwhelmed Elsa that she wondered how she could never have seen it before. *Because I was in love with Peder.* Dear Peder, her beloved husband. No one could ever take his place. But her love for Karl felt so new and vital that it pushed her love for Peder back into the dim shadows of her heart and mind. It was as if she had opened heavy dark curtains and let in the light. She blinked and everything came into focus.

While Elsa had long since packed away her mourning black, there were still vestiges of her heart that belonged to Peder, clashing with the other parts that were increasingly drawn to Karl. Perhaps it would always be this way. When one woman loved two men, perhaps she would always feel a little split. She hoped it would ease as time went on. Already she felt more comfortable with Karl, more ready to enter his arms when he embraced her, eager to lift her lips to his without the image of Peder lingering in her mind.

A quick rapping at her door startled her. "Yes?" she called, walking toward it.

Five children stumbled inward. "Auntie Elsa!" Jessica said. "Look!"

"Look! Look!" cried the others. Eve was jumping up and down. Between them they carried a bulky wooden crate with her name neatly printed on the outside label: CAPTAIN ELSA RAMSTAD, C/O JUNEAU HARBOR MASTER, ALASKA, NORTH AMERICA.

She had long since made the acquaintance of Harvey Shalinger, Juneau's harbor master and town barber. The box looked much like the seven other crates that had arrived for her with identical labels. She smiled at the children. "Shall we see what it is?"

"Yes! Yes!" they cried.

"I will need a crowbar."

"Let's go downstairs!" Charles said. "I think there is one in the kitchen."

They tumbled out of her room, pausing at the stairs to watch her come after them, then cascaded down to the restaurant, lugging the bulky crate between them. Elsa was careful not to look outside, through the restaurant windows. She didn't want any potential glimpse of Kaatje and Soren to sour her mood.

"Who could have sent it, Auntie Elsa?" Jess asked.

"I wish I knew."

"Whoever sent the others probably sent this one," Kristian said in his best grown-up voice. "Look at the label."

"I agree." She pried the top of the crate upward.

The children practically pushed her aside as they pulled straw away from all sides of the box, digging for the buried treasure. She laughed under her breath. "What is it?"

"There! There!" Kristian cried.

"Careful," Elsa warned. "It might be fragile."

"It's a stereoscope! A stereoscope!" Kristian shrieked, his voice rising an octave. "Jimmy Lansing has one at his house!"

"A stereoscope," Elsa said, excited herself. The one-and-a-half-foot box had become a parlor room standard, featuring an eyepiece at the top, and a turning knob at the side that would rotate the two-dimensional images. "Are there any pictures?"

The children dived back into the crate, and each came back up with a box of photographs. "Here! Here!" they cried, all pushing them at her at once.

"Just a moment," she said, leading the way to the kitchen sideboard. She carefully set the stereoscope down and found the latch to open the top. "Hand me your boxes, children." She pulled up a chair and looked at each one. "Let's see. Let's start with Asia, then go to North America, South America, Europe, and Africa."

It was fairly simple to attach each group of photographs onto the rounders, placed two to a sheet so the viewer's eyes gained greater scope. The children had resumed their hopping they were so eager, but Elsa waved them off. "It is my present. I will look first. Then you shall each have a minute to look yourselves, in order of age."

"Ah-uh-ah," Eve whined.

Elsa stood and leaned over the stereoscope, staring at images she had once seen herself in India, Burma, and China. She grinned as she spun through the pictures, wanting a quick overview before the children attempted mutiny. Seeing the sights was like taking a trip around the world. Whoever had sent the present knew her well. How perfect it was to get something like this in the dead of winter! It chased any sense of melancholy and longing for the sea away.

She sat back, and Charles climbed atop a chair to take his turn. Elsa laughed aloud as a thought struck her. *She* had become like her column readers, traveling vicariously by gazing at the pictures! After all her years on the sea, writing about and illustrating her exploits, she was at home in a warm kitchen, pouring herself a cup of coffee and musing about places far and wide, seen and unseen. It seemed contrary, this road on which God had taken her. Every time she figured out her role and place, it was apt to change. Perhaps it would be so all her life.

Tora leaned her head to one side as Trent took her in his arms and nuzzled her neck. They were staying in a villa he had purchased on Hawaii, a sprawling house with open windows and huge verandahs. There was a white sand beach just steps away that they could walk along for hours, splashing in the water. On the other side of the house was a freshwater waterfall that cascaded several feet in a long, smooth sheet to a lush pool below. The previous owner had diverted some of the water toward the house, so the staff had easy access for cooking and cleaning. It was idyllic, and Tora couldn't imagine ever wanting to depart.

"What do you want for Christmas, my love?" Trent murmured, between kisses along her neck.

Smiling because it tickled, she pushed him away with the back of her head. He remained behind her, his arms about her waist. She felt safe, protected, loved. "A baby," she said, dreamlike.

Trent laughed, his chuckle coming from deep within his chest. "I'd like that too." He turned her toward him, and his expression sobered. "It will happen in time." He lifted her chin and kissed her on the nose. "And then you'll be complaining about how much work the baby takes."

She wrapped her arms around him and rested her head on his chest, feeling comforted by the steady beat of his heart. "Sometimes," she almost whispered, "I'm afraid that I will never have another child."

"It's only been two months since we married, Tora."

"No, sometimes I wonder if I'll never have another child because I cannot."

"What?" Trent asked, pulling away to look at her. There was no accusation in his voice, just concern.

Tora could not bear to look at him, so she gazed instead out to the cresting rollers grumbling to shore with wet rumbles. "Sometimes, I wonder if Jessica is the only child I'll ever have."

"Why?"

"Because maybe the Lord is punishing me for…my transgressions."

Trent wordlessly enveloped her in his arms again, resting his cheek on her forehead for several unbearable moments.

"Say something, Trent."

He paused, then said, "Tora, we've all transgressed in one form or another. You've confessed your sin and followed the Lord's lead for years now." He lifted her chin and waited until she looked him in the eye. "If you don't have another baby, you don't. We can adopt a child or explore life as a couple only and be glad of finding each other. But you must do something—you must forgive yourself. It is not God that is punishing you, Tora; it is you. Let go of your sin as God has. Let go of it." He kissed her then, on the forehead, and quietly padded inside, leaving her to study the azure sky and contemplate the idea of forgiveness. Of forgiving herself. Of forgiving Frank Decker.

She shivered at the thought of him and again looked out to the sea. Somewhere in the tropical forest around them, an exotic bird let out a call she had never heard before. How could she forgive Frank Decker? She had tried before, but the same horrifying images came to her mind, keeping her from finding true peace. The bird called again, and Tora looked toward the sound. Perhaps it was like the bird, she thought, perhaps she should listen for a different call than she had ever heard before.

He was my child once.

She sighed and closed her eyes. That was it. That was the key. To look upon Frank Decker as her heavenly Father looked upon him. With pleasure once and sadness at seeing what he had become. When she thought about how God probably wept over Frank Decker, it made her tear up too. A good and right creation gone wrong. What had happened to him to make him so evil? So cruel? So angry?

The empathy pulled away all her own anger and fear. All her desire for retribution, leaving only sorrow. And in that sorrow, Tora at last found a way to forgive Frank Decker. "I forgive you, Frank Decker," she said. "You did terrible things to me, but in the name of my Lord Jesus Christ, I forgive you. I am sorry I could not tell that to you in person."

She looked up into the sky, watching as the golden-edged clouds grew to a deep pink, then purple and gray. "Is it the same for me, Lord, in order to forgive myself? It's still hard for me. I feel as if I have to constantly work to repay Kaatje, to repay you for the things I did. As if I'll never be able to do enough to be worthy of forgiveness."

She bowed her head and waited, but God did not reassure her with his still, small voice. He did not give her another word that made her understand this, too. She knew the answer already—her sins had been forgiven, her transgressions paid for by the blood of Christ. "I know, Lord," she whispered, "I know. I have to keep reminding myself that no one else has to do it. By your grace, I am free." Her eyes swam with tears. "By your grace. I'm trying to remember, Lord. I'm trying."

It was time to forgive Soren and give him a chance to be her husband once again. Besides that, Kaatje thought, she could not bear the physical tension between them any longer. If he did not hold her, kiss her, kiss her as a husband ought to kiss his wife, then she was liable to scream. She relished the feel of her hand in his as they walked toward the door, content after a cozy supper for two in the corner of the restaurant, discontent at the thought of separation. Half of her longed to ask him home, to tell him she was giving him another chance; the other half screamed to run away, to pull her hand from his. He was so handsome, with his sparkling eyes that smoldered as they studied her.

He was...magnetic. She had seen women turn and look back at him as they passed. Thankfully she had never discovered him looking too. In the three months he had been in Juneau, he had never given her cause to wonder. Everything was beginning to feel so...right.

"What is it, kitten?" he asked softly. He ducked his head to catch her gaze, and, in doing so, his face neared hers.

Kaatje was silent, only looked back into his eyes, and then allowed her gaze to drift down his straight nose to his full lips.

He apparently understood her feelings, her desire, because he took a step closer. "Kaatje, are you ready?"

"I am getting closer every day," she whispered.

Soren took her hand and pulled her along the porch of the roadhouse, then along a narrow alleyway, a shoveled track that led to the back. The snowdrifts were deep, and they were suddenly alone in a white cavern, away from the prying eyes of passersby. He waited no longer. Placing his large hands on her back, one between her shoulder blades and the other at her tailbone, he slowly, agonizingly slowly, pulled her to him. She gave in to his touch, all too willing to surrender to the desire she felt for the husband she had not lain with in seven years.

His breath was sweet and warm on her face as he brought her to him in quiet, languid passion. Kaatje fought the desire to fling herself toward him, giving in to the ecstasy of being sucked into marital pleasures. He was teasing her, testing her to make sure she really was right about her feelings. Barely touching her lips then pulling slightly away, watching as her eyelids drooped with desire, studying her like a tutor with a student finally learning how to solve a difficult problem.

A bolt of electricity suddenly shot through Kaatje from head to toe, and she wrenched away, taking a step backward. He was using his body as a means to controlling her. She could see it clearly now. He followed her, a look of confusion and concern lurking at the edges of his expression, seemingly trying to recapture the moment. To regain control. *Control.* He pulled her to him again.

She put a quick hand on his chest and turned sideways, fighting to contain her composure. "No."

"Kaatje, say yes…"

"No! I will not do this! Don't you see, Soren? I need to forgive you with my heart and mind before I forgive you with my body. It has to be…*straight*. Or else it will never be—"

He pulled her even closer, pushing away her hand and pulling her tightly against him. "You desire me. I felt it. I know you, Kaatje. You want your husband again. You want me."

His tone was victorious, driving her fear deeper, as if seducing her would be the final battle. She had been so close to giving in. She was still fighting the heat inside her, the desire to let Soren win and give herself up as the spoils. He cupped her chin, urging her lips toward his.

"No," she gasped. "Stop!" she shouted, when he did not.

He dropped his hands, his face filled with the confusion she felt. "I'm sorry, Soren. I've…made a mistake. I still need time."

"Time?" His confusion turned to anger. "You think you can do that to me? I've been waiting a long time for you, Kaatje. A long time!" His voice was rising too. He turned to pace away from her and then back. "Have I not proven myself to you? For three months, I've been the model citizen. The model husband! I go to church with you! I shovel your walk! I take whatever crumbs you give me. Now, it is time to take what is mine," he said lowly, angrily pointing toward his chest and advancing upon her. She backed up and stumbled over a fallen icicle.

He was instantly beside her, pulling her up, toward him.

"No!" she shouted. "No!"

"Kaatje—"

"What is going on here?" Kaatje knew the voice behind her. It was James. "What are you doing to her?" Suddenly he was right behind her in the narrow alley, shouting over her shoulder at Soren.

"I was only helping her up," Soren grit out. "And besides, this is none of your business."

"Even if it wasn't Kaatje," James ground back, "I would come to the aid of a woman under attack."

Kaatje was beginning to feel stupid. After all, she had come with Soren...

He echoed her thoughts. "I wasn't giving her anything she hadn't asked for for weeks."

"I did tell you to stop," she protested.

"Only after you kissed me," he returned.

Kaatje shook her head, feeling woozy on her feet. "I need to go."

"What?" Soren asked.

She turned to James. "I need some time. To leave. Leave Juneau for a while."

"What?" Soren repeated, looking bewildered.

"James, will you escort me to Ketchikan? Tonight?"

"You cannot be serious," Soren complained, following them out of the snowbound alley. "You're going where?"

She turned back to Soren, but held on to James's arm. "To Ketchikan, Soren. I need some time, time away from you. Being with you has helped in some ways, but now I'm simply...confused."

"But why have *him* along?" Soren spat out, nodding toward James.

"Because he's a gentleman and will see me safely to the Storm Roadhouse in Ketchikan."

"Like he saw you safely along the Yukon?" he sneered.

Kaatje lowered her eyebrows in consternation. "Yes. Exactly." She turned away from him then, her skirts flying, but did not miss James's victorious look back at Soren.

"I'll bring the sleigh at three," James said when they reached the front door. "We can catch the four o'clock ferry to Ketchikan."

"Fine," Kaatje said, not looking at him again. Her stomach was a mass of knots as she rushed to the front door of the roadhouse. Inside, Karl and Elsa looked up from their armchairs beside the fire, at the end of the restaurant. They had taken to reading books aloud to each other for an hour every afternoon. Kaatje suddenly wondered why they hadn't come to her aid. Was it the distance and their dialogue that had kept them from hearing her? Or had James been close by, spying on her?

"I am sorry," Kaatje said. "I did not mean to disturb you. But now that I have, I need to speak with you." Quickly, she walked the length of the room, appreciating the warmth of the flames as she neared. "I need to leave for a week's time and wondered if you two could manage the children and restaurant for me."

"Well, certainly," Elsa began, clearly confused. "With it only being open for supper this winter, and a good staff, that's no hardship. But where are you going? And in such a hurry?"

"To Ketchikan. I've been meaning to check on the Bresleys and their progress on the roadhouse. It's only a few months before you will be bringing tourists to stay the night! And things with Soren have become…"

"Complicated?" Elsa guessed.

"Yes. I need some—"

"Room?"

Kaatje shot her an irritated look.

"Forgive me," Elsa said. "I wondered if it was going too quickly. I know, I know, I'll quit with that. I think a brief holiday will help. Yes, I'm game for managing the restaurant. How hard could it be?"

That comment worried Kaatje. She looked toward Karl. Surely, between the two of them, they could manage. And another chance to be alone together would be good for them, not like her and Soren...

"Yes, I'm game too," Karl said. "At least I am if you promise you'll return at week's end. Tell us what we need to know."

James Walker pulled up promptly at three, talking lowly to the sleigh's horses. His heart was twisting with conflicting emotions. Should he have said no when she asked him to take her? Should he have found someone else? But he was so relieved to spirit her away, away from that devil of a husband. More and more he was convinced that Soren was only acting, that given enough time, he would show his true colors. Had he not done just that today in that alley? What if James had not been nearby? Would he have taken advantage of Kaatje? And if he had, would that have put a stop to her falling in love with him again? Perhaps if James had just let Soren continue, Kaatje would've seen him for what he was. But James couldn't bear the thought of Soren hurting her.

He cradled his head in his hands. The questions had barraged him for hours now, and his head hurt so much he could barely see. The restaurant door opened and James raised his head, even tried a smile.

"You look the worse for wear, man," Karl said, clambering down the steps and resting his hands on the side of the sleigh. "You're seeing Kaatje to the ferry?"

"To Ketchikan."

"To Ketchi—" Karl stopped abruptly. "She asked you to take her all the way to Ketchikan?"

James shrugged, ignoring the pain slicing through his head. "She trusts me, I guess."

"Yes. She trusts you."

James did not let his gaze waver, understanding Karl's unspoken warning. "I know, Martensen. I know. You're not thinking about anything I haven't thought myself a hundred times."

Karl leaned his forearms against the seat of the sleigh, his expression one of complete understanding. "You're walking on delicate ground, James."

"Yes."

"The best thing you could do would be to be her friend. Keep your distance."

James shot him an irritated look. "Not that it's any of your business."

"I'm afraid it is. Kaatje is a dear friend, and I'd like to say you and I have started a friendship too. But Kaatje comes first for me." He dropped his tone. "I've been where you are, man. Wouldn't it be best to simply leave? To come back after Kaatje makes her decision? Give your feelings time to cool?"

"I cannot. Not until Kaatje makes her decision. I'll go just as soon as she can look me in the eye and tell me she trusts Soren to treat her right. If she can do that, I'll be gone. But I can't get past the idea that she needs me. Needs me here."

"Is it she who needs you here, or you who needs to be here? Check yourself."

"I do. A hundred times a day." He sighed heavily, surprised that he felt no defensiveness with Karl. Perhaps because the man looked at him with such empathetic eyes. He obviously had struggled as James was struggling now. "So you think I should send her to Ketchikan by herself?"

Karl looked him dead in the eye. "I do. She's looking for time to straighten things out. The Bresleys will be with her in Ketchikan—"

He was interrupted by Kaatje coming out, saying good-bye to the children, giving Elsa last-minute instructions. Karl opened a pocket watch, one with an anchor on the face, and whistled. "You had better get going. The ferry's going to leave without you."

"Ach, yes."

Karl put her bags in the sleigh and then helped the bundled woman onto the seat beside James.

"Take care, Kaatje. See you in a week," Karl said, smiling up at her.

"I'll be praying for you, Kaatje," Elsa added.

"Good-bye, Mama! Good-bye!" called her girls, waving and looking a little wistful that she was leaving them again.

"Go, James. Hurry. Before I turn back."

He clucked to the horses and flapped the reins, turning them in the street back toward the harbor and waiting ferry. Tiny bells rang as the metal skis of the sleigh *swooshed* over the fresh snow, taking them toward the coast. James purposefully avoided looking at the mercantile, knowing Soren was probably in the window. He noticed Kaatje raising her head and then lowering it as if seeing someone and saying a silent good-bye. He did not care to see many more interchanges between the woman and her husband. It was about more than he could bear. It kept him up at night.

They were to the harbor in a few minutes. "Kaatje, I wanted to ask you... Do you think... I was thinking it might be wiser for me to stay home. For you to go to the Bresleys' and have some time to think. Without me. Without Soren."

She looked at him quickly, her eyes furrowed in confusion. "Go alone? No, I couldn't do that. If you don't wish to come with me, I could stay. There's so much to take care of back—"

"No! No, that's not it. There's no place I'd rather be than with you. And I think you should spend a little time away. Thinking on things. But I wonder if I might be confusing the issue by going with you."

"Nonsense. You're the perfect gentleman, James. I trust you with my life."

He sighed heavily again. "I wish you wouldn't. I'm afraid I'll let you down someday. Do something that will deflate that big balloon you have me riding on." He pulled the horses to a stop. "So you won't go alone?"

She squinched up her face and shook her head slowly. "I do not think so. You are my rock, James. I want you with me." She took his gloved hand softly in her mittened one. "I know this isn't fair of me, but I don't know what else to do. It's all so much... If you cannot come with me, I do not think I care to go."

"Kaatje, are you trying to find time for us to see if there's a future for us before deciding whether to take Soren back or not?" He didn't like the sound of it. Or rather, he liked the sound of it too much.

"No, no, my friend. I love being with you, but it isn't right... And yet, I need you. Oh, I must drive you to the brink of insanity with my aimless chatter!" She threw up her hands in self-disgust. "You see how confused I am? This is why I need to get away. To get my mind clear!"

James swallowed hard and then jumped down, pulling her valise from the back. "Come, Kaatje. I'm taking you to Ketchikan."

"Are you sure, James? I do not want to push you—"

"Come on. We're going."

twenty-one

Tearing off a chunk of jerky with his teeth, Kadachan leaned against a black pine. He ignored their collective grumbling as he observed the group of six men that James Walker had hired. It was unheard of, hiking through the mountains of Alaska in the dead of winter. Only doubling their salaries and promising them a portion of any gold strike kept them moving when most miners were holed up for the winter and didn't come out again until May's ice break. But they were almost at the claim.

They were a rough lot, but sturdy. James had chosen them well. And he had firmly stood behind Kadachan when he announced his requirements to them all. "You will obey this man's orders as if he were me. If you do not, you will not collect on your pay. And if he doesn't return with you come ice break, I'll have all your heads." The thought of obeying an Indian on a work site was so disagreeable to two that they had left, muttering under their breath about "filthy injuns." But the rest had remained, willing to earn a buck through the winter rather than spend it on poker. Two of the men were Inuit, which helped Kadachan. He doubted that James had chosen them on a whim. As with most things, James knew exactly what he was doing. James Walker was a careful man.

Except when it came to Kaatje Janssen.

Kadachan agreed with James that Soren was not all he appeared to be. But he also knew that James's love for the woman was bound to cloud his thinking, alter his perspective on things. Kadachan hoped, for James's sake, that he was right—that Kaatje's mine would produce a small fortune and drive the true Soren to the surface like a hungry salmon after a fly.

"It's time to move again," Kadachan stated, pushing his back off the tree. He began walking, not waiting for the others to follow.

"When you think we'll get there?" called one of the miners, a shiver in his voice. It was cold in the wind coming off the river's ice. The man was obviously feeling it too.

"Ten, eleven days."

"If we're not caught in a blizzard," called another.

"If it begins to snow, we will build shelter. We have provisions." Kadachan knew this land, these woods, the water. A change in weather did not frighten him.

"For the whole winter?" grumbled the fattest man, already huffing from the exertion of walking in snowshoes.

Kadachan paused and eyed the whole group. "It will be enough."

Joseph Campbell had arrived in Saint Michael five days prior, exactly as Trent Storm had requested. It had been a long journey from the Montana Territory to Seattle and northward to Alaska, but it had been undertaken with impressive speed. Between rail and sea, travel these days was certainly efficient. He hoped he could accomplish this latest mission for Mr. Storm and return as speedily to his family.

It was always financially worthwhile, seeing to Mr. Storm's requests. And gratifying. Why, who would have ever guessed that the woman he trailed through Montana and Washington would later become Mrs. Trent Storm? It made him feel as though he had a hand in the matchmaking. He hoped marriage would not make Trent less…fiscally generous. Keeping a woman—and presumably a family at some point—in fashion and comfort took resources these days.

Donning his hat and raising the collar of his wool coat, he left the small hotel yet again, determined to follow up the latest lead in finding Soren Janssen's castoff lover. A Catholic priest had approached him after services on Sunday and told him he had heard that Joseph sought information about a woman and child who had recently lived with a white man off the Yukon River.

"It is not an uncommon occurrence," the priest had said, his English thick with a Russian accent. "There are many lonely white men who take Indian brides and then abandon them when they decide to return to the cities of their birth."

"He never married this woman. And I believe she had a son." He had gathered that much, if she was the right woman, from correspondence with others along the Yukon. He motioned toward his own head. "She is said to be tall for an Inuit. And beautiful. A princess once."

The priest shook his head, his eyes conveying his sorrow. "It pains me to see such things."

Joseph respectfully waited for the priest to go on.

"There is one woman that could match such a description. A nun here found her on the streets, her child almost frozen with the first snows. I believe the nun found her a job as a washerwoman a block west." The town was only two blocks long by three short blocks wide; it would not be difficult to find it. In fact, Joseph remembered seeing the sign for washed shirts for five cents.

"I appreciate your help, Father," Joseph said with a curt nod. "I shall be adding to the offering plate this Sunday."

"That is not needed, but appreciated. What is needed is that you care for the lost, my son, and that woman sounds as if she is in need of help. Go with God."

"Thank you, Father." He departed and went back to the hotel. A finicky man, Joseph had few soiled shirts, but after a few minutes' search, he found one that was reasonably dirty. He bent and rubbed it along the face of his boot sole. Then he left again for the washer-woman's place of business.

In five minutes, he was there. All around were shirts drying on lines. Four Indian women peeked at him from amongst them as they stood beside wooden tubs, scrubbing against washboards. "I have a shirt to be laundered," he stated, still looking at the women. None of the four were what he would call striking. They stared at him through slitted eyes in wide, bland faces. A movement to his right caught his eye, and he realized there was yet another approaching him.

She was beautiful, worthy of her royal heritage, if she was indeed the woman he sought. Somewhere, some father was ready to kill Soren Janssen for stealing her away. "Shirt?" she asked. She quickly met his eyes and then looked away. Joseph knew then that he would never forget those obsidian orbs—they were filled with sorrow.

"Here. You see? It is soiled."

She took it from him, and he noticed long, slender fingers with broad nails. He could tell that she wondered how a shirt could get dirt like that on it, and yet she said nothing.

"Does the name Soren Janssen mean anything to you?" Her quick glance cut him off. She knew Soren, all right. "Listen, I need some information. Some help. Can you take a short break?"

She shook her head. "No. I cannot leave my work. They will not pay me."

"You can bet a pig's nickel on a butcher's table I won't pay her." A big man emerged from a back room, apparently drawn by the lull in the washerwomen's chatter. Instantly all four women began scrubbing again. He neared the counter and snapped at the woman attending Joseph, "Get back to work! Or you can leave and never come back!"

"I beg your pardon," Joseph began. "There's been a misunder-standing. It was I who detained—"

"You here to get your shirt washed?"

"Yes, but—"

"We have your shirt?"

"Yes, but—"

"Your name?"

"I'm Joseph Campbell," he said loudly. "I'm staying at the Hawk's Eye Inn."

"Very well, Joseph Campbell of the Hawk's Eye Inn," the man said with a smirk. "Your shirt will be ready tomorrow noon." His eyes narrowed, and he leaned over the counter. "These girls are not for sale. But you can find your whore over on the next block. At least that's what they tell me."

Joseph stepped away, feeling defiled. There was no use explaining the situation to an idiot like that. He would wait and simply hope that the woman came to him with the information he sought. He walked outside and took a deep breath of the frigid air. "Alaska, Land of Opportunity," he muttered under his breath. "Even the worst can make a living here."

He was eating supper, just finishing a half-decent meal of roast beef and potatoes, when he caught a glimpse of her outside the window. She was looking in, as if searching for him. In a rough-and-tumble town like this, he decided he had better hurry. A beautiful woman like that wouldn't be alone for long.

Joseph wiped his mouth with the cloth napkin and quickly laid it and a coin beside the tin plate. After a quick swig of coffee, he rushed outside. "Come, come in," he invited. "Let us go to the hearth where you can get warm."

"No," she said, her eyes conveying real fear. He guessed that more than Soren Janssen had abused her. It had taken courage for her to come to him.

"Fine. Where shall we go? I want you to feel comfortable."

Wounded and afraid, her eyes searched his. After a brief moment, she turned and walked away, apparently assuming he would follow. She led him to a row of shanties, behind the second block of ramshackle shops and houses—a pitiful line of tiny homes for those less fortunate than the rest in town. Joseph swallowed hard and entered the dirty hovel, right behind her. It took his eyes a moment to adjust to the darkness. Shortly, a movement by the fire caught his attention, and he saw an old Indian woman holding a small child, perhaps a year old. A half-breed.

"You seek Soren Janssen," said the woman.

He turned back to her and sat down on the dirty blanket at his feet. "Yes."

"I was his companion for the last several years."

"I see." He waited for her to go on. When she didn't, he said, "And then?"

"And then he left me here one night while I was asleep."

"You do not sound surprised."

"It was his intention from the start. As soon as we heard at the fort that his wife was there, seeking him, offering a reward."

"I see," he said again. The wounds were deep in the tiny shack. The child moved but made no sound. What terrible thing had transpired that this child uttered no sound? He thought of his own rowdy, noisy boys back at home.

"He knew she had come into some money, which was the star he always sought."

"You know English well," Joseph said, momentarily distracted.

"I attended a school in Juneau for some years. My father knew the coming of white men would make a difference to our lands. My brothers and I all attended a Catholic boarding school there. My father...my father thought it would help. Instead..."

Joseph did not push her, feeling as if he were prying. "Tell me your name."

"Natasha Dances by Moonlight."

Joseph paused again, thinking on the combination of an obvious Russian name—probably bestowed upon her by some Orthodox nun—and the Indian sounding name given to her by her father. "Natasha..." The name seemed so incongruent and wrong for her! "When did you arrive in Saint Michael?"

"Just as soon as Soren could get us down the river. He told me that he wasn't leaving, but I knew. I knew from his eyes."

"Your son... Is Soren the father?"

"Yes."

He paused, measuring his words. "Natasha, I am prepared to pay you a large sum for the following information. I know this might be painful, and I do not wish you harm. But my employer is looking out for Kaatje Janssen, Soren's wife. He fears that Soren is not all he claims to be."

She snorted a laugh in response, the first semblance of humor he had seen in the woman. Then the smile left her face. "I have nothing. Anything you give me will be used to help my son."

"I will give you enough money to purchase lumber and build a decent house. Enough money to begin your own laundry business and give your...employer some competition. You have already given me lots of information, but I need more. You said Soren never mentioned his wife until she came looking for him?"

"Yes. I had seen her picture, but he left it behind at the cabin. I thought it meant she was dead to his heart, too."

He swallowed hard at her visible pain. "And it was the promise of a financial reward that caught his attention?"

"Yes. He said that if she had enough money to pay for guides and a reward, she had come into some money."

"So he emerged again because he thought she was rich?"

"He told me that he would get his share and come back for me. I do not believe I will ever see him again."

"Because you refuse to?"

"Because he will never come back. Soren is out to care for himself. He wants to do more, care for my son." She paused and glanced at the child. "But eventually it always comes back to Soren."

"One last thing." He pressed his lips together, hating to cause her any more pain. "He told his wife that he saved you. That you were falsely accused by your tribe of...lying with a man out of wedlock.

That you were being beaten for it. That he took you away to save you. Is that true?"

Her eyes did not leave his. "I was with another man. It is true. But the man was Soren Janssen. And my father was so angry he threatened to take me home and beat me. But it was Soren Janssen that tore me from my tribe, from my...honor." It was only at the last word that her gaze dropped. "Soren was betrothed to my sister, but he wanted me. I was a fool and went to him. I was weak. He never asked for my hand."

Joseph rose. "You will have three hundred dollars waiting for you at the hotel desk tomorrow."

She gasped.

"It is good information that you gave me, Natasha. I want you to use the money to get back at Soren Janssen. To do what he could never do. Take care of yourself and your son. You will do so?"

"Yes. I will. I will do as you say. Build a home and another laundry. There is more than enough work, and it will be much better than working for... I deeply appreciate it, Mr. Campbell."

"It is the least I could do." He placed his hat on his head and tipped it toward her, then turned to go, relieved to smell fresh Arctic air. He was so angered by what he had seen, so furious at the devastation Soren had left behind, that he decided to put in a hundred and fifty of his own money toward relieving Natasha's situation.

Kaatje poured herself a cup of coffee and took another out to James, sitting in the cold, on the porch of the Ketchikan Roadhouse. He spent much of his day away from the house, telling her he was looking for new trails to take come spring in search of beaver or elk. The snow was deep, so he could not have gone far from the house. Kaatje knew it was her he needed to escape.

She opened the door, and her eyes grew wider at the cold. James glanced up at her, and then away, as if forcing himself to do so. He was a good man, a strong man. An honorable man. "Here," she said. "For you."

"Thank you."

Kaatje sat down beside him on the step. "I am sorry I made you come with me, James."

"You did not force me."

"I did. In a way. I said I couldn't come without you. But you didn't want to come. Still you came."

"You're wrong," he said, the steam of his coffee rising up to his face. He did not look at her. "I wanted to come. That's why I knew I shouldn't. Karl tried to tell me."

"Karl? What would he know about—?" her words halted suddenly, knowingly. "Ah, Karl. Yes."

James shot her a curious look but did not comment.

"You've spent five days outside. Aren't you tired of being cold?"

"It is fine. The cold gives a man the chance to think."

They sat in companionable silence for a minute. "James, you've seen me safely here. As I asked. Now I want you to go back. You're miserable, and I don't want to live with that responsibility for the next few days. Take this afternoon's ferry and head home."

He looked down at his coffee, then took a sip. Kaatje studied his profile—a slightly large nose that was compensated for by a strong chin, seasoned skin the color of nutmeg from the sun, even in winter. Rough whiskers the same golden color as his hair... Before she could stop herself, she reached out and ran her fingers down his jaw line.

He caught her hand, turning toward her. "Don't." He seemed desperate.

"I'm sorry." She shook her head. "That was stupid. I just want... I just wish..."

He stood abruptly. "I'm getting my bag, Kaatje, and taking that ferry today. I can handle being near you, watching out for you, but not this near."

"James, we can't continue like this."

"No, we can't."

"Why haven't you gone away? Given up on me? Why do you keep taking this punishment?"

"Why?" he blew out a breath of frustration and gave her an incredulous look. "Why?" He ran a hand through his hair and then put his hat on, watching her all the while. He straightened the brim. "Because I'm in love with you, Kaatje Janssen. In love with you. I've been in love with you since that day you got mad at us for killing the baby bear. I love your strength and your resolve and your dedication. I love everything about you. And until I hear that you love your husband and are giving him a chance, that you want me to go away and never come back, I'm going to stay close enough to hear you say you love me back."

He left her then. Never touching her. But it felt as if he had. Every inch of her was warmed by his words. She had wanted to hear them, yet dreaded hearing them. But it was true. She was in love with James Walker, and try as she might, she could not find the love she once had for Soren anywhere in her heart.

But she was trapped. Trapped in a marriage to a man who had betrayed her. She did not believe in divorce. Yet she could not allow herself or her girls to be hurt again. So there she sat, in limbo. "Why, Lord? Why?" She felt crushed by the agony of it all. "Finally, here is a man who could love me. Who wants to love me. Who wants to return my love. But Soren holds me still. Please, Father. Please. Show me your way. Show me the path. And give me the strength to take it."

twenty-two

March 1889

And when Charlie came in to tell us that ten more men"—Karl paused to laugh, barely able to breathe so great was his amusement—"had been seated, the look on your face..." He could not even finish his sentence.

Elsa giggled along with him, half miffed and half bemused by his enjoyment of recalling their mismanagement of the roadhouse when Kaatje was away. "And you were no picture of perfection yourself, Captain Martensen." She gazed fiercely over their table aboard a small, elegant steamer. When the weather had turned unseasonably warm for March, Karl had convinced her to come with him to Glacier Bay on a scouting trip. She had assumed there would be others along and was overjoyed when she discovered that it was just the two of them and a crew.

"No—a picture of perfection I was not. Every day I rise and am thankful to our Lord that I was born for the sea and not for the kitchen."

It was Elsa's turn to laugh. "So are all those guests from the road-house!"

Karl hooted along with her. Their turn at running the Juneau Storm Roadhouse had been more challenging than originally thought. One cook had up and quit, and the other had come down with

264

influenza. Mrs. Hodge had had a terrible cold and was in bed. They tried valiantly for three days to keep it running, relying on the children and remaining staff to assist them. But the two of them were simply no good at keeping hungry men fed. "What were we thinking?" Elsa asked, wiping tears from her eyes. "We haven't cooked in years." She lifted a fork, filled with her last bite of a succulent crab and cheese soufflé. "And for good reason."

Karl pulled a handkerchief from his pocket and wiped his nose. Then he picked up a crystal goblet. "Shall we toast to never running a restaurant again?"

"Never again," she agreed gladly, listening for the delicate *clink* of their glasses. "I can't remember being so relieved when you suggested we compensate Trent, Tora, and Kaatje for lost days at the restaurant and simply close it."

"It was a stroke of brilliance." He paused and gazed at her tenderly. A quiet moment passed. "I am so happy you came with me, Elsa. This trip would've been interesting because of the locale but somewhat lonely."

She smiled back at him and then reached across the table for his hand. "You've done a great deal to ease my loneliness, Karl."

"I am glad you've allowed me to do so."

"Tomorrow we go to shore?"

"Yes. I've arranged for a Hoona guide to take us in kayaks amongst the glaciers. It's a bit dangerous with the warm weather, but we'll take care. Are you game?"

"Of course. I wish the children could see all of this!" Kristian and Eve were back home with Mrs. Hodge, who'd recovered from her cold and could manage the passel of them and help Kaatje with the restaurant with greater ease than Elsa or Karl.

"Perhaps we could bring them up here someday."

His use of *we* did not go unnoticed, and Elsa's heart skipped for a moment.

"I have a present for you," he said mysteriously.

"You do? For what occasion?"

"The maiden voyage of this ship and her first guest." The small steamer was one that Lucas Laning had brought over in pieces across the Panamanian isthmus and built on the western shore.

"I'll accept gifts under any guise."

He rose and went to a corner cabinet, then returned with a large box wrapped in elegant white paper. Seeing him there, with the gift in hand, made her think of all the boxes she had received in the past couple years. "Karl," she said, as she accepted the box and set it on her lap, "have you ever sent me presents before?"

"Presents? Of what sort?"

She studied him, and he looked truly confused. Elsa could feel the heat rise on her neck. How foolish to ask in such a straightforward manner! What would he think of her, accepting gifts from strangers? Though what she was supposed to do with them she did not know...

"Elsa?"

"Oh! Well, the last gift was a stereoscope with pictures from around the world."

"A stereoscope? And you do not know from whom it came?"

"No, I—"

"There was no note?"

"No. I am sorry I broached the subject. Please, forget I said anything." She hurriedly turned to the package on her lap. Would he think she had another suitor? Did she? It was all very puzzling. "What could you have purchased me?" she asked, but did not wait for him to comment. She ripped at the paper and opened the large box while he rose to stand by her side. Inside was a beautifully made sealskin coat, with a hood lined with lush fur, and matching trousers. "Karl!" she said in awe.

"When in Rome... We cannot be touring the glaciers in the latest fashions from Paris."

She rose and, clutching the jacket to her breast, stood on her tiptoes to kiss him. "Thank you, Karl. It was most thoughtful."

"It was not all generosity, I confess."

"Oh?"

He grinned again. "I would pay good money to see you in that outfit."

She swatted him. "Next time we meet, I'll be wearing it. No charge." She rose and gave him a quick buss on the cheek. "Until tomorrow?"

"Until tomorrow, my love." His eyes told her he wished they did not have to part.

She turned and walked from the dining room, aware that he was watching every step and treasuring every second of it. *My love. My love,* she repeated silently.

Karl took a sharp breath as he watched her emerge from her cabin the next morning. She was as lovely as he had envisioned when he first saw the jacket and pants on sale in the marketplace. The pants were slim and shamefully showed off her legs. He tried not to look. And the jacket clung to her curves, apparently meant for a more willowy Indian than Elsa Ramstad. She raised the hood and gave him an impish look.

"You are beautiful, my princess of the Far North." He bowed deeply.

She held the small fur-lined hem of the jacket in a slight curtsy. "Let's get on with it," she said urgently. "If I don't get into that kayak shortly, my insides are going to reach the boiling point."

He knew what she meant. His own Inuit sealskin coat had him uncomfortably warm this day. He eyed the glaciers in the distance. They were beautiful, and yet he knew their shifting forms could easily snuff out the life of the most experienced kayaker. Was it safe?

"Come on!" she said, a girl in Bergen again. She tucked a strand of white blond hair back under her hood. Her cheeks were ruddy and her eyes alight. So different from almost three years ago when he had discovered her in the Skagit Valley mourning Peder.

She made her way down the ladder, to where an old Hoona had pulled alongside, with two other kayaks in tow. "Be careful, Elsa. They are extremely tipsy. Toyatte, here, wished to bring his canoe. But I told him we'd prefer the maneuverability of the kayaks. Don't fall."

"Like this?" She pretended to tip as she entered, sending tiny wakes away from the kayak on either side.

"Elsa!"

"Oh, come, Karl. I have walked lanyards a hundred feet above deck and shimmied up masts in storms around the Horn." She scowled at him.

"All right. You cannot blame me for caring." He nudged her under the chin and then gestured toward the kayaks. "You're saying you've been in a kayak before."

"Once or twice," she quipped, gripping the tiny hole and gingerly stepping in. It barely tipped as she settled to the bottom and maneuvered the oilskin drop cloth about her waist to keep water out. The old Hoona gave her a rotting-teeth smile and a nod, then waited for Karl to enter his kayak. Once he got into his own tightfitting little kayak, they were off, skimming across the waters toward the glaciers.

He could not stop smiling. An adventure with Elsa! As they neared the closest iceberg, he could not keep his eyes off her. She was gazing at it in childish delight, then squealed as she glanced down in the water. "Look, Karl, look!"

Beneath them the iceberg spread out in ghostly, frozen waves, a monolith just beneath the surface. He nodded at her, and she looked at him strangely for a moment, as if she could sense his joy. He was transparent in his feelings for her, he knew. Perhaps it was a mistake, but he didn't think so. From the start on the *Majestic*, he had been honest in his feelings for her, letting her proclaim them first, but never turning back. He wanted it all to be out in the open, this love he had for her. Besides, it was easier to enjoy it that way. There were no games, only pleasure and joy. It was as if God had ordained it himself.

Like this day! The small steamer had entered Glacier Bay, or as the Hoona called it, *Sit-a-da-kay,* or Ice Bay, two days prior. Yesterday, past the smooth marble islands along the southwestern shore, they passed Geikie Glacier, the first of many. By late afternoon they had passed the Miller and later reached the head of the bay and the mouth of the northwest fjord. It was there that they had met Toyatte as they neared the Hoona sealing grounds. Above them rose the magnificent Hoona and Pacific Glaciers, named, as they all had been, by John Muir during his explorations of '79.

The Fairweather Mountains surrounded the fjord, like titanic sentinels standing guard. They were spotless white, from base to summit, making them appear all the more formidable. It was easy to see how they'd inspired the Hoona name of "Ice Mountains." Karl ceased paddling for a moment and raised his face to the sun in a crystal sky, relishing the warmth on his face, the cool spray of the waves against the kayak on his hands, the sounds of the sea. He was startled when it sounded as if he had hit something.

"Seals!" Elsa cried, ten yards ahead of him now. "They're everywhere!"

He laughed aloud. Seals had been hunted in this area for decades now, and it was unheard of to see more than one or two. Now more than ten frolicked about them, if he was counting right.

Once ahead of them, their guide grunted and nodded, intent upon his task. They paddled along, watching as the seals dived and circled, coming alongside them again and again, all big brown eyes and long, stiff whiskers.

After paddling for a mile up the fjord, they neared the Pacific Glacier, making their way through a tangled jungle of ice, taking care not to be squished between two of the slow-moving, bone-crunching bergs. When they had cleared the largest of the fields, Toyatte ceased paddling, gliding to a stop in the dark waters. Karl pulled alongside, while Elsa paddled on ahead in relaxed fashion.

"Come, let us go to the glacier's face," Karl urged.

Toyatte shook his head.

Karl scowled. He had paid the guide with tea, rice, flour, sugar, and tobacco. The terms had been set then. So why was the Hoona being so stubborn? "We will beware of the calving."

"Not glacier," Toyatte said in stilted English. He waved about him. "Weather no like. Bergs come."

Karl frowned. Toyatte's hand motion was from the bottom, not from the top. He had been prepared for the tremendous separations of ice from the mother glacier that formed the floating icebergs around them. But from the bottom? It made sense, that icebergs would release from the bottom as well as the top. Karl simply had not thought of it. His head whipped around.

"Elsa!" he called. "Elsa!"

She turned and laughed, suddenly sprinting ahead with her paddle. She thought he wanted to race; she obviously had not heard Toyatte's warning.

"No, Elsa! Wait!"

All he could hear was her mad paddling, and he assumed she could not hear him. Or she thought it a game and was ignoring him. "Elsa!" He put his shoulders into it, leaving Toyatte in his wake in the sudden urgency to reach her.

By the time he caught up, she was staring up the face of the glacier, a frozen cliff of fifty feet above her.

"Isn't it remarkable—?"

"Elsa, listen! We're in danger. Come. Come away."

"You must be joking. Look how beautiful—"

"Come away!" he demanded.

She frowned and paddled after him.

"It is the icebergs shifting from the bottom that Toyatte fears, not from the top."

Her eyes went out to where the old Hoona bobbed on the surface of the fjord's choppy waters. "From the bottom?"

"Yes." He was not looking at her; he was looking down, searching the icy depths for any rising dangers. "We should not even be this close."

Elsa sighed, and his eyes met hers. "I understand, Karl. But look!" She pointed toward an icy glacier cave not a hundred feet above the waterline. "If we could make it to that, and inside—"

"No, Elsa."

"Really, have you ever—"

"No."

When she set her shoulders back and her chin rose, he knew he was in for an argument. "I have not made it across the seven seas and through hurricane-force winds without taking a risk now and then. This life is made for living, Karl. Yes, we ought to take care. But Toyatte is a super-stitious old Indian who doesn't like the smell in the air. He has proba-bly seen comrades capsized and perhaps drowned, but he will not on this day. Come. Come, beloved. I want to see something new with you."

She gave him a lingering look and then turned to paddle toward the shoreline, to one side of the glacier. Knowing he could do little to stop her short of turning her over himself, he followed behind, scouting the waters below them. Every ten minutes the thunderous groan and creak of the glacier let yet another berg free of its bound-ary, allowing it to crash to the surface with a tremendous splash.

"The sounds remind me of the storms around the Horn," Elsa said.

He agreed in silence. There was the same primal scream and groan that the Cape Horn skies gave passersby in fierce storms. Karl breathed a sigh of relief as their kayaks crunched along the sharp-edged shale of the rocky shore and they scrambled to get out of the kayaks. After a brief stretch, they began climbing.

"Careful, Elsa," Karl said over his shoulder. "Beware of crevasses." But the ice seemed sturdy there, old. And the rock beneath could not be farther than ten feet below them. Karl made footholds and hand-holds where he could in the snow and ice, and Elsa followed at his heels. In minutes, they made it to the top. Elsa gasped when she saw it, and he put his arms around her.

Carved into the face of the glacier was an ice cave, presumably cut by a warm spring waterfall above them that trickled through one end and out the other. The ice was a vitriolic blue, so smooth and hard that it resembled a metallic surface. "It's unearthly," Elsa whispered.

"Aye," he whispered back. The icy dampness emanated in waves off the walls, as if it were actually water, moving so slowly one could not see it, only feel it.

She turned within his arms and bent her head for a kiss. He gladly obliged, relishing the cool smoothness of her lips and the warmth behind it. "I love you, Karl Martensen," she said, her eyes shining.

He took a quick breath. They had hinted at it, both knowing this was coming. But he could have never said it first, not with their past. And the words—to him they signified commitment, a future. It was true! She loved him! Him!

"I love you too, Elsa Ramstad." He bent and kissed her again, pulling her closer, not able to get close enough. When he released her, he stared into her eyes. "Do you think Peder would approve?" It was the question that plagued him, rode him every day like a cougar on a deer's back.

Her eyes never left his. "I think so," she said, and smiled on the last word. "After all this time, after all we've been through, it simply seems *right*. Even Peder, in all his stubbornness, could not deny it."

He laughed, the sound of it sharp and then soft in the echoes of the cave. Despite the warmth of the moment, a shiver suddenly went down his back. He looked to the deep blue ceiling of the ice cave, ten feet above them. It was then they heard the groan, closer than any before them. "Elsa—"

Karl was cut off by such an ear-splitting creak that both covered their ears with mittened hands and winced. But they had no time to comment. Beneath them, the ice shook and groaned as a portion of the ceiling splintered and fell toward them. A shard cut Karl's cheek. He grabbed Elsa's hand, intent upon making their way out of the cave, when the bottom gave way beneath them.

Elsa screamed when the crevasse opened to her left, and she felt herself lean perilously close to the edge. Only Karl's hand on hers stayed her fall for a moment, and it was as if time was suspended. She looked over her shoulder, watched his frightened expression, glanced to her hand, and gazed as only her mitten was left in his hand, and his hand was sliding away, away…

She fell for ten feet, grunting as her back hit an icy edge, and then her forehead another. Thankfully, her body came to a stop as her thighs and hips became lodged in the triangular opening. And the groaning had stopped. For the moment.

"Elsa! Elsa!" She became aware of Karl, high above her.

"Oh, Karl," was all she could mutter, wincing as she moved one of her feet.

"Are you hurt? Can you move?"

She took a moment to take stock. "I'm in a bit of a spot. I seem to be wedged down here, and my right ankle is somewhat hurt. Sprained, maybe. I don't think it's broken."

"Can you move?" His tone gentled, as if he were trying to calm himself in order to calm her.

She reached about, searching for any strong handhold, but there was nothing other than an inch of leverage here or there. "Thank you for the sealskin."

He looked upward and then down at her, shaking his head. "You can thank me later."

"No, I'd be much more cold if I hadn't this to wear."

"You wouldn't be down there if I hadn't suggested an exploration."

"I wouldn't be down here if I hadn't insisted upon the ice cave."

"No matter. How do we get you out?"

Elsa sighed and again examined her predicament. She could only look up and to one side, her head kept from looking straight on by the closeness of the icy wall. "I'm pretty well wedged. We'll need rope."

Another tremendous groan and tremor within the glacier caused Elsa to raise desperate eyes to Karl.

"I know, darling. I know. Hold tight, I'll be back in a moment."

He left her then to find the rope, and Elsa never felt so alone in her life. She remembered the day after she lost Peder at sea, awaking to an empty bed, with no hope of him ever returning. "Oh, please, Lord. Please. Forgive me my foolishness. I call Peder headstrong, but it was I who was headstrong today. Please, Father in heaven. Allow me to return to my children. Allow me to return at Karl's side…" She shut her eyes and leaned one cheek against the hard ice.

"Ayee," Toyatte muttered lowly, suddenly high above her and staring down. Karl appeared on the other side. She watched as they stared at each other, chin to chin, without another word, then let down a short length of rope. It teased Elsa's fingertips, dangling just shy.

Karl let out another few inches. "That's all I have, love."

Elsa could hold it then, but not with any of the strength she needed to pull her out. "It's not enough. It's not enough!" She could hear the desperation in her own voice.

"I'm coming down."

"No! No, Karl. You can't do that." The glacier groaned and trembled about her. "Do you hear that? This crevasse could close any minute. Then we'd both be lost. And there's nothing here to hold, so you'd simply get in your own predicament." She swallowed past the lump in her throat, willing the ache in her stomach back until she could cry in private. "You have to go, Karl. Back to the ship. Bring back more rope."

His eyes screamed in fear of leaving her, but acknowledged the cruel truth of it. "I will move faster than any Hoona and be back as soon as I can. Toyatte will stay here with you."

She nodded slightly, unable to say another word, afraid she would break down.

"You hold on," he said firmly. "You understand me? You hold on!" His voice broke on the last word, and she watched as a tear left his eye and dropped toward her like a raindrop from a forest tree.

That was all it took. The ache moved from her stomach to her throat and she stared up at him. "I will. I will, Karl." She was saying good-bye. Chances were good that she would die before he returned.

Good-bye! After they had just said hello! Just professed their love! *O Lord!* She cried silently. *O Lord!*

"I love you, Elsa." He wept openly. "Hold on to that."

"I love you too, Karl."

He rose, and a sudden thought came to Elsa. "Karl! Karl!"

He knelt by the edge and waited. "Karl, if... Karl, take care of the children."

He stared at her for a moment. "I will. With you. With you, Elsa." He left then, and the crevasse grew colder.

Karl practically tipped over the kayak as soon as he was in the water, so great was his urgency. He left the tears streaming down his cheeks, not wanting to take even a moment away from his deep digs into the water of the fjord to wipe them. He cursed the icebergs that blocked his way drifting back and forth. What was once a playful labyrinth now kept him from the rope aboard ship, from the life of his beloved.

"Please, Father God," he prayed, gritting his teeth as he cleared one of the last fields of icebergs and gave all he had to getting to the ship. "Please don't let me lose Elsa now. I beg you. Please." He dug into the water again with his paddle, ignoring the slow burn in his shoulders and across his upper back. He had crossed a hundred yards of water when another field of icebergs closed in. Forced to stop and consider the most expeditious path, he screamed to the sky, shaking his paddle at the ice mountains with the fury of a foiled warrior.

Unable to pause for yet another second, he paddled toward the first opening he saw. As soon as he passed the first berg, he knew it was a mistake. He looked over his shoulder, intent upon backing out, but another iceberg had blocked his path. He was stopped on all four sides, unable to go anywhere, in danger himself of being crushed. He screamed out his fury again. *"God! Lord! Where...are...you?"*

He panted, his chest heaving with great effort. *"Where are you?"* he screamed again.

Be still and know I am God.

"Father, I—" he panted.

For I know the plans I have for you. Be still.

Karl suddenly knew the meaning of stillness. It was quiet where he was, completely quiet. The outside fjord's wind was blocked by the bergs about him. His vision was of nothing but white to the side and blue above. Beneath him, there was little of the open sea, just the haunting blue iceberg bottoms, scraping here and there as they passed. There was naught he could do but sit and wait upon his Lord.

"I love her, Father. Please help me. Help her to live. We have made just a beginning. I want a whole life with her. Please, Father. Please."

He waited and knew to the marrow of his bones that he had been heard. A moment longer, and the icebergs journeyed on in their own directions, opening a path to Karl that led nearly straight to the ship. He took a deep breath and then paddled onward.

"You not cry," Toyatte said, high above her. "Strong," he said, clenching his fists as if the vision of him would shore up her dwindling courage.

There had been two more frightening moves of the glacier. One had squeezed her tight, so tight that she could barely breathe. She'd thought all was lost. The other had released her, just as she neared fainting from lack of breath. "My children, my children," she had moaned in the beginning. As the ice's frost pierced even her sealskin coat and wool sweater, she began to detach, to feel apart from her body. She was tired, so tired. Her mind, her soul, she supposed, began to contemplate death. And not what she left behind. What was ahead. Would there be the magnificent blue of the ice about her? Of course. Along with the rubiest of reds and sapphire blue the color of her father's eyes…

"Missy? Missy!" Toyatte's voice brought her back to the present.

"What?" she whispered, irritated that he interrupted her delightful vision.

The old Hoona grinned at her, exposing his black-and-white checkerboard of teeth. "He come. The captain. He come." He gestured from his eyes to the fjord. "I see. He come!" He left her then without another word, presumably to get the rope and come back to her while Karl untangled himself from the kayak's oilskin folds. It would be so easy to just let go, surrender to the overwhelming drowsiness that urged her eyelids down, her breathing to slow...

Karl had shouted for his spiked ice-deck boots while briefly aboard ship, and now was thankful for them as he easily ran across the ice to the crevasse that held Elsa. Back in the fjord, two of his crew were rowing toward them, with blankets and coffee, in a lifeboat that would hold Elsa, if necessary.

One look down at her, and he knew it would be necessary. "Elsa! Elsa!" He refused to believe that she had died. Surely she had simply passed out! The trauma of her fall, the frigid temperatures in which she was encased... *Lord, protect her as if you were holding her in your hands instead of this ice holding her. Please, God.* If he hadn't been so busy, he would have been on his knees pleading with God.

Quickly he fashioned a sliding knot, creating a large loop. Looking down, there was perhaps enough room to drop the loop about her head and under one arm. Yet he did not want to risk hanging her. "Elsa! Elsa!" he continued to repeat. She did not stir.

He dropped the loop once, then twice, trying to get it past a knob of ice to her armpit, but to no avail.

Karl looked over at Toyatte, crouched on the other side. "I need to go down to her," he said slowly, hoping the man understood. He quickly tied another slipknot in a second rope and tightened it under his own armpits. With neither the velocity of a fall nor a slim form to aid him, he prayed he could get low enough to reach Elsa. He tossed the length of the rope to Toyatte and showed the Hoona how to hold him, a much larger and heavier man, with little but the strength of his squat body.

He had no time to worry over the guide. Then he lowered himself so that his straight arms held him above and to one side of Elsa, as if guiding him through a small hatch to belowdecks. He dug an ice boot into one side, grunting in pain at the odd angle of his ankle, then did the same with the other. In like fashion he descended as low as he could go, eventually turning upside down to dangle low enough to reach Elsa.

Karl breathed a sigh of relief when he could touch her. The pulse at her neck told him she lived, and with a little more maneuvering he was able to slip the rope around both her arms. He tightened it, then frowned. Unconscious, her arms might simply move up with the motion of the rope and she might slip right through the knot.

His men reached the crevasse with a shout, and Karl sighed again, relieved. Three men were certain to be able to get them out again. And two now spoke English. "I need to stay down here! I'm afraid she'll slip through the loop as you lift her."

"She's unconscious?"

"Yes."

Karl's temples were throbbing from the pressure of being upside down, but he ignored the pain. He touched Elsa's silky hair, rubbed her scalp. "Elsa, Elsa. Come back to me. Come back."

"Ready up here, Captain," one yelled.

"Okay. Leave me here. Pull gently on her rope on the count of three." He looked anxiously about, wondering if there were obstacles that might impede her progress, but there was little he could do in his position even if there were. He swallowed hard. "One... two...three!"

She lurched upward, and as he had feared, her arms squeezed together over her head. Karl let out a cry.

"You all right?" yelled a man.

"Yes. Yes! You got her legs loose. But she's in danger of slipping through the rope. Send down another!"

In two seconds, another rope came down, narrowly missing Karl's head. Quickly, he fashioned a seat out of it. "Try to get her up another few feet!" He grabbed hold of her coat at the collar, conscious of the danger she was in. If she slipped through the rope with the next heave, she could go deeper into the crevasse. But he had to have her higher in order to reach her feet and slip the rope about her. "On my count! Very slowly, please! Very slowly! One...two...three!"

She rose another two feet, and the rope slid to her chin. *She might choke!* he thought desperately. As fast as he could, he pulled her calves toward him, slipping the double loop around each foot and then sliding them to her thighs. Thank the Lord for the sealskin pants! They protected her from the cold and the cruel bite of the rope. "Good! Good!" he called. "Pull up on the second rope. Use it as your mainstay, and the first as only a means to steady her. She needs to go up fast. The first rope is too close to her throat!"

Obediently, they counted as one above, and Elsa sailed to the top. When he lost sight of her over the edge, Karl screamed, "Now get me out of here!"

He was pulled to the top then too and unceremoniously heaved to safety. The glacier groaned, and Karl rubbed his face. "Let's get her off this glacier and back to the ship." He rose, gingerly testing his sore ankles. The two men carried Elsa, one holding her under the armpits, the other her legs, carefully following Toyatte down the side.

When one fell and the three slid ten feet to the bottom, Karl let out a cry of frustration and picked Elsa up himself. "Let me do it! I've got her. Get the boat! Hurry! She's barely breathing! I said *hurry!*"

Elsa awakened to the sensation of sweat rolling down her spine.

"Welcome back," Karl said, kneeling beside her chair. Her feet were on a footstool, raised to a wood stove. She was covered in blankets, and by the fur visible around her face, still in her sealskin.

"Thank you, Karl. For getting me out. I thought...I thought I was going to die there." Visions of her children, laughing aboard the *Majestic,* shot through her mind. She reached out a hand and caressed his face. "I thought we weren't going to be together anymore."

He looked down and then back to her, his gray eyes shimmering. "I thought the same."

"Are you trying to kill me now?"

"What?"

She cast off a wool blanket, then peeled off another. Elsa laughed as she counted the coverings. "Ten blankets! And a bearskin!"

Karl's laugh joined hers, a pleasant cello sound in accompaniment to her alto. "I wanted you warm, really warm, after almost losing you. By the time we got you to the lifeboat, your lips and fingernails were blue."

"And now I'm perspiring so that I'm probably as red as a beet." She tossed several more blankets off, then winced at a pain in her ankle. "It's sprained, don't you think?"

"If I were to hazard a guess."

Elsa raised her eyebrows and cocked a smile at him. "It could've been worse. We just proclaimed our love, and suddenly it looked as if we were going to have to separate forever."

His eyes did not match hers in merriment. "It did look that way." He took her hand in his. "I was frightened, Elsa, terrified that I was about to lose you. When you had just been found."

She nodded, feeling the same intensity of emotions. "I did not want to die. To leave you. My children."

Karl reached out and gently traced the contour of her forehead, brow, and cheeks. "I don't ever want to lose you again. Elsa, my love, would you do me the honor of marrying me?"

She wet her lips and studied his eyes. "I would love to spend the rest of my days by your side, Karl." An impish thought ran through her head. "As captain of your ship."

He laughed and looked to the floor. "We'll discuss who captains our ships." Then his expression turned serious. "But you'll marry me? Soon?"

"I will, Karl. Gladly. Just as soon as we can."

twenty-three

*S*oren tapped his boots against the boardwalk, shaking the street's sticky mud from them, then leaned against the storefront wall to read the story in the *Juneau First Edition*. GOLD STRIKE! the headline screamed. TWENTY-FIVE MILES SOUTHEAST OF FORTY MILE. He had been right in his first reading. He shook his head as he stared at the subheading again. Twenty-five miles southeast of Forty Mile would put that strike so near his own mine that he could practically spit and hit it. He went on reading until a name caught his attention. *Kadachan*.

Surely there were several Indians named "Kadachan" in the Alaska Territory. His heart started pumping. He hadn't seen the man who traveled with James Walker in some time. Months. Kadachan. Was it coincidence that a man of that name was so near his old stake? He crumpled the paper to his lap and looked up and down the street. He had a sick feeling in his gut, a sense of foreboding. There were several sizable claims within striking distance of his own. It could be one of many that struck it lucky.

But what if it was his? What if a claim-jumper had taken over his spot, his tools, and hit it right? What if they were hauling out bucket-loads of gold—his bucketloads—until the vein was emptied? His pulse raced. He raised the paper again, trying to read the rest of the story, but his hands were shaking. It was his. Something deep down told him it was so. Someone had jumped his claim.

He dropped the paper to the ground and hurried down to the roadhouse. He did not plan to report to work that day. Not that day or for some time.

Kaatje hurried toward the door. The breakfast crowd had been fed, and they were in the midst of setup for lunch. Since ice break, the town had boomed with trappers and miners ready to enter the riches of Alaska's Interior.

She smiled when she saw the man at the door. It was Soren. Things had cooled between them since her time away in Ketchikan, but they were still friendly. All in all, it was all right with her. The separation gave her time to think, to be right about her decisions. It was as if she was naming the direction of the wind for once with Soren, and the sensation calmed her. She did not know what was next for them, but she would be deciding it when she did.

"Soren, I—"

His hat was in his hands, and his troubled expression stopped her midsentence.

She hadn't seen that look since the day he left her on the Dakota plains. Her heart pounded dully in her chest. Perhaps he would make the decision for them after all. "You're going then?" she whispered.

"Kaatje, look. I won't be gone long. I need to leave for a while on business."

"For the store?"

The question caught him off guard. "No, on personal business."

"For the mine." She, too, had seen the headlines that morning.

"Yes." His eyes did not leave hers. He reached out a hand to touch her shoulder, but she shied away. "It's only to go and make sure it isn't my claim they want to *stjele* from me." He moved forward and took her hands. "I must stop them. It's our claim, Kaatje. Our future."

She laughed under her breath and gave him an incredulous look. "You must be joking."

He moved away and set the hat on his head. When he turned back to her, his eyes told her he was decided. "This is for us."

"No, Soren. It's never for us. It never has been. It is for you, Soren Janssen. Every move you make is for you. You don't have a giving bone in your body!"

"What are you talking about? I left Bergen for you! I went to the Dakotas for you to start the farm you always wanted!"

"What? Is that what you think? It was for me?" She spat out the last word. "I don't believe you. That's a convenient little excuse you've made in your mind, Soren, but it is not the truth. You left me on that farm with a baby! With a baby! And I don't believe you ever intended to come back." She hoped her eyes sparked all the fire she felt.

"You cannot believe I never intended to return to you. To Christina. I did. I did!" He grabbed her arm, keeping her from running back to the kitchen. "All I wanted was to make something of myself. How many times do I have to tell you that?"

Tears came then. "Don't you see, Soren? Will you never see? You were always *something* in my eyes. You were my husband, my man. You were my daughter's father. You were making a living, however lean the times. But we were together. That was all that was important to me. Together we had made something of ourselves. But not for Soren Janssen. No, for Soren Janssen, it was never enough! It was never enough!"

She turned away to leave him, determined not to watch as he walked out of her life again, but then she paused and spoke over her shoulder without looking.

"What hurts the most," she said through her tears, "was that we were not enough, Soren. Your wife, your children. And we still are not."

She walked away, not looking at him, even as he yelled, "I'll be back, Kaatje. For you and our girls."

"No!" she cried, turning. "Don't bother! Don't bother to come back. If you go away, stay away!"

"It'll be all right, Kaatje," he said, ignoring her words. "Because I'll be rich. It'll be all right! I'll be back!" She let the kitchen door swing shut behind her. Christina and Jessica stared up at her, tears in their eyes, obviously having heard most of the argument. They moved as one—as if to go to Soren—but Kaatje held them back. She pulled them into her arms, embracing them, wanting them to feel her determination to never let them go, even if their father did again and again.

"It'll be all right," she oddly found herself saying, crying with them, stroking one head of hair and then another. "It'll be all right."

James watched as Soren left the roadhouse and jogged over to the mercantile. In half an hour he was out again, with a satchel of supplies in his hands and new boots on his feet.

It had begun. And as suspected, Soren was running to the gold mine like a grizzly to a fat salmon. James kicked the boardwalk on the opposite side of the street and waited for Soren to see him, but the man did not see anything other than his own visions of sugarplums. He hurried down the street toward the ferry gate, apparently intent upon buying his way to Skagway and then hiking over the pass.

James smiled for the first time since his days with Kaatje in Ketchikan. The dog was leaving town! But his smile quickly fell. Soren's departure didn't clear his way to Kaatje. On the contrary. To remain faithful to his decision in Ketchikan, he would need to steer clear. The thought made him ache inside. She would need support now, but he couldn't be there for her. The thought of it threatened to pull him into parts like a man drawn and quartered.

He clenched and unclenched his hands as he paced along an alleyway, wanting to be away from prying eyes. He needed a task, a vision, something to keep him busy and away from Kaatje while Soren was away. While Soren was away! Suddenly an idea came to him—James would follow the man back into the Interior. Every panting breath, every aching step, every decision of Soren Janssen would be echoed by James Walker until he knew the truth.

With luck, he would be the one to show Soren the new deed to the mine and the name on the paper.

By the third day on the trail, Soren knew that he was being followed. On the second, he had decided that it was a coincidence, that another party had simply departed Skagway the day after him, as he had the day after the party before him. But on the third day he knew. He could sense it, as he could sense a claim-jumper working his mine. And he could guess who it was. James Walker.

The man was like a flea on an alley dog's hind leg. Soren had not been able to take a decent drink while in Juneau, to say nothing of satisfying his pent-up frustration from being without a woman for too long. He could see why Walker would shadow him while in Juneau, waiting for him to trip up, so he could lay claim to Kaatje. But why here along the trail? What would Soren's journey mean to the lout? Walker didn't care anything for him. Unless he was in cahoots with the Indian who'd stolen his claim. If anything, Soren's departure could have been his chance to move in on Kaatje, to tell her what a fool Soren was for leaving her. Why not stay with Kaatje and make the most of the time he had with her before her husband returned instead of trailing him? And Soren was not meandering along the trail. He was moving along, like a man possessed. But James was matching his speed.

And he kept matching his speed, day after day. Somewhere between Lake Laberge and the river, Soren lost him. Perhaps Walker had turned back or taken ill. He cared not. All he cared about was getting to his mine and returning with his fortune. With some gold nuggets in his pocket, he could win Kaatje back with pride. What did James Walker have, after all? Years in the Interior? Superior hunting skills? Ha! As if that could satisfy a woman. No. A woman needed fine things to wear and a husband of whom she could be proud. He was going to make Kaatje proud, build the finest mansion Juneau had ever seen, and buy his daughters anything they wanted. He stayed up nights, thinking about all that he could finally accomplish with the wealth he would bring home in shimmering gold.

James passed Soren one night along the end of Lake Laberge and, by hiking into the night, assumed he was gaining at least a half-mile on him each day. If he calculated it right, that would put him a day ahead of the man in reaching the mine, more than enough time to find out what had transpired in the mine and prepare for the confrontation that was as sure as the river's flow.

He passed familiar sites—where he and Kadachan had saved Kaatje from the grizzly, where he had pretended to ignore her as she gathered early berries but could do anything but, and finally, the mine, where he had first come to care about Kaatje's tender heart. Even the glimpse of it as he rounded the bend of the river made his heart palpitate and his lips clench together. Hadn't this place been the place of incredible pain to Kaatje? Where she saw the evidence of an ill-begotten love, a family abandoned? As if it were the same day, he could remember following her deep into the woods, her slim form racing through the trees and columns of light cascading from the canopy above. He could hear her guttural cry of anguish.

It made him want to shake his fist at God, those memories. But for now, he willed himself to follow the direction he had found in Ketchikan—to remain Kaatje's silent protector, to flush out the truth in Soren before leaving her alone with him He spent his frustration on the effort of getting the skiff to the river's edge, which was no small task in the spring ice melt. The whole journey had been trying, as difficult as last year's, except that now he missed Kaatje, so it was much lonelier.

Kadachan was at the river's edge as he approached, and James caught his attention with an owl call. It was a poor imitation, and Kadachan thought it hilarious each time James tried. The Tlingit Indian was a master at it, as he was at ten other bird calls. The man smiled broadly and lifted one large hand in greeting. He waited for James to float near, then waded to thigh depth to help bring him to shore. Once there, they clasped hands and walked toward the makeshift shelters the men had built of cedar boughs and small logs, not wanting to wait any longer than necessary to get the mine up and running.

"It is as they say?" James asked. "You have struck gold?"

Kadachan smiled again and went to a corner trunk. He opened it and then tossed a huge nugget, twice the size of the one Kaatje had found, to his old friend. James whistled under his breath at the weight of it. "And there are others?"

The Indian bent and then, with some effort, carried the small trunk over to James, who whistled again, at a loss for words. The trunk was filled mostly with smaller nuggets, but here and there were other sizable rocks, of similar diameter to the one Kaatje found in the water. James shook his head. "I thought it would be a ruse. I truly thought it would only be something to flush Soren out of the thicket, not a real mine."

The other men sat around, smoking Indian cigars and watching their boss appreciate their work. "You all have done a fine job. You will be compensated as promised."

"How about now?" grumbled the fat man.

"How 'bout it?" James repeated with a smile. He searched the trunk for seven nuggets that were comparable in size, then tossed one to each of the men. "You need to understand that what I say is true," he said quietly. "I will treat you fairly. This is not a bait-and-switch game. You will get what I promised you."

They hooted and swore and laughed, looking at their individual prizes. They had accomplished all that James had hoped and more. And he would fulfill his promises to them as he had said.

And in thanks, they would back him up when Soren came the next day. He was sure of it.

Soren grew excited as the shoreline became more familiar. He was nearing home or the closest thing to it that he recently remembered.

He loved these deep forests of cedar and pine and maple. Yet he would have to be careful. He had not left on good terms when he had spirited Natasha off to distant lands. Her father would still like to have words with him, he was sure, if not a good flogging. They were a fairly peaceful tribe, but Soren knew that he had crossed the line in taking Natasha away from her family.

Briefly he thought of his son and his beautiful brown eyes. His quick smile. But Soren put him out of his mind. His first obligation was to his elder children. When he was rich and Kaatje and the girls had all they wanted, then he would go back to care for the mother of his son. But that would be a quiet affair—he never wanted his affiliations with another woman to hurt Kaatje again. The pain was deep in her eyes, and Soren knew he was close to never winning her back again. This was it. As a fellow Irish miner once said to him, if he did not find the gold at the end of this rainbow, there would certainly never be a rainbow again.

He rounded the last bend in the river and scowled as he saw a group of men encamped on shore. Prepared for the worst, he paused and strapped on a gun belt, a Colt .45 secured low on each hip. Both were loaded, as was his shotgun that lay across the center seat of the rowboat. He thought about getting it, bringing it closer to him, when a man rose and pointed in his direction. He had been discovered.

Setting his chin in determination, he poled toward the encampment. This was his land, his claim. It would be harder if they had indeed struck gold on the property. They would be infinitely more reluctant to depart. But nonetheless it was his. He was feeling fairly confident until he saw the form of James Walker edge out of the group and walk to shore. Right behind him was Kadachan. He swallowed his surprise at seeing James ahead of him when he had thought him behind.

The skiff ground into the pebbles, and Soren walked to the end, hopping out and turning to pull it more firmly onto shore as if the men were not there. Then he turned and walked right to James, his heels sinking in the soggy ground with each determined step.

"You're on my land."

"No, we're not."

"Yes, you are." He walked past the men toward the cliff side where he had left tracer mine materials. "These are my tools you're using."

"You left them behind. We have made this claim our own since you abandoned it." James's expression bothered Soren. He was too confident.

"I left them behind only for a season. Here I am again," he said, pulling his arms out to the sides as if greeting old friends. "Now it is time for you all to go." His hands came down to rest on either pistol. "And you are to leave any gold you have found."

The men stayed where they were, a formidable lot.

"You did find gold, right?" Soren asked. "It was my mine that was reported in the newspaper? There aren't many others up and running yet that I've seen, unless things have changed since last year."

"Oh, we found gold, all right." James turned, picked up the heavy, small trunk, then dropped it to the fine gravel before him and lifted the top.

Soren fought the urge to gasp. He let a thin smile split his lips. "Do not worry," he said to the other men around James. "I will reward you for your work. You will be paid."

"With what?" James asked, his voice little more than a rumble.

"With this."

"This is not yours."

"It most certainly is." He picked up the biggest gold nugget in the trunk as he searched his vest pocket and produced a land deed for James to read. How could the man be so stupid? Did he think he could send a group of men here to rob him blind and Soren would not see? He held it out to James, and the man calmly took it.

"Yep," he said with a nod. "You have a serious problem, Soren."

"Oh?" Soren bantered back.

"Yes. This deed here expired some months back. The land claim has been refiled under another name."

Soren's eyes shot up to meet James's laughing gaze. James didn't drop his eyes as he reached into his own vest pocket and took out a leather case. Gingerly, he removed a pristine white document and read it, as if to remind himself. "Mm-hmm, that's it. This mine is no longer in the name of Soren Janssen. This claim has been filed in honor of Kaatje Janssen. It looks to me like your wife is a wealthy woman, Soren. And you're out in the cold once again."

twenty-four

May 1889

*J*ames had watched the blood drain from Soren's face as his eyes
scanned the land deed again and again. It had given him infinite pleasure to watch the man turn away, his shoulders sagging
in defeat. But what truly bothered James was Soren's expression as he
climbed back into the boat and pushed off into the river. His eyes
never left James's—and they were cold, so cold.

His first inclination was to celebrate with the men, to toss them
each another nugget of gold and dance around the campfire. But there
was no joy in his heart at beating Soren that day, and it came as a
cruel surprise. He immediately walked deep into the woods to exam-
ine what he was feeling. Following the deer path that Kaatje had once
followed, he hiked to where the forest canopy high overhead was so
dense that the light grew dim and the shafts of sunlight all the more
intense.

He leaned against an old pine, then sat down amongst the moss
and peat and pine cones, cross-legged, near a column of sunlight. He
stared as it slowly moved closer to him over a half-hour period, content to think of something other than himself, Soren, and Kaatje. First
the column illuminated a tight green pine cone—most likely dropped
by a squirrel—then brilliant, yellow-green moss on a log, then an

intricate spider web strung between the roots of the tree against which he sat… The shaft came closer and closer, showing him different details of the forest floor as though God was showing him different parts of his own heart.

James sighed and leaned forward as the sunlight touched his shoulder and then climbed his neck until he could feel the subtle heat of it on his head. "I have sinned, Father."

His Lord knew that already.

"I wanted to protect Kaatje, but more than that, I wanted to beat Soren. I wanted to hurt him."

He knew that, too.

"I wanted him to fall, Father, to know defeat. I wished him ill, and it is not my place to wish such things. I wanted him to feel pain, because I feel it. Because I couldn't have his wife. I wanted her more than life itself. Forgive me."

The sunlight moved off his head and to his left shoulder. He watched through bleary eyes as it moved on, mourning the loss of Kaatje and the fact that hating Soren would not bring her to him. He swallowed hard. "I will leave her, Lord. Leave her in your hands."

James felt the indistinguishable desire suddenly to go home. To Juneau? It was as close to a home as any since he had left his wife's graveside in Minnesota. But that took him back to Kaatje. "How can that be, God? How can I be close to her when…?"

Home. He was to go home.

Now. It was so clear to him it was as if God had audibly spoken.

But he had just promised to leave her. To stay away from her. Why was he to go home? Why now? Instinctively he knew—Kaatje was in danger. He leapt to his feet and started walking quickly to camp, then padded to a jog, then to a full run.

Something was wrong, desperately wrong. The respite of the forest floor and the gentle sun was pushed away like an Arctic wind on a warm eve, and inside, James shuddered. All he could think of now were Soren's cold, cold eyes.

He ran until his lungs burned. When he reached the claim, the men looked up at him in confusion and concern. One spilled his tin cup of steaming coffee, swearing, but James had more on his mind than a man's mild burn. "I need to get back to Juneau. Right away."

Kaatje brought a mug of coffee to Elsa, who sat sketching one of the totems on Ketchikan's seaward banks. It was a cold, drizzly day, but Elsa had insisted on going out to sketch. "I'm going mad," she explained. It had been a long month of convalescing as she let her sprained ankle heal.

It had been Kaatje who had come up with the idea of sailing to Ketchikan for a holiday, of sorts. Her girls were eager for a break too. So they all went south on Karl's small steamer. He had left them there while he took a trip to Seattle on the *Fair Alaska* to pick up his first group of tourists. They would arrive in two weeks for the grand opening of the Storm Roadhouse of Ketchikan. Kaatje could tell that Elsa was itching to see him, could tell that she was restless, so restless that she had even insisted on going out on such a dismal day.

Bradford sat beside her on a huge, sea-grayed log, stripped of any bark or moss by the driving wind and rain of the region. He held an umbrella above them both, silently watching as Elsa sketched the eagle, bear, and salmon on the giant totem pole before them. Beyond them, in the trees, Christina and Jessica were chasing Elsa's children and the Bresleys' little boy with joyful shouts and screeches, oblivious to the fact that they were getting soaked. They had been as fidgety as Elsa to get outside, regardless of the weather.

Kaatje sat down on the other side of Elsa, taking the umbrella from Bradford, who immediately left to join a game of tag with the children. There was so much moisture in the air that Elsa's paper curled at the edges, but she ignored it, seeming to be in another world as she sketched madly, as if the totem would fall any minute and her opportunity would be lost forever.

"How do you do that?" Kaatje asked in a hushed tone.

"What?"

"That. Sketch so well. Did you always know you would be an artist?"

"Not always." Gradually, a bear's paw took shape at the top of the pole on her paper. "I simply started. You never know what you can do until you start."

Kaatje smiled. She'd come to know that too. From crossing the Atlantic to America, to farming the land by herself, to co-managing a roadhouse, Kaatje had surprised herself at what she could accomplish if she simply began the process.

Elsa completed her sketch and sat back, looking from totem to pad, then shifted her swollen, wrapped ankle a bit.

"You miss him, don't you?" Kaatje asked gently.

"Horribly."

"What happened in Glacier Bay? I mean, beyond the accident."

Elsa smiled and shot her a quick look. Then, gazing out to sea as if hoping his *Fair Alaska* might emerge from the mists, she said, "He told me he loved me."

"Finally."

"Finally?"

"You two have been in love all year. What gave him the courage to tell you?"

Her grin grew more broad. "I told him I loved him first."

Kaatje giggled. "Brazen girl!" she chided. "You never are one to wait, are you?"

Elsa laughed with her. "That is true. But he needed... I don't know, I think he needed me to be the first one to say so since we had shared so much in the past. It was as if he was terrified to speak again and be rebuffed. But all I wanted was to hear him say those words. To confirm all I was feeling."

Kaatje looked down and kicked the fine, rounded sea gravel with the toe of her boot. "It is good that you two have found each other. It is right."

"You think so? Really?"

"Really."

"It relieves me to hear you say that, Kaatje. I think it's right too, but sometimes I get a niggling doubt. That somehow I'm not honoring Peder's memory by staying on my own without a man."

"Peder would not have wanted that. You are a young woman. You have a whole life ahead of you. And it will be all the more rich with a companion."

Elsa gave her another quick look. "As it would be for you."

Kaatje scoffed at her words. "I fear I am destined to live my life as an old maid. The man who has me tends to throw me to the winds, and the man who wants me cannot have me."

"And you? What do you want?"

Kaatje stood, suddenly uneasy. "I want...I want things to be settled, one way or another, as I have for almost seven long years."

Soren moved more quickly toward home than he had to the mine, and James shadowed him, finding himself surprised and challenged by his pace. They traveled hard, taking risks in riding the river and walking the trails until the last vestiges of twilight faded from the sky. Fortunately, the days were slowly getting longer, the light staying with them until nine o'clock.

James sank to his bedroll one night, rubbing his aching calves and knees. It had been a hard month on the trail. He wondered if Soren— just a half-day ahead of him, judging from his last campfire—ached as much as he. Would it slow him down any? And yet part of him wanted to get on with it, to get to the conclusion of this grand puzzle they were putting together. There were still several questions that had to be resolved. How would Soren react to Kaatje when he confronted her with the facts of ownership? James had not told either of them that it was he who had changed the registration when the deed lapsed. He needed to be there when he confronted her, to tell them both the truth at the same time. He feared what the man would do to her otherwise.

And how would Kaatje react? James wished now that he had found the opportunity to tell Kaatje what he had done and why. That he'd only wanted to protect her. But doubts about his own motive jabbed at him. Had he done it solely to beat Soren? Would it all backfire, providing Soren the means he sought to settle down and be the man Kaatje always wanted? One thing was clear to James: He would witness the resolution to all of this and then leave town. Staying near Kaatje, but unable to be with her, only tore him apart, and it had to stop. To say nothing of what it did to Kaatje as she sought to rebuild her marriage.

He would simply make sure that all was resolved, that Kaatje was safe, and then he would say his forever good-bye. James swallowed hard. He would not cry again over it. He would not.

Soren punched the wall of the Storm Roadhouse of Juneau in fury when he found out Kaatje was gone. Had she run away? Hidden herself away to enjoy his hard-earned money without sharing any with him? "Where is she?" he ground out, glaring at the shaking waif of a waitress in the roadhouse door. "Where is she?" he screamed.

Sara tried to shut the door in his face, but he shot a foot out to block its progress. He fiercely grabbed her arm, then looked down, panting, his hand throbbing, trying to get control. "Listen to me. I need to speak with her. It's urgent. Where is she?"

"Ketchikan," Sara whispered. "She went down there for the grand opening of the roadhouse. It's in four days."

He dropped her arm so suddenly, she cried out. It surprised him. Did she think he was going to strike her? He was not a violent man. Ordinarily.

"Thank you," he muttered, turning and wiping a hand over his sweaty upper lip. He winced. Had he broken some fingers pounding on the door? The pain only fed his fury.

Slowly he pulled out his pocket watch. Four o'clock. There was a ferry leaving in the morning to Ketchikan, as there was each morning. And he aimed to be on it.

When Sara related to James what had transpired, he did not wait for the morning's ferry. He went directly to the docks and hired a decrepit old steamer south. He wanted to be in Ketchikan, with Kaatje, when Soren arrived. If he could beat the ferry.

It would take them three days to reach Ketchikan, if they hit the tides right. The old ferryman insisted upon going down Stephen's Passage and hugging the western shoreline, rather than going out to sea. "I must beat the morning's ferry to Ketchikan. You're sure you can beat it?" James asked for the fourth time.

"As sure as mosquitoes," the man drawled.

James sighed. What were his options? He could do little but trust that the Lord had put him in this place, at this time, for his purpose.

But the next day, he cradled his head in his hands as the old man worked on the broken-down boiler. He had spent a difficult night in the tiny, cramped cabin with the pilot, who snored incessantly. And now he was growing frustrated and frantic. James paced back and forth. "You swore to me you'd get me there ahead of the ferry! Hurry, man! It's important!"

"I'm doin' all I can. You just settle your drawers on that seat over there and leave me be." He gave James a sour look and ceased working, chewing on a wad of tobacco, until James did as he bid. By noon, James was ready to start running along the coastline toward Ketchikan, as mad as it sounded. Anything was better than languishing there, with the old man.

It was then the engine started.

"Hurry, man. Give it all she's got. We'll have to run past dark."

"We'll do no such thing! These shoals would be the death of us!"

James leaned closer. "I waited for you to get the engine started. It will not idle until I tell you it should do so."

And as it happened, after their delay, long days among the islands and archipelagos of the rough coastline caused them to reach the small dock of Ketchikan just as the ferry did. James groaned. There was no time to warn Kaatje, to tell her what he had done. He could only be there to witness what transpired and to do what he could to ease the truth into light.

Kaatje looked out the window at a group of Tlingit Indians disembarking from the Tuesday morning ferry, then looked again. Was that Soren? And then from the other small steamer—was that James? Soren walked straight down the dock and toward the roadhouse while James hung back a little, obviously preferring not to be seen just yet. A bead of perspiration cascaded down her spine. Both of them, here, in Ketchikan. It did not bode well.

"Clarify my feelings, Lord," she whispered. "Help me to see your path and follow it every step of the way." She moved to one side of the window, watching as Soren climbed the freshly hewn timber steps and rapped on the front door. She did not answer it for a moment, staring at the man who was once her husband. Who still was, legally. Elsa came down the stairs, but Kaatje waved her back. Taking a breath, Kaatje opened the door.

"Kaatje," Soren said. There was anger and disgust in his voice. No joy or welcome.

"Soren?" she asked in confusion. "What…what are you doing here?"

"I could ask the same question." He pushed her hand aside and made his way through the foyer and into the front room, a large sitting room with giant windows looking out toward the ocean. On the other side of the room was a doorway to the restaurant, and on the far left, a doorway to the hotel rooms upstairs. The huge Victorian was built to accommodate up to fifty people a night. It was the largest Trent had ever constructed.

Elsa stepped forward with a slight cough, as if to reassure Kaatje of her presence, obviously concerned by Soren's demeanor.

"It's all right, Elsa."

"Is it?" Soren asked. He unrolled a newspaper and showed it to Kaatje. It was the issue from the day he left her in Juneau. "Remember this?"

"I do."

"So do I," said a low voice at the door. It was James. He entered and closed the door behind him. "I need you both to sit down. I think I should say something first."

"Not until I have a word with my wife."

"Don't say something you'll regret later."

"Like what?"

"Hear me out, Soren. Take a seat."

James looked miserable, almost repentant. What had he done? What could he have possibly done to look as he did?

"I prefer to stand," Soren said.

"As do I," Kaatje said, steeling herself for the hard news that James obviously had to deliver.

"Forget it. I'm having my say," Soren said.

"But—"

"Kaatje, why didn't you just tell me?" Soren asked, before James could go on. "You thought you could steal my mine out from under me? Why? A means of paying me back? What was going on in that little head of yours? Were you thinking you'd divorce me, marry him?" He stepped closer to her, menacing in his shaking anger. "Well, you cannot have it. The mine belongs to me. I discovered it, worked it, staked a claim. And you stole it out from under me."

"What are you talking about?"

"I'm talking about this gold strike!" He threw the old Juneau paper at her. It hit her waist and fell to the floor.

"Stop it! Stop it, Soren. I don't know anything about that mine… I made no plans to divorce you—"

"You think I'm an idiot? Okay, say you don't want a divorce. But if I want you back, I have to come on your terms, is that it? You have to hold the purse strings? I'm a man, Kaatje. I need my own means."

"Soren, I'll ask once more. What are you talking about?"

"This," James said, his tone miserable. He unfolded a leather pocketbook and pulled a parchment from inside, handing it to her.

Quickly she scanned the document. It was a land deed, for a claim. Her eyes flew to Soren and then James. On the bottom line was her name. "You mean, I own the claim?"

"Why pretend you didn't know?" sneered Soren.

"Because she didn't," James said.

"You're telling me that she didn't go and put her name on the deed when it lapsed? That she didn't intend to use this as a final insult? To laugh in my face when she deposited the gold at the bank?"

"Final insult?" Kaatje asked. "What does that mean?"

"I am saying that you've had me groveling at your feet for months. Eight months now, Kaatje. A loving wife, a wife who hadn't gone frigid, would've welcomed me back right away."

Kaatje took deep breaths as her own fury grew. "I do not know how you could have expected anything else of me, Soren. You left me for more than eight months—it was seven years! You were as good as dead as far as I knew. And I know nothing of this deed."

He took another step toward her, but James put a hand to his chest. Soren pushed it away, his eyes still on Kaatje. "Sure you did. You strung me along, making me think you would take me back, distracting me until you could get your hands on my mine. My only hope for a future, and you thought you'd steal it out from under me. Trying to pay me back, Kitten?"

James shoved him backward with a roar. "Stop it! Quiet! She knew nothing of the deed. It was I who changed it to her name when I discovered the deed lapsed. It was I who figured you owed her every cent you had, to say nothing of your heart on a plate."

Kaatje sat down heavily on the edge of a green velvet settee, and Elsa came around and sat down next to her, putting an arm around her shoulders.

Soren paced a bit, like a wounded dog, ready to strike out in fear as much as anger. Suddenly, Kaatje felt very sorry for him—it was as if all that had been good and hopeful in him once had been lost. Who was he now? What was he about? His eyes were hollow, his expression deadly cold.

"Yes, I see the truth now," he said, so low they could barely hear him. "You two were working together. Two lovebirds making the most out of the ex-husband. String him along, Kaatje. Yes, make him think you're going to welcome him home, while I steal the land out from under him. He's *idiotisk*—he won't find out until it's too late."

"It wasn't like that," James said.

"Oh yes, it was. You never intended to give me a chance," he said to Kaatje.

"Yes, I intended to give you every chance."

"And when I kissed you. When we were in the alley and you pulled away, your lover was right there to intervene."

"Coincidence."

He laughed mirthlessly. "Do you think I am so thick?"

"Soren," she said, rising, "You have it all wrong. There's been—"

He didn't wait for her to finish speaking. He shoved her back to the settee and Elsa yelped. James was there, grabbing him by the shirt at the collar and pushing him back toward the door with a growl. "Get out!" he yelled. "Don't ever touch Kaatje again!" He opened the door with one hand and shoved Soren out.

Soren stumbled and then rose, wiping his upper lip with the back of his hand. "You'd like that, wouldn't you, Walker? If I never touched her again?" He looked from him to Kaatje, through the windowpane. Then he turned and walked away.

Kaatje was trembling. She had never seen Soren like that, and the strangeness of it unnerved her. Just what was that man not capable of doing? Suddenly she feared for her life, for James. For her girls and Elsa...

James walked back in, his face a mask of sorrow. "I need to apologize, Kaatje."

She rose and walked to him. "There is no need, James. I understand."

"I wasn't thinking straight, only of Soren and making him be truthful to you. I wanted to hurt him where it would hurt most. Rob him of his future, as he did to you again and again."

Kaatje couldn't help herself. She moved to him, wrapping her arms around his chest, holding him close. She could tell he was surprised and reluctant to hold her. But she didn't care. She needed reassurance. A man's reassurance, right now, when she was so frightened.

"I wanted to know his true motivation in coming back to you. Whether he had really changed as much as he led you to believe."

"How did you know that he was lying?"

"I didn't. It was gut instinct." He released her and paced away. "But I confess, there was more to it." Elsa rose and left the room, obviously realizing they needed the privacy. As the door closed behind her, he continued, "I wanted you, Kaatje. For myself. I had such strong feelings for you; you're the only woman I have loved since my wife. And it burned to give you up. I wanted Soren to fail you, to give me a chance." He rubbed his eyes as if suddenly weary. "Will you forgive me? For wishing ill upon your husband? Upon your marriage?"

Kaatje walked to him and took his hands. "You are a good man, James, regardless of the poor choices we made. We both made choices, together. You have honored my marriage more than most men would have and have remained my true friend. I could not have asked for more. My ultimate welfare was on your mind—I know that. Otherwise, you would've made the claim out in your own name."

He looked down at her, his face still mired in confusion. "Where do we go from here?"

"I do not know." She went over to a secretary behind the front reception desk and pulled out a locked box, then a key from under the collar of her high-necked dress. She unlocked the cherry box and pulled out a letter. "I received this last week. It's from Trent's detective, the same man who located Tora for him. Trent had him investigate Soren, set him on Soren's trail before leaving on his honeymoon." She smiled ruefully. "I have a lot of friends looking out for me."

She walked out from behind the heavy desk. "Soren did have an Indian companion. She was not beaten by members of her tribe, as Soren claimed, but was an outcast for...taking up with Soren, her sister's intended. She bore him a son. They were living in poverty in Saint Michael, where Soren abandoned them in favor of seeking me out again. She told the detective he had come just as soon as he heard that there was a reward and that I had hired guides to search for him. She told him that Soren came running because he thought I was a woman of means. And that poor girl was left living in squalor."

James sighed and stroked her face. "An owl never stops hooting."

Kaatje rested her cheek against his chest. "He hasn't yet. And one never knows what is beyond the corner when it comes to Soren Janssen. I want to send her money, James. Make sure she is all right and her child cared for."

"You can't take care of all of Soren's messes."

"I can take care of those I know about. The detective left her some money, but I intend to send more. Apparently I now own a prosperous gold mine."

James laughed mirthlessly. "That you do, my dear. That you do."

Just outside, hidden in a dense cedar grove, Soren watched as Kaatje and James finally embraced. It was obvious that he was right. Kaatje was a conniving wench who had cheated him out of his rightful wealth, and James, her lover in the wings. They hoped he would go away and never come back. But they would not be so fortunate. No, he would be back. And soon.

twenty-five

May 1889

Tora loved being Trent Storm's wife. She loved having his ring on her finger, the passion of a shared marital bed, the security of having him nearby. There was an intimacy in her marriage that she would never have believed possible prior to exchanging vows with her husband.

They were at sea once again, making their way back to Alaska. After supper that night in the dining hall, Trent bid good night to their companions and offered Tora his arm. She took it, and they left the hall to stroll the teak decks, kept pristine by an endless line of sailors scrubbing, sanding, and refinishing. The captain had told them that they had begun the process on the first voyage of the elegant steamer, and it would be an ongoing venture. As soon as they refinished the entire deck, they began on the rails. When they finished the rails, they went to the wood walls of the bridge and the numerous doors. When they finished that, they began again with the deck. The attention to detail aboard the ship had paid off. She was magnificent, one of the finest ships under steam in 1889.

"Thank you, Trent," she said, holding on to her dainty hat as a moist gust off the sea threatened to pull it from her head.

"For what?"

"For marrying me, for taking me on this trip. Hawaii, Japan, all of it. It has been delightful."

"Not nearly as delightful as you. I am proud to be your husband, Tora."

"And I your wife."

Two sailors passed by, and the couple fell to silence. It was a companionable silence, and they strolled onward, each appreciating the song a quintet of sailors sang at a capstan, unfurling a sail, to counterbalance the new wind off the water. They paused at the bow, where a boy slung clay discs—or "pigeons," as they called them—from a sling, while another shot each one as it arced toward the water.

"Care to give it a go?" the man with the gun asked Trent.

"No, thank you."

"I would!" Tora volunteered.

The man laughed, a merry sound that emerged from low in his gut. "My own wife is quite a shot. Do you mind, sir?"

"Not at all. My wife seems capable of surprising me at every turn."

"Keeps a marriage fresh, that's what I always say." He handed the gun to Tora and could tell that she found it surprisingly heavy. "Held one of these before?"

"No."

He turned to the boy who handed him another shotgun. "Raise it with your left hand, here," he said, holding the shaft. "Then use your right hand to pull the trigger. It's cocked and loaded. Be ready for some kickback—it'll feel as if someone has suddenly pushed you on the shoulder. So keep your stance wide, your knees slightly bent."

She did as he instructed, tensed for the pigeon.

"Ready?"

"I suppose."

"Pull," he called, and with that the boy sent the pigeon flinging into the sky.

She shot too high, and then the man caught it with his gun just before it struck water, shattering it into tiny shards.

"Well, perhaps you ought to stick to sewing, eh?"

She looked him in the eye and gave him a level smile. "Let's go again."

They repeated the cycle, but this time Tora wasn't so far off. "Once more, please?"

"How can I resist a question put to me like that?" he asked Trent. He waited as Tora, after watching him load his, reloaded the gun and cocked it herself.

"Pull," she said. This time, she kept the pigeon in her sights, just ahead of it, and pulled the trigger as it began to descend.

Trent shouted his approval as the pigeon disintegrated into a hundred pieces and the man's shot went long, without a pigeon to stop it. The man echoed Trent's hoot and set his gun aside. "Forgive me for not making a proper introduction. I am Hunter Gainsley."

"Mr. Gainsley," Trent said. "I am Trent Storm, and this is my new bride, Tora Storm."

"You did a fine job, ma'am."

"Thank you. And thank you for the opportunity to shoot."

"Any time, Mrs. Storm."

The couple resumed their walk until Tora took a deep breath and paused at the rail. "What do you think they're doing at home?" she asked dreamily, suddenly anxious to see Elsa, Kaatje, and the rest.

"Probably preparing for the Storm Roadhouse grand opening in Ketchikan. If the Bresleys kept it on schedule."

"Goodness! Is it that time already?"

"We've been away six months, darling."

"Are you sorry to be missing your second Alaska opening?"

"Not half as sorry as I'd be if I weren't here with you." He smiled at her, then, scanning the deck, pulled her between two lifeboats. Hidden there, he kissed her, a deep, searching kiss, until she squirmed in his arms. "Trent, what if someone else is strolling the deck?"

"Then, my love," he said tenderly, "they'll see a couple in love stealing a scandalous moment together."

"Come," she said, slanting her eyes at him as she took his hand. "Let's go somewhere proper for a married couple intent upon privacy."

When they reached their room, Trent popped the cork from a deep green bottle.

"Champagne? What are we celebrating?" Tora asked. Trent was not ordinarily one to drink.

"Us. Our union." He poured two flutes and handed her one.

"And to our friends at the Ketchikan roadhouse. May we soon be reunited."

"To our friends in Ketchikan," Trent repeated.

"Karl, where are you?" Elsa muttered in exasperation. The children hopping up and down at her side had not helped her growing impatience either. Finally, she sent them to the house to wait with Kaatje's girls. First the guests disembarked from the *Fair Alaska,* coming down a wide, canopied gangplank to the pier below. It had seemed to take the crew an eternity just to set it up, and another lifetime to wait for all the guests to come to the pier. At last he appeared, her beloved, coming toward her. Elsa thought her heart would burst with joy. It wasn't until the moment she saw him that Elsa realized how much she had missed him.

As he walked toward her, she moved uneasily. What if things weren't as she remembered? What if he did not feel this intensity that had overtaken her as soon as the *Fair Alaska* drew near? What if he did not love her as she loved him? What if things had changed in the three weeks they had been apart?

Yet as he came closer, she could see the love in his eyes. And she knew that all her fears were for naught. Karl Martensen loved her with all the passion and intensity she felt for him. When he reached her, he took her hand and, bending low, kissed it with reverence. Then, before anyone could see, he quickly kissed the inside of her wrist. It sent butterflies to her stomach, and she grinned back at him as he straightened, still tenderly holding her hand.

"I've missed you, Karl."

"And I, you. I told you that you ought to come with me." He offered Elsa his arm, and they walked up the beach on newly constructed stairs to the Storm Roadhouse.

"It wasn't the place for children. It being your first voyage with passengers and all."

"Kristian and Eve are well behaved. And at some point they'll have to travel with us."

"At some point," she repeated, relishing the idea of traveling together and never parting. "Is that when I captain your ship?"

"How about we make a deal? You take her out of port to our destination, and I'll bring her home."

"I will be content with any arrangement, Karl. Truly. I agree with you. This last separation proved to me that I don't want to leave your side again. If we are to be together, let us be together. And soon," she said urgently, squeezing his arm.

"It can't be soon enough for me," he said in a suggestive whisper as they entered the grand house. "Remind me why we're waiting to marry?"

"Tora waited on me for months. I ought to be able to wait a few weeks for her return."

"She obviously wasn't as much in love as we are," he said lowly, making Elsa laugh. They walked through the front foyer and into the dining hall.

In one corner the small orchestra that traveled aboard Karl's ship entertaining the guests was setting up as Christina and Jessica—dressed in their finest—brought guests elegant hors d'oeuvres of smoked salmon, caviar, shrimp, and red beef. A waiter served the finest beverages available in the Storms' crystal wedding flutes.

The clinking of glasses brought Bradford Bresley forward, and he waited patiently for the crowd to quiet. "Thank you for joining us for the thirty-fifth Storm Roadhouse opening. As a joint venture, Trent generously allowed a few of us to take stakes in his roadhouses in Juneau and here in Ketchikan, so it is with some mirth that I now can call myself an innkeeper."

The crowd laughed obligingly.

"Trent and Tora Storm could not join us today because they are otherwise engaged." He coughed conspiratorially and again was rewarded with laughs. "But we neophytes at innkeeping will try to get through this on our own. So, a toast." Every adult in the room raised a crystal flute. "To prosperity and fond memories."

"To prosperity and fond memories," the crowd said as one.

"Do I dispute a land claim here?" Soren asked, as soon as he was inside the door of the Juneau land office.

"You can take it up with me," said a clerk, moving to an open portion of counter and waving him forward.

"I had parcel 1155 registered in my name, Soren Janssen," he said, spreading out his original deed. "I worked it, had tracer mine materials on site."

"And?"

"Another man brought in a crew while I was here in town, used my equipment, and found the gold that was meant for me."

The clerk looked more closely at the deed. "Claim-jumpers, eh? Parcel 1155… Yes, I read about this one. They struck it big, didn't they?"

Soren only responded with a scowl.

The clerk's smile faded, and he looked again at the deed. "Says here that your claim was up in November of last year. You renew? Pay the taxes?"

"I was here in town, working. I assumed I could renew it at my leisure."

"You assumed wrong. When the taxes go unpaid and the claim lapses, it's fair game." He turned to a large book behind him and let it slam to the counter, then he paged through until he found what he wanted. "Didn't you say your name was Janssen?"

"Yes."

"This mine is registered to a Janssen."

"I know."

"Hmm. Cat-gee," he said slowly, trying to sound out her name. "A brother or cousin? Seen that a time or two. Liable to tear a family in two."

"Kaatje. My wife."

The clerk snorted and then hid his smile behind a hand. He swatted the clerk nearest him. "This man lost his claim to his wife." They both broke out in undisguised laughter. "Not getting along with the missus, eh? I'd suggest you reconcile, or you're out your gold. There ain't a lick I can do for you."

Soren turned and left without another word, ignoring the second peal of laughter exploding behind him. Would the humiliation never end? It wasn't enough that she blocked his every attempt to make something of himself. Now she had gone and stolen from him. And there was no getting it turned back around.

He placed his hat on his head and straightened the brim. Reconciliation. He and Kaatje had never been further from it. Not that he was ready to pursue it again, after all the embarrassment she'd put him through.

She had taken up with Walker. She'd led Soren on while cheating on him and cheating him of his gold.

Sure she didn't know about it.

He didn't buy that explanation for a moment. Soren looked one way and then the other as he stood at the street in front of the claim office. What was there for him to do now? No wife to win, no mine to claim. He felt all tied up inside, like an angry bull brought down and bound at the hooves. It made him want to run or chop down trees or swim back to Ketchikan and give that James Walker the licking he begged for.

310

Ketchikan. He would go back, and one way or another, set things to rights.

But first he wanted a drink. It had been far too long since he had indulged in a decent pint of whiskey. If there ever was a perfect night for it, this was it.

Karl smiled as he smoked a rare, celebratory cigar with the other men out back of the hotel, and then walked farther out, away from the lights of the house. Kristian followed every step he made, as he had since Karl's arrival. "Yes, there they are!" Karl exclaimed. He bent to point the northern lights out to the boy, and Kristian hopped up and down.

"Can I go tell the others?"

"Yes. Let's do. They'll all want to see them." It was a remarkable show, in deep red and purple against a black sky. He dropped his cigar to the ground and mashed it with his heel until no spark remained. Then he hurried toward the roadhouse after Kristian, taking the stairs two at a time. Since returning from Seattle, he had been aching to get Elsa alone, to properly bestow his engagement treasure on her. Now was the time—he knew how much she loved the northern lights.

"Hey, everyone!" Kristian yelled. "Come and see. The northern lights are out! The northern lights!"

As Karl knew they would, the people came at once, chattering and laughing, a party en masse. But he grabbed Elsa as she passed. "Not you."

"But I want to see!"

"And so you shall. But it'll be a private showing." He gently took a sleepy Eve from her arms, handing the girl off to Mrs. Hodge, and then offered Elsa his hand. It gratified him as she coyly slipped her long fingers in his. How good it felt to hold even her hand! What would it feel like to hold the rest of her in his arms, with no need to relinquish her again? They walked around the house to the back as the others went to the front, and continued on, climbing the high hill. From the ship he'd seen that there was a clearing at the top—he hoped it was as perfect as he thought it might be.

It was. Elsa gasped as he helped her sit on a wide stump, then knelt at her side. Trees angled down on either side of their private auditorium giving them a perfect view of the mountain range and the colors that climbed the sky in slashes above them. The aubergine lights were vertical as the magenta stripes crossed them.

"It looks like a wild Scottish plaid," Elsa whispered.

"Or a very rare zebra."

Elsa laughed, the sound of it like a wind chime in his head.

"Elsa, I bought something for you in Seattle."

"Oh?"

"Yes." He reached inside his pocket for the velvet-covered box. "It's a ring. I want to put it on your finger. You can see it once we're nearer the house. But I wanted to give it to you here, on this perfect night." He took her hand in his and slipped it along her finger. "We'll have to get it sized—"

She hushed him with the fingers on her other hand. "It's perfect."

"But you can't see it."

"Karl, it's perfect." She leaned over to him, tilting her head slightly for a kiss, and he gladly obliged.

"We have to wait until Tora returns?" he asked urgently, as they parted.

"Until Tora returns," she said firmly.

He rose and nudged her to the side of the giant stump, then sat down beside her. He put an arm around her, liking how she fit in the crook of his arm, and pulled her close. "Have you thought about what we'll do once at sea? I mean, really thought about it? You've been a captain for some time, and, truthfully, it will be difficult for me to stand down as first mate."

"There needn't be such conflict. My joy is just being at sea. Let's begin together, with the children, and see where it leads. I will be content for some time simply to be your wife and the mother of my children, if not forever. I have much to keep me busy between Kristian, Eve, and my painting."

"It would bring me much joy if it could work that way."

"And if it didn't?"

"Then we'd have to reassess."

"Good. As long as there's freedom to reassess at any time, then I will feel free to relax and enjoy my lot."

"Your lot? It sounds like a prison sentence."

"Hardly." She turned his chin to her and kissed him. "I cannot wait to begin our life together, Karl. You have brought me such joy… What I feel inside is almost inexpressible."

"I know what you're saying. I never knew joy could be so… complete."

"Our Father in heaven has been merciful in letting us find each other. As more than friends this time."

"I agree. There isn't a day that goes by that I am not on my knees, praying for his protection over you and the children. Thanking him for all I've been given. Life is rich, Elsa, so rich with you."

She leaned her head against his shoulder and watched the lights. "They're waning."

"Saying good-bye."

"They can go. I'm content after their show. And eager to see my ring."

"Then come. I am eager to see your reaction." He pulled her up and tucked her hand in his arm, taking care as they picked their way down the rocky hillside in the dark of night. When they neared the roadhouse again, they paused underneath the warm light of the kitchen window.

"It is magnificent, Karl. Thank you. I am honored."

"There are rubies to signify our deep love, sapphires to symbolize the deep blue sea on which we'll travel together until the end of our days, and emeralds for the trees along the shoreline of our home."

"I think there are more traditional meanings to the jewels," she teased.

"You don't care for mine?" He pretended to be hurt.

She laughed. "Of course. I would take your explanation over a jeweler's any day of the week."

"Good. Then come."

"Where are we going?"

"Why, to announce our engagement, of course."

twenty-six

June 1889

With each bottle of whiskey Soren consumed, he became more clear of what had to happen. Yesterday's newspaper story had proved the mine was a roaring success, sending hundreds of others to begin their own mines all around what had once been his. But it wasn't as if he could go out and begin again. Not after he had been the one to start it all. No. He had to reclaim what was rightfully his, and to do that he would have to win Kaatje back. As her husband, what was hers was his. Her punishment would come later. After they lived again together as man and wife. Then she would understand her place again. Oh, how she would understand!

"Hurry up!" he demanded of the small steamer pilot as they made their way to Ketchikan. After three days on the boat, he figured they were close. All he cared about was convincing Kaatje that they could not tarry any longer. Again he ran through his mind his rationale to convince Kaatje. They had a life ahead of them; it was as God ordained, for a husband and wife to be together; there were the children to think about; and they were set financially. What else did they need? Eventually, love would be rekindled.

As the thickly forested banks drifted by and the small boiler rattled on like a wheezy old man, Soren's mind drifted back to their days together on the Dakota prairie. They had been happy for a time there. He had sworn off other women and focused on desiring only his wife. And their union had been fruitful; Christina was born within the year. If they had had a son, perhaps it would've kept him home—a boy needed his father. But in time, his attentions had drifted, to their French neighbor, so enticing with her long, dark hair, and then on to the promises of Montana, and still later, Alaska.

He hit his fist into the palm of his other hand. His drifting had paid off, had it not? The mine was what he had been led to. All his work, all his wandering, had led him to it! He had worked so hard. For them. For their future. And she had stolen it from him! Yes, Kaatje had two choices. She would return as his wife, or she would sign the claim back over to him. But he didn't want just the mine. He wanted Kaatje. He wanted his wife. He had worked since last September— nine long months—to win her back. Soren hit his palm again. How could she tease him like that? Pretend she was interested, then run off with Walker? Plot against him? It infuriated him.

"There she is," the pilot said, the only three words he had spoken in the days they had traveled together. Soren had not minded the silence.

His heart pounded as they got closer. He looked from the road-house to the *Fair Alaska*. He needed a drink, but he had thrown the last empty whiskey bottle over the edge of the steamer the day before. He could see children playing on the banks in front of the roadhouse, collecting treasures from the rocky beach.

He easily picked out Christina and Jess from the others. His eyes focused on his girls. They needed their father now, he told himself, convincing himself with the very words he planned to use on Kaatje. They would soon be of marrying age, and in this land, where there were a hundred men for each woman, they would need him around to protect them. When they saw him, they hopped up and down, waving. He waved back. Kristian sprinted off, to share the good news of his arrival, no doubt. Jessica ran out on the pier to greet him.

The ferry pilot pulled alongside the pier and expertly tied her off. Soren grabbed his satchel, slung it over his shoulder, and climbed the wooden ladder to them. "Hello!" he bellowed, picking up Christina and kissing her loudly, then doing the same to Jess. "How are my girls?"

"Very well, thank you," Christina said properly.

"We've missed you, Father," Jessica said.

"I've told you to call me Papa!"

"Yes, Papa." She slipped her hand in his.

"Let's go see your mother." Jessica kept her hand in his, and Christina walked backward in front of them, chattering about the grand opening of the roadhouse.

"Is the pilot going to stay overnight?" she asked.

"I suppose. I didn't ask. Watch your step!" he said urgently as they reached the end of the pier. She turned and rushed up the stairs, waiting for him to get to the top. Once there, she took his other hand. Soren grinned. With one of the girls on either arm, how could Kaatje rebuff him?

Guests meandered about, watching him as if he were a circus curiosity. Kaatje emerged from among them, wiping her hands on a linen apron over her hips. There was no smile on her face as he neared, just an expression of sorrow. "Soren."

"Kaatje."

"Girls, would you excuse us, please?" They parted but a few feet. "Inside." Kaatje looked at the girls, her tone sharper this time. They scurried into the roadhouse.

"Kaatje—"

"Come. Let us walk."

He offered his arm, but she ignored him, leading the way toward the small grove of cedars that he had hidden in the previous week, as he'd watched his wife and her lover. As soon as they were away from the guests, she whirled. "What are you doing here, Soren? I thought after our last conversation that you would be off to some new territory."

"Not without my mine," he groused. *Hold*, he told himself. *Watch it, Soren.*

"I have thought about the mine," she said, leaning against a tree with her hands behind her. "Let us talk this out, Soren. Can we not do that? There was a time—long ago—when we could speak without arguing."

He nodded, hoping to look conciliatory, and did as she bid. "You have thought about the mine…"

"Yes. And I believe it is good that the mine is in my name. I will use it to assure the girls of an education and the upbringing they deserve. It will not be used for me, not a penny. It will all be for the girls. They have suffered, Soren. Done without too many times. I want to use the earnings to make it up to your girls, Soren. And to…others you've hurt."

Soren paced away, biting his lip, looking out to sea. He had not expected this tactic. What could he say without looking like a cad? If she was determined to keep it, there was only one card he could play. "It can be as you say on one condition."

"That is?"

"You give me another chance."

It was Kaatje's turn to stare out to the water. He studied her profile. He squelched the desire to walk over and kiss her, to remind her of their marital passion and what could be again. No, now was the time to talk.

"You're thinking of our girls. They've needed a father. Will need one even more in the coming years as suitors come around. Their real father," he added, lest she be considering Walker for that role. He gentled his tone. "We would no longer have financial problems, with my gold mine and your stake in the roadhouses." He could not bring himself to call it anything other than *his* mine. It was his. Should be his. He paused, waiting for the final, winning card. "Kaatje, we spoke our vows before God and our people. We promised to live out our lives as man and wife."

He expected it to melt her. Instead, it set her on fire.

"Do not speak to me of vows, Soren," she hissed, her eyes narrowing. "You have done little to honor them, when I have done everything to do so."

He nodded, hoping he looked contrite enough. "I know. I have failed you. I have failed our marriage. But I've told you again and again that I want another chance. And are you not to forgive me? Is that not the Christian way? To give me another chance?"

She turned away, silent, but shaking her head, anguished over his words. "I am to forgive you, Soren. And I am trying to give you another chance, but I keep telling you that I need more time."

"I am afraid of time, Kaatje. When I gave you time before, you ended up running here with Walker." He coughed. "Where is he now?"

"Off chopping wood."

"You see? He remains near you. If I give you more time, you're liable to fall as I have fallen in the past."

"James is here because he doesn't trust you. He fears what you might be capable of." For the first time her anger was replaced by a hint of fear—he could see it in her eyes.

Soren snorted. "He doesn't trust me to give you up. That's what he doesn't trust. He wants me to walk away from my wife so he can have you." He moved toward her, falling to his knees amidst the pine needles, taking her hand in his. "We cannot take more time, Kaatje. If we want this marriage to work, we must seize this moment. No more games, no more time. Let's just take it! Let's say we're going to make it work, come what may, and do it. Please, Kaatje. Send James away. Let us live again as man and wife. Day and night." He hoped his meaning was clear.

Kaatje looked into his eyes, staring, searching. She pulled her hand from his and hugged either arm, as if barricading herself from him. He was making headway, wheedling close, but teetering on some unseen precipice. Was he to push or not? He rose, brushing off his knees, choosing his words. "Isn't it time, Kaatje? I know I've hurt you

319

too many times to count. But for heaven's sakes, woman. You came across the length of the Yukon, looking for me. And here I am," he exclaimed, spreading wide his arms. "I cannot believe that a woman who was destined for another would go to such great lengths to find her first love."

"She went to prove you were dead," said James, suddenly with them in their small enclave of the forest. He wore a pistol at his side, as Soren himself did on either hip. "After you had abandoned her and not written for years."

Soren scowled at him. "We're having a private conversation. Please leave."

"You left such an incredible woman that she was willing to risk her life solely to know what became of you."

"And I came to her as soon as I heard."

"As soon as you heard there was reward money. As soon as you heard that she had the means to hire guides along the Yukon."

Soren's eyes went to Kaatje's. She knew. She was watching him, waiting to see if he would acknowledge the truth. He took a risk. "Yes, I came as soon as I understood those things. But I also realized right away what I had lost. What an amazing woman Kaatje is, had always been. And I fell in love all over again." He was speaking to Kaatje, not Walker.

"Because she didn't fall into your arms on first sight of you," James went on.

"No, because—"

"You do always want what you cannot have, Soren," Kaatje said softly. "What if I were to say yes to you now? How long would it be until you tired of me, left me again? And now I have more than myself to think of."

"Yes, of course," scoffed Soren. "There's James—"

"The girls," she interrupted. "They were so young when you left last; they'd never known what it was to have a father, so they didn't miss you. But now, they're at an impressionable age. They're already attached to you, attached to the idea of your return. If you were to live with us again, then leave—"

"I wouldn't. I swear it. There would be three of you to hold me home, not just one. Don't you see? It would be three times as easy to remain with you."

She was silent, studying him. "You said 'hold me' just now. I do not wish to hold you, Soren. I want—I've always wanted—for you to simply want to stay with me. To want it above all else. I want to not live in fear of being unable to 'hold you.' A marriage is built on trust, on love, on devotion. If I cannot trust you to remain, even when times in our relationship are difficult, then I cannot live by your side. I would rather go on in our separation."

"You're speaking of divorce."

"No. You are speaking of divorce, a divorce of emotion, spirit. I want a marriage. One of love and devotion and trust. But you do not allow it."

"It is you who are not allowing it. I am here begging for it."

Kaatje sighed. "You do not hear me, Soren. I cannot live in fear that you will run off with another woman as soon as my back is turned."

"I will not."

"And what of Natasha and your son?" She stared at him as her words stole the breath from his lungs. She did know all of it. How long had she known? It was little wonder that she had been distant, difficult to convince. His eyes shot to James, wanting to blame him, accuse him of spoiling it all, but that would not be effective. It was the truth they faced him with, not false accusations. He had to fight back with truth. It was the only way Kaatje would believe him.

"I told you about the woman."

"But not the truth about how it began. It began as it did with all other women, Soren. It was not different. You were not saving her. You were simply satiating your desires, as you always have. I plan to give a portion of the money from the mine to provide for her and your son."

Soren turned away, thinking. He had to fight, strike before he was struck. "It had been years, Kaatje. I had not seen you for years. You cannot believe that a man could wait—"

"A man can wait," James said steadily.

Soren pointed a finger at him. "Stay out of this, Walker. This is between me and my wife. I know you want her. But you can't. Kaatje, tell him to leave. This is between us."

Kaatje looked down at her hands.

"You cannot say no to me without him at your side, is that it? Perhaps you have your own little tryst," Soren continued.

"No! And I resent such an accusation from you, of all people!"

"Then why is he here? It is spring. There is work to be had for a guide. Why remain here?"

Kaatje raised her chin. "James Walker is more a friend to me than you have ever been."

Her words made Soren's blood boil with fury. With a guttural cry he lunged at James, taking him unaware, catapulting them both out of the woods and into the clearing in front of the roadhouse. Soren hit the ground and rolled with a grunt. He could hear the air pound out from James's chest. The man gasped for breath as Soren pulled him up by the collar and struck him with the full force of his fist. James groaned and moved away, trying to protect his face while regaining his breath.

"Stop it! Soren, stop it!" Kaatje was beside him, pulling him backward. "This is no way to convince me to come back to you."

Soren laughed, wiping his lip. "You have no intention of coming back to me. You never did."

"That is not true. I have tried, every day I have tried, to find the reasons, the strength to give you another chance!"

James rose to his knees and then to his feet. Blood dripped from his nose and eye. "Stay away from her, Soren. There is nothing left between you two. What is left is between us, is it not?"

He pulled his pistol from his belt and tossed it to the ground, daring Soren to do the same with his. "Come on."

There were gasps from the porch, the sound of people spilling outdoors to find out what the commotion was, but the trio ignored them.

Soren stepped away from his wife. "I will take care of him, Kaatje. I will get rid of him, and then you and I can be together. He's the obstacle. He's the menace to our marriage."

"No, Soren." She was crying; he could hear it in her voice. "You were always first to me. You were the biggest obstacle to our marriage."

Soren glanced from her to James. No matter what she said, he knew. She was just trying to protect him. If he could get rid of James, then Kaatje would have no choice but to take him back. She needed a man. Her husband. And Soren would be there for her. He did not take off his own gun belt. Instead, he pulled a Colt revolver from his belt and cocked it. *"Nei!"* Kaatje screamed.

"Adjø, James Walker," he said.

Kaatje screamed again and lunged at him as the bullet left the pistol.

James ducked and rolled, but the bullet caught him in the thigh. He neared his own gun as he fell, and immediately reached for it, his face a mask of pain.

Soren shook Kaatje off and aimed again at James on the ground. Kaatje rushed to James, getting in his way. Soren erupted. What was she doing? Trying to protect him? Soren took aim again.

But James had already squeezed off a shot, hitting Soren squarely in the chest. He fell backward as if pushed, falling to the ground. Dimly, he could feel the dust settle around his head and hear Kaatje wailing. Determined, he ignored the burning hole in his chest—it felt a foot wide—and rolled to his side. He took his second pistol from his belt and watched his wife with her lover. They were liars, both liars. He had been cheated, of his wife, of his mine, of his life. They would pay.

"Oh no!" Kaatje wailed. "Oh no!" She brought James to a sitting position, examining his wound. She hadn't come to Soren. To see his wound. His own mortal wound.

They had to pay. *Look at them,* his mind screamed. *Look at them!* Together they represented all that had gone wrong with his world, all the reasons why his life had not come together as he had always wanted. With a shaking hand, he brought the pistol forward, pointing toward Kaatje, toward James, he didn't care which. He wanted them both to die. If he was dying, they should die too.

"Kaatje!" a woman screamed from the porch. Maybe Elsa, he thought.

"Soren!" yelled another, that sounded like Karl Martensen.

Kaatje's eyes came to rest on Soren, and he teared up suddenly, at the thought of it all ending. It was over. All over. *"Adjø,* Kaatje," he whispered, squeezing off a shot. He thought James moved then, as if to cover her, but he couldn't be sure. There was a wall of black moving up before his eyes... The curtain was falling, he mused, thinking of a burlesque show he had seen in Skagway a couple of times, blocking his view of shapely legs and high skirts. The curtain was falling...

"No!" Kaatje screamed. *"No!"* she wailed, crying through her keening. She moved James off of her, laid him down on his stomach, staring at the gaping hole in his back, a vertebra exposed. She glanced over to Soren and knew he was dead. Karl confirmed it with a quick shake of his head.

Elsa ran to Kaatje, pulling her away. "Stop it, Kaatje. Stop moving him." She pulled the burned fabric of his shirt delicately away from the wound in his back. "Go for the Tlingit medicine man," she told a wide-eyed Charles. "Tell him to bring supplies to pack the wounds," she cried after him.

She looked to the porch, now full of staff and guests. Then to Kaatje's girls, standing motionless, aghast at the scene before them. "Christina! Jess! Get wooden planks!" They took off immediately for the back of the house, obviously thankful for the task. "I'll need them fashioned into a wooden cot. We need to move him inside, but carefully."

Swallowing hard, she looked at the wound in his thigh where the bullet had gone clean through, maybe nicking an artery, judging from the amount of blood. A man nearby offered his handkerchief, and she pulled him over, motioning to the wound. "Push down here, hard," she emphasized. "I need another man and cloth! Get more cloths!" Another gentleman of about fifty emerged. He knelt beside the first man. "You hold yours on this side," she said, showing them how to staunch the blood. "We need to keep the pressure constant, so when you tire, ask for someone to take over."

That done, she moved back to the wound that concerned her more. It was difficult to concentrate as Kaatje wailed. Elsa could see the end of the lead slug, barely. It looked as if it was lodged against his spine. What was she to do? Try and take it out? Or leave it and sew up the wound? She had read of patients surviving, living long lives with bullets still inside them, the muscle and skin growing back over them. Kaatje wailed again. Elsa moved to Kaatje and placed a hand on either side of her head. "Kaatje, please. Please try to quiet yourself. I need to listen to see if he's still breathing." Kaatje bit her lip, sniffling, trying to be quiet.

Elsa bent beside his head, where she could hear quick, shallow breaths. "He's still breathing," she told Kaatje, who resumed crying, then rose, as if to go to Soren. Karl stopped her, enfolding the woman in his arms. Elsa wanted to help her devastated friend, comfort her, but she knew time was critical if James was to be saved.

The medicine man came running with Charles at the same time the girls arrived with three wide planks of wood.

"I don't know whether we should try and take out the bullet or leave it."

The medicine man, smelling of oil and soot, leaned forward and calmly examined the wound. "It is lodged against the bone," he said. "Leave it. He might live then. He might not walk, but he is more likely to live." The elderly man gestured toward the shoulder wound, and Elsa understood. James probably wouldn't survive the bullet extraction after losing so much blood from his thigh.

"All right," she said as she exhaled. "Let's get him inside."

t w e n t y - s e v e n

The next day, Ketchikan

*W*e are ready to bury him," Elsa said quietly, squeezing Kaatje's shoulder gently.

Kaatje was at James's bedside, as she had been all night. He remained unconscious, sweating profusely. All night Kaatje had dribbled water into his mouth, hoping some of it made it down his throat. He winced every once in a while, and then moaned, as if reliving the scene again and again. Each time, Kaatje envisioned his face, close to hers, as he took the second bullet in protecting her. His eyes had not been afraid—they had been filled with love.

"Mrs. Hodge will stay with James. She'll let us know of any change."

She heard Elsa, but as if through a door. Soren had died. The man she had waited so long for, the man she'd secretly hoped was dead, now *was* dead. Because of her, she thought for a moment before correcting herself. *No. He died because of his own selfish choices.* She was sad that it was the truth, that Soren had never looked to God for his fulfillment, had blamed everyone else for his unfulfilled life. She felt bad for him, but she did not mourn him. Not as Elsa had mourned Peder, as a wife who'd lost a true companion. Soren had never truly been that to her. She'd come to accept that in the years he was gone,

326

and his actions the day before only confirmed it. She rose wearily and pushed aside the muffin Elsa had offered her.

"You need to eat something, Kaatje. It will help."

"Help what? Help bring Soren back? Help James rise out of that bed?" She broke down in sobs and leaned against the doorjamb. She was not really angry at Elsa; she was angry at herself. For not seeing it coming; for not doing something to stop the two men in her life from killing each other.

Elsa walked over to her and rested a hand on her shoulder. "There was nothing you could do."

Kaatje shook her head. "I should've said something. Or I shouldn't have said all I did."

"Soren was bent on his own destruction. It was only a matter of time before something like this happened."

"Exactly. I should've seen it coming."

"And what could you have done to stop it? Perhaps you could've stopped it yesterday, but you would have had to stop it the next day and the next. Soren was going to have you back or die trying. And you simply weren't ready to take him back; you were wise in not taking him back. You sensed he was not being truthful; you saw the holes in his story. You had no choice but to wait. And he could not abide by that."

Kaatje soaked in her words like a dry sponge and then walked out the door, wiping the tears from her face, past a silent Karl, never turning back to Elsa. She moved down the stairs and sat just above her two girls, who sat on the second step waiting for her. "I'm sorry, girls," was all she could say. She cried again for the loss of her children's father, and for all that James was suffering now. She couldn't bear the thought of losing him, too.

They rose as a group, hand in hand, and walked out of the roadhouse and up the hill behind, where Karl had proposed to Elsa. It was clear, and there was a view of the mountains in one direction and the wide sea in the other. "I figured it was a good place for Soren to rest,"

Elsa said gently, suddenly beside her again. "He always had his eye on the horizon."

The crude wooden coffin was already deep in the grave. Kaatje knelt and took a fistful of dark earth and then sprinkled it over his coffin. "*Adjø,* Soren," she whispered, and then nodded to the girls to do the same. They did as she bid, each saying, "Good-bye, Father."

Kaatje nodded at Karl, standing at the front of the grave, and he began shoveling dirt into the hole, along with Bradford Bresley, standing on the opposite side. In minutes it was filled, taking a hundredth of the time it took to dig. Much like Soren unraveling our marriage again and again in minutes after months of rebuilding, Kaatje mused. She knew she should say something. There was no minister to say a few words over the grave, and the nearby missionaries had gone to Juneau for the month. But no words came to mind. Not a single thing. She looked to Elsa, helpless.

Elsa looked down at the grave, as if choosing her words carefully. Kaatje knew it would be difficult for her friend to find anything good to say about Soren. She was glad Elsa was taking the awkward task for her.

"Let us pray. Father God, thank you for the sunshine on our backs and the sea breeze on our faces. Thank you for the good you created in Soren. His laughter, his optimism, his hope for the future. He had so much potential, Lord. Be with Kaatje, Christina, and Jessica as they move on in life without husband and father. Amen."

Kaatje turned away, the tears on her cheeks dry by now. She accepted the condolences of those around the grave and then watched as they moved down the hillside. Even Elsa somehow knew that she wanted to remain alone with her children, and she left them with quick kisses to their hands and tears in her eyes. Kaatje stood, with an arm around each child, looking out to sea. There had been no real hope of salvation for Soren—he'd never seen his own need of it. She thought of those good things that Elsa had scrounged up in her prayer about Soren. It had probably taken all her friend could muster to come up with even those words. Kaatje was thankful for what had been spoken. And thankful he'd left her two beautiful daughters.

"Your Auntie Elsa was right," Kaatje said, squeezing the girls' shoulders. "Your father died in a horrible way. But let's remember all the good things about him, shall we? His laughter. No one could laugh like Soren. And his vision. He was always so optimistic." She knelt in front of them and looked from one sad, confused face to the other. "I sincerely hope that you have inherited his laugh, his hopeful nature. That would be his gift to you. Something we could celebrate in your father's memory."

"But he almost killed Mr. Walker," Christina said in consternation. "He almost killed you. Isn't that bad?"

"Yes. That was very bad. But your father was sick, confused. He made a poor decision, like when he decided to leave us in Dakota. But I honestly don't think he meant evil. At least at the start. He simply fell into the devil's hands again and again. It is sad, isn't it?"

Jessica nodded, huge, billowing tears in her eyes. "I wanted a father. I wanted him to live with us."

"I know, sweetheart." Kaatje's thoughts went to James. Perhaps there was still a chance that they would one day have a father… "Will you two pray with me?"

They nodded as one.

"Dear Lord, we pray that you will be with us as we mourn Soren's passing. Please give us thy comfort and strength. Sustain us all our days through. And let us be right with you, Father, throughout our lives, that we may someday know heaven's grace. Amen."

"Amen."

"Amen."

She rose and walked back to the roadhouse, holding tightly to each of her girls, feeling some peace. At last her life with Soren was at an end. And the future, however bleak it looked, was at least hers.

There was no husband in the shadows, half in her life, half out. It was just her, Christina, and Jessica, as well as their loyal friends.

And maybe, by the grace of God, James.

On the second day, James awakened. Elsa had been walking past his room with an armload of linens when she heard Kaatje exclaim, "Oh, James! You're awake! Welcome back."

Elsa leaned her forehead against the doorjamb and whispered a silent prayer of thanks before entering the room. If James could recover, all would be well again. She was sure of it. "What's this? Our patient finally decided to rejoin us?"

"Yes, yes," Kaatje said. "Isn't it wonderful?" She stroked his forehead, pushing dirty hair back, smiling into his eyes.

His eyes did not smile back, in fact, he looked troubled. "I...I'm having trouble moving my legs."

Elsa sat down in a chair on the other side of him. "There was a bullet, James. Lodged right by your spine. You had lost so much blood from your thigh wound, that we were afraid to even try for it. I'm sorry. I hope we made the right decision."

"A decision's a decision," James said matter-of-factly.

There was a knock at the door. Karl. "He's awake! Hello, James." "Karl."

"Memory's all right, I'd say, if you're remembering names. Do you know what year it is?"

"Eighteen eighty-nine."

"Who is the president of the United States?"

"I was hit in the shoulder and back, not my head. I'm fine. That way." Karl frowned. "What is it? Pain?"

"Yes, that. But moreover, I'm having trouble moving my legs."

Kaatje whisked away the blankets, exposing legs covered in pajamas. His feet were bare. "Can you move your toes, James?"

The patient frowned and furrowed his brow in concentration. There was a small wiggle. Then he gasped.

"What? Are you hurting?" Kaatje asked.

"No, not that. Soren. What happened to Soren?" His eyes were desperate, searching as if he'd just remembered the awful ordeal.

"He is dead, James," Karl said. "As I understand it, you shot back when he hit you. Then, from the ground, he shot at you and Kaatje."

"You covered me," Kaatje said. "Saved me from the bullet with your back."

James sighed. "I'm sorry, Kaatje. I never meant to kill him. Just stop him."

"I know that. You had little choice in the matter. I'm so sorry...for not stopping it myself...before it got started." She started crying again.

"How? How could you have done that?" James asked.

"I keep asking myself that...time and...time again."

"You come to no conclusion?"

"No."

"Then you must not punish yourself over it. What's done is done, Kaatje. I am only sorry that it had to be done in such a fashion. Did the girls see what happened?"

Kaatje nodded. "It was horrible. You in a pool of blood, Soren..."

James sighed again. "We're going to have to pray. For all of us. That we might get past all this. But especially for the girls." His thoughtfulness, in the midst of his own crisis, touched Elsa. He truly was a generous, giving man. A man Kaatje deserved. If only he could get well! Walk again!

"You're perspiring again," Elsa said. "We had better let you rest."

"I'll stay with him," Kaatje said. Elsa and Karl left them and walked down the stairs and out to the porch. They sat down to talk. There were thunderstorms brewing. A great, dark cloud in the distance sputtered lightning bolts and grumbled ominous thunder.

"I need to get the ship out deeper and get her anchored," Karl said, eyeing the cloud. "I don't like to leave her there with only that small pier to hold her."

"Do what you must, Captain."

He rose as if to go, but the second mate was rushing down the pier, she assumed to ask him the same question. Karl met him halfway with instructions and then returned to her. "Elsa, I was thinking. Perhaps we should take James back with us to Seattle. I'm due to pick up the guests in Juneau the day after next. We could stop here on the way back south. Get James into a proper hospital and let the doctors look at him. See if they think he should undergo surgery and have that bullet removed."

"It would ease my mind, at least, to know I did the right thing."

"You saved his life. You got the wounds to stop bleeding, sewed them up tight."

"Perhaps leaving him without legs for the rest of his life."

"At least he lives."

"How would you feel if you were paralyzed? Would you be glad to live?"

He did not answer her right away. "It would be harder to feel like a real man, a provider, now that there's you and the children to think about."

Elsa nodded. "Perhaps you could speak to him," she suggested gently. "As a man who could empathize with his position."

"Perhaps." But there was little hope in his voice.

James refused to go anywhere, refused the idea the day Karl suggested it, and the day after. When the *Fair Alaska* was about to leave without them, Kaatje began to lose hope. But as if deposited by God himself, Tora and Trent returned home. Their exuberance at seeing old friends was quickly hushed as they heard the news of Soren's death and James's struggle. He had lost over twenty pounds in two weeks, eating little more than clear broth and water, and he vomited even that up. More and more, Kaatje worried that he was willing himself to die.

It was Tora who reached his soul, awakened his spirit.

The day she and Trent arrived, she spoke with Elsa in low tones downstairs, then the two of them rushed to Kaatje and James. Kaatje

had been reading to James from the new *National Geographic* maga-
zine and looked up in surprise after the quick knock. "Tora!" she
exclaimed, rising and hugging her friend. "And, Trent! Don't you two
look refreshed and happy!"

She looked Tora over again, wondering if that glow in her eyes
signaled pregnancy or simply happiness, then dismissed the idea. It
was not the time nor the place to ask. Tora immediately sat down
beside James's bed and took his hand.

He offered her and then Trent a wan smile. "Welcome home," he
said, grimacing as he struggled to sit higher against his pillow. Kaatje
rushed to help him.

"Thank you," Tora said. "I hear you've been leading an unevent-
ful life around here."

"It has been kind of dull," he answered in kind.

"And we hear you refuse to go to Seattle for expert medical care?"
Trent stated, worrying his hat with his hands.

"I have all I need. If I die, I die."

Kaatje felt as if he had struck her in the stomach. Never had she
heard such words leave his lips. There was little hope, just desperation and sorrow.

"Listen, here, mister," Tora commanded. "You will not speak that
way again. You have been spared. And look! You have the loveliest
nurse available." She rose and went to Kaatje, making her blush.
"Which should be reason enough to live. So buck up!"

"Tora," Trent warned.

"No! You paid this man good money to get Kaatje through the
Interior alive and well. He did. If he did that, he can get himself
through this."

"Tora," Kaatje said, adding her own warning. She was being so
hard on him! Couldn't she see how weak and frail he was?

"No," she insisted. "Our Lord has spared your life, James Walker.
Are you going to spit in his face by lying down to die? I think not."
She leaned closer to him, as if examining every pore on his face. "You're

made of more than that, much more. It's in you. You just have to reach for it. Where is it, James? Where's the strength, the gumption that gave you the might to fight off a bear for Kaatje? To ride the river with a woman on a mission you could never understand? To stand beside Kaatje, honorable to the last, as Soren tried to win her back? No, there is great strength within you, James Walker. *Use it.*"

She stared into his eyes for a long, uncomfortable, silent minute.

And then James laughed. It pained him to laugh—Kaatje could see by his wincing how much it hurt—but he couldn't stop. And the sound of it made her laugh too, then Trent, and finally Tora.

"Who let this ball of fire into the room?" James asked, when he was finally able to speak.

"That would be me," Trent said ruefully. "Do you wish for me to take her outside where she can burn without singeing anyone else?"

Tora tolerated his teasing with good humor. She had known what she was doing. Exactly what she was doing. And Kaatje was grateful. Tora had said all that Kaatje had wanted to say since the day James had awakened and started losing ground. Trent urged his wife to her feet, to lead her out, but Tora resisted for a moment more. "I'll be back at suppertime. And I want to see you eat something besides broth."

"Yes ma'am."

Kaatje smiled. The Storms were back. It was so good to have them home, for many reasons. She took James's hand and smiled into his eyes. "She said all I've longed to say myself."

"It was good you didn't. I wasn't ready to hear that until today, I think. And somehow it was easier to hear coming from Tora."

Kaatje nodded. Perhaps she was too close, too dear to say anything that might hurt him. She put her other hand around James's, so it was nestled between both of hers. "James, I want you to go to Seattle. I want to take you to the hospital there, make sure we've done all we could. Perhaps there's a procedure—"

"Perhaps not."

"Still. In any case. Let's go. Let's go and make sure that we have done all we could with the resources God has given us. Karl will stop by tomorrow and has to leave, with or without us, for Seattle."

"There will be other trips after that, through the summer, right?"

"Yes, but..."

James sighed and closed his eyes. "I don't know, Kaatje. Let me consider."

It was her turn to sigh. "All right, James. You rest now. Dream of living a full life." She bent and kissed his brow, feeling his eyes widen at her touch. Then she left the room.

The *Fair Alaska* prepared to ship out the next day. Tora and Trent were staying behind, needing to get to the Juneau Roadhouse to settle into their home and let the Bresleys settle into theirs in Ketchikan. After they had said good-bye to all their friends and family, Elsa placed an arm around Kaatje as they walked the gangplank to the ship. "He'll be all right. We'll find him the finest care."

"I know it. I still worry. What if they want to operate?"

"Then we'll pray that the operation will restore him to health."

"And what if they...do not?"

"Then we'll get through that, too. One morning at a time, Kaatje. Otherwise, you might get overwhelmed. Concentrate on the fact that he has at least agreed to go."

The girls ran back to them, dressed in their finest dresses, which were already ill-fitting and snug. Elsa added shopping to her to-do list. And while they were out shopping for the children, perhaps she could find an elegant, simple ivory dress. Something in which to marry Karl.

"Elsa?" Kaatje had obviously been speaking, and Elsa flushed at her self-centeredness. Her friend was in anguish, and there she was, daydreaming about her wedding to Karl!

"Forgive me. What were you saying?"

"I was saying that while we're in Seattle and James convalesces, we should go shopping."

Elsa laughed. "I confess I was just daydreaming about a visit to Madame de Boisiere."

"Oh, wonderful! That's something happy to keep my mind off of James."

"We'll come up with other ways to keep your mind, and your girls, occupied."

"Good. Anything." They reached the top of the gangplank. "Point me toward my room, will you?"

After directing Kaatje to her quarters, Elsa watched her go and prayed for the hundredth time that James would find health, and Kaatje, happiness.

Her own happy husband-to-be gathered her in his arms. "Alone, at last."

A giggle behind them told them they were not, and Karl immediately dropped his warm arms. She felt a jolt of sorrow at his absence. "Girls, why don't you go and find your rooms?" she told Christina and Jessica. "Try 103, right by your mother's room. Mrs. Hodge already took Eve to our quarters."

"Next to the captain's quarters," Christina said slyly.

"Are you two ever going to get married?" Jessica asked innocently.

"As fast as we can," Karl said, taking Elsa's hand.

"As soon as we get James back to health," Elsa added.

They nodded as one and then disappeared behind the door Kaatje had gone through earlier.

"We have to wait on James, eh?" Karl asked, pulling her toward him for a warm hug. He kissed her hair and then moved back, obviously not wishing to be caught again. It was unseemly. But so unavoidable…

She took his other hand and looked him in the eye. "I need to wait. I want everything to feel right. You understand? And right now, all is not well. Let us get James to some decent medical care, Kaatje and the girls settled. When we're sure of that, then we'll marry. In Seattle, if necessary."

"What about Tora?"

Elsa smiled. "She gave me specific instructions to marry you just as soon as I could. To not wait as she waited on me. I think her honeymoon gave her...new perspective. Would you mind? Marrying me alone? Perhaps with just the children?"

"Not at all." He stepped closer and caressed her face. "I want to marry you anytime, anywhere, Elsa. As soon as possible. I only want you to be satisfied. So tell me when all is right, will you?"

"The second it is."

twenty-eight

*K*aatje paced the floor, wringing her hands as she awaited the surgeon's arrival.

"It will be all right," Elsa said for the hundredth time, almost as if to reassure herself.

"I know," Kaatje returned in a monotone. Inside, she could see the surgeon emerging from behind the heavy wooden door, telling her that James had died in surgery.

Prior to the operation, he had informed them all, in very grave terms, that it was dangerous, a risky operation. It was James who ultimately decided to take the risk, as it had to be James. It was worth it, he told her in a whisper, to have the chance at someday standing by her side. "As your man," he said, staring into her eyes.

"Do you not realize," she had urgently whispered back, "that you are my man already? That there is no one else who could ever replace you? You don't have to do this, James, to be with me."

"I have to do this," he had said, "for me first. And for you. And for the children."

So it was with tears in her eyes that the nurses herded her out the night before in order that "Mr. Walker can get his rest." She had not even been allowed to see him that morning before surgery. Elsa had

338

said that they expected to start about noon. It was five now. How long could they keep his back open? A gaping wound? There was gangrene to worry about and…

Be still.

That's right, Kaatje thought. They were in a nice clean hospital where they did this kind of thing all the time, not on a field of battle. But what if they didn't get the bullet out? What if James was permanently injured? If they could not heal his body, she wondered if his spirit…

Be still.

All right, Lord, she prayed silently, leaning her head against the cool tile of the hallway wall. *I'm here, Father. And you hear my cry. I know you do. I'm begging you to bring James back to me, in a wheelchair or not. Just let him live, Lord. Let him be with me.*

Suddenly after losing Soren once and for all, the thought of losing James seemed unbearable. What if he had died that day? Without Kaatje ever having the chance to say good-bye? The thought brought her to her knees, literally, and she sobbed into her hands.

Karl and Elsa were immediately by her side, lifting her to her feet, guiding her to one of the few hard wooden chairs that lined the hallway. "I…I'm sorry," she said through her tears. "It is all…so much."

Karl left to get Kaatje some coffee while Elsa hugged her tight. "It will be all right, Kaatje. These doctors are good at what they do. One way or another, it will work out for good. I promise. I promise you."

Kaatje clung to her and her promise, hoping against hope that James would live. It mattered not whether he would walk again. It only mattered that he would live.

As Kaatje watched the nurse approach, a Catholic nun in a bleached-white uniform and large hat, she steeled herself for the worst news. The nurse's expression was cold and distant, exactly as it might be if she found herself the unwelcome bearer of bad tidings. Kaatje grabbed

Elsa's hand and squeezed it tightly, as if she could pull in some of her strength and borrow it for a while.

"Mr. Walker has made it through surgery," the nun said crisply.

Surprised, Kaatje gasped for air, so sure that it was bad news she would be given.

"The doctor was successful at extracting the bullet, and shall be out shortly to tell you more of his prognosis for Mr. Walker's future."

"Thank you," Elsa said, apparently seeing that Kaatje could not speak. "We'll wait here for him."

The nurse gave them a curt nod and was off down the hall, writing on a chart as she went. Kaatje smiled through her tears. James was alive.

She turned to Elsa and embraced her, still crying, but in joy, not fear now. "Oh, Elsa."

"He's alive, dearest! He's alive!" Elsa's voice expressed all the celebration Kaatje herself felt inside. When Elsa released her, Karl hugged her too, throwing social custom to the wind.

They all stood then, waiting for the doctor.

"He's gone out for a four-course dinner before speaking to us," Elsa complained in a whisper, twenty minutes later.

"Shh," Kaatje said, eyeing a couple of nurses as they passed, even though she felt just as impatient as Elsa. At last the doctor arrived, looking at his chart as if reading a speech instead of looking them in the eye.

"Our patient has done well," he began. "The surgery went as expected, although the bullet was more difficult to dislodge than we had originally anticipated. It is good that you left it in at the time of the accident, for if you had tried to remove it outside of the hospital, you would certainly have killed him." He eyed Elsa with a hint of appreciation in his eyes; Kaatje had told him how Elsa had cared for James that day.

But the flicker of anything good in his eyes left the next second. "Because of the trauma Mr. Walker suffered during surgery in extracting the bullet, I am afraid that he has a reduced chance at regaining the use of his legs. But again, it is good that we went in and took it out. There was scar tissue forming that would eventually have caused him great pain, and perhaps cut off all feeling to his legs, and ultimately would have killed any chance to walk. This surgery, at the very least, has assured him of a decent life span."

"Then he will live?" Kaatje asked.

The doctor frowned at her as if she were questioning his license to practice medicine. "Of course. He is weak and cannot have any visitors for a day or two. But he should live."

Kaatje breathed another sigh of relief. "There was no sign of infection?"

"No."

"And in regard to his walking. Although you think he has a reduced chance, there still might be hope?"

"The spinal cord is intact, but damaged. To what extent, I could not ascertain. But if I were a gambling man, I would say his only hope is a miracle from God."

Elsa put her arm around Kaatje again. "We've seen them before," she said without batting an eye. "We'll pray for another."

The following day, still blocked from visiting James, Elsa drew Kaatje away from the hospital to take the girls for an appointment with Madame de Boisiere. "Come. We'll have her make you something smashing. More beautiful than you've ever had before. A ball gown! That's it! And then we'll go and buy a ready-made suit for James. For when he walks again. When he can take you dancing."

Kaatje looked out the window of the carriage. "I do not think James danced even before the accident," she said. The girls glumly stared from their mother to their aunt.

"Remember the last time we did this?" Elsa asked, waggling her eyebrows.

"You were pregnant with Eve!" Christina said, her face melting from a worried frown into a smile.

"And now she's with us!" Jessica said, giving the youngest girl a sisterly hug. "Do you want a pretty dress, Eve?"

"Yes, yes!" the small girl replied.

"I want a hat," Christina announced. "A grown-up hat."

"You are looking more and more grown-up," Elsa said, nudging Kaatje. Her friend sat up straighter, seeming to refocus on the girls. They mattered most at that moment.

"You are," Kaatje added. "Perhaps you could get a grown-up hat today."

"And me?" Jessica asked hopefully.

"Yes."

Eve quickly followed suit.

"No, no," Elsa said good-naturedly. "Someday. When you are nine or ten years old. And not until then."

"But what color gown for you, Kaatje?" Elsa asked. "What color would make you feel pretty and alive and glad for everything?"

Kaatje shot her a strange look, but curbed whatever was at the tip of her tongue. "Green."

"Ooh," Elsa said, nodding. "Like the color of your Christmas dress?" She grimaced as soon as she said it, remembering that Soren had given the fabric to her friend.

But to her credit, Kaatje just nodded back, with a wistful smile at the corners of her mouth. "Yes, like that. But with a little more blue in it."

"To better match your eyes."

"If I am allowed to be so vain." She blushed a bit, making her cheeks spotty with red, while a wave of pink went up one side of her neck. "And in a heavy silk."

"Will you make it a ball gown with yards and yards of fabric to tie up in a bustle?" Jessica asked excitedly.

"No," Kaatje said thoughtfully, staring out the window for a moment. She turned back to them all with resolution in her eyes. "I want Madame de Boisiere to make me the most stunning traveling suit she can. Something to encourage James to stand and walk beside me. And something to wear on Karl's marvelous ship," she added.

"That's a lovely idea," Elsa said.

"Especially with no ball invitation in hand or expected," Kaatje added. Juneau and even Ketchikan were growing, but had never had an occasion more formal than a town dance. "We could come here for a ball," Elsa said.

"No. I think I want the traveling suit."

"Why not both?"

"Both?" Kaatje scoffed.

"Both," Elsa returned evenly. "You are a woman of some means now, Kaatje. Even if you only use the proceeds from the gold mine to care for your children. You have lived long on little. Why not indulge a bit? What about a perfect traveling suit in green and a ball gown in a lovely rose?"

Kaatje smiled at her girls, and Elsa could practically see the visions from *Godey's Ladies Book* dancing through her head. "Indulge?"

Her daughters stared back at her, wide-eyed.

"Well, maybe just a little."

All three girls squealed together as if it were Christmas morning. After a few more blocks, they were there, admiring the dresses in one window, and then another. But as they entered the store, there was one last window. Elsa stopped dead in her tracks.

It was the most beautiful wedding gown she had ever seen. Striking in its simplicity, but elegant from bodice to hem. Kaatje wrapped her arms around Elsa's waist. "Oh, Elsa. You must have it! You must!"

Elsa's hand went to her mouth. "Do you think so? It's right? For me?"

"Perfect. It was made for you. Come. Let's have Madame de Boisiere bring it into the shop for you to try on."

"All right," Elsa said excitedly. They went into the shop, relishing the tinkle of the doorbell as they entered, and the smell and sights of rich fabrics all around them. Madame de Boisiere was with a customer, but once she saw them, she beckoned an assistant to take over and came to greet them. In minutes, she had brought the dress in from the window.

"It eez about your size," she said, nodding with approval as she looked Elsa over from shoulder to hip like a butcher eyeing a cow.

Elsa's pulse raced as she touched the smooth ivory silk of the dress. It had short capped sleeves that were trimmed with heavy satin fringe and a deep drape across the bust and at the back. Underneath the tight bodice, the skirt was gathered at the waist and then continued in luxurious horizontal folds to the floor. It had a modest train, and intricate embroidery at the bottom of the entire skirt—done in a continuous swirling, Greek flourish—before meeting the matching trim of satin fringe.

Elsa was excited to dress in the gown, and she forced herself to walk sedately toward a dressing room to the right. Wordlessly, an assistant came with her to help her undress and then don the gown. When Elsa had removed her own summer dress, the assistant frowned at her and then left, holding up one finger. When she returned, she had a beautiful corset in hand, decorated with delicate lace and satin ties. Compared to her own utilitarian corset, it was lovely, but Elsa shook her head at the folly of the idea of it.

"It is your wedding day, no?" said the French maid.

"It will be. But—"

"No buts. You simply cannot wear this wedding gown," she said, gesturing to the window-display gown, now hanging on her dressing room door, "over that."

Elsa laughed and then shrugged her shoulders. Why not? It would be her wedding day! She had encouraged Kaatje to indulge a little. Why not do so herself? In short order, the assistant had her dressed and was fussing with the sleeves. "Madame will want to take these in a leetle. Otherwise, it eez perfect, no?"

Elsa shook her head while she smiled. It was perfect. Perfectly lovely. Taking a deep breath, she exited the dressing room to see what Kaatje and the girls thought. Judging from their reaction, it was as wonderful as she thought. The girls clapped their hands together, all talking at once, and Kaatje came to her to fuss with the drape of the skirt.

"You look like a princess," Kaatje said.

"Wait," Madame de Boisiere said. She left them for a moment and then returned with a choker of pearls and gold beads, fastening it around Elsa's neck. Elsa laughed as the girls aahed in appreciation—she would be purchasing the choker too.

"Well, that was simple. Perhaps we should get on with finding the girls' dresses and those two you spoke of, Kaatje." Madame de Boisiere turned to help Kaatje locate the patterns she desired in a large book on a side table. The girls moved to the bolts of fabric, admiring this one, hoping they could get a dress in that one, while Elsa turned to the long, oval mirror and stared at her reflection.

She was going to do it. She was going to marry Karl. And she hoped that everything on her, from corset to choker, pleased her husband-to-be. Her smile faded. If they ever found the chance to marry. Life had gotten complicated. Scheduled to take another trip to Ketchikan, Juneau, and Glacier Bay, Karl had ruefully left Elsa and the children behind to stay with Kaatje and her girls as James convalesced.

Elsa had thought about planning a wedding in Ramstad House for when he returned, but that didn't seem right for them. The idea of waiting until they could get back to Ketchikan seemed distant too. Who knew how long they would be here with Kaatje and James? She sighed. Someday, somewhere, somehow they would marry. She ran a hand over her smooth bodice. Soon.

James stared out the window at the limb of a great pine outside, as he had for weeks now. It was his one tie to his old life. The thick forests of Alaska had sheltered him, warmed him, even fed him once or twice when he shot squirrels from her limbs. Those days were gone now, he thought sourly. He supposed his future was filled with beds and white linens and sterile rooms. And yet his eyes could focus on little but the tree limb outside his window.

Kaatje came each day, bringing drawings from the girls—they were not allowed inside the hospital—and occasionally Elsa visited. Karl came for a while, before he had to ship out again. For a moment each day, when James first caught sight of Kaatje's bright eyes, he had to force himself to remember his infirmity, not to stumble out of bed as he eagerly tried to greet her. After that first moment when he practically forgot where he was, why he was there, then his mood would plummet, leaving him despondent. If only he could get out of bed and greet her as a man! If only he could leave his bed and run out of the hospital, out of the city, into the heavy forests that surrounded Seattle. That would heal him. That would give him strength.

But God had not answered his prayers. James had prayed, prayed specifically for the gift to walk again. To be able to kneel in front of Kaatje and ask for her hand. But it was obviously not meant to be. He could barely sit unaided, let alone kneel. And with each day, he became more and more convinced that he should release Kaatje, send her away if she wouldn't go on her own.

So when she arrived that day, cheerfully arranging fireweed and daisies in a vase by his bed, he grabbed her arm more gruffly than he intended. She immediately halted her flower arranging, and her look of confusion and concern made James want to sink under his covers. But he did not. "Kaatje, stop. Please stop chattering as if all is well, as if all will be all right. We need to talk. Really talk."

Kaatje did as he bid, pulling a white wooden chair to his bedside. "Anything, James. We can talk about anything."

James cleared his throat, glancing to the tree limb outside his window then bravely back to Kaatje. "We have done it. We went through the surgery, hoping I would regain the use of my legs, but I have failed you."

"That's not true, James. With each day you gain a little movement…"

He held up a gentle hand to hush her. "A half-inch here and there does not add up to walking."

"A half-inch each day eventually adds up to a foot of change."

"I think it's stopping, Kaatje. My progress. There has been little change in the last few days."

"You've stopped pushing yourself, James."

"Because it's not worth it. I don't see the end of it. Why work so hard? It would have been better for me to die on that table."

Kaatje rose, shaking, and walked toward the window. The blood had drained from her face. Then she did something James never saw coming: she turned around and shook her index finger at him. "You listen to me, James Walker. We have been through too much for me to watch you lie down and die. Tora Storm told you how it was, and you listened. I agreed with her, afraid to say all that she did, but agreeing nonetheless. You think I don't see you, gazing out to the trees, day after day? You don't think I know the longing in your heart to be free of this cursed hospital and that bed or chair? I feel your pain, James," she said, shuddering, pointing at her chest, "as if it were me. I wish it were me. I wish it had been me that took that bullet. Because if it were me, I wouldn't give up. I would give life every possible chance. Because I had my girls. Because I had you."

Tears were streaming down her face. "I am obviously not enough. It has to come from inside you, James." The door opened behind her as an anxious nurse appeared, alerted by the noise, but Kaatje ignored her. "You have to reach down, down past the hurt and exhaustion and fear, and find that will to live, let alone walk. You have to remember that life is worth something, even if you are confined to a chair forever! Just because you have lost the use of your legs does not mean you have lost the power to be a man. On the contrary. You could show me you're even more a man than you used to be, by doing all you can from the seat of a chair. Yes," she said, nodding in response to the subtle shake of his head. "It's true. Think about it. There are ways to be a man, even when you cannot be on a river just after ice break. It takes more here," she said, pointing to her head, "and more here," she said pointing to her heart, "but it is possible."

"Leave us," he directed the nurse.

"I must ask you to keep your voices down."

"Leave us," he said just as insistently, but not any louder. Miffed, the nurse turned and left. He could not look at Kaatje. "Kaatje, I want you to leave me. Leave me here and get on with your life in Alaska. I promise I will not haunt you as Soren once did." He laughed, without merriment. "Not that I could. But I won't come to you; I won't write. I want you to be free."

"Don't you see?" She knelt and took his hand, forcing him to look at her. Pain was etched in every line of her face. "I am hopelessly in love with you, James. If you send me away, you will break my heart in a more cruel way than Soren ever did. He was thoughtless. But you have put great thought into this."

"I am not the man you need, Kaatje."

"You are exactly the man I need. The only man I need."

Her calm, steady voice forced his eyes to meet hers. He licked his lips. She did not want out, was not taking his offer to run while she still could. Could it be that she could still love a useless man? What would it take to become the man she would admire, the man she described who was able to tackle a river just after ice break, a man who could fend off a mother bear for her?

Staring into her eyes, feeling her warm hand in his, James had no choice.

He had no choice but to fight again.

For the chance to walk. For the chance to live. For the chance to love.

twenty-nine

⟨design⟩

On the eve of James's homecoming, Karl and Elsa threw a celebration party at Ramstad House. James sat in his wooden wheelchair and tried to be as merry as he could, in spite of being clearly uncomfortable. He was the kind of man who was in his element deep in the Yukon, not at parties in mansions, Elsa mused. She hoped he would be able to someday return to the Yukon.

"He's made tremendous progress," Elsa said, reaching Karl and taking his arm. They stood together in the corner of the parlor and looked back at James and Kaatje.

"Mm-hmm," Karl muttered, as he drew closer to her, clearly not thinking about James.

Elsa glanced at him and then swatted his arm. "Karl! Somebody might see you!"

"Mm-hmm," he repeated. He leaned closer to her, making her bare clavicle and neck break out in goose bumps. "Come away with me," he whispered suggestively.

"To where? We leave for Alaska next week."

"I don't care. Anywhere. Let's just go. Away. Together. Let's get married and have a bit of a honeymoon before we go to Alaska. I can't stand waiting even another month."

"Away from Seattle? But Tora—"

"Tora told you to get married as soon as you can. She doesn't care if she's there—she just wants you to marry when the time is right."

"But Kaatje—"

"Just got James home. She'll be concentrating on him for the next few weeks."

"Week," she corrected. "Kaatje told me today James wants to be on the *Fair Alaska* when we sail home."

"Can't blame him. Alaska might be just what he needs. The inspiration to get a man on his feet again."

"That's what she says too."

"Well then, good. Kaatje and James will be here. Trent's business will keep him away another week as well. Between Tora and Mrs. Hodge, the children will be well cared for. Let us go. To the San Juan Islands. To Vancouver. Or just out on the water. All I want is to be at sea with the woman I love. Married."

"Just us? No one else at our wedding?"

"I like the sound of it, if it's all right with you. We can have a big reception with all our friends and family once we return here or to Alaska." He moved even closer to her, wrapping his arms around her shoulders and kissing her temple. "What about it? Are you ready to become my wife, Elsa?"

She looked back into his gray eyes and smiled. "Yes. There's nothing I want more."

"Good. Tomorrow. Let's sail at ten. I'll surprise you with the rest. Is that all right?"

Elsa laughed. "You mean I don't get to plan my own wedding?"

"If that's all right with you. If you trust me…"

"I do, Karl."

"Good. That's all you have to say tomorrow, too, and I'll handle the rest. Now if you'll pardon me, I need to leave and get our affairs in order."

"My, aren't you mysterious?"

"I hope so. I want you to be a little surprised every day we're married, Elsa. That a man can love you as I do, that a marriage can be so sweet, that I can be a good father to your children. I hope I can do that for you, in honoring Peder's memory and to complete my own joy as well."

Elsa reached up and caressed his face. "I will pray for that too, Karl."

"Until tomorrow, love."

"Until tomorrow." She smiled, the thought of tomorrow's promise thrilling her.

"I will send a coach for you at ten. Let me go and say good-bye to the children, and then I'll be on my way." He held her hand until the last minute, staring into her eyes, as if he wished he did not have to leave her for even this last night.

At last, at last they were to marry! Elsa grinned and finally focused on others in the room. The party had waned, and suddenly Elsa knew that she and Karl had been quite a spectacle. When she spotted Kaatje and Tora staring at her, giggling, she understood just how much of a spectacle.

She walked over to them. "Tell me you're laughing over something not at my expense."

"Oh, you can afford it," Tora said, taking her arm. "Karl told me he was going to suggest getting married tomorrow. Are you going to do it?"

"Yes. Are you sorry you won't be there?"

"Not as sorry as you'd be if you missed such an intimate, romantic opportunity. We'll celebrate afterward. And I want you to wear your gorgeous wedding dress to the reception." She leaned back and stared at Elsa for a moment, then leaned forward again to hug her. "You're going to be so happy, Elsa. That's all that matters."

"Thanks for sharing my joy," Elsa answered.

"You are welcome." There was a wistful look in Kaatje's eyes, and Elsa hoped against hope that someday James would feel well enough to ask for her hand in marriage. Kaatje deserved that kind of happiness.

As if hearing her thoughts, James wheeled over to them. "So what is the big secret?"

"Secret?" Kaatje asked, cocking an eyebrow.

"Secret," he said, playfully lowering his eyebrow and taking her hand.

Kaatje bent down and whispered in his ear, and James smiled in approval. "Exactly as I hoped. Karl is a good man, Elsa. You two will be very happy."

"As will you and Kaatje," Elsa said, before she could think through her words. "Oh, forgive me for being so presumptuous! I'm in such a high mood, it makes me feel I can say whatever is on my mind!"

"Not that being in a low mood has ever stopped you before," Tora teased.

"No, that's all right," James said. "I aim to never leave Kaatje. And I hope to soon be out of this chair so I can get down and propose as a man should."

"James!"

"What? It is true. No sense in hiding it. You were wondering about it, weren't you?"

"Well, yes, but I never...I didn't...I couldn't..."

"Perhaps we had better excuse ourselves," Elsa said, nodding at them both and pulling Tora away.

Dimly, Kaatje knew they had left her side, but she only had eyes for James. "You think one day we can marry? You want to marry me some-day, James?"

He looked chagrined at being caught, for opening his mouth and hinting of it before he was ready.

"I do, Kaatje. More than anything else. But I have to be out of this chair. You've seen the progress I've made. Doctors say it won't be long before I can try to walk with a couple of canes. Just as soon as I can, sweetheart. That's the moment I'm going to get down on my knees and make things proper."

Kaatje swallowed hard. It was true—he had made tremendous progress. Even getting out of the hospital and coming home, getting through the party—it was all remarkable for a man shot twice just six weeks prior. But she had to ask. It would eat at her every day until the day he spoke of if she did not. "And if…"

"And if I cannot get out of this chair? That's what you were going to ask, wasn't it, Kaatje?" His voice was soft and had a quiver to it.

She could only nod once.

"If that's the case, and I'm praying to God it isn't, then I aim to be the kind of man you could respect, even in a wheelchair."

"I already respect you, James, wheelchair or not. You must know that by now."

He stared at her, still holding her hand, but was quiet. "I guess I do. I suppose I'm the one who has to learn to respect myself in this chair."

"Not that you shouldn't try to get better, to regain use of your legs," Kaatje said, kneeling beside him. "But I don't ever want it to come between us. We can have a life together regardless of what transpires."

"You really think so? You wouldn't ever look back and curse the day you took a cripple for a husband?"

His words made her angry. "James Walker, the day I take you as my husband, I would be taking James the man. There is no wheelchair in my heart, because it is your heart, your spirit, I fell in love with. Don't get me wrong," she said, suddenly a bit shy. "You are a fine figure of a man, James. And I would love it if you could walk again someday. But it has no impact on the way I feel about you. No impact on the way I'd feel if we could never be together."

He nodded silently, her words apparently making sense to him. "I will think on these things, Kaatje. You have done much to get me to where I am tonight, and I am grateful. Thank you for remaining by my side through this." He reached up and caressed her face, much as Elsa

353

had caressed Karl's face earlier. His broad, warm, callused hand felt good and reassuring. Someday James Walker would rise out of that chair and walk to her. He would bend on one knee and ask her to marry him.

She knew it. With all the clarity of prophecy that Jeremiah or Isaiah ever knew before her. And she was filled with peace.

"Whew, I had better sit down," Tora said. "It's been an awfully long day."

Elsa glanced at the mantel clock. "It's only quarter past seven. You've gotten soft since you became Mrs. Storm. What you need is a little hard work..." Elsa stared hard at her. "You've been tired a lot lately."

"Yes. I had to have a nap just today. I was wondering if I was coming down with something."

"But you've been that way ever since you arrived in Ketchikan."

"Yes. I chalked it up to being weary from our whirlwind honeymoon. My husband is no old man, despite his gray hair."

Elsa was staring at her so hard! Tora gave her a silly face. Did she have a spot of an hors d'oeuvre stuck at the corner of her lip? Quickly she ducked behind her hand to check. No. "What? Why are you looking at me that way, Elsa?"

"I'm looking for a glow."

"A glow? A glow?" Finally, she understood what her sister was after. No. It couldn't be.

"How long since your last monthly?" Elsa whispered.

Tora started thinking back. "It's been...sometime before... After Japan, before Hawaii on the way back."

"So that was two months ago?"

"About that, yes," Tora said, nodding and getting excited. "But I haven't been ill in the mornings," she whispered, wanting to be talked out of the possibility before she got too excited.

"Not all women get sick," Elsa whispered back, her grin spreading.

Tora ran through the calendar again. "I guess when we reached Ketchikan, and with Soren dying and James's injuries, I simply didn't pay attention. But yes, it's been two months!"

"I'd say I have another niece or nephew on the way. You'll know for sure in another month."

"Oh, do you think so?" Tora asked, clinging to Elsa's arm. "How wonderful it would be! I was so afraid, Elsa, so afraid I'd never have another baby."

"Yes, I think so," Elsa said. "I think Trent's in for a shock when he gets back from his business trip."

"It's not like I've kept it a secret that I wanted a baby," Tora said.

"No. But a man is never prepared for the news like a woman is."

"Oh, I cannot wait! For another month to pass by! For the chance to share my hope with Trent!"

"When is he due back from Minneapolis?"

"Not until the week after next."

"Well, don't you worry. Another two weeks will give you all the more confirmation that our prayers have been answered, or that you'll just have more opportunities to try again. In any case, Tora, someday you're going to be a mother. I know it."

"I hope so, Elsa." She leaned her head against her older sister's shoulder. "I hope so."

A card was delivered early the next morning, telling Elsa that Karl's plans had taken longer than he had expected and that a coach would not pick her up until three in the afternoon. She was disappointed, having arisen early to begin packing and preparing for her big day. "Silly man," she said, sinking into a deep settee beside Kaatje. "This is what happens when you leave things to a man to plan."

"Get used to it. You have been too long without a husband— you've forgotten their ways."

"You are one to talk."

Kaatje laughed and looked down at the knitting in her lap. "That is true. Maybe someday I'll get the chance to wait on my own husband-to-be."

"I hope so too," Elsa said, squeezing her hand. She looked back to

Karl's stationery, imprinted "CAPTAIN KARL GUSTAV MARTENSEN, JUNEAU, ALASKA at the top. She ran her hand over the letters. She had been a Ramstad for a very long time. It would take some getting used to, being called Elsa Martensen, Mrs. Martensen, Mrs. Karl Martensen... Fortunately, she liked the idea of any and all of them.

"Never mind the delay," Kaatje said. "We will fill it. Why don't you take a long walk with the children? It's a lovely day. And when you return, we'll have a bath waiting for you. After that we'll have a light luncheon, and I'll do your hair and get you dressed. You'll marry tonight, right?"

"Yes. I believe so. I'm going in my gown!"

"I cannot believe that our Karl would let one more night slip by without you in his arms," she said conspiratorially.

Elsa flashed her an excited grin. The idea of being with him and never letting him go again... Of being his, body, mind, and soul... She rose quickly and wrung her hands. "A walk. A lovely idea. I'll go gather the children and be off."

Everything was perfect. The sun had reached its zenith and was beginning to descend. Karl double-checked his watch. Three o'clock. The coach would be picking her up now. He had rented the finest available in Seattle, a white phaeton with gilded wheels. He wanted Elsa to feel like a princess on her way to her prince. She deserved nothing less.

The *Fair Alaska* was bedecked with ivory roses and tulle fabric draped in gentle arcs along its railing. Mrs. Hodge had arranged the delivery of hundreds of ivory pillar candles, and Charlie—after begging to live aboard with Karl for even a short time—and the crew had helped him distribute them throughout the ballroom and his stateroom. There were fresh, luxurious linens on his new, double bed. The minister was due to arrive just before Elsa, and Cook had supper under way. If they could manage to eat anything, Karl mused. His stomach was so tied up in knots, he could not fathom eating even a bite. Only Elsa's safe arrival and sailing with her out beyond Bainbridge Island would ease his frazzled nerves. They would anchor in a deep harbor on the leeward side, for Karl wanted their evening and night to be at sea, but without the accompaniment of the noisy boilers. He wanted it silent, nothing but the lapping of the sea they both loved and the sounds of lovers in their marital bed...

Karl paced, barking orders at men who deserved no punishment. He knew he was tense. He patted his jacket pocket and felt the velvet box tucked safely there. He'd have to tell Elsa that night that it was he who had sent the presents over the last few years. He'd felt so mischievous when she'd asked about it earlier and he'd played innocent. He pictured fastening the sapphire pendant around her slim neck and confessing. Knowing Elsa, she had probably already guessed. Either way, he longed to tell her that he had been thinking of her all this time, never knowing that she would give him the ultimate gift—herself in marriage. Their marriage...their wedding... Thoughts of it sent him pacing again. What if something went wrong? What if her carriage was in an accident?

He was sure the entire crew breathed a sigh of relief when he went to the rail and saw the ivory phaeton come into view. He paused, straightening his pristine black suit and tie, then walked sedately down the gangplank as if he had all the time in the world. Looking back, he noticed most of the crew leaning over the side to watch. He whistled once and pulled his head back. They disappeared, hopefully to stay out of sight for the remainder of the day.

The phaeton driver pulled the matched grays to a halt, and a coachman stepped off the back. Karl grinned in satisfaction. Three men to serve her. She ought to feel like a princess! The coachman opened her door and offered his assistance.

A slender hand emerged from the shadows, and then a small ankle, clad in white hosiery and a delicate slipper. It was her smile he saw next, her lovely smile. She ducked through the small doorway and carefully made her way down the steps, dropping the coachman's hand to take both of Karl's.

"You…," Karl breathed, looking her up and down, "are a vision." He bowed slightly.

"You do not look poorly yourself," she quipped, straightening his tie.

The two men appeared behind her, laden with luggage.

"Packing light, are you?"

She raised her chin. "My fiancé would not tell me where we were going. I figured I ought to be prepared."

Emboldened by their play, he escorted her along the gangway and leaned to whisper in her ear, "We will be married. Who will need clothing?"

She colored prettily, and Karl sighed. Their time to retire to the bedroom suddenly seemed a very long time away. Fortunately, he was distracted by her elation at the decorated ship. Seeing her reaction, it was well worth the effort to do all he could to make the evening magical. Two crewmen and Lucas appeared to take Elsa's luggage from the coachmen, whom Lucas paid. Karl nodded at him and knew that Lucas would get the ship underway without further delay.

"Come, my bride," he said to her, offering his arm. They walked to the bow and stood there as the *Fair Alaska's* boilers churned them out of Seattle's harbor and along Puget Sound.

"Where are you taking me?"

"Not far. I thought it appropriate that two captains be married at sea."

She smiled up at him, the ivory of her dress making her smile all the more bright. She had perfectly rounded lips, turned up a little at each corner. He bent and kissed her, wanting more of her as he tasted the sweetness, but pulled away. In time he would have all of her, and she of him.

"Will you pray with me, Elsa?" Karl asked softly. "I am overcome with what God has given me, given us."

"Yes, Karl. I would like that." She bowed her head, drawing closer to him as she did so.

The wind off the water was cool, and suddenly Karl realized her arms were bare. Quickly, he slid off his jacket and draped it over her shoulders. She smiled, her eyes still closed. Karl bent and reverently, slowly kissed each lid, then pulled her into his arms, resting his cheek against her smooth, golden hair. He kept his eyes open—he wanted to remember every moment of this day and wanted the visual memories to accompany his thoughts.

Beyond the ship, over the small, silvery blue waves of the Sound, the rounded, thickly forested hills abruptly dumped into the water, trees clinging to the very last rocks. Several sailing vessels hurried over the waters, making the *Fair Alaska*'s leisurely pace seem decadent. The sun was warm on the bridge of his nose and cheek, but not hot. The air was mixed with the pleasant scent of Elsa's lavender toilette water and the salty sea.

"Karl?" Elsa whispered.

"Yes, beloved?"

"Are you going to pray?"

His smile grew larger. "Yes, beloved. Pray with me now. Dear God, thank you for this miraculous day. For the sun on our heads and the wind on our faces and the sea below us. But most of all, thank you for the love that Elsa and I share. May it be strengthened with each day we are together, an honor to you as our God. Help me to be a good husband—"

"And me a good wife."

Karl laughed softly. "And Elsa a good wife. Let us be good parents of Kristian and Eve. We pray that you will grant us long lives to celebrate this love we've found. Thank you, Father. Thank you. Amen."

"Amen. Amen and amen."

Karl released her and held out his hand. "Come, love. Let us make our vows and begin our life as man and wife."

"Indeed," she said, her eyes shining like the most brilliant day on the Pacific. "It cannot begin soon enough for me."

e p i l o g u e

A year later

℮lsa and Karl had walked out onto the porch to escape the joint squalling of Tora and Trent's twins. The cool evening breeze off the water and the last vestiges of a sunset's burnt red and orange—giving way to the deep purple and blue-black of Ketchikan's night sky—immediately calmed Elsa, and she took a deep breath as Karl enveloped her in his arms. She leaned her cheek against one of his biceps, liking the scent of him, the heat and closeness of him. How good it was to be in love and married to her best friend! Her joy was complete. They were hidden away, in a corner of the porch, while Karl leaned on the rail with Elsa tucked firmly against him, staring out to sea in companionable silence.

Kadachan, James, and Kaatje joined them on the far side of the porch, but surprisingly, they didn't spot the couple in the corner. Content to share the quiet majesty of the moment, Elsa said nothing, closing her eyes and listening to the hoot of a horned owl and the crickets step up the volume of their evening symphony.

By the time James began speaking, it was too late to announce their presence. Indeed, Elsa was holding her breath, watching the scene unfold before them like a moving oil painting created by a master of old.

"Kaatje, I've waited a long time for this moment," James said.

Kadachan moved to his side and helped him rise from the chair, then slowly, with agonizing effort that made Elsa want to break out into a sweat, James drew near, wobbling with each step it took to reach her at the rail. He shook Kadachan's hands off his arm, bent one knee, and came down hard. "Oh!" was all Kaatje could say, her hand over her mouth. In the deep shadows, Elsa could not see her face, but her voice conveyed all the joy Kaatje was feeling. "Oh!"

Elsa admired the strength it took for Kaatje not to reach out to help James. She seemed to know that this had to be all on his own, without assistance. And it had to have hurt James to fall that last foot to his knee, but he did not cry out. Instead, he smiled, the broadest smile she had seen on his face since before the accident, visible even in the dark, with his face toward the water. He took her hand in his and kissed each of her fingers in a tender, reverent fashion.

Then he proposed. And Elsa's hand went to her mouth. Joy for Kaatje made her choke up, and tears formed in her eyes. Karl hugged her close, watching with her. She was sure he was smiling too.

And though they weren't visible there in Alaska, suddenly Elsa knew that somewhere the northern lights were dancing as never before.

*If you've enjoyed Lisa Tawn Bergren's Northern Lights series,
be sure to look for her contemporary novel,* The Bridge,
releasing September 2000 and available at your local bookstore.

THE BRIDGE

p r o l o g u e

July, 1961

Ernie Powell smiled in satisfaction as he closed the creaking screen door of the cabin behind him. He took a deep breath of the Swan River morning. There was no place like northwest Montana in July, and today was a day to prove it. He reached for his forty-year-old fly rod and made his way to the riverbank, admiring the view before him like a treasured old friend. There was always something familiar about the river, yet always something startlingly unique. This morning a thin layer of fog hovered just above the still pools held back by boulders and snags, creating an unearthly golden glow above deep-water green. Here and there, rocks were beginning to emerge from waters that were waning from their snowmelt zenith to the more subdued level of midsummer.

About twenty-five yards downstream was his favorite fishing spot, near the old bridge he had watched being built as a boy. The trout favored the darkness that shielded them from the sun just coming up and were often hungry at this time in the morning. Although the air was cool, Ernie could tell the fog would soon be gone. It would be a warm day.

With rubber boots on, he waded in until the river reached mid-calf. The icy waters licked at his bones, making ankles and knees, too old to walk a mile, ache in protest. He smiled again. Ernie liked the challenge of the river, her silent shout to turn and leave the fish alone. *Not a chance, old girl.* Martha was planning on trout for breakfast, and after sixty-some years of marriage, he knew better than to disappoint her.

Ernie reached into the basket at his hip, studying the ebb and flow of the river, and pulled out and attached his fly—hand tied just the night before—to the line, then cast it out to the sweet spot the fish favored. The emerald-and-red Royal Wolf was just floating down past the deepest pool when he heard a car approaching. *Odd,* he thought, *at this hour.* He grumbled under his breath, knowing vibrations from cars on the bridge scared away the trout.

He hated the increasing number of automobiles that crossed the rickety, old wooden bridge, but growth was inevitable, he supposed. The other side of the river now had more than eighteen cabins. Twenty years ago only he and Rudy Conway had places along the Swan. With so much traffic, the county would have to get around to replacing the old bridge soon. Why, even from where he stood, with eyes that weren't what they used to be, Ernie could see the rot that ate at the pilings.

Ernie swore mildly under his breath. He had missed his opportunity over the deep pool. He pulled in his line and cast again as the car left the gravel above him and began crossing the one-lane bridge. Planks creaked, and it seemed the entire structure moaned under the weight. Ernie frowned. It was a different sound than its normal protest. What was usually a *chu-chunk chu-chunk* was now a keening, splitting scream.

The car had just reached the center of the bridge when Ernie heard the crack of a thousand broken bones and watched in horror as a central piling collapsed. "Oh no," he muttered under his breath. The next piling went too. "Dear God in heaven…no!"

The silver Buick slipped backward into the sudden crevasse, and Ernie heard a woman scream. He dropped his rod and shouted, not knowing what he said, too stunned to move. The back of the Buick hit the water with a tremendous splash and immediately started sinking, the front still sticking upward. A baby began crying. As the woman kept shrieking, a cross section fell from the bridge, crashing through the windshield. The shrieking stopped. The baby's cry went on, increasingly furious.

Without another thought, Ernie pulled off his boots and ran downriver toward the bridge, wincing as rocks bit into his tender flesh. He had not been swimming for nearly twenty years, but he did not hesitate. He ran into the water, watching as the car yanked against the bridge that held it, filling with waters that urged it downstream. The river reached his waist, and Ernie dived in, gasping at the cold that took his breath away. *Dear Father,* he prayed again as he made his way to the wreck, shuddering from the cold that chilled his flesh. *Dear God in heaven, please let me help them. I'm just an old man. Give me the strength...*

His gnarled hand grasped at the window of the driver's open door, and he carefully hauled himself upward, conscious of the precarious hold the decrepit bridge had on the Buick. What he saw inside took his breath away faster than the cold. A young woman, her face nearly under water, her body pinned beneath the rotting wood sticking through the windshield, gazed at him with soulful brown eyes. Her face was serene, and Ernie saw blood pool in the water around her waist and filter away like fiery sunset clouds in a strong wind. She held the baby boy mostly out of water above her, and his bright red, squalling face was near Ernie's. His fury startled the old man back into breathing.

Ernie glanced at the woman, wondering how to get them out. Her eyes told him everything.

He could not save them both.

She was handing him her child, her love, for him to save. The car groaned, and the mother slipped beneath the water, bubbles rising to the surface, signaling her last breath. Swallowing hard, crying, Ernie grabbed the babe from her icy thin, shaking fingers, which immediately sank. He cast himself away from the wreck, sobbing, holding the child above water until he came back up himself, then, resting the boy on his chest, swam with everything in him for the river's edge.

Dear God, it's cold, he prayed to the Savior who had long been his friend. *Please let me get this child to the shore. If I can do this one last thing...* His heart pounded painfully against his ribs, and Ernie considered for the first time his own chances at survival. The babe quieted on his chest. *Probably going into shock,* Ernie assessed, remembering soldiers in trenches during the Great War. There was a bright light, and Ernie wondered why the sun was so high in the sky at this hour. He felt rocks beneath him, and he stumbled to his feet, desperate for a foothold. His arms felt like they were asleep, and Ernie struggled to hold on to the baby. It was bright, so bright...

He collapsed on the mud and grass of the Swan's bank one last time. He inhaled the sweet, mossy scent and felt the long river reeds on his cheek and the life squirming on his chest. It was too bright for him to see much, but there was a man beside him then, a powerful giant of a man, and Ernie was glad, so glad that help had arrived. "The child—"

"The child is well," said the man kindly. "And you will be too. I am proud of you, Ernie. Now come. Come with me."

Dear Friends:

Thanks for reading my third book in the Northern Lights trilogy. What fun it was for me to travel vicariously to Alaska and watch as Kaatje and Soren and Elsa and Karl and Tora and Trent and the rest came to some state of peace. I loved finding a new heart's home for Kaatje and fell in love with James right along with her (sorry, Tim!). I hope you did too.

Things are well on the Bergren home front. Emma is one and trying to say all kinds of words, as well as most of the "animal sounds." She's steadily attempting to steal our hearts, the little thief. Olivia is attending her second year of preschool, feeling quite grown up at going three afternoons a week. And Tim and I have passed right through our seven-year-itch milestone, feeling itchy only on rare occasions. What a joy to be a wife, mother, writer, and editor! Life is good. Even when I'm stressed, I work at thinking about how good it is. The best book I've read in the last year is Richard Foster's *Prayer*. It's life changing. It has helped me keep things right, centered on the Savior.

And so it ends. No, I'm not planning another Northern Lights installment, in case you're wondering. (I've been asked that by several people who read the manuscript.) I'd rather leave the Bergensers to find their way, continuing on the road we all travel. I'm excited about returning to a contemporary setting. This fall, *The Bridge* will be released, and I think it will be my best yet!

I hope this letter finds you well and settled, understanding that we all must take time to bask in the warmth of the Midnight Sun. I deeply appreciate you all.

In Christ,

Lisa Tawn Bergren

P.S. Let me know what you thought of the Northern Lights series!

LISA TAWN BERGREN

Lisa Tawn Bergren is the best-selling author of eight novels, three novellas, and two gift books, with over half a million copies in print. Her first children's book, *God Gave Us You*, will release in September 2000. Her current work-in-process is *The Bridge*, a contemporary novel that will release in September 2000. Lisa lives in Colorado with her husband, Tim, who is an artist and designer, and their two daughters, Olivia and Emma.

To find out more about Lisa Tawn Bergren, please visit her Web site at www.LisaTawnBergren.com, where you can send her an e-mail. She loves to hear from readers.

You may also write to her the old-fashioned way!
Lisa Tawn Bergren
c/o WaterBrook Press
5446 N. Academy, #200
Colorado Springs, CO 80918